Advance Praise for *Paper is White*

"*Paper is White* is a wonderfully tender, inventive exploration of survival, secrets, memory, and love. Zaid's characters are wholly original and riveting, and this story is funny, moving and necessary; you will love this book."

—Karen E. Bender,
National Book Award finalist for *Refund*

"Written across histories as seemingly varied as Lithuania's Jewish Kovno Ghetto and Queer Nation San Francisco, *Paper is White* connects them in a very different sort of adventure novel, where remembering someone you love becomes one of the most radical things you can do. Zaid is fierce, a rebel with a cause, and her breathtaking leaps of imagination make new worlds possible."

—Alexander Chee,
author of *Edinburgh* and *The Queen of the Night*

"Hilary Zaid has written a beautiful, heartbreaking book about the stories that haunt us, about the ways silence can wielded as a weapon and ultimately about how love between women can be redemptive."

—Nayomi Munaweera,
author of the critically acclaimed no͏vel
Island of a Thousand M͏

"*Paper is White* draws you in, word by word, senten͏ sentence, until you're so immersed in its world you stop reading. Exploring the relationship between int͏ and truth-telling, as well as how past secrets com͏ present-day commitments, this beautiful novel r͏ generations of love."

—Lucy Jane B͏
author of *The Evolution*

Lafayette, 2018

To JoAnn —

PAPER
IS
WHITE

HILARY ZAID

A champion of Jewish causes! Thank ya!

Hilary

Bywater
BOOKS
Ann Arbor

Bywater Books

Copyright © 2018 Hilary Zaid

All rights reserved. No part of this book may be
reproduced, stored in a retrieval system, or transmitted
in any form or by any means, without prior permission
in writing from the publisher.

Print ISBN: 978-1-61294-113-4

Bywater Books First Edition: March 2018

Printed in the United States of America on acid-free paper.

Cover designer: Ann McMan, TreeHouse Studio

Bywater Books
PO Box 3671
Ann Arbor MI 48106-3671
www.bywaterbooks.com

Portions of Elizabeth Landau's testimony are derived from personal
conversations with Lucille Eichengreen, Fall 1996. Ms. Eichengreen
has published her own account of her experiences in the memoir
From Ashes to Life: My Memories of the Holocaust (1994).

Lyrics from Tanja Solnik's "PapIr is Doch Vays,"
from Love Songs and Lullabies. Traditional.

To my mother, who loves to tell stories

and in memory of my beloved

Rose Reiser and *Deborah Levi*

( )

There's an Indian tale you may know, from a collection called A Flowering Tree. *It's about a woman who knew a story and a song, but she never told the story, and she never sang the song. One day the story said, 'Bahin [sister], this woman will never let us out.' So the next day, while the woman's husband was away, the story turned itself into a man's jacket, and draped itself near the door. The song turned itself into a pair of men's shoes, and sat partway under the bed. When the man came home that evening, he saw the jacket and the shoes, and accused his wife of unfaithfulness.*

March 1997

On the night my best and oldest friend sped three thousand miles west to hear the news of my engagement, it struck me finally and with the force of revelation that I couldn't get married without telling my grandmother first. My parents had loved me in their own, distracted way. But my grandmother, a widow, had cherished me. That night, as Fiona's jet dipped into the thick, blurred batting over San Francisco Bay, I lied to my fiancée about where I was going and crept into the shadowed living room of the house we shared to dial my grandmother's number. She had been dead for five years.

It was March. Through the French doors, small squares of milky, urban late-evening light glowed against the East Bay darkness. Lola's collar jingled when I walked in; she lifted her head, then settled her muzzle down again between two paws. I was glad she wouldn't be able to tell Francine what she saw as I palmed the phone from its cradle and stared at it, rehearsing the digits in my head. I had punched those numbers into the keypad so many times in my life that I could have sung the tones. In the years since my Gramma Sophie died, I'd often tapped my fingers lightly over the buttons, but I'd never actually dialed them. That night, though, as Fiona's jet trembled heavily into view above the lights of San Francisco, I felt a desperate longing to press my thumb down into the numbers just to hear the song they made. I knew it was childish. I knew the phone wouldn't ring that night in the little Culver City apartment that smelled like old carpet and leaking gas and chicken soup. I knew the old tin canisters lined up on the counter—*Flour, Bread, Tea*—wouldn't shiver with the extra loud buzz of her phone. It wouldn't ring anywhere she could be found. But I didn't care. The search for a blessing: No matter how revolutionary we think we are, that's what marriage is. I let the plastic hook slip from under my thumb and waited for the dial tone to call me back to the present.

It didn't.

Silence blanketed the line: It was the sound of sitting with my grandmother on the couch watching *The Price Is Right* with her hand on my back, of perching across from each other at the kitchen counter, playing 21. I pressed the phone to my ear like a shell, like a landlocked sailor listening for the sea. I thought I could hear her breathing. "Gramma?" I pressed my lips to the receiver, but my voice had gone weak, tremulous, as if *I* were the ghost.

Finally, a woman's voice answered, an old woman's. "Hello?" she asked, as if she were lost between this world and the next. "Hello?"

In all the times I had imagined speaking to my grandmother again, I'd pictured myself crying out "Gramma, I love you!"—words I had never managed to say during her life. But when it came to an actual, breathing presence on the telephone, I panicked and hung up.

A few seconds later, it rang, like a bomb going off in my hand.

"Hello?" Francine, in the kitchen, had picked up at the same time.

"I've got it!" I called through the house, trying not to sound sneaky, feeling as secretive as I had in high school when my girlfriend called and I pulled the phone as far as the cord would stretch into the depths of my closet. Francine hung up.

A woman's voice, gravelly and lightly accented, wondered languidly: "Is that your *roommate*?" My neck pricked hot and cold at the base of my skull. I had picked up the phone to call her, but I had never for an instant believed that I would end up speaking

3

to my grandmother's ghost. Longing and shame, surprise and accusation, peppered my nose. I didn't answer. "Yes." She sounded pleased with my silence, with the way she had caught me up when she said: "That's what I thought."

Outside the French windows, beyond the low-hanging clouds, the comet Hale-Bopp inched across the late-winter sky, an ancient glimmer ambered in the blackness of night. If there's anything dangerous about calling up ghosts, it's believing that you've found one. Her voice was familiar. But finally, I realized: This wasn't my grandmother.

How many voices had I heard with that faded accent, with that cultured lilt, with that softness that muted a half-century of loss? Dozens? Hundreds? In the five years since my grandmother had died, it had been my job to entice those voices out of their decades-long silences, to capture them and cork them in a bottle. I worked at the Foundation for the Preservation of Memory in San Francisco, where I recorded and archived the testimonies of the last living survivors of the Holocaust. As the Assistant Curator at the Foundation, I spent my days across from the placid, silent faces of people who for fifty years had picked up the bread and the cheese, and merely blinked at a stranger with a familiar accent, who grabbed the mail and sidestepped dogs; those quiet ones who sat down to tea and *kuchel*, played cards, and in the still, polite moments between other people's words, refused resolutely to let certain phrases take shape on their own lips, applied entire atmospheres of silent pressure to their history until, spurred by mortal urgency, they decided: *Now. It's time.* The San Francisco main library may have been jettisoning books by the thousand, but I was holed up just blocks away, collecting as many stories as I could before they vanished from this earth.

My clients and I met on the Embarcadero, down in the interview rooms of our bright new SoMa office; we exchanged our words within the safety of its sealed glass walls. My supervisor, Wendy Rosenberg, would never give out my home number to a client; she wouldn't let me give it out myself. There were too many survivors, too much need; they were too vulnerable and,

4

if we thought we could save them, so were we. "*There are limits,*" Wendy often reminded me. There was a code of conduct. It was very, very clear. Whoever it was, I should have told her to call me at the office. I should have gotten right off the phone. I should have remained professional. I should have wondered: *Why are you calling me at 7:30 on a Friday night?* But I didn't. I felt so comfortable with my clients, so familiar. That was why Wendy had hired me. And that, she had told me, was the primary danger.

Silence hung between us on the line. I stared out the French doors at the gauzy gray mist darkening the bricks on the patio. That word—*danger*—hovered in the periphery of my consciousness, as I imagined deep crow's-feet fanning out at the corners of her eyes. "I can't talk right now," I whispered, like someone who was already guilty. Francine was clattering in the kitchen, collecting my mixing bowls. The thick static of the faucet wrapped my words, offered in the darkened living room, in silence. Francine had encouraged me to take my job at the Foundation to contain an interest in old ladies she thought was bad for me. A client calling me at home would *not* reassure her. Never mind why I'd picked up the phone in the first place. On the mantel, two silver filigree candlesticks sat slightly tarnished, one cup half-filled with hard white wax. Absently, I flicked a drop with my thumbnail; it popped off with a satisfying click. "Who is this?" Urgency edged my words with furtiveness, ±but the doorbell had started to ring; the dogs had begun to bark.

"Are you having company? For *Shabbat?*" the woman asked, her voice as curious and sly as if by bending it just so, she could look through the phone and see into our house. My hand curled reflexively around the tarnished candlestick. In her tone, I thought I heard some version of my parents' own second-generation scorn: "It's fine to be a Jew," my mother liked to say, "but you don't need to make a career out of it." I remembered our screams, my mother's and mine, trailing each other through the house, when I refused to wear dresses for High Holidays. But the idea that we might actually pursue it beyond the age of thirteen. . . . They'd wanted their children to be Jewish, but not *too* Jewish: kosher-keeping, Old Country, provincial. Suddenly, I ached to get off the phone.

The soft, insinuating voice prompted me, insistent as the barking dogs, "Are you having *friends?*"

"Yes," I answered. "I'm sorry," I told her, not sorry but relieved. I didn't need another voice of disapproval in my world. This was supposed to be one of the happiest nights of my life. And I was speaking with a *dybbuk*. "You're welcome to call me at the Foundation." Finally, I made it clear that she was from my other world and she would stay within its bounds. Immediately, I felt more professional. I sounded chillier. This person didn't belong on my home phone. None of my clients did. None of them even knew I was gay. (Would that change, I wondered, if Francine and I were married? Wouldn't it have to?)

But maybe I'd been too harsh. Now the woman seemed to hesitate. The barking had become an eager whine. Behind the closed door to the living room, I knew Fiona was standing in the hall. "We'll see." She remained unhurried, or was it uncertainty I heard in her voice? I didn't get a chance to find out.

"Hell—ooooo!" Fiona called through the house. "Honey, I'm home!"

"I'm sorry. I—" I needed to get off the phone before Francine realized I was talking to an old woman.

But she cut me off, as if she, too, were too familiar with keeping secrets. "Go," she said, as if she knew me well enough to tell me what to do. And then she hung up the phone.

"So what is it? What's the big news you couldn't say on the phone?" My best friend Fiona stood in the little foyer of the tiny Rockridge bungalow Francine and I shared, the three of us crowding the corner where we always piled our shoes. Fiona hadn't slipped off her shoes; she hadn't even dropped her bags on the mat. Twenty times more impulsive than I'd ever be, she had hurtled west at 400 miles per hour on a maxed-out credit card at the merest suspicion of a secret. But now that she was here, what

6

she really wanted was to guess. "You're not sick?" Fiona whispered, her voice grainy with dread. Fiona had recently been promoted to Volunteer Coordinator at Gay Men's Health Crisis in New York. "Of course not!" I reassured her. I felt like I, too, had just hurtled into this room from somewhere far away, a place somewhere between the present and the past. I tilted a little with jet lag, a vertigo I hoped neither Francine nor Fiona noticed.

Fiona didn't. In a black turtleneck and jeans, Fiona, as always, looked dramatic. Her shining black hair hung in curtains around her face; her cheeks glowed like two round spotlights over high cheekbones. (Sometimes it was hard to be friends with someone so stunning—my own hair too frizzy, my nose too "striking." It probably helped that Fiona was straight and I wasn't.) We had been best friends since we were slight enough to slip behind the ball shed at Hillside elementary, and tough enough, when discovered hours later, to withstand our mothers' frantic rage. If I was going to get married, Fiona would want to be the first to know. But Fiona was on a roll.

She narrowed her eyes, which were almond-shaped, huge and green as a cat's, to slits. I could practically hear her thinking. Her voice dropped to a confidential murmur. "You guys aren't breaking up?" Fiona brushed the dark curtain of hair from her forehead. She glanced from me to Francine and back again with those huge, circumspect green eyes, as if she assumed the answer must be *yes*. I wondered where *that* one came from. And Francine didn't leap in to correct her. A preschool teacher, Francine could be preternaturally patient with people prone to drama. Though this rightfully should have been our moment, she was thoroughly enjoying the full spectacle of what she called "the Fiona show." Her mouth crinkled mischievously at the corner. I shook my head. "Of course not!"

Fiona blinked beneath thick lashes. The surprise on her face lingered for only a second, chased by a wild, hopeful guess: "Are you moving? To New York!" Fiona's smile could sell used cars. *Moving to New York?* No matter what I said now, Fiona was bound to be disappointed. Come to think of it, this was how this game always ended, Fiona creating an outsized reality I could never be part of while I stood next to her and didn't say a thing. Fiona's huge personality had always cast a comfortable shadow in which I could slip out of sight. It had always been so much easier for me that way. But tonight I needed things to be different.

Francine stood at my side in her jogging shorts and Clinton/Gore T-shirt. She looked at Fiona, still clutching her bags, and laughed. "You two really pick up just where you left off, don't you?" Her comfort with the enormity of this friendship was one of the things I treasured about Francine. Her auburn curls still damp, her pale cheeks flushed, she slipped a declaring arm around my waist. I looked at Francine with her kind, quick eyes, eyes I had stared and gazed and blinked at for the better part of seven years, and I knew again how much I wanted to marry her. Why couldn't I just interrupt Fiona and *say* it? I wasn't in the closet. I had been a Queer Nation girl, slapping Day-Glo orange stickers onto lamp posts and chanting in the streets. But, when it came to sharing personal things with the people closest to me, I shied in a hereditary way from what my mother would call "shouting it from the rooftops." When my sister finally admitted she was engaged to her Chinese boyfriend, my mother had indicted her: "I don't see her shouting it from the rooftops!" She inferred shame, rather than sensible defensiveness, from my sister's shy, reluctant tone. But who was my mother to talk? Marilyn Margolis would no sooner want me to shout the love-that-dare-not-speak from the chimney tops than watch me fiddle from a shingle while the pogroms roared. It wasn't *only* personal. The demons of this world have always hunted down our plaintive cries of joy and pain. Love, fear, devotion: We never spoke about those things.

Francine cleared her throat. Presented with the torment of small and suffering creatures, she would always be the first to put a broken thing out of its misery. "Ellen and I are getting married." It was strange to hear the word out loud. *Married.* It was the right word, but, like a word in a foreign language or adopting a different name, it had never belonged to us and it was going to take some time to get used to.

8

"*Married?*" Fiona's eyes went searchlight-wide. "Oh my god!"

There was a moment as Fiona inhaled, the long rush of her indrawn breath, that was like the whistle of a rocket streaking upward, and a noiseless moment as it arced, a moment of breathless silence as Francine and I waited to see if it would crash back to the ground. I remembered the years in college after I started dating my girlfriend Sam, two years during which Fiona and I hadn't spoken, and I hoped not. Fiona caught her breath. "Do you mean, like, *married*-married?" Her eyes narrowed again as she glanced from me to Francine; her voice dropped. "Can you actually *do* that?" But Fiona wasn't really waiting for an answer. After all, she'd just flown three thousand miles to hear big news. She jumped up and down in the little foyer, dropping her bag on the mat. "Oh my god! My best friend in the entire world is getting married!" Bewildered, the dogs began to leap and bark. Fiona leaned forward, threw her arm around my neck, her other arm around Francine's neck, and drew us together. "We're getting married!" She screamed. A light went on behind her eyes. "In Hawaii?" Fiona shot me a *let's-do-something-crazy* look.

There were rumors of legal marriage in Hawaii, but they were only that: rumors. "Hawaii hasn't happened yet." My boring tendency to cling to reality would inevitably keep disappointing her.

"So then . . .?" Fiona popped the question we ourselves hadn't answered yet. How would we be married, exactly? What were we going to do? We didn't have a clue. But logistics had never troubled Fiona too much, especially in the face of large emotions. She turned to me with glistening eyes. "I can't believe it." She took my face in both her hands and stroked my cheeks, an intensity I did my best to bear. "We're getting married!" she announced to the house. Francine and I laughed, awkwardly. This was why we were doing it: We wanted to be celebrated. But we had learned to expect so much less.

Fiona and I walked slowly to the kitchen, arm in arm. "My li'l *segotia*," she crooned, squeezing until my pinky knuckle popped. Then, as if she suddenly remembered something important, she pulled on my hand hard enough to spin me toward her. "Who

9

were you on the phone with before?" Her chin jutted, accusing, but her voice had dropped to a confidential murmur, a voice obviously meant not to be overheard, a reassurance that, marriage or not, she would always take my side. "In there. On the phone." Jealousy sharpened her words.

"Huh?" I stepped toward the kitchen, eager to exit the spotlight. "I baked you cookies," I added quickly. I told myself that Fiona liked to make a bigger deal of things than they were. I'd managed to conceal having a girlfriend from her through most of high school.

Fiona knew me well, but emotions moved rapidly through her. At the mention of cookies, she shot me a shy, hopeful glance, her eyes huge with desire. I had seen boys cross the street for those eyes. "Gramma Sophie's?" A fixture of my childhood home, Fiona knew that creaming together butter and sugar was the way my grandmother and I had marked the change of every season, that our Hanukah miracle came from the cookie press and that we frosted every birthday with yellow buttercream. My Gramma Sophie may not have been a religious person, but she was religious about baking, and springtime always reminded me of her delicate *hamentaschen*, the little "three-cornered hats" she spooned with strawberry and apricot jam. (Pressed together by sticky little fingers, these were the sweetened, condensed form in which, each spring, Francine's preschool students celebrated good Queen Esther and her triumph over yet another plot to make the Jews, as the under-five set called it, "go away.") From the time she was seven years old, Fiona had walked into my parents' kitchen every March, headed directly for the corner where she knew my Gramma Sophie kept the tin lined with waxed paper. These were the baked treats Fiona in the full fledge of her baby Irish pride called "your grandma's St. Patrick's Day cookies." I nodded. Fiona shrieked: "Those are my favorite cookies on the entire planet!"

Mine were also the messiest cookies on the planet. I hadn't checked them while they were in the oven, distracted by my ghost on the phone. Now, on the tray set cooling on the counter, my *'taschen's* sharp edges sighed apart, golden islands in a sticky sea of molten jam. These were some kind of mutant, late-twentieth-century descendants of Gramma Sophie's tight little triangles jeweled with a single, glittering dollop: bigger, more impulsive, indiscreet. The usual disaster. I had overloaded the centers with jam, as Gramma Sophie—"No more than half a teaspoon, doll!"—had warned me a thousand times not to. On the radio next to the sink, Alanis Morissette was singing a familiar song: "*Isn't it ironic?*" On the cover of the *Newsweek* Francine had tossed onto the kitchen table, the ceasefire in Ireland had blown apart again.

Grabbing a mitt from the stove, Francine bent over the hot tray. Francine has the most beautiful hands of any woman I know, pale and small and bony at the knuckles. Carefully, with a single slender finger, she lifted the drooping lip of a *hamentaschen* and pushed it back up to form the edge of an equilateral triangle. The dough was still soft, dewy with heat and butter, and the fallen side re-formed without a crack, without any evidence of its breaking. One after another, she repaired the entire, limping tray. Because Francine is practical that way; she doesn't believe in leaving a mess. She straightened up, compact and lithe as a dancer, though she no longer danced, and licked hot jam from her fingertips.

"Strawberry or apricot?" I lifted the spatula to Francine's face. It was damp outside with early spring rain, but the kitchen was humid, and the windows in our little bungalow had misted over with the heat from the ancient Wedgewood stove. In the kitchen, the air had filled with the burnt-sugar sweetness of memories. We leaned against the counter, blowing on our cookies. The crumb, I had to admit, was perfect: moist and just vaguely citrusy. The kitchen smelled like my Gramma Sophie, warm and sweet.

Licking jam from her fingers, Fiona opened the fridge—a privilege of friendship, she'd always said: unfettered access to the food. Her green eyes twinkled. "Got milk?" At the top of the fridge door, right next to the cream, a small, chilled black Kodak canister shifted instead of rattling. "You still have *that*?" Fiona's huge eyes got huger.

The canister was a souvenir of Ponar, a small village outside the Lithuanian city of Vilna, where the Nazis had dug huge execution pits. A glade fringed with trees: a blank in the forest, a million leaves scattered on the fall earth; the pits, perfect circles upon which the forest, just held back, impinged. My parents had visited that part of Europe on a "roots trip" arranged by my mother. After the guide's perfunctory historical coda on the site, as visitors wandered the vale in silence, something had possessed my unsentimental father, drifting to the edge of the pit, to crouch down and, in a move more Jewish and unconscious than anything he'd ever done, scoop up the dirt in which a billion atoms of our tribe had returned to the earth. This was the film canister in which my father had spirited away a tubeful of dirt. One hundred thousand murdered souls blended with the Ponar dust.

"Of course I still have it," I answered. I suppose there are people who live entirely in the present, as if the past were not available at the merest gesture, the small familiar touch, but I had never been one of them. If you've ever ridden one of those black coaches through the Haunted Mansion at Disneyland, you've seen the specters that appear when your coach passes by the mirror: a third figure between you and your friend, a Victorian ghost, laughing and smiling, someone you otherwise can't see between you, but only when you look in the mirror. I am the kind of person who knows the spirit of the past is right at our shoulders on our ride through this world, and I'm the person who is always looking for the mirror.

Francine, of all people, knew that about me best.

Who called? Francine mouthed. But in the hubbub of Fiona's chatter, I pretended not to hear her.

And that's how, seven years into our relationship, on the night we told my best friend that we were going to get married, I lied to Francine for the very first time. A lie, like so many, of omission. As the three of us stood in our kitchen, Francine, Fiona and I, eating my grandmother's cookies, I wondered: What would the Jews of Ponar have said about that? I imagined I could hear them sigh as the refrigerator door swung shut.

I know what my Gramma Sophie would have said.

Nothing. She would have been the first person to tell me to keep my mouth shut.

( )

When I was twelve, my Gramma Sophie overheard me on the telephone, reporting that my sister was having her appendix out. She didn't wait for the phone to hit the cradle to wag her finger in my face. "That's not to share outside the family!" Her hazel eyes, huge behind the huge, round frames of her glasses, were round more with fear than with anger. It was one of the only times in my life she scolded me. I had been talking to my uncle.

She practiced her own rule religiously. In the twenty years after my grandfather died, how many days and hours did I sit out on the back patio of my parents' house by my grandmother's side, my legs skinny and brown, hers knotted and blue and stretched out in the sun, while she lovingly, tenderly, never once mentioned his name? I never took her reticence for distance. My grandmother, more than my parents or even my sister, was the person I spent the most time with as a child. Across from each other behind a fan of playing cards, at her elbow breaking eggs into the mixer, side by side on the couch watching *Let's Make a Deal*, most of those fond hours were spent in companionable silence. Only once in my life had I seen my grandmother cry.

But it wasn't just terrible things. It was the good things— maybe most of all the good things—that we had to hide.

People often assume, because of my work, that I'm a daughter of Holocaust survivors. I'm not. My mother's family left Europe, fleeing pogroms, in the Great Russian Jewish exodus of 1882. And my father's family made it out of Ukraine just before the Russian Revolution. Those who didn't—two of my great-grand-father's brothers, who stayed behind in Zhitomir with their wives and children—died at the hands of their neighbors; the one brother who escaped fled to his end in the service of the Czar. All three brothers, bare, truncated branches on the Margolis family tree, typed up on smeary onionskin. My family had survived the erasures of a different time and place. But the immigrant tradition of keeping quiet about the past, of keeping quiet about sorrow, of keeping quiet about joy, that had been sown in our shared blood centuries before, as old as the Evil Eye, as old as the *dybbuks,* as old as the ghetto and the *shtetl* as well as the Camp, was something we shared: the conviction that, if we only stayed silent about the things we loved most, no one would come for them to take them away.

Though I would have said that my longing for my Gramma Sophie was the reason I ended up working at the Foundation, the truth was more complicated. I was drawn to my survivors not only because they were old, but because they were ancient treasure boxes, as beautiful for the jewels of story inside them as for the silence whose strength they proved by breaking it.

As a graduate student doing research at the Foundation for the Preservation of Memory, I had occupied a dark carrel down in the media room, crammed with notebooks and loose paper, working on my dissertation research. Then, five years into what the University of California calls "normative time" and three chapters into a dissertation provisionally titled *Ikh Ken es Nisht Fargesn: Mother/Daughter Holocaust Narratives, The Persephone Myth and the Recuperation of Memory,* on a Friday afternoon in spring, I stepped through a turnstile at the Strawberry Canyon pool and discovered that my graduate adviser Annie Talbot—the smart young professor who welcomed me every week into her home to read through my pages, my guide and companion through the War's dark thicket of loss, my only real link to the university I was finally seeming to pass through—had gone home the night before and killed herself.

It was early spring—all those little white flowers in all those trees blending so sweetly with the smell of chlorine and the watermelon-rind whiff of fresh-cut grass. My hair dripping with salt and bromine, a towel snugged tight around my waist, my shoulders bare in the atomizing late afternoon light, I saw her picture on the front page of the *Daily Cal*. Pert, blond, intelligent. "Renowned Professor Annie Talbot Dies Suddenly at Home." I read the article fast, and then slow. Then I stepped into the dirt and vomited.

At the funeral, students and professors queued up outside the black-shingled Episcopal church, chatting in dark clothes under a bright spring sun. The small, dark beds huddled against the black church were crazy with poppies. Behind me, a man I didn't know leaned close into my hair and whispered, "How did she do it?"

Inside the dark church, Annie's sixteen-year-old daughter Camille stepped up to the lectern, her mother's doppelganger down to the blond ponytail and the soft patrician lilt. I wasn't the only one whose mouth dropped. Perched above the lectern's golden eagle, Camille spoke fondly of movies under the covers. Her mother, she said, had been more like a best friend. And then she said, "My mother had dark times, too. In her academic work, she was becoming drawn to the post-War suicides. In death, she thought that she, too, might find an end to her suffering." Camille spoke with Annie's impeccable timing, her absolute grace. She was a sophomore at Berkeley High. Would academic understanding, I wondered, be enough to inoculate her against the legacy of a suicided mother? Not long after the funeral, I saw Camille chatting with a friend outside of Semifreddi's. She looked just like an ordinary sixteen-year-old. I hoped she would rebel against Annie by staying alive. I wondered, glancing at her fresh, teenage face, where she hid the scar.

I was barely hiding mine.

The year ended. The History Department didn't bother to assign me another adviser. I turned from *Ikh Ken es Nisht Fargesn*

16

to game after game of computer solitaire. Jeweled faces against a field of green. The solemn, one-eyed Jack had Annie Talbot's nose.

The next spring, on the anniversary of Annie's death, I joined the hordes of dispirited doctoral students in the humanities and quit the program ABD, "All But Dissertation." And, then, because every new loss invokes the first, I started following old ladies down the frozen foods aisle.

The first time it happened, I trailed the woman all the way to the Mrs. T's frozen *pierogies*. Francine and I were doing our Saturday shop at the little Safeway on College Avenue; sometimes, they played disco oldies late Saturday afternoons. Francine had gone ahead to pick up cheese. (Though we liked to laugh secretly at my sister Rebecca and her husband, Ted, and their rich, stinky French raclette, I often found Francine looking for a "not too salty, not too smelly taleggio.")

I was drifting behind Francine, draped over the handle of the shopping cart when the woman pushed past. I recognized her instantly. She was small, her back rounded. She wore plum slacks and a gray wool jacket with loops circled around knotted silk buttons my mother called *frogs*. Her hair was dark gray, streaked white at the temples, brushed sensibly back to reveal a lightly powdered Semitic nose. She examined a jar of marmalade with an age-spotted talon, the label up close to her glasses, then set it gently in the child seat and rolled past, trailing a single deep inhalation of something floral. I knew her right away: She was part of my tribe. I followed her to frozen foods, where Francine found me, dazed.

The second time it happened, the same Safeway, a different woman, Francine *saw* me, saw my stare lock on the little humped back drawn up behind the chipped red cart handle, the taupe purse draped over the swinging, doughy arm, saw my hands swing the cart into line behind her, saw my feet lock into step at her heels, mesmerized, all the way to cat food, pulled after her by invisible strings. Francine watched me, unconscious, breathe in her wake, my lids half-closed, dreamy with desire. If it had been a younger woman, Francine would have pinched me. Since it

17

wasn't, she just stared. Because it was obvious: What I felt toward that woman was longing.

That afternoon, Francine and I had a "talk." "Call Wendy Rosenberg," she told me. It was an order.

"Why?" I wasn't too depressed to be petulant.

"You've been walking around here for weeks like a fucking zombie. That's why. Tell her you need a job." I resented the hell out of her; I knew she was right.

A child of close-mouthed people, I had always craved the hidden. Preserving Holocaust stories gave that craving a name, an urgency. And I believed passionately in the need to save these truths from annihilation, from deliberate erasure. But I had preferred the safe distance of a book. The fact was, I didn't want to meet another old Jewish lady, the loose skin at her throat sunk in the center to a flour-soft bowl; I didn't want to consider the plump, polished fingers, the brown blotches contoured like countries on the back of the hand, to smell Jean Naté and hair spray, to hear the smattering of Yiddish words and remind myself, *Like her, but not her*, while, inside, the big, dumb dog of my heart following an old, well-known scent, tumbled heedlessly along toward something primal, familiar, old as life. Let's just say, I know how that story ends.

In the end, I took the job. I convinced myself I could maintain a distance.

My clients, after all, were Titans of emotional containment, the poster children of Silence. One of the first survivors I worked with was Elizabeth Landau, a member of our Speakers' Bureau, whom I met up with on the campus at UC Berkeley where she was going to speak with a class of undergraduates about her experiences during the War.

We met on the marble steps of Wheeler Hall. She was petite, well-coiffed and articulate, a woman who had served on the Foundation's Speakers' Bureau for years. Lodz Ghetto, Auschwitz, Bergen-Belsen. She walked through the doors beside me, her short legs set squarely apart.

"We still have the four," she told me. "My brother, my two sisters, and me. We used to be thirteen." I hoped that my conversation with Elizabeth might lead to an interview with at least one of her surviving siblings, but Elizabeth was not encouraging. "They never talk about it, you know. My sister, whenever she hears about it, she faints."

How was it, I wondered, that after thirty-five years, Elizabeth had decided, "I've still got time left, and I'm ready to talk," while her seventy-one-year-old sister passed out cold when she saw trailers for *Schindler's List*?

"Some people want to make these kids cry," she confided on the way to the classroom. "I don't believe in that," she rasped with the coffee-thick traces of her Polish accent. "They have to have hope."

The instructor who had contacted the Foundation to invite Elizabeth, a graduate student named Emily, met us at the door of Wheeler 21, excessively polite, profusely grateful. I thought I recognized her large front teeth from campus, a lifetime ago. Twenty students gripping ready ballpoints sat in a murmuring horseshoe; their voices dropped when Elizabeth walked in.

Despite what she'd said about hope, Elizabeth was a survivor from the school of aggressive normalcy. After fifty years of withholding it, she had come to handle the truth like a blunt object. When she described wheeling her mother's emaciated body to the graveyard in the Lodz ghetto, when she told them how she and her sister scraped their own shallow pit with their raw fingers, how they heaved their mother's corpse into a grave they could mark only with a stick, Elizabeth did not grow soft, or press her fingers to her face. She coughed once, then sipped slowly from the paper cup sitting on the corner of the table. It struck me: She had learned how to open the locked box inside of her without stepping outside of it.

"Does anyone have any questions?" Scanning the class, I raised my eyebrows encouragingly.

An athletic girl with blond hair looked at Elizabeth. "Do you forgive the Germans?" she managed to ask.

"Forgive?" Elizabeth's hand flew up like a dazed, wheeling bird, injured, widowed, off course. "I cannot forgive," she pronounced, "what only the dead can forgive."

Elizabeth did not fully appreciate that her answers were showstoppers. "For the fiftieth anniversary," Elizabeth offered—the anniversary of the Liberation—"they had a big reception for us, for the few of us who came back," she told the students, her mouth moist. "*They* stood on one side of the room, and we stood on the other, but no one approached us." Blank stares. "I went back to Lodz," she continued, "to look for my mother's grave. Of course, it was impossible. Nonetheless," Elizabeth shrugged. "I went to the caretaker's office to ask. Two men were there in long coats. 'Who are you?' they asked me. 'Why do you want to know?' 'My mother is buried here,' I told them. 'I am a Jew.' 'Impossible!' the man said to me, 'There are no Jews in Lodz.'"

After the talk, bodies streamed out through the classroom door with polite, demure thanks. It was Wednesday at noon. From across the Bay, air raid sirens droned through the afternoon sky. Elizabeth blew her nose into a wadded tissue pulled from the corner of her sleeve. "These young people are very shy, very timid about the past." She folded the tissue and tucked it back into her sleeve.

Elizabeth Landau wasn't a fainter. Hers was the stolid, compartmentalizing gaze on the past that allowed people to survive. Jewish history of the late twentieth century was practically built on it. Little boxes. The morning after my sister's wedding, while my mother sat at the turquoise kitchen counter ticking off complaints on her still freshly lacquered fingers, my father offered his wisdom about how to handle the things that upset her, a philosophy that seemed to have informed the worldview of so many of my clients: "We each have little compartments inside ourselves, and we just need to lock things up and put them away." Sometimes it worked. Sometimes it didn't.

Up in the Campanile tower, the carillon bells clamored. Elizabeth Landau, I remembered, had had a husband who died recently, a husband of forty years, who, like herself, had been a Holocaust survivor. She hadn't mentioned him. "What was it like to be married to another survivor?" I asked her. "Did you have similar experiences during the War?"

"Ellen," Mrs. Landau spoke my name for the first time; her accent made it sound truncated, somehow, like "Helen" without the "H," the initial sound swallowed in a soft swirl across her palate. "We never talked about it."

I nodded. "But you know what happened to him?" I nodded again.

But Elizabeth shook her head.

I expected her to confess that it had been a terrible mistake, a source of perpetual regret, this history they had never shared. But she didn't. Her gaze fixed on the wide waters of the Bay. "We never spoke of those things to one another," she said tenderly. "We never," she added, "never needed to. It was already between us. And the details," Mrs. Landau paused again, her tongue resting along the edge of her teeth; she waved the details away with a flutter of her hand. Sure, I realized, she was a talker *now*; but for fifty years, she'd been a withholder, and a very successful one. At the time, I judged her for that.

Elizabeth Landau turned from the students streaming through Sather Gate. She looked at my face so long I had to force myself not to look away. "Are you married?" she asked me. She glanced at my hands. "Do you *have*," she asked, "a boyfriend?"

I had felt my face flush. I hated that a simple, honest answer had the power to derail the entire conversation, and Francine and I weren't engaged to be married then. Would I have said I had a girlfriend? A lover? I said: "I'm in a relationship." Elizabeth smiled, a polite, disinterested smile. "Yes, of course." Her lips had been frosted with a pale pink that had faded, now, to the deeper red-brown of her mouth showing through. Then her smile, too, faded. "You understand, Ellen. You allow each other separateness, things you do not speak of."

"Privacy," I suggested, remembering my grandmother's quiet hand on my back.

"Dignity." She corrected me firmly, and with finality. In her shining pupils, two tiny versions of me looked back.

Before Francine and I decided to get married, though, I didn't see my reflection in those mirrors. If anything, I feared I would always be the fainting sister. Compared to my tight-lipped parents, to my cool, MBA sister Rebecca, I'd never been able to keep my feelings under wraps. Not well. I'd had a passionate, painful, and very secret first love in high school, and that had ended terribly.

Then, in college, I'd started dating Sam, a petite half-Cubana Canadian with thumbprint dimples and Chairman Mao pants. Brilliant, charming, and sometimes melancholy, Sam had coached me through my coming out. Coming out in college had seemed like the antithesis of all that familial withholding, life out of the closet a repudiation of silence, a path to power. Pinned to the straps of our book bags, buttons draped our chests like the insignia of decorated generals: *Lesbians Ignite!*, *Defeat Homophobia*, *SILENCE = DEATH!* But that powerful outspokenness was never native to me. Sam went her own way after college and I went mine. All her effortless intelligence that I loved, and admired, and was leaving. By the time I moved to Berkeley, I'd become a girl who picked up a carton of *mu-shu* vegetables every night and shared it with her dog.

I didn't feel like I was hiding, though. I believed I was just waiting for someone to share my stories with. Then one full-moon Friday night in early October 1990, Francine and I met on the steps of her little wisteria-covered East Oakland cottage, got into Francine's car together, and drove to Club Q. My college friend and grad-school roommate Debbie had introduced us because, according to her super-scientific formula, "you both have dogs." The wind was blowing in my face, and, for just one unfraught second, my heart skipped with the vacant joy of all the things it stood just on the other side of knowing.

The dark, strobe-lit room smelled like perfume, beer, sweat, and smoke. I found an empty chair at the edge of the dance floor. It was still early, not quite ten. "Scoot over?" Francine tapped my knee. She was wearing black jeans and a navy blazer with the sleeves rolled up over a white "Queer Nation" T-shirt. She nudged in next to me and we sat, not trying to talk over the music, watching dykes in vests and T-shirts snap and grind to Soul II Soul. Then they started playing Sister Sledge.

Francine closed her eyes when she danced; her hair flashed auburn under the lights; her body moved like liquid. Afterward, we stepped out onto the sidewalk, our ears hissing with the static after the music, our bodies chilled in our damp T-shirts in the cold night air. That night, alone in my bed, I lay awake, stricken with panic, fallen hard, in knee-knocking, cold-sweat, can't-sleep love with a red-haired girl. Eventually, Francine fell in love with me, too. We thrilled ourselves with our abandon. *Have you done this? This?* But it was never just literal with me. I was trying to reach under her skin more deeply than anyone before me; I thought that if I could reach far enough into her heart, she wouldn't want to let me go. I thought I'd let her all the way into mine.

We stayed true to each other. We withstood trials. A year into our relationship, Francine had gone back to school for her master's. Two years after that, she finished, precipitating the crisis I'd been anticipating since she took her first class at Mills.

"So." I'd perched next to her on the futon we'd come to think of as *our* futon, in the house on Manzanita Court that had become *our* house. "You're leaving. I mean, you've finished grad school, and now you're leaving." I wanted to say it first. I'd wanted at least that much control. Early in our relationship, Francine had talked about how much she'd liked living in Ann Arbor, where she went to college. She said she wanted to see Boston.

"What are you talking about?"

I didn't answer. After my preemptive announcement, I'd found it suddenly difficult to speak.

"Ellen." Francine looked at me. "I'm not leaving. I love it here. I like my family. And I love you. Did you really think you were getting out of this that easy?"

"Liz and I loved each other," I countered. My high school girlfriend. "Sam and I loved each other, too." We'd left each other, it seemed, so easily.

"Liz was straight," Francine pointed out, getting up. "And I think you left Sam."

"People fall in love," I went on, following her into the kitchen, "graduate from school and then leave each other. It's practically a rule." I'd only ever broken up with anyone through attrition. We'd stayed together until we drifted thousands of miles apart. I ground my teeth miserably. Nothing was wrong between me and Francine. It's just the way it was.

"It's not my rule," Francine said, laying two plates out on the table. "And since I'm the one graduating, I get to decide. I love you, I want to be with you, and I'm staying." The thing about Francine was, when it counted, she had this remarkable clarity about things I found impenetrable. Then she added, handing me a glass, "When you graduate, you can decide and you can leave, if you want to." I felt desperately sad and thrilled at the same time. "But, Ellen Margolis, you'd better not. Want to."

Francine frowned at me, her chin breaking into a dozen tiny dimples. A mock scowl. I threw my arms around her. I hugged her so tightly, I broke the glass in my hand. At the ER, they told us the wound was clean. I got a shot of Novocain, six stitches, and a Band-Aid, and they sent us home.

In this way, I forgot something I knew about myself: that as much as I strove in true lesbian feminist fashion for openness and honesty and real communication, I believed deep in my bones that silence was safer. Did I think by coming out of the closet I had excised my entire cultural history? That by slapping on Day-Glo orange stickers (*Loud, pushy, Jewish dyke!*), my secrets and longings were visible from outer space? My parents and their generation had shed Jewish ritual observance like their *bubbe's* old *shmatas*, but they couldn't shed the old fears and superstitions that come with centuries of expulsions and pogroms, the glance over your shoulder to make sure no one is looking, the pinch of salt tossed in the eye of the devil, the *kine hora* twined into the DNA. Neither could I. I wasn't really loud.

Or pushy. No matter what I said, I was still my grandmother's child, still my parents' daughter. I was a Jew of the late twentieth century, and silence was my legacy. But when Francine and I decided to get married, I couldn't see it then. Because the best way to keep a secret is to keep it from yourself.

( )

Despite the three-hour time difference in the other direction, Fiona, characteristically, slept until eleven, dead to the world in the middle of the house while Francine and I attended to the usual, domestic routine. Francine and I still lived in our tiny Craftsman bungalow at 6156 Manzanita Court in Rockridge, just off Broadway. "More of a *schmungalow* than a bungalow," Francine liked to say, because sometime in the early '70s, someone thought it made sense to turn the six-hundred-square-foot, one-bedroom, one-story house into a six-hundred-and-eighty-square-foot, one-bedroom, *two*-story house. Aside from the wooden coffee table and the futon, the secondhand desk and the bed, we still didn't have any real furniture, which was fine, I reassured Francine whenever I saw her curled up with the Pottery Barn catalog, because we didn't have room for anything else. *Yet!* I always added, at Francine's frown. (I thought of style as something we would grow into; she saw it as something we perpetually did without.)

We'd moved into Manzanita Court six and a half years earlier, the second weekend of October 1991; the very next weekend, the Oakland Hills went up in flames. The sky went coal black; hot dry winds pushed the fire to the hills just above the house. We packed the dogs and ran. We didn't come back until the next day; in the yard, a single, complete page from someone's diary, only its edges charred, had blown up on the lawn.

Water rushed through the pipes. Then the dogs swirled into the living room to the crooning of Fiona's voice. Francine and I were holed up in the kitchen, the first big announcement behind us, relieved to have to decide only what to eat.

Francine stood scrubbing the potatoes at the sink. She was making her "famous" potatoes, little red ones chopped in wedges, baked on a tray with olive oil, salt and pepper, in honor of St. Patrick's Day weekend. Italian, not Irish, but still: potatoes. It was all gourmet to Fiona, whose mother, Cait Collins, I had never seen take anything out of the kitchen cabinet besides a glass. I kept one eye on the phone, but it didn't ring. "I'll never forget how strange it was, the first time I saw your mother and your Gram peeling the mushrooms." Francine shook her head, scraping at the crevice of a potato with a fingernail. These were the bits of history we carried for each other, the small shared accumulations of a lifetime together.

"But now you think it's normal, right?"

"No," Francine answered. "I think it's kind of like ironing your underwear."

Fiona appeared in the doorway in rumpled boxer shorts and a big gray sweatshirt, blinking away sleep. "Good morning, little lovebirds," she cooed. She looked significantly from me to Francine. "So, do we have plans?"

"Tea?" Francine offered.

Fiona reached for a mug. "For *the wedding*."

The last wedding I had been to was my sister's. It was two years before, and on that morning my mother galloped down the hallway to the bride's bedroom, bony ankles visible between the hem of her cotton nightie and her high-heeled bedroom slippers, belting "I'm Getting Married in the Morning!" Passing through the hall with all the melody of a lone Canada goose, she burst into my sister's room and grabbed Rebecca fiercely. Unmoving, Rebecca touched three fingers absently to the twin gold braids wound in a coil at the top of her head.

Never mind that my mother didn't want Rebecca to marry

Ted Hsu. (Shelling a pistachio with a long, pink nail the night before, she'd offered coolly, "I'm sure *his* parents feel the same way.") From the half-opened door of my childhood bedroom, I watched my mother disappear into my sister's room, propelled by the urgent, purely generic truth that this was a wedding, her daughter the bride. Standing inside my own former bedroom's closet, Francine had pulled her camisole over pale, damp shoulders. Her brown suit hung on paper-covered hangers over the top of the door. I stared at the tops of her thighs, white in her white cotton underpants. The closet smelled strongly of plastic, faintly of groomed leather. Francine and I exchanged glances; she rolled her eyes, but in her forehead I saw a faint wrinkle of real distress; Francine was costuming herself for the euphemistic role in which my mother would always script her: Ellen's "friend."

It didn't matter that Francine, unlike Ted, was Jewish, a coupling my mother should have approved as within the Tribe. Women did not "marry" each other. Not in the pages of the Sunday *Times*.

Was it pathetic that some part of me wanted my mother's frenetic displays of fake enthusiasm? I knew she would never sing that song for me.

"Well," Fiona, ever eager to be my chief problem-solver, started, "what kind of weddings have your *friends* had?" Fiona always imagined we knew *all* the lesbians. We lived in the Bay Area, didn't we?

Francine moved to the chopping board and whacked the potatoes into wedges. "No kind," I admitted. We'd never been to a lesbian wedding, had never even heard of anything besides a "commitment ceremony." And we hadn't even been to one of those. In retrospect, given that Bill Clinton had sold us down the river with the Defense of Marriage Act—or maybe it was *because* Bill Clinton had signed the Defense of Marriage Act—I don't quite know what gave us the *chutzpah* to decide we *would* have a wedding, except that maybe, like the recent *Newsweek* lesbians and the *Dateline* lesbians and the Queer Nation lesbians we had been, we were just tired of waiting.

Fiona put the kettle on. "I saw a *Dateline* exposé," she started again, as if there were upsides to our ignorance. "They sent fake brides out to caterers for quotes. Then they sent in guys allegedly planning bachelor parties, and old ladies throwing luncheons for their church groups." Fiona picked up a raw potato, stuck it absently in her mouth, made a horrible face and spat it back out. "They all asked for the same food. They all had the same number of guests. But the bachelors and the church ladies paid less." What was she saying? That people who want to get married are chumps? Or that we'd get a discount if we pretended not to be getting married? That would be ironic. Or, did she mean that, if we said we were getting married, we'd pay the price? I should have been wondering: Why was Fiona watching exposés on wedding caterers? The kettle whistled, more whine than whistle, something else Francine thought we needed to replace.

"Sure," said Francine, scraping a pile of potato peels into the paper bag she'd set at her feet. Scraps clung to her wet fingers. "Who wants to skimp on their own wedding? The biggest day of your life, the symbol of all your potential future happiness as a couple."

The biggest day of our life? The symbol of all our future happiness? Was that what Francine thought about our wedding? (Even as a kid, I had never dreamed about being a bride. Rebecca had conscripted the role. Five years old, Rebecca rubbed her old baby blanket experimentally against her cheek, then swirled the soft knit fabric high above her and let it settle against her fine, blond hair. "Let's play brides," she announced. "You be a bride and I be a bride." She tilted her chin up and lowered her lashes coquettishly. "It's like princesses." "You be the bride," I'd answered. "I'll be the house painter.") I felt a new pang of guilt about lying the night before to Francine. It seemed like a small thing: a phone call from an old lady. But if a wedding was all about symbols, what was a marriage that began with a lie? I decided I would tell her when Fiona wasn't around.

"Obviously, no one wants to pay more." Fiona blew into her steaming mug. Her upper lip was a little thin, like her mother's. "The caterers take advantage of all the cultural baggage around a wedding, and the couples are so wound up in it themselves that they don't revolt and boil spaghetti at home." Maybe I was more indoctrinated than I realized: I may not have thought much about weddings, but I knew I didn't want to boil spaghetti at home. Without a real wedding, a big public statement, what would getting married to Francine really mean? We were already a couple—had been a couple for over six years. No one was going to think of us as *forever* unless we made a statement. But *our potential future happiness as a couple*—somehow the dimensions of the thing were becoming enormous. There must be some kind of middle ground. I waited for Francine to inject her opinion, but she just chopped the wedges harder.

"And I'm sure, if the bride's family is paying," Fiona mused, "there's the guilt factor. If they're not paying enough, do they really love their daughter?" I didn't want to think about whether my parents would offer to pay—I guessed they wouldn't.

As if she knew I was thinking about her, my mother called. She's always had a preternatural sense for calling when I least wanted to talk to her: All through college if Sam and I were pulling off each other's clothes in my tiny dorm room, the phone would ring. But I had forgotten about that. Now as it trilled through the invisible center of the house, thinking only of the woman who'd called the night before, I leapt for the phone, and then it was too late.

"What's *new*?" my mother sounded suspicious. In point of fact, she *always* sounded suspicious, a fact that I tended to forget when she happened to have grounds.

"Nothing," I told my mother, cradling the phone between my cheek and my shoulder. Fiona and Francine were still sitting at the table, talking about catering and its discontents. My mother was definitely *not* the next to know. "Actually," I admitted, tossing what I thought was a red herring, "Fiona's here." It was always safer, with my mother, to talk about someone else.

"From New York?"

"Mmm hmmm."

"What's the occasion?"

"No occasion," I lied. "Just visiting."

"No *trouble*?" my mother pressed.

Trouble. My mother didn't mean, *Is Fiona pregnant?* specifically, though she might have meant that, too. She meant any of the kinds of trouble Fiona had been in and out of throughout the long history of our on-again, off-again friendship. Family trouble. Boyfriend trouble (Fiona had had more than her share). School trouble, job trouble. Fiona and I had known each other practically all of our lives. Our mothers were never friends.

"No trouble," I reassured my mother.

"Well, say hello to Fi-ona for me," my mother answered.

Francine stood up and slipped the potatoes into the oven. Fiona got up, too. Their voices trailed through the living room and out onto the back patio, a world away.

"There's something I'd like to talk to you about." My mother's stern tone reeled me back to the small kitchen. (Could she *know*?) "Your father has worked very hard for over thirty years," she started.

My father David was a real estate agent in L.A., commercial real estate, i.e., the Beverly Center. He'd started his business on the sale of a piece of the Atlantic City shore that became one of its biggest casinos. Then, fleeing their own Old Country, my parents moved to L.A.; my unlikely Uncle Irwin, who was only a teenager at the time, joined him a decade later. They never went back. If you spent any time in Los Angeles in the early '80s, you probably saw their names on big white placards rammed into huge, empty lots, fixed to the corners of shining steel boxes: Margolis & Margolis. "There have been ups and downs, but he's been very successful." That was putting it mildly. My father's success in real estate was huge, and both of my parents constantly measured my work at the Foundation against it as a failure. They had invested so much in me, my mother always reminded me, and what had I done to show for it? My mother herself had gone to school in fashion and textile design, gotten married, and kept a room full of lace antiquities locked up in the back of the house. "We don't have you and your

31

sister living here anymore, and there aren't any grandchildren."
Was she blaming me for not giving her grandchildren? Did
she *want* me to? I kept quiet. I couldn't tell where this was going.
"Your father and I would like to travel more." For the same past
thirty years that my father worked late every night, my mother
had maintained a nominal membership to the American Society
of Travel Agents, with her own Sabre number, which she used
exclusively to book a spring and a fall trip to Europe for herself
and my father. Now she announced my father's retirement warningly, as if I didn't know she had been waiting those thirty years to
finally have my father all to herself. It was a paradox, I realized,
waiting for whatever it was my mother had to say; my closest role
model for romantic intimacy was the relationship from which I
had been most painfully excluded. My mother paused dramatically.
"We're selling the house."

"Oh." I bit off the word before any others could come out
after it. That's how it was with my mother: the strongest feelings
compacted into the fewest syllables.

The house on Dunsmuir Drive was where I had learned to bake
at my Gramma Sophie's elbow, soaking up the sweetness of her
silent, flour-and-sugar love while my mother retained her mystery
behind the locked door of her secret room, the egg whites glossed
to white waves in the bowl. That house and baking with my
Gramma Sophie were synonyms for each other. "Here, *puppe*."
Doll. Gramma Sophie would hand me the beater, frosted white
with sweet meringue to travel with my tongue when my mother
and Rebecca went shopping for clothes without me, when my
sister moved on to boys, when I stayed home to study for my AP
exams. Together, we baked the tin of chocolate chip cookies
Gramma Sophie sealed with raisin-soft fingers and tucked into
my suitcase the night before I left home for good. Without a place,
where would those memories belong? That house was the
Haunted House mirror in which I could still see my grandmother's face. And my parents were throwing it away.

As I stared into the empty fireplace, it seemed suddenly that
scraps from every album of my life, every era, torn, curled, burnt

at the edges and all out of order, were being borne off on an eddying gust, swirling down everywhere. Among them, a single memory flared and settled like a page ripped from my gramma's book of recipes: A day in winter. L.A., late February, hot and smoggy. A day like so many other days. My father was still at work. Outside, Rebecca and I were killing the hour before dinner, pedaling our bikes in circles up and around the sloping edges of the driveway on Dunsmuir, pretending we were gliding at the bottom of an ocean. Gramma Sophie was in the house making lasagna, stretching slick, white noodles blank as papyrus across the bottom of a Pyrex dish with wet fingers, shaking tomato sauce in runic letters across the top. Our mother stepped out, looking for the mail, waiting for something to change. She shaded her face, hovered on the step for a minute, and then disappeared behind the kitchen door, through which I could see Gramma Sophie, spaghetti sauce on her apron, looking up just as the door started to close.

We each have little compartments inside ourselves. I could hear my father's voice again. I reminded myself: I didn't get to protest. I was the one who'd left.

"When?" I asked her.

My mother went on in great detail about my father's predictions for the spring real estate market. "As soon as possible," she concluded. My father would keep working, but they'd travel half the year. "I just wanted to let you know," my mother added. As if she might not have.

I hooked my fingers on the mantel of the old clinker fireplace in the living room, the phone tucked under my chin, my mother's breath sucking hungrily at my ear. I thought of that old woman the night before with her mysterious phone call, her insinuating voice. Of course, it all made sense. My parents with all their clubby intimacy had never needed anybody else. Now they were scrubbing themselves of us, my grandmother and me. (In the new condo, there would be a climate-controlled, locked room for my mother's secret collection of antique lace.) Why did it matter what my parents did? Getting married was supposed to make

Francine my home; it was supposed to give me a new foundation, make my hearth the new family hearth. But as I stared into the ashy fireplace, I felt less like an adult about to start my life than like the child I had been. It might have been different if I knew that all of society, or if at least my own parents were behind me. But I knew they weren't. "Okay," I said. I couldn't bear to be on the phone with my mother anymore. I could hear Francine's voice, not the words but the music, drifting in from the backyard, and I wanted to go to it. "I guess that's what you have to do."

In the backyard, Francine and Fiona were talking about breaking the glass. You don't have to know anything more about Judaism than *Fiddler on the Roof* to know the sound of a Jewish wedding is the crash of glass, followed by a hail of cheers. The familiarity of it comforted me. After all, my parents had rejected most of Judaism, too, and the Jews still managed to survive. (If our wedding was "too Jewish," would that part repulse them, too?)

I pulled up a chair on our small brick patio, shaded by the overspreading redwood, bordered by a small, dry garden of river boulders and feathery native grasses, and let my fingers fall against the back of Francine's hand. I'd interviewed a survivor of Lodz, once, whose sister had gotten married in the ghetto. They'd shattered a broken pane of window glass. "When the glass shattered," Roman said, "it returned them to our hell. But there was hope in that sound, too. Continuity. Life." Continuity—that's what I wanted, for a wedding to connect me with my culture and my past, instead of causing the line to break.

"It represents the woman's hymen breaking." Fiona made a face. She'd majored in Women's Studies.

Francine bristled. Fiona had violated a rule torn from the same book as "No one criticizes my mother except me": No one tears apart Judaism except Jews. The problem was, Fiona had spent so much time on the West side of L.A., she didn't always realize she wasn't a Jew.

"Actually," Francine, who knew a thing or two about Jewish holiday traditions, cleared her throat, "breaking the glass is about the destruction of the Temple in Jerusalem." A jay darted down to the patio, hopped along the warm, dry bricks, and was unceremoniously barked back up into the redwood by the dogs. Francine got up and went inside for more tea.

"She doesn't have to get so pissy," Fiona whispered. But she left it at that. Maybe she realized, if forced to choose, I'd choose Francine. When Francine came back out and handed her a fresh mug, Fiona chirped, recovering, "I know how we can find out." She disappeared into the house; when she returned, she was holding a brand-new copy of *Jumping the Broom: Weddings in Every Culture*. Francine and I glanced at each other. *A wedding guide?* Francine mouthed. I raised my eyebrows. Fiona certainly hadn't bought it for the two of us.

Fiona plopped back into her lawn chair, her pale feet bare on the warm bricks, and, dropping her finger between the pages of *Jumping the Broom*, she guffawed. "This is great!" she roared. "'The breaking of the glass is a symbolic enactment of breaking the hymen.'" Francine frowned. Fiona held up her hand. "'Which explains why it was considered important that the groom 'accomplish' the deed. If the *bride* stepped on the glass,'" Fiona raised her voice significantly, "'the groom's traditional role as *paterfamilias* was threatened.'" Fiona looked up, her face bright. "I *love* it!" she roared. "So," Fiona sipped her tea, "which one of you two *brides*," she raised her eyebrows, "is going to do the 'deed'?"

Fiona was hopeless. I shrugged, as if I hadn't already started imagining stomping on it myself.

"Ellen," Francine answered, leaning back in her seat. Her shoulders were pink with heat against the worn wood.

"Why?" I think my mouth hung open. I'd expected at least to put up a fight for it.

Francine considered me under her eyebrows. Just like my grandmother, who always sliced the frosting off her piece of cake and handed it to me, Francine said simply: "Because I know you want to."

I reached for my tea, shifted my weight in my chair, and came down on a sharp pinprick of pain in my foot. "Ow!" I tapped Francine on the knee.

"It's a wart," she said. I grimaced in horror. Francine had just gone to the spa, for God's sake, to celebrate her best friend June's birthday. There was not being girly and then there was being a toad. I had to get rid of that thing.

Fiona looked up from the book. "When *is* the wedding?" she asked, eagerly. "I need to get plane tickets."

Francine looked at me, uncertain, as if I'd already promised Fiona a wedding date. "Did you tell your mother?"

"Are you *joking*?" I turned my foot wart-side to the ground. Of course, with my parents, I'd eventually face the usual unpleasantness. I wasn't in any hurry to seek it out.

I knew she wasn't looking forward to telling them, either.

"Are we calling up Betty and Sol?" I gently tugged her earlobe. Francine's parents, who lived in Berkeley, had always been more approving. They were older than my parents, inspiring a comfortable rapport with them Francine ascribed to what she called my AARP-o-philia.

"Don't be ridiculous." Francine shook out her curls.

When you grow up different from your own family, you need to find your own "people" first, friends who can support you for who you are, before you expose yourself to the people whose disapproval will crush you most of all. Regardless of our different parents, we were no different that way.

Leaning back into her patio chair, Fiona, pale from a New York winter, rolled her boxer shorts up to the tops of her thighs. She squinted at me, her left nostril rising. "You could run off and elope." It sounded like a dare. It sounded like something Fiona herself would do.

"Oh, come on," I protested, "you can't just," I snapped my fingers, "get married." Of course, you could. Just drive down to the county courthouse, or zip over to Reno. If you were straight, that is. We couldn't just do that. We couldn't do that at all. We had to do all the other things. Or else, what was it?

Francine started to open her mouth. Inside the house, the

phone rang out. Probably my mother again. She never called just once. Francine got up. Fiona and I sat in the quiet garden, the soft breath of March in our faces. Inside the house, Francine's voice murmured, grew sharp with interrogation then with impatience. It wasn't my mother.

Adrenaline spiked my veins.

Francine came back and announced: "We just had a crank call."

Not ten minutes ago, I had decided to tell Francine the truth. But now, a sharp and immediate fear of discovery told me that I would do no such thing. In a cheater's way of thinking, I rationalized it quite easily: Francine, after all, encompassed her own worlds. Why shouldn't I?

( )

Anya Kamenets appeared at the Foundation on the last bright morning of March, windswept and without an appointment, a diminutive woman of about seventy, wrapped in a gray rain jacket, wearing surprisingly fashionable, fine leather shoes. It had been a week since Fiona had packed up her wedding guide and headed back to New York. Francine and I, having decided nothing more about what it meant for two people outside the law to get married, had gone back to work, where Anya Kamenets was lying in wait. I actually noticed her as I rushed from the Embarcadero BART station toward the Foundation, into the office late after an interview off-site, but the sidewalk was full of people rushing places and I didn't know her. She was just another stranger. I didn't stop.

Laid out right over the bones of the old Gold Rush steamers, San Francisco's northern streets angle off Market into the Financial District like the tines of an old TV antenna, acute angles creating intersections where you don't expect them. The Foundation for the Preservation of Memory sits right there on the seams, in five floors of an old building made new with internet money.

Just five years ago, the Foundation hunkered, a one-room archive, in the fog-damp basement of a house in the Sunset. Then one cold summer day the grandson of an Auschwitz survivor and the grandniece of a Lodz resident met on the steps, fell in love, and decided to start a database company. With the IPO of Max^2, the little archive run by Wendy Rosenberg moved its load of fog- and sea-salt-heavy boxes out of the Sunset District basement into the big, blue-carpeted new archives building south of Market, a wide Bay-facing window in the entry-level reading room looking east toward the sharp, white compass point of the Claremont Hotel.

Foundation visitors entered on the fifth floor to a large burlwood reception desk and a tasteful black-and-white photo montage. A bank of computers provided access to the archive's catalog; behind them, rows of polished cherry work tables, wide and smooth, ran between glass display cases of camp uniforms, lockets, photos and even hair, as well as framed archival letters; beyond these, in big, wooden file drawers and tall wooden bookcases, shelf upon shelf of memory books, manuscripts and transcripts lined the walls, mute and black as mourners at graveside. That's where she was standing when Jeremy, the temp subbing for our regular receptionist Mi'Chelle, called me down from my office twenty minutes later: gazing toward the window, her hands folded together in a knot. She introduced herself.

"Ms. Kamenets." I offered my hand.

"Anya," she corrected me without unknotting her own. Her eyes, a pair of sideways parentheses arcing up above her high, rosy cheeks, naturally asquint almost to the point of closing, squeezed tighter with a charming, close-lipped smile that sent a fan of wrinkles spreading out to all the corners of her face.

I introduced myself, too. "Do you have an appointment, Ms. Kamenets?" If Ms. Kamenets—Anya—had an appointment, it was news to me. My boss Wendy was out. Mi'Chelle was out. Francine and I were getting married. My parents were selling the house. So much had changed. Maybe I'd forgotten. "Does Ms. Kamenets have an appointment today?" I asked Jeremy, the temp, a disconcertingly skeletal guy with drooping, shoulder-length brown hair, sounding as calm as possible and hoping to god I hadn't fucked something up. But Jeremy had burrowed his head back into a worn copy of *A Brief History of Time*.

Anya smiled again. "I would like to talk," she consented. Her hair, which was perfectly straight, was pulled back and tied with a black silk ribbon.

39

We never took interviews with people off the street. No one ever came in like that. I tried again. "Do you have an appointment with Wendy Rosenberg?"

Anya shrugged, a big comic shrug, shoulders up to her ears, hands held open at her sides, eyebrows shooting up. She nodded encouragingly. "We can talk?" Was it her, the woman from the phone?

"Ms. Kamenets," I asked her gently, "are you a survivor of the Holocaust?" Weird as it may seem, there were any number of reasons people showed up at our door, and weird things had been happening.

"*Anya*," the small, parenthetical woman corrected me. "Yes," she answered, nodding; her face broke out again in joyful wrinkles, as if she'd just agreed to something delightful, while her mouth turned down in a regretful smile of abject misery.

"Let's make you an appointment," I offered. We never interviewed without preparation. Some research, an intake, so that when I met with a client for the interview, I knew the context, I had some questions to ask. People think of the Holocaust as one monolithic event, but it wasn't. It happened in different places to different people. There were six million different stories. I turned to the reception desk to use Jeremy's computer. "What day would be good for you?" I asked, my back to Anya Kamenets.

Then something weird happened again. "What day would be good for me for what?" answered my boss, Wendy Rosenberg. Small, warm, and curvaceous as a round of challah, Wendy had stopped behind me, still pulling off her coat. Anya Kamenets was nowhere to be found.

"I thought you were out for the morning?"

"I forgot my laptop." Wendy shrugged.

There was no way I was going to tell Wendy Rosenberg that a mysterious woman had called me at home, that a mysterious woman (the same one? A different one? I decided she must be the one) had shown up here and disappeared. (Had she been here, or was I imagining things? I glanced at Jeremy, who didn't look up from his book.) There was no question in my mind what Wendy would say: *Make it stop.* I didn't want to.

I walked into the large, upstairs office I shared with Wendy as if it were just a normal day at the office and, while Wendy picked up her laptop, glanced at my phone: no messages. Then, as soon as Wendy walked out again, I hurried down to the card catalog of survivor testimonies to look up *Anya Kamenets*.

I found her. Down in a booth in the media room, I learned that Anya was one of the few survivors of Lithuania's Kovno Ghetto. It was a very typical interview, conducted just nine months earlier, right there in the new Foundation building, in the glassed interview room with its fresh blue carpet and its slightly uncomfortable, homey, overstuffed blue chairs. Wendy and Anya Kamenets. Same raincoat, same smile. I had probably seen her walk in.

Anya had gone from Kaunas's Jewish intellectual elite to the ghetto, to the partisans, the hard-labor camps of the East. I usually loved to hear stories about the Resistance, proof that we fought back. But there was no joy in Anya's tale, no spark. Kaunas. Kovno. Slobodka. She recited a hero's tale. Told with great detail. Little feeling. She often smiled. The smile seemed to be a reflex of her face, a habit of survival. It hid her eyes.

Anya had already left her testimony. So why had she returned? Emerging from the dark media carrel, rubbing my eyes against the brightness of the late March day streaming through the big bay-facing windows, I decided that she must have disappeared because she'd seen Wendy. I was convinced that she was the woman from the phone and that for some reason she had come to see me.

Sam, my college girlfriend, disagreed. Instead of going straight back to my desk, I'd stepped outside onto Market Street and found myself at a phone booth, where I'd pulled out my Sprint card and called the one person I knew who would never call up Francine.

Sam was a blazing intellect, and, by virtue of coming out nine months before I had in college, she had always seemed exponentially more certain of our place in the world. (As newly hatched gay college students, we matured in dog years, frantically making up for the true adolescence we had missed.) She'd spent the bulk of our senior year holed up in a windowless room we called the Monk's Cell, smoking cigarette after cigarette, typing out a thesis on medical history and eighteenth-century French literature called *The Anatomy of Desire*. If anyone would have a brilliant insight about what it meant that I had fallen into a state over a little old lady, it would be Sam. She tended to dicourage obsessional thinking in others, having found it was much harder to nip the habit in herself.

Sam surprised me by picking up the phone. She was a medical resident now in Toronto, working days at a stretch, a far cry from the girl who had smoked on Sunday mornings in bed, picking out Tracy Chapman songs on her blue guitar. "Hey. You called me!" She went on to tell me that she had just met someone, another intern. It occurred to me that I should tell her Francine and I were engaged. But, as Sam told me more about this new girlfriend, she drawled a little ruefully, it seemed to me, for someone who was newly in love. I knew, too, that she was prone to epic fits of melancholy, to bouts of depression. Sam was my ex, the woman I had left in order to meet Francine. "I just had a strange visit," I told her instead.

"She came in for an interview with you, even though she'd already interviewed with your boss?" Immediately, Sam sounded thoughtful, right in her element. She'd always been a magnet for confidences. "Do you think she's a chronic?"

It was a term we'd used in college, back when Sam and I staffed *SHOUT!*, the GLBT sexuality/coming-out hotline run out of a basement room on batik-draped couches. Our supervisors had warned us about the *chronics*: not students, but lonely relics of a not-so-distant age who called year after year, hoping to tell the same agonized stories, to say the same forbidden words to a sympathetic, eager gay college student. (I glanced over my shoulder at the Foundation building, guessing my life hadn't changed so much.)

Could Anya Kamenets be a "chronic"? I'd never heard that term used to describe a Holocaust survivor. Mostly because, more than anything, they were people who had chosen not to talk. But if Anya Kamenets wanted to tell her story over and over, compulsively, who would dare to call it *chronic*?

"If you're not sure," Sam suggested, "you should talk to your supervisor."

"Hmmm," I traced my finger along a heart scratched into the phone booth's glass, "I'm not sure I should do that."

"Because you already feel like you've done something illicit," Sam offered. The illicit had always been Sam's area of expertise, in literature and in love, but she sounded tired of it now. I *did* feel like I had done something illicit. As if, even though I didn't know anything about Anya, I'd invited her there myself. (I hadn't mentioned the mysterious phone call.) That was natural, Sam said, a kind of projection and counter-projection that was normal in these cases. As long as I didn't act on it. Maybe she had grown up; even Sam didn't think that everything needed airing anymore. "I wouldn't worry about it," Sam reassured me with the air of someone who had left the intrigues of *Liaisons Dangereuses* for the white coat and stethoscope. "Unless you hear from her again, I wouldn't let it bother you." She already sounded like a doctor. Though I knew I should take her advice, the idea that Anya was simply a chronic left me feeling strangely deflated.

After we hung up, I kept wondering what "acting on it" would mean. A normal person wouldn't be thinking about how to have an illicit conversation with an odd old lady. A normal person in my shoes would be obsessing about wedding cakes and—and— wedding stuff. Clearly, I wasn't a normal person.

For a long while after I stepped out of the phone booth, I watched the F-line trains glide up and down Market Street like colorful fish. Though the line was fairly new, the trains were old—refurbished, antique cars from cities around the world. This one was bright orange, and angular. *Milan,* it read. Underneath that, the original date: 1814. As I walked back to the Foundation, the F-Market sailed on, fresh, shiny and new, still haunted by the people to whom it had once belonged.

( )

But as Francine and I got ready to go to her parents' house for dinner the next Sunday night, I decided I was being too hard on myself. I was starting a new life with the woman I loved. Not just the woman I loved—her family, too. Sunday dinners with Francine's family had always comforted me with the idea that I could have a future that was better than my past. Her parents seemed so different than mine in such fundamental ways. What Francine always said about that: "Because they're not *your* parents."

Francine's parents Betty and Sol lived in North Berkeley, in the house where Francine grew up, at the top of a dead-end road on the oak-gnarled outskirts of Tilden Park. The first Sunday night I met them, when we pulled up to the house on Laurel Road, Sol and Betty were working in the garden, Francine's father pruning roses, Francine's mother kneeling by the thick green sod, pulling weeds.

They'd been older than I'd pictured. Betty had straight hair that she kept short and almond-shaped hazel eyes, the color of Francine's. Her cheeks were round, but loose under the jaw, and the skin on her neck looked slightly papery. Francine's mother wore sensible, outdoor clothes that were the antithesis of any outfit in which I had ever seen my own mother: a plaid shirt, relaxed-fit jeans, dirty sneakers. (I could no more see my mother and father working in their garden together than I could imagine them scrubbing their own toilets.) Standing on the grass, Betty wore no jewelry, with the exception of a simple gold wedding band that cut slightly into the soft flesh of her finger, and, just visible in the *V* of her Oxford, a round gold locket, big as a silver dollar, the kind that held a photo. In her greeting—"Nice to meet you, Ellen"—I detected the faint traces of an accent.

"South Africa?" I asked.

"Very good." Betty's eyes twinkled with sardonic appreciation. "The really thick guess, 'Scotch?' That's not even a language; it's a drink!" She laughed just a little acridly. Her gaze, when she laughed, focused on a point far in the distance. "We came over when I was a little girl."

Sol had put down his pruning shears. He took my hand in a big warm grip and shook it, grabbing my elbow with his gloved hand before he turned to hug Francine. He was short and compact with tendrils of pure white hair curling in a cultivated patch at the top of his head, mowed clean and straight around his nape and ears.

Next to her parents, Francine looked like a living model of the Mendelian genotype chart: her mother's hair and eye color, her father's hands and curls, evidence of a neatly split genetic merger. Unlike me, the genetic replica of my father, for whom my mother had apparently provided the services of a pod. (I do think she loved me for the resemblance, and resented me for the lack of representation.) Together, they looked a lot like people who had done it right.

Every Sunday for years, we'd returned to dinners and conversations over their French country table. And over the years, Betty and Sol felt more like family, more like parents, in a way, than my own parents, because the things Betty and Sol cared about were the things I cared about, too. For years, after Sunday dinners when Francine rose to help Sol with the dishes, Betty crooked her finger for me to follow her into Francine's old room to talk politics while she sewed. "I have a feeling you're going to be around here a lot," was how she'd long ago put it, "we might as well teach you something useful"—but she was in fact sounding me out. Betty had a dangerously sharp little pick with which she tore out old stitches. While we talked, she picked out little details about my thoughts and opinions like bits of old thread. It was an interest in my life so different from my mother's that I mistook it for reciprocity, for openness.

Though we hadn't announced anything, Sunday dinner, now that we'd become "engaged," had taken on a new weight. ("Will you love me when I'm fat?" Francine asked, pulling on a pair of jeans in front of the mirror. She'd started anticipating a married future in which we watched each other get lumpy and old.) We sat at the old French country table in our accustomed places, Sol and Betty just back from a trip to England. Betty told us all about Japan Centre. And then: "Your father took me to an interesting lecture about carbon molecules . . ."

Francine's little brother Jerome, who went by "Jigme," had come back from Tibet in 1994 after two years away and surprised us all by announcing that he had decided to major in civil engineering. (We suspected he was a converted Buddhist, but didn't want to tell his parents. Not because, like my ambivalent mother, they would think he had betrayed his people, but because Sol didn't believe that God was subject to proof.) His brown hair stood in soft spikes all over his head, like firmly beaten egg whites. He pushed his glasses up his straight, blunt nose with the middle finger of his left hand and looked at Sol. "I thought this was vacation," he said, swallowing a mouthful of penne.

"That *is* his vacation," Betty teased dryly.

Francine and I had agreed not to tell her parents about our engagement until I'd told mine. Rather, Francine had *announced* to me that she wouldn't be telling her parents until I told mine because she knew that, otherwise, I might never do it. If not telling Betty, Sol, and Jigme that we were getting married felt something like an itch, it was an itch soothed at least partly by the balm of their conversation. The dinner table banter at my own home always orbited around places and things—*that* parcel, *that* condo, *this* car—solid, finite, and, to me, uninteresting; at Sol and Betty's table, we talked about books, movies, ideas, a medium in which I found I could swim, weightless. If Sol had a tendency to pontificate, so did my father. If Betty had a tendency to be wry, my mother did as well, and more pointedly. Sol always expected us to talk back, and challenging him was one of the sauces of the meal. If there were yawning silences, I was too used to them to notice. This, I thought, was family happiness.

That night, after dinner and sewing-table time, we collected quietly in the living room. Betty, carrying in tea, paused to touch Sol's crown after setting his cup on the table. Outside the living room windows, hidden frogs croaked the spring night from puddles down in the park, where silent salamanders crept the night roads on sticky orange feet. Jigme padded across the hardwood floor in his socks. He settled down beside Betty on the couch with a copy of *Snow Crash* and a bowl of Phish Food. Betty's eyes flicked over the top of her *Gourmet* magazine, while Francine and I sat on the floor, our knees crossed under the coffee table, playing chess, which Sol had taught me. She moved her knights aggressively across the board, forcing me, once again, to choose between my bishop and my rook. "Mmmmm hmmmm," Sol cleared his throat.

"Dad, don't help," Francine protested. "He never wants to play, but he always butts in."

Behind us, the glass door to the yard reflected the quiet figures in the Jaffes's living room like still, luminescent creatures at the bottom of a silent ocean.

"I wish we could bottle this," I said out loud. It was something I never would have said in front of my parents, even when we were happy together. It would have spoiled the happiness.

"Chess?" Sol and Jigme asked at once.

I glanced up at Francine, her features warm and familiar in her soft, pale face. "Family happiness."

Jigme blushed and looked at his socks. Sol guffawed and Betty, her pencil poised in the air over her puzzle, looked at me aghast, as if I'd just suggested praying together. "You've gotten too fond of us, dear." She returned to her puzzle. A sharp wit, a dry humor, a powerful, self-effacing art of understatement: These were the things I loved about Francine, too.

When I looked down at the board, Francine checkmated me. It was time to go.

We were still standing in the light of the family home when Francine squeezed my hand and said, "You really see my parents as old people, don't you?" Having an older mother, someone who never understood about fashion or music, had always been a sore point for Francine, who envied all of her school friends their young mothers. It drove her a little bit crazy that their white hair made Betty and Sol so appealing to me. But it seemed unfair that Francine had her old people and I didn't have any. I protested, "What? You have a happy family." Betty and Sol had a quiet, regular domestic life. It wasn't fancy, just comfortable, and that seemed just right to me. "I want to be like them. Is that so bad?"

It seemed like an answer when Francine stroked my palm, the one with the pale, thin scar that had replaced my life line, and blurted, "Let's get rings." I didn't realize she was changing the subject.

"Really?" I asked her. Of course, all the married people had them. "Rings?"

"Just because we're queer, doesn't mean we shouldn't have sparkly, sparkly rocks," Francine opined, reminding me, again, why she and June were friends. And there was a certain appeal to it. With a big rock on your finger, you didn't have to make announcements; you just slashed your shining finger through the air and people understood you were engaged.

I started totting up figures on my fingers. "There are two of us, so, it's not two months' salary. It's four months'," I pointed out. "But, you know, I think it's four months of *that guy*'s salary."

"What? Who?"

"The guy in the diamond ad. 'Isn't two months' salary worth something that will last forever?'" I parroted. "He's probably a stock broker, or a corporate lawyer. Even if you take both of our salaries together—" I did some more calculations on my fingers—"we'd probably have to multiply our salaries by a factor of seven or eight."

Francine shrugged. "Ok. So we'll get diamonds later."

"Okay," I agreed. "Let's get rings." But then something else occurred to me. "But we can't *just* get rings." When Sam and I were in college, Melissa and Diti, the sweetest couple we all knew, had sat down at the long, Formica breakfast table in matching pajamas and, with a sly smile, lifted their clasped, newly ringed hands and announced, "We're married." They had gone out into the moonlit garden and promised to love each other forever. I could see them, two nymphs glowing in the pagan moonlight like a tableau by Maxfield Parrish. And who better suited? But, even at the time, I'd wondered: Couldn't something so simply and privately done be just as simply undone? They wouldn't be the first couple in the GLBSA to announce "We're married," and then split up. No one really expected them to stay together; they didn't have to get divorced.

Francine hadn't let go of my hand, as if she might not let it go until she had actually slipped a ring on it. But now she let it drop. "Right." Francine had come out in college, too. She knew that, without community property behind it, a couple of rings and "We're married" didn't sound real. She glanced back at her parents' door, which had closed behind us long before, as if the answers might be in there. The fact was, we were making this up on the fly.

"I'll talk to Debbie," I offered. Debbie, my college friend and former roommate, the person who had introduced me to Francine, had been the biggest campus activist I knew and was now a civil rights lawyer. Queer Nation East Bay had started up in our living room. "If anyone will know how to make a lesbian wedding a wedding, she will." Francine agreed. I picked up Francine's hand and held it. "But you still *want* rings, right?" I smiled what I hoped was a Fiona-wattage smile, bright enough in the dark driveway to convince her that we were going to figure it out.

49

"Are you kidding?" She winked lasciviously, as if she were talking about sex or chocolate. "I want the most fabulous ring you can buy."

I laughed out loud, partly out of relief and partly out of guilt, because I planned to ask Debbie to meet me at SFMOMA, where I'd confirmed with an anonymous phone call Anya Kamenets still worked part-time as a docent.

( )

Debbie readily agreed to meet me under the shining quartz oculus of the San Francisco Museum of Modern Art. Debbie was a style hound who wore crushed velvet dresses to Whole Foods, a former law student who had once spent our first weekend in the apartment alphabetizing the spice rack. Debbie was as eager to see the frowning Kahlos, as I was to spot Anya and her black-ribboned hair, her stylish shoes. I wanted to know if Anya really was a *chronic*, like Sam thought, or if there was something more to it. I was curious. Who wouldn't be? And if I happened to spot her there at the museum, who could say it was any more than a coincidence?

Debbie and I met in the lobby. High above, hung from an invisible wire, a toaster flew in lazy circles through the vaulted air. I'd forgotten how large the museum was, how honeycombed with darkened galleries. Debbie buzzed toward the paintings, a cloud of cucumber and cinnamon, telling me all about the women she'd had over to watch *Ellen*, while I glanced toward the hidden alcoves, the doors that nearly melted into the walls, marked "Staff." I might push through one of them and find Anya behind it. But then what would I say? Frida Kahlo stared down from the walls with heavy-browed disapproval.

Debbie nodded at the picture on the wall, one of the few self-portraits in which Frida had let her dark hair down. "How's Sam?" A thousand years before, Debbie had introduced me and Sam in the busy portico of Sever Hall, where we realized that we both sat in the third row of *Beauties & Beasts: Medieval Bestiaries*. For the rest of the semester, Sam scribbled satyrs in the margins of my notebook. For a second, I looked at Debbie, elegant in her linen dress and leather purse, and flashed on the college girl in Doc Martens and cutoffs, pink triangle and "Silence = Death" buttons stuck like scales to her ratty black messenger bag. Though Debbie had congratulated me and Sam on not pretending we were going to stay together as a couple after we left for separate coasts, she still had a soft spot for our love. "She's seeing someone new."

Debbie's eyebrows tilted with appreciation. "I can't say I'm surprised." As soon as Sam had moved to Toronto, she had hooked up with someone new. It was how she kept the demons at bay. Even though we weren't together anymore, it had upset me at the time. But that was ancient history. Sam was my ex. Francine and I were getting married—whatever that meant. "What do you think about gay marriage?" We wandered below the shadows of the people passing overhead on the translucent bridge.

Debbie shook her head, knowingly. "With a woman for five minutes, and this is where it goes?" The urge to merge, she meant. It was the oldest joke in the book: *What do lesbians do on the second date? Rent a U-haul.*

I was *going* to say, "Not Sam. Me and Francine." And that might have made a difference. But I'd never been the kind to say something straight out, especially if I could sense disapproval brewing. My mother had taught me that. Instead I said, "No. Seriously. If you were with the right person, would you get married?" Along with Sam, Debbie was the person who had drawn me into a bold, forward, public life out of the closet. *We're here! We're queer! Get used to it!* Long-closeted professors had come out in our wake. Debbie was the person who had introduced me first to Sam, then to Francine. She was practically single-handedly responsible for my entire adult romantic life, and she was an adult, a person whose opinion mattered to me. More than her political opinion, I really wanted her blessing. But that's not what I'd asked for.

"Married?" Debbie shrugged toward a strange portrait of Frida Kahlo and Diego Rivera. The two of them were holding hands, but Kahlo stood behind him, and, in the perspective of the painting, she appeared weirdly small, almost doll-like. "I wouldn't get married to a man if I couldn't get married to a woman." The security guard, a burly woman in polyester pants, glanced over, her face to the side, as if she weren't listening. "And I wouldn't get married to a woman if I couldn't do it legally." Debbie's tone grew clipped, the same quick, hyper-articulate tongue that reminded me she'd grown up in New York, went to Hunter High and then to Harvard and Boalt Law, the same cadence in which she'd demanded an anti-homophobia resolution from the Undergraduate Council. Biracial, Jewish, bisexual, Debbie was not a person who trucked in half-truths. "Marriage is a civil institution. Without the framework of law behind it, a wedding is just a pantomime played out at our own expense." All around us, couples pressed closer to the paintings, serious-looking, comfortable, older men and women holding onto each other's arms. People who had the support of the law. "You can tell yourself you have a right to something," Debbie picked up a fat coffee table book of Degas dancers, flipping through the pages. To her, this was just a hypothetical conversation, a talk about politics. She didn't know that, to me, it was personal. If she did, would she have gone on? I'm pretty sure that she would have. "If you don't have that right and you convince yourself that you do, you're just abetting the enemy."

Abetting the enemy? A chunk of my heart broke off right then and plunged straight through the floor, like a modern art exhibit called, "Girl, Falling Through Space." Just as it did, I spotted an elegant figure with blond hair and a black ribbon. Had she heard what I was saying? It seemed to me, as I raised my head in alarm, that the parenthetical eyes caught my eyes and smiled, a slow, knowing smile, before she melted into the crowd.

( )

Anya had a knack for making me feel like she was the cat and I
was the mouse, and I was too eager to be wanted by someone like
her to realize it had quickly turned the other way around. Seeing
her at the museum made up a little bit for my stinging conversation with Debbie, and I tried to hold onto that feeling by
steeping myself in my work: the world of old ladies with their
secrets to tell. I was at my desk, late, when Fiona called with big
news.

"Well, hello!" Typical Fiona. It was part of her claim on me
that she didn't even need to say her name. "What are you doing?"

"Working," I told her, glancing over at Wendy's empty desk
and massaging the back of my neck. I'd just spent the past four
hours going over microfiche articles on the Piaski Ravine, preparation for an interview with Mrs. Hannah Weiner, a survivor of
Janowska, the final endpoint of Lvov's few surviving Jews.

"Are you sitting down?"

"Practically prostrate," I assured her.

"I met someone."

Growing up, Fiona and I had been tomboys together, until just
like the dandelions that appeared overnight in their big, badly
mowed lawn, Fiona had sprouted huge breasts and the magnetic
attraction of every boy in West Los Angeles. It's no wonder so
many of the transformation myths involve young women. Briar
Rose, *kitsune*, seal-into-selkie, Fiona was all of them. Her straight

black hair, which used to fly wildly behind her on her bike like October wind, now swayed seductively around her shoulders, a spring breeze; her cat-like green eyes had gone glinty. I had always been her sidekick.

"Mmmm." I rooted around in my desk drawer.

"Someone different."

Three loose peanut M&M's rolled out from behind a pile of paperclips. They tasted stale, fragrant with pencil shavings. I loved Fiona. But, having heard these phrases for most of my life, I'd lost some of my itch to inquire. "So?" I prompted Fiona, "*Nu?*"

"So . . ." Fiona started hesitatingly. "I think you'll really like *her.*" Excitement shimmered at the edges of Fiona's silence. She went on quickly. "I've decided that I just can't limit myself, you know?" This was a test.

"Like an omnivore?" I suggested.

"Right." Suddenly, I saw Fiona walking down the streets of Manhattan, *every* pair of eyes on her, the delivery boys and the young, bleach-blond dyke bike messengers, the preppy lesbians with their briefcases under their arms. I reminded myself: Fiona was impulsive. She liked to do things just to see what would happen next. But she didn't always follow through.

"*Mazel tov.*"

Across the line, I could hear Fiona break into a smile. "Ooohhh. I knew you'd be happy for me," she thrilled. I could hear her clap. "I'm breaking up with Chris," she told me. "And David."

"Wow." Breaking up with *both* boyfriends. That sounded serious.

"Chandra and I have so much in common," Fiona effused. "She gets the whole Irish mother thing."

"Ex*cuse* me." I had practically grown up under Cait Collins's roof. "I think I know a thing or two about the whole Irish mother thing."

"Wow." Fiona paused dramatically. "I can't believe it. I mean, I expected it, but I can *not* believe it. You're actually jealous." I should have asked her if that was the point. She didn't sound mad, though. In fact, she sounded mildly pleased.

"I'm not jealous," I objected. Despite my best friend's radiant sexuality, I'd never been in love with Fiona. I'd known her too long. At least, I wasn't jealous of Fiona's girlfriend. I was mildly jealous that Fiona got to fall in love with brand-new women. After eight years with the same person, who wouldn't be?

"You're the one who's getting married," she felt the need to remind me, as if she'd just discovered the joys of eating meat, right when I had decided to become a vegetarian. "Who knows," she mooned, "I might even end up getting married before you!"

That was too much. Francine and I had been together for years. Our relationship was serious, and we were taking the whole idea of what it meant to get married seriously, too. "Oh, please!" The words leaked past my lips without thinking, fueled by my misplaced anger at Debbie. I never criticized Fiona. Supporting her no matter what crazy thing she did had always been my job. Until now. "You've only known this person five minutes!"

Fiona answered slowly, thoughtfully, like this was something she'd been considering for a while. "You've never been in love at first sight, have you?" That was low. Francine and I hadn't fallen in love at first sight. At least, she hadn't fallen in love at first sight with me. And Fiona knew it.

Ages ago, after Francine had my knees knocking with her liquid dance moves, we had gone on a half-dozen discouragingly platonic dates. Finally, I invited myself over to Francine's East Oakland cottage; Francine and I were together, alone in her little house. It did not go as planned.

I headed for the bathroom while Francine filled two water glasses. On the wall opposite her bed hung a small corkboard on which she'd tacked up a handwritten copy of the Emily Dickinson poem, "Wild Nights," which I found too suggestive to look at. In the bathroom, bright sunlight flooded the walls and white enamel fixtures like an overexposure on Francine's most intimate stuff: a loofah sponge, a hair scrunchie and a thread of copper hair, a pyramidal bottle filled with clear, olive-colored liquid. All along the edge of the tub thick white candles stood sentry in thick glass votives, their wicks black with use. For whom—or with whom?— had Francine lit them?

When I came back to the living room, a woman's voice sang a haunting melody, a medieval sound Sam would have liked. Francine was sitting on the futon. "I brought you a book," I said. Maybe it was admitting too much. But Francine didn't show it.

Francine glanced at the cover just long enough to read the title: *I Never Saw Another Butterfly*. Then she tucked her legs up under her and looked intently into my eyes. "Tell me."

I had to look down before I told her about the camp outside of Prague called Terezin, a model camp set up by the Nazis to prove to the Red Cross that the Jews were being treated humanely. Francine nodded, biting her thumb and narrowing her eyes. "They brought in Jewish artists and intellectuals to create the impression that it was a cultural haven; one of them decided to give secret art lessons to the children, and someone else had the foresight to smuggle a bunch of the drawings and poems out."

"Did the children . . .?" Francine began.

"All of them." I squinched my lips to the side. "Just about." Suddenly I wondered why I thought it was a good idea to court a woman with the most horrific story ever.

But Francine didn't seem repulsed. She studied the drawing on the front cover, a paper collage of red-roofed buildings held in the grip of twin scissor blades, the sky behind them black. She leafed through the pages slowly. "This reminds me of something else." Then she got up and returned with a slim, hardcover book. I recognized the sailboat docked in choppy water, the huge sleeping beast with its human feet, from childhood: *Where the Wild Things Are*. Francine held it toward me so I could see the pictures. "The night Max wore his wolf suit . . ." As she turned the pages, I fell rapt at the melody Francine's voice made, and when she read, "And Max, the king of all wild things was lonely, and wanted to be where someone loved him best of all," I felt the old longing at Max's table set with soup and milk and cake, and at the mother who forgave him his wildness, and knew what he wanted.

Francine turned back and began flipping through the pages. "I always notice that the first picture is quite small." She touched the rectangle framed by inches of white, in which Max nails a bedsheet to the wall. "But, gradually," she flipped slowly to the next page, and the next, "the pictures get larger and larger, and the white parts start to disappear, and the forest grows and grows," Francine paged ahead, "until the ocean spills over and there are no words at all." Max, eyes pressed shut with joy, swung from the trees; Max, eyes closed in regal contentment, rode through the leafy forest on the backs of his beasts.

"I start thinking," Francine murmured, closing her own eyes for a long moment, "about how the pictures grow and shrink, and I wonder about the order we impose on kids, the limits, and about how big the world of imagination is, inside us." Francine opened her eyes and blinked.

I took the book from her hands and turned through the first pages, stopping at the picture of Max, banished in his room, a forest canopy beginning to bloom above his bed. The way the children at Terezin had made worlds bloom inside their barbed-wire cage. She was right. It was like *I Never Saw Another Butterfly*. At least as Francine saw it: the closed world opening up.

My gaze dropped to her mouth.

That's when Francine shot up from the futon. "I forgot all about your drink!" In three steps she was in the kitchen, pouring lemon water from a pitcher. I studied Francine's pale, smooth cheek, the line of her jaw, taut above her pale throat. I couldn't read her at all. The opening world suddenly closing inside of me.

Fiona was the one I had called when I got home, the one who'd said, "I'm sorry, honey."

But that was the point. What a person felt at the beginning wasn't necessarily the same as what a person felt later. I tapped my pencil against my desk. "I believe in love after many, many sights," I told Fiona, the love-struck baby dyke. *Let's see how Fiona feels about this woman Chandra six months from now*, I thought.

But I worried: What if Fiona, with her guidebook and her

new love-at-first-sight, managed to waltz right up to the altar, nary a care for the law or lesbian feminist politics, while Francine and I were still dickering around, trying to figure out how to get married?

After work, I poured from the BART station on a wave of commuters into the smell of spring as familiar to me as the first bike ride of late February on Dunsmuir Drive between my house and Fiona's, the smell of bursting out of doors to pedal wildly up and down the hills of the neighborhood. A smell that went with the returning call of the mourning doves. I was happy for Fiona. But, just this one time, I wanted my life to come first. I had a plan and I couldn't wait to tell Francine.

When I put my key in the lock, the front door pulsed like we were throwing a frat party. That was odd. I walked into a tsunami of sound, bass throbbing louder in our little house than I'd ever heard it, the wooden coffee table in the living room vibrating to the deep, groaning pulse of the Gap Band. *Gap Gold.* Francine had been thrilled when she'd picked the used CD out of the bin at Amoeba. The living room was empty. The dogs were outside. Francine's jeans and sweater lay in a heap at the foot of the bedroom stairs. The thick hair on my arms rose up.

"Hi!" I called out. But the music, blaring from the downstairs speakers, swallowed my voice. I set my backpack down by the front door, stepped out of my shoes, and started for the stairs.

So I've got to get up early in the morning, the Gap Band crooned over the wonk of synthesizers, *to find me another lover.* The synthesizer growled, a piano throbbed, and a cowbell punctuated the beat with a steady, disarming clank. What if Francine had already realized that getting married meant never falling in love with another woman? What if she'd decided to do something about it, before it was too late?

I crept halfway up the bedroom stairs. The bedroom door was ajar. But I didn't see Francine until I leaned in close, low. She was standing near the foot of the bed, her face contracted in intense focus. No, not standing: moving. *Undulating.* Dear god. Sweating, flushed, Francine threw her head back, throat exposed, and pulsed, her curls tumbling to the side of her face. From where I squatted on the steep staircase, I couldn't see below her waist. My heart thudded with the bass. Francine pulsed again, her eyes rolling from the shoulder, a look of total intensity on her face. From below, the music pounded . . . *Young and wild. I even wanted her to have my child*. Francine's eyes stayed shut.

I crept a slow step higher—I was pulling myself up the stairs by my fingertips now, my head hunched low—then another, until I could see everything. From top to toe, Francine's whole body throbbed, her hips rocking, her head and arms swaying, the fluid line of her movement shifting easily from one bare, arched foot to the other.

I stared, thrilled and breathless: Francine in her tank top and shorts was dancing alone.

I wanted to crouch there and watch her all night, the sexy, self-confident girl I had fallen in love with on the dance floor. What did new love have on this? I wanted to get up and put my hands on her hips, to move with her motion, to seal her mouth with my mouth. But, as much as I wanted to watch her, to join her, in the pit of my gut, I also had the same strong feeling I'd had the time I'd found the notes for an auction catalog my mother had sketched out in black ink on a Margolis & Margolis pad, tucked high behind a hat box at the top of her closet—the unmistakable sense that I shouldn't be looking. *Privacy. Dignity*. Mrs. Landau's words whispered in my ears.

I crept back down the stairs, stepped noiselessly into my shoes, and stepped out again into the evening. When I crossed Broadway, I glanced over my shoulder, behind the redwood that stood outside our bedroom window, I thought for a moment that I could see the silhouette of her arms, outstretched above her head, moving in time with some invisible music against the blinds.

I came home an hour later. The house was quiet, Francine stretched out reading in the living room, the *Journal of Early Childhood Education* folded back in her hand. As if nothing had happened. That was okay. That was normal. I cupped her soft

60

cheek in my hand, leaned down, stretched out along her body and kissed her, and Francine, flush with her own sensuality and anchored deep in her own body, kissed me back.

Then Francine noticed the museum sticker still clinging to the jacket I'd last worn a week before to SFMOMA. "Remember, I met Debbie there?" I prompted her, though, in fact, I'd never brought that part up. Francine squinted and bit her cuticle. "*You* agreed to go to a museum?" She stared at me as if trying to x-ray my skull. "Huh," she stared at me, "that's odd." Though I hadn't told her where we'd met, I'd told Francine what Debbie had said. Debbie's disapproving stance on gay marriage hadn't surprised her. ("Put four lesbians in a room and you'll have a debate about it," she reminded me.) She'd been disappointed, but not in the same way I had been. According to Francine, a person like Debbie should know better than to wait for the law. Francine's confidence had been enough to turn our disappointment into fight. Now she was picking the sticker off my coat like a tick.

I plucked it from her fingers and rolled onto my elbow. Francine had her secret life, I reminded myself, remembering her dancing silhouette on the shades. These were the distances married people gave each other: privacy. Dignity. "Fiona's dating a woman."

Francine blinked up at me. "Oh my."

I sat up and pulled her up next to me. "Are you surprised?"

Now Francine pursed her lips, which were still wet from mine. "*Am* I surprised?" Staring out the French doors, she squinted into the distance and tapped her chin with a finger, until finally she answered. "Yes." She paused. "But also, no."

I nodded. "We need our own damn wedding book."

Francine turned to me like a gangster who had just agreed on a hit. "Yes," she sucked her teeth, "we do."

But when it came to looking for wedding guides, Francine's bravado seemed to desert her. We agreed to meet after work at Cody's Books on Telegraph, the biggest bookstore around. On Tuesday evening, I walked into Cody's and started cruising the aisles for Francine's hair. This is probably not the most intimate, her-soul-knows-my-soul means of seeking out one's beloved, but Francine's auburn curls are pretty easy to spot in a crowd. No hair in Psychology, *New York Times* Best Sellers or Gay and Lesbian. I headed out to the Children's Annex, but she wasn't there, either. Finally, sidled up by the magazine racks, I found her. Despite the warm, late spring weather, she had her denim jacket pulled tightly around her, and her hair carefully tucked up under her dad's old fishing hat. The cap on her head—Francine never hid her hair, which she thought was her best feature—gave her a distinctively furtive look, like a PTA mom out on a porno run.

She looked up, startled, her eyes wild. "I found these." She revealed the magazines she'd stuffed behind the covers of an open *New Yorker*: *Bride*, and *Modern Bride* and *Contemporary Bride*. Wedding porn. My sister had collected stacks of them.

"Are we modern brides?" I flipped through about a hundred reeking pages of ads for perfumes and makeup. Stick-thin models in body-hugging, white satin dresses leapt from every page, yards of lace running riot behind them like fantails. "Don't they have one called *Postmodern Bride*?"

Francine looked concerned. "I haven't seen that." Her sense of humor had drained away with the color in her cheeks.

"Why are you acting so freaked out?" Francine and I had agreed we needed some game plan for this. Why was she acting weird about it now? I stuffed the magazines back into the rack. "You're not afraid someone is going to find out you're marrying a woman, are you?" That didn't seem like Francine's style. But she wasn't officially "out" to the parents at the preschool, either. In other parts of the country, that could cost you your job. Francine worked in Berkeley, but *the parents*, I remembered; *the parents* . . .

"Ha!" A single, explosive laugh burst from her throat. "Did you *see* that crap? I'm afraid someone might think I'm *a bride-zilla!*"

I held up *The Essential Guide to Lesbian & Gay Weddings* I'd spotted in the Gay & Lesbian section. Francine turned the pink-pearlescent cover over in her hands. "Were there inessential guides, too?" She pulled off her cap and shook out her curls.

In the line snaking toward the registers, a young woman with long blond hair and a huge diamond ring glanced down at the book in my hand. "You might want *Here Comes the Guide*, too," she offered. "It's *really* good."

( )

Francine and I were starting to get excited. Maybe not first-lesbian-love excited, but, for the first time since we'd used the word "married," we started being able to imagine what a wedding could look like. Debbie might not approve. But we weren't alone. Someone had written a book for *us*! It was in this mood of hopeful anticipation about claiming our rightful place in the world that I waited at the elevator banks for the arrival of Michael Freund, seventy-one, who had shimmied up a light post to see Hitler's smudge of a moustache as the Führer marched into Austria.

Mr. Freund arrived precisely on time, a tiny, adorable man with a twinkling smile and sweetly wrinkled cheeks who reached out to pinch my own. "You're Ellen?" he mimed complete surprise. "I expected a middle-aged lady! But you're so pretty!" He was so effusive in his neat gray slacks and charming smile, I took it as a compliment. As we walked down to the interview room, Mr. Freund kept exclaiming over my lovely dark hair. "Do you have a boyfriend?" he wanted to know. "A husband? Do you have kids?" It might sound creepy, coming from an old man, but it was sweet, the way all of my clients' polite questions were sweet. They had suffered terribly in their own lives and, for me, they wanted unadulterated happiness. They wanted me to have a future.

I turned to Mr. Freund and smiled as widely as I could. Debbie had accused lesbians who "marry each other" of pretending. So, I would stop pretending. "A girlfriend," I winked, "and she's a beauty." If he had been an old lady, it would have been harder, but I had never known my own grandfather, and I'd always had a certain collegiality with male friends on the subject of women. It was the most natural thing in the world.

But Mr. Freund did not seem to think so. His face fell flat, toneless, the face of a person who has just suffered a cardiac event. "I'm sorry." He rooted around in his pockets, as if he'd just realized he'd forgotten something. "I think I would feel more comfortable with someone else." At that, I could feel my face go flat, too. One survivor I knew had had a gay brother, had seen him suffer doubly for being gay and Jewish. Some of them had seen the original pink triangles. Sometimes that didn't matter. I was glad he wouldn't look at my face, so he couldn't see me blink back tears.

I paged Wendy. When she came down, she assured Mr. Freund: "Ellen is the best we have. She's a trained oral historian."

But Mr. Freund repeated, "I'd be more comfortable with someone else." And what else could she do? Our clients needed to be comfortable. This was about them, not us. That's why we didn't tell clients things about our personal lives. Or, at least, why I didn't. Mentioning a husband wouldn't be the same.

Afterward, when we debriefed, Wendy was apologetic. But she was also curious. "What prompted you to come out to him?"

"He asked if I was married."

"Huh." She looked puzzled. The springy little curls around her glasses trembled. "I'm surprised no one has asked you that before."

"They always ask," I told her. "I just never answer."

"It'll change," Wendy reassured me. I imagined Anya's parenthetical smile folding down.

Maybe it would change when these people were all gone. I loved these tribal elders and their sweet, wizened faces. But their quiet discomfort hurt more than any random "Adam and Steve" ever could. Their personal lives and mine were two worlds that had to be kept apart. That was the day I decided once and for all I would stop trying to run into Anya Kamenets.

"Hard day at the office," I told Francine when I got home. It was early May. The mourning doves were cooing in the eaves, and it seemed right then they mourned for us. I worked with the very old and Francine worked with the very young, and this would always be a problem.

"The very young aren't a problem at all," Francine corrected me. "Their parents are. For now." She kissed me sweetly, and I disappeared to work on the one thing I could maybe sort of control: my wart.

As I sat on the lurid, red-tiled floor of our little bathroom, I remembered the first time I lay in Francine's queen-sized bed watching her dress for work. "Why do you always put your hair up?" I'd asked, as she clipped in a barrette. Much as I loved the notion of Francine uncostuming herself from her public life, pulling her hair loose at the end of the day just for me, I also loved her long hair and wondered, selfishly, why she smoothed every curl away from her temples every day.

"Lice," she answered.

"Oh." I'd tried to sound unconcerned, and resisted the urge to scratch. "Um, isn't there anything you can do about that?" I'd tried to sound casual. I'd waited how long to get into her bed? I couldn't exactly go flying from her room at the first sign of . . . animal imperfection. ("There's nothing you could do," I'd told her, trying fruitlessly to seduce her, "that would make me stop wanting you." Bad habits, I'd meant, or finding out she didn't like popcorn with Raisinettes. Not being infested with parasites. What else didn't I know about her?)

I slipped a finger nonchalantly against my scalp. *There must be some chemical you could use to kill them. Napalm, maybe?*

Francine was staring at me. "Oh my god!" She laughed nervously. "I don't HAVE lice!" She stepped toward the bed and pushed her head into mine. "Ellen!" she scolded me. "You're such a hypochondriac." She pulled my hand away from my head. "Here." She sunk her fingers into my hair and I went limp with delight. Gramma Sophie had used to scratch my head like this in front of Marlin Perkins's *Wild Kingdom*. "I work with children. Putting my hair up is a *precaution*."

Francine had always seen my weaknesses, I realized. It was a good thing I had decided to forget about Anya, because, no matter how clever I thought I was being about sneaking around, Francine would definitely find out.

I was still sitting on the bathroom floor, scraping away at the wart with a small plastic scalpel, congratulating myself on my good sense, when the phone shrieked by our bed. The knife slipped. The point caught in the thick skin at my heel, where I would soon sprout another wart.

"Have you seen *Die Hard with a Vengeance*?" My mother pronounced the name of the movie gingerly, the way a woman in high-heeled shoes might lift her own dog's shit out of her garden, delicately, with the tip of a spade.

"Have *you*?" I answered.

"No. But the assistant to the associate director was here yesterday." My mother waited importantly.

"And?" I prompted her.

"And," my mother ignored me pointedly, "they're buying the house."

105 Dunsmuir Drive. "Oh."

"Escrow closes in two months." I studied the blade in my hand and shut it absently. "We've lived in this house for almost thirty years."

"Right."

"We had a good life in this house." Her voice got all chunky, clotty with swallowed tears, but she didn't say more. Why did my mother do this to me?

I wished that I could share this simple sadness with her, but I'd known her all my life. I squeezed a single word out. "Right."

Downstairs, I could hear Francine flipping channels on the TV.

"Well," my mother inhaled loudly through her narrow nose, "if you want to save anything, you're going to have to come clean out your own crap, my dear."

( )

My crap would have to wait. I had a very important interview with Mrs. Hannah Weiner, survivor of Janowska, a transit and forced labor camp on the outskirts of Lvov, serving the German army as part of the German Armament Works. The camp had been liquidated in 1943. But before it closed, the Jews at Janowska, ordered to burn all the bodies in the mass graves, "struck back with what we could find, what we could muster," and a "very, very few escaped." Mrs. Weiner was one of these. She may have been one of less than a dozen who were not rearrested and killed, deported to Belzec or shot in the Piaski ravine. This was not an interview to miss. People changed their minds. They were old. They died.

Mrs. Weiner came to the door of her eighth-floor apartment in a pale blue silk blouse and a straight skirt, her belly pressing outward in the shimmering fabric like a waxing moon. "Come in, come in," she said, her accent familiar, thick and warm. The skin at the bridge of her nose was thin and pus-colored, like a scab recently picked away. She'd had cancer, I remembered, chemotherapy followed by a series of tenacious infections. *Don't*, I reminded myself, *think about it.*

Mrs. Weiner slipped behind the counter of the little kitchenette, struggled to fit the mouth of a kettle underneath the tap of the little porcelain sink. The apartment was small, but light and clean, its cozy sitting area squared against Mrs. Weiner's miniature

67

veranda. An angular loveseat, clean lines and match-stick legs, drew close against a spare wooden coffee table. Perched on a stand, a potted philodendron trailed a small jungle of heart-shaped leaves across a side table strewn with intricately carved walnuts, their shells knotted with twined, pleading faces. They looked merely knotty, until you picked one up, and then the eyes stared back at you, face upon twisted face. Disarmed, I set the walnut back down. I'd come to claim something more elusive, and rare: the tale of a survivor of Janowska.

In 1939, Lvov had the third-largest Jewish population in Poland, some 200,000 Jews. Between the Soviets and the Nazis, ghettoization and "reduction," the population dwindled to 86,000. From the ghetto, only 2,000 of Lvov's Jews made it to Janowska. Of those, a mere 120 were used for forced labor. All the others were killed. Of the 120, how many had escaped? Five? Ten? A dozen?

"I have been so unlucky," Mrs. Weiner murmured. "To lose them all—my father, my brothers, my sisters. All except for me."

Mrs. Weiner had begun her story, like many, at the end.

I hefted the camera to my tripod. "Mrs. Weiner, could you tell me your maiden name?"

"My name? Was Hannah Schwarz. I came from Lvov, Poland." Mrs. Weiner came around the corner of the kitchenette, forgetting the tea kettle and the tea. She picked up a paper napkin, which she folded, unfolded, then refolded into a perfect square. "Very big city, there. Factories. Both of my parents worked during the day. We were not having much money, you see. I stay home to take care of my sisters and brothers. My parents, they can't afford a person to care for the little ones so we older children could go to school. We all learn together at home, in the evenings, until I get my first job."

"What was that?"

"What?"

"What was your first job?"

"Cleaning. I clean houses for other people. Other people's houses." Mrs. Weiner pressed her lips firmly together. Crowds of

68

wrinkles huddled around her mouth, drawing it down. She had survived. But she looked beaten. *Cancer*, I reminded myself.

"Even after I'm married, I stay with my parents and my sisters and brothers at home."

"When did you get married?" I set the camera in the tripod, grateful that Mrs. Weiner had sat down facing the full light of the window. Her features were sallow and drawn. *I've been so unlucky.* ("We like our survivors cheerful," Wendy had observed, smiling wryly, after an especially depressing speakers' bureau event at a large public high school. The principal, a stocky man with a silver whistle around his neck, had pulled her aside afterward and said, "We were hoping for something more . . . inspirational.")

I took a breath.

"I'm one of the last—one of the oldest and the last. But, you know, we can't afford to all get married and have children so young."

The white walls of the apartment filled with silence. Mrs. Weiner stared straight into the camera. She cocked her head, waiting.

"What was your husband's name?"

"Aaron?" It came out as a question.

"Aaron?" I prompted her. "Do you remember Aaron's last name?"

Mrs. Weiner smiled nervously, pulling her hair back off her forehead. She looked down, away from the camera. Presumably, Aaron's last name had become her own.

"Do you remember," I asked more gently, "what Aaron did? For a living?"

Mrs. Weiner stared at the camera, spittle gathering at the corners of her lips. She seemed mesmerized by the cool, dark witness of the lens. She shook her head minutely.

I nodded. Mrs. Weiner and I sat, again, in silence. I felt my initial irritation at her tone of complaint slipping away, dissolving to nothingness. Next door, through the walls, a telephone rang. "We all work. My parents, they worked at the factory for nothing. And so many Jews coming in. Even after we were married, we waited to have children so that I can work."

"You had children?" I asked, my tone solicitous, detached. I considered the daughter who called to arrange her interview; I hadn't realized she was born during the War. I wondered how it could be that not only Mrs. Weiner, but a small child had survived both the Lvov ghetto and Janowska. Miracles, I reminded myself, were possible.

"A beautiful daughter," Mrs. Weiner said. She smiled. Her eyes filled. "A perfect girl, so beautiful. 1939." Mrs. Weiner looked at me, for the first time, gravely. "And then," her voice grew thick, "they came. Oooh," she shook her head, "then they came." I made sure that I looked at her without flinching, through the violence she described as relentless and inexorable as waves: Soviets. Nazis. Pogroms. Beatings. Murders. "My father they march with the old, the sick," she said, "over the Peltewna bridge, to the ghetto. That's where they shoot them all, on the bridge to the ghetto."

We pass by the corpse of her father. She has not mentioned Aaron. By the time she reaches the ghetto, she and her daughter are alone. "It is good to have each other. To look out for each other. It is essential." I nodded. Mrs. Weiner nodded, smiling bitterly. "Filthy, cold, no food. But. We get by.

"So, you know. They stop us in the street there. Soldiers. Nazi police. He orders her: Come! My daughter. So young. And small. She was frightened. She hung on me. 'Please,' I tell her. 'Go to the man. Go.' Because if she did not—

"She would not go. My daughter. She cry so hard. The soldier take her from me. And then—"

Mrs. Weiner looked up, past the camera, past my face, out the glass sliders, past the low porch wall into the pale blue of the fading sky. "They shoot her."

Mrs. Weiner's face closed in concentration, the way the aperture of a camera closes, from the edges to the center. "'We should shoot you, too,' he says to me. 'For raise your child so badly.'"

She stood abruptly, and turned to the kitchen, the linoleum counter lined with old, matched tins labeled "Coffee," "Flour," "Bread." Unlatching the largest of these, Mrs. Weiner extracted a bag of cookies, its top wrinkled soft from folding and unfolding, pinched shut with a wooden clothespin. Her worn fingers pressed, clothespin-like, against it. She shook out six butter cookies, one by one, onto a small blue plate.

"Her name?" I asked, as gently as I could. My voice, like the afternoon light, had grown soft. "What was your daughter's name?"

The tea kettle shrieked. Mrs. Weiner shook her head. Then she carefully refolded and clipped the bag.

When at last I walked out of the apartment and shut the door, the camcorder packed back in its padded bag, the mugs from tea rinsed by the sink, the thing that felt surreal was the sound of voices in the hall, the little *ding* of the elevator arriving, the BART ticket still tucked, perfectly straight, in my jacket pocket: the evidence of the world, still going on everywhere around me. So it was unsurprising, in a way, when the elevator opened on the downstairs lobby and there, among a group of women waiting at the door of the big, mauve dining room, stood Anya Kamenets, laughing. "Ellen!" she greeted me like an overdue guest. She acted like she already knew me. She seemed so glad to see me. "So!" She reached for my hand and gripped it, hard, in hers. "I was waiting," she murmured, mysterious as a fortune-teller, "for you to come."

Even her elusiveness felt very familiar. At that moment, I was tired, wiped out after Mrs. Weiner's testimony, by the idea of a world evil enough to make a mother forget her daughter's name. I was glad, at that moment, to be with someone who recognized me, someone who wanted me to be there. I didn't pull away.

Anya introduced me to the women standing with her: Mrs. Shaeffer, who nodded politely, glancing through the double doors of the dining room, where old people, mostly women, sat murmuring and adjusting silverware, waiting for baskets of rolls. She introduced me to Mrs. Gilbert, who appraised me frankly, from the pleated black pants Sam used to call my lesbian uniform to the tips of my frizzy curls. "Ellen what?" Mrs. Gilbert wanted to know, looking from me to Anya Kamenets, her blond hair held back today with a fabric band above the forehead. Anya regarded me with suppressed amusement, her mouth a frowning smile, revealing nothing. "Margolis," I answered. And then, even though I guessed from her avoidance of the Foundation that Anya probably hadn't wanted me to, I added, "I'm from the Foundation for the Preservation of Memory." When Mrs. Gilbert looked at me as if I had uttered a phrase in Mandarin, I translated, "Holocaust testimonies."

The hand Mrs. Gilbert had put out toward my cheek dropped to her side. "I was just telling these ladies," Mrs. Gilbert began, "about my grandson Liam." Anya's eyebrows, her parentheses, lifted almost imperceptibly. *I told you so*, they seemed to say. Mrs. Gilbert resumed what I could only guess had already been a long monologue, whose particulars blurred away into the perfectly familiar buzz of something normal. I listened without hearing the words, and noticed as the colors returned to what I saw: Mrs. Shaeffer's dusty, rouged cheeks, Anya's blond hair. "Well," Mrs. Gilbert's carefully set head bobbed indulgently, "boys will be boys." A male nursing aide, sleek in his blue uniform and clogs, his brown hair pulled back in a smooth, shining ponytail, pushed a bent woman in a wheelchair noiselessly through the dining-room doors. Mrs. Gilbert raised her chin as they passed. "Except when they're girls," she murmured; the corner of her lips curled down.

Mrs. Gilbert, Mrs. Shaeffer and Anya Kamenets all gazed after the wake of the Puerto Rican nurse as if to pick up the trace of his gender-defiant scent; Mrs. Sheaffer's chuckle sounded like a cough you try to hold in.

Here we were again.

My last semester of college, I'd come home for spring break, a ghost in the house. Gramma Sophie sat out on the patio in her robe, the crossword in her lap, her eyes closed behind her glasses, her round knees flashing white under the hot pink hem of her short cotton robe, the tips of her toes a familiar collection of corns and bunions, just touching the pink velour slippers she'd let drop onto the bricks beneath her chair. "*Mechiadich*," she murmured. *Delightful.* Her hand fell on my thigh, squeezed it. "What's that?" Gramma Sophie jabbed a painted fingernail into the leg of my pants. I was wearing a pair of Levi's on which Sam had ballpointed a triangle tattooed, "Gay '90s."

"Nothing." I shifted in my chair, twisting slightly away. Gramma Sophie wore thick glasses. She always held the *TV Guide* close to her face. And yet she saw this, blue-on-blue at twenty paces: "Gay."

"It's just an expression," I fudged, my face warming. "For the '90s."

"What kind of expression is that?"

Mrs. Shaeffer looked after the nurse. "If that one helped me, I wouldn't feel comfortable."

What was I doing here, talking to Anya? What had I expected? "It's nice to meet you," I told the ladies gathered around her. I had always been drawn to the elderly, but I would never fit in with them. Except as a child. Except as a sexless child. I told Anya Kamenets I was sorry; I needed to go. I stepped away from Anya Kamenets and her friends. But Anya took hold of my arm. "We need to talk. *More,*" she encouraged me, as if she were spooning me porridge. *More?* Was she admitting she was the one who had called me at home?

I looked toward the dining room, which smelled of white rolls and disinfectant.

Anya wrinkled her nose. "The food," she whispered, "is terrible. Come." She tugged at my sleeve. "I have food in my room." I glanced at Anya's purse. The idea of the food Anya Kamanets might have squirreled away in her room horrified me, the thought of going up in those elevators, into another one of those apartments and listening, once again, to one of those godforsaken testimonies . . .

But Anya wouldn't let me see her as one of the others. "Come up," she urged me. "Now, you are here," she reminded me that she'd been waiting for me to come to her, that, to her, I wasn't just a recording device. She couldn't know how enticing she was. Taking me by the sleeve of my shirt, she turned back toward the elevators and, while the rest of the Rose of Sharon Towers descended, buzzing innumerably behind the white double doors, clawing at the hems of white-clothed tables, reaching for the soft, white-floured puffs of packaged dinner rolls, I followed her up to her room.

Anya's apartment on the eleventh floor was the mirror-image twin of Mrs. Weiner's and, remarkably, not a thing like it. Opening to the right, instead of the left, the apartment gave way to the same kitchenette, the same sitting room and veranda, the same glass sliding doors. But Anya's porch framed a different sky, a big, flat Hockney sky, a wide, rising Georgia O'Keeffe sky. A sky without history, but without possibility, either. Just openness, emptiness, endless.

Anya had decorated the apartment as if to frame the sky. The furniture she'd assembled—a marble-edged glass table, pale, veined; leather couch, polished, sober, circumspect—didn't look like the accumulation of a life, nor like the stripping away of it, either (Mrs. Weiner's pieces still smelled of the parlor), but like the stylish installation of the new Museum of Modern Art, as if, like the museum, she'd started again, right at this moment. Stepping into her apartment, I realized that Anya Kamanets was the first person I'd met for whom moving into the high towers of a senior independent living facility was not an act of culmination, or resignation, but simply another iteration of self.

I stood in front of the sofa and gazed, marveling, at the sky.

"Sit."

Why not? I reminded myself that I hadn't sought her out, that I was only here at the Rose of Sharon Towers because of my job. But I didn't take out my camera. Anya set two pieces of cake on the glass tabletop, slices pink and precise as a Thiebaud. We were sitting down together over food. Between the sweet, moist layers of sponge and buttercream, sharp red fruit burst with startling tartness, both disconcerting and joyful. We didn't speak until we had scraped the last smears of buttercream up with the sides of our forks. Then, as if setting a record needle down on a familiar groove, Anya began to tell her story, the same one she had recorded with Wendy, the one I had watched five or six times. These were the words she knew how to share.

It was like listening, once again, to a long and complicated composition, like Bartók's *Concerto for Orchestra*. At first, all of it had sounded to me like breaking glass. Then, gradually, I had learned to hear the patterns. *Obbligato:* dark, rhythmic movements, intercut with the frantic complaint of strings, the *staccato* of machine-gun rounds. *Kovno. Sloboka.* The words made a brutal poetry. I liked the sound of her voice; her consonants were as rich as cake. It was the oddest of seductions—this old woman, the sweetness of dessert, the softness of her voice. There was the story of the War. And underneath it, around it, between it, there was the quiet minuet of our glances, of our hands moving across the same tabletop, of our being here together. The Ninth Fort, the Seventh Fort, the Fourth Fort. Ghettoize. Deport. Exterminate. Two thousand, three thousand. Hunt, burn, gas, shoot. In the close, clean space between us, her voice, and not her words, drew us together.

Anya's lullaby led me down into the forest, with the partisans. Damp peat. The crackle of pine boughs mingling with the crackle of machine-gun fire. The sounds of death spattering the dripping green sounds of the primeval, concealing forest. Anya had been blond and young. There were ways, if you were lucky enough, and clever enough, to pass. "We'd come back with food." Who did she come back for? Anya didn't say. She had made compromises she didn't wish to describe. Anya was twenty-two years old when the war ended. "I was lucky," she said.

Lucky.

Because it was early in the summer, the high, framed sky stayed light a bit longer. Still, the color washed out of our faces. Anya's window faced east. It faced the same sad, hopeful light in which my mother used to sit, waiting for the mail.

Anya had stopped talking. I glanced at the camera bag, untouched, at my feet. I had been hypnotized. So, when she startled me with the question, I felt defenseless, exposed. "You're not married." Anya prompted me with a slight incline of the head toward my left hand. When she smiled, her face was *all* parentheses, the eyebrows, the eyes, the closed, upturning mouth, the cupped demitasses of her cheeks. It was the same old, impossible question. But I had learned my lesson. These were questions I knew very well how to deflect.

"Were *you* ever married? Did you have children?" I leaned forward in my seat.

Anya hadn't mentioned a husband. Not before the war and, more atypically, not after. Marriage, children, normalcy: Those were the antidote.

"You're a very pretty girl. Do you have a boyfriend?"

She was persistent. But why should I answer her? I had answered Mr. Freund, to no good end. Were Anya and I more intimate, because of a secret phone call, a glance in the museum, tea and cake? There were things I had never talked about with my own family. What did I owe to this person, this stranger? This wasn't how this relationship was supposed to work.

I turned from Anya, considered her high, framed sky. "Well . . ." I said. I stood up, pulled down the legs of my slacks.

"Just a moment." She tapped her fingers together gently and then I could see, from out of nowhere, she held something in her hand. A small, warped square. A photo. She didn't want me to leave.

I glanced at the photo with careful interest, as if it were a prize butterfly that might disappear on the breeze. Survivors of the Holocaust left Europe with nothing but their skin. But I had read that, in Kaunas, a man named George Kadish had taken photographs through the buttonhole of his coat. I wanted to leap from my seat and, in a single neat bound, swipe the photo clean out of her hands. She cradled it like a bird in the nest of her fingers. She held it face down. There would be a price to pay.

As Anya cradled the photo, I understood that this must be the reason she had lured me here. And I wondered: Why hadn't she shown it to Wendy? Had she just discovered it? Or had she been keeping it for some secret purpose? Had she been waiting for this moment??

Anya looked out the big windows toward the sky. "I knew a woman in the ghetto. A woman from Kaunas. She worked the kitchen. Food a dog shouldn't eat. 'Rations,' they called them—only potatoes. Black, moldy, potatoes. Potatoes breakfast, lunch, dinner. If there was dinner. But hardly potatoes. More like lumps of earth. No one could survive on such a ration, mind you. But that's how it was: Work to death. Starve to death. Both at once," Anya pursed her lips and blew the Nazis' casual unconcern for human life into the air, "even better. One day something came over this woman—God knows what came over her; some people just went mad—but something came over her. Sometimes it happened. She put one—" Anya made a quick gesture with her hand, and the photo disappeared, "right into her pocket. A potato no person could eat. But she took it. That same night they took her. The woman. And for no reason at all, they took her sister."

Anya's lips, often turned down in her half-smile, half-grimace, twisted horribly, like a bone out of joint. But she fixed me in her slitted eyes; in them, I saw something like defiance. Then she was holding the photo once again in her hand. All the tension had gone out of her face, out of the room, out of the rest of the day. The little sitting room was dark, and I looked around, switched on the light.

Anya held out the photo in her open hand, an offering.

Carefully, I took the photo, cradling it. To peer into it was to peer into a looking glass and see the dead. Two girls. One of them, dark and intense, stared straight into the camera, her school bag slung over her shoulder. Dark skirt, white blouse, pure teenage attitude. The picture was old, taken from a distance; even so, you could see that her eyes were dark, sultry, and indescribably sad. In the photo, the other girl looked at her, laughing. Blond hair, drawn straight back behind her head. The other young face was turned a little to the left—Anya's face. I looked at Anya, willed her closed face to open up, to tell me something about what I was looking at. "This is from before the War," I commented.

Anya's mouth folded shut more tightly. She gave a single curt nod. I studied the picture again, the school clothes, the backpack. I wondered again why Anya had kept this photo from Wendy, why she was showing it to me now.

"From Kovno. From school. A friend." Anya paused, a silence in which the word bloomed into something ripe and whole. *A friend.* How strange this phrase sounded in relation to everything else Anya had described. "She came to the ghetto with me. My friend."

At the end of the phrase, a silence of complete finality, of emptiness, the silence of a hundred other silences coming to rest, like a sigh.

Holding it by the edges, I handed her back the photo.

Anya smiled the beguiling smile which, finally, was utterly mournful. I had so many questions. But she wouldn't tell me any more.

( )

I needed to tell someone about my meeting with Anya, but I had
already convinced myself I couldn't tell Francine. Francine and I
were slowly but surely moving into the next phase of our life, and
telling Francine would drag us back to a past we were freeing
ourselves from. She would worry about me. She would tell me
to stop. To Francine, this would seem like a much bigger deal
than it was.

So, I decided to tell Jill. Petite, half-Chinese, half-Indonesian,
with hair the color of lava rock and fierce, dark eyes the burning
black of a Javanese god of love or war, Jill had been coming to
the Foundation every second Wednesday morning since the fall,
reviewing warped manuscripts in her small, tapering fingers. A
graduate student at Stanford, she knew more about Babi Yar
than possibly anyone on Earth besides Dina Pronicheva. (For-
merly of the Kiev puppet theater, Pronicheva had managed to
leap into the Kiev ravine *before* being shot, lay for hours among
the thousands of corpses, under the groaning wounded, and
remained silent when a suspicious Nazi kicked her breast and
trod on her hand until the bones cracked. Then she dug her way
out.) Which is to say, Jill was on the track to a very hot tenured
position at a place like Princeton or Yale, the kind of places to
which my own tepid academic ambitions had not led me. But
there was a natural sympathy between us, the knowledge that
what I cared about, she cared about, which made me feel like

entrusting the secret of Anya to her instead of Francine was somehow not a terrible, unforgivable thing to do.

I was rushing from work to an airport shuttle coming for me at home when I finally ran into Jill at the elevator bank. Smooth and prescient as a Jakarta *dukun* summoning a pain-relieving charm, Jill asked me, "Need a lift?"

Jill's car, parked in a ten-dollar lot off of Market, was small and graduate-student ancient, a little white hatchback she probably bought from an *emeritus* professor for a thousand dollars. The doors shook audibly when we pulled them shut. Almost immediately, we got stuck in a line of idling cars trying to cross Market. "Presidential motorcade?" Jill suggested. Bill Clinton was back in town, milking the big cash cow of Silicon Valley.

We were jammed in the middle of the block between a Roadway eighteen-wheeler and a moving truck when I asked her, "Have you ever gotten drawn in by one of your subjects?" Jill didn't work for the Foundation. Whatever I told her wouldn't get back to Wendy. "There was this woman. At the Foundation. Well, not exactly *at* the Foundation . . . ," I started.

Even though I told myself that nothing had "happened," talking about it made me feel guilty. But Jill overflowed with empathy. And empathy can be very enticing. "It's impossible to explain to other people," she gazed at me with her dark and thoughtful eyes, "how the lives of the people I study move me. It's so much more than intellectual, isn't it?" She blinked at me. "It's a kind of passion."

Passion. Had I ever noticed that Jill's eyes were almost completely black? Smoldering, actually. It was hot outside, the smoggy, still heat of early summer. The little white car fidgeted. In twenty minutes, we hadn't moved an inch. I cracked my window, took a huge whiff of diesel smoke and cranked it back up again. As Jill talked more about this shared passion for the things we both cared so much about, I stared straight ahead at the moving truck and wondered what was happening to me. I'd let my boundaries down with Anya and now *all* my boundaries seemed to be dissolving.

Jill was smart, and garrulous in a way that always made me feel like I had a million things to talk about. For reasons I rationalized as the infrequency of our meetings, I'd never mentioned her to Francine. Now, suddenly, huddled against the worn velour in Jill's flimsy hatchback, walled in by looming eighteen-wheelers, shuddering diesel engines pressing in on all sides, I felt there might be a different reason I hadn't. Jill's hand, smooth and shiny as polished wood, rested on the gearshift just inches from my arm. It wasn't so much that I wanted to, as that I felt an overwhelming, elemental force—like nuclear fusion—pulling the atoms of my body toward the atoms of hers. The air in the car felt alive with charged particles. Together in the close, tinny vehicle, I could smell the honey and sandalwood smell of Jill's skin; I could feel the heat rising off her arm.

Jill cleared her throat. "I think I've gotten you into trouble."

"Huh?" My ears scorched. If Jill could read my mind, I was in deep shit indeed.

Jill nodded at the unmoving truck. "We haven't moved more than a car length in the last thirty minutes. If you don't run, I'm afraid you'll miss your shuttle."

I grabbed my bag. "Right." I slammed the tinny white door with a clap. *You don't even know if she's GAY!* I yelled at myself and fled toward the BART station as fast as I could.

( )

My parents picked me up at LAX, my mother immaculate in a crisp linen suit, my father sporty in his tennis whites, a beautiful couple to whom I was, as always, the awkward third wheel. After the usual pleasantries, I sat in the back, staring out the window, while my mother talked about a new acquisition in confidential tones with my father. "You would not believe this piece of lace. Point D'Angleterre lace with crowns in each corner." My parents loved me in their own way, but their lives had sealed up over my absence like water over a stone. I had never fit in.

Darkness had dyed the Western sky a rising fade of blue by the time my father turned off Sunset Boulevard into the gated, rustic silence of Dunsmuir. From the time I was born, my family had lived in the rustic nook of West Los Angeles incongruously named the Dunsmuir Estates, on the eponymously named Dunsmuir Drive. All the streets in the neighborhood bore the names of Scottish castles and cloudy lochs; recently, huge faux thirteenth-century stone castles with ice-cream cone towers and their twentieth-century counterparts in boxy concrete, brushed steel and glass, had risen up on the chaparral ridge of the Pacific ocean, on the old Spanish land grants where red-tiled Mediterraneans and low post-War ranch houses had once clustered. Ours was one of the original ranch-style houses, which my father, despite his professional interest in real estate, and my mother, despite her personal commitment to impeccable taste, had never bothered to update. I guess it didn't matter now.

As always, after a very light dinner in which lettuce was served along with some leafy greens and the thing that was grilled was me, we retreated to our corners.

Since I'd left, not much had changed in my pink bedroom, either, except for the emptying of my grandmother's closet. That night, standing in front of the closet doors, I felt the same anxiety and dread I'd felt standing outside the closed double doors of the cardiac ICU, staring through the glass into the blinking warren of monitors, diodes, EKGs, bodies swathed in blue and white. Between the flaps of her gown, a long, knobbed ridge bulged from the center of my gramma's chest, a thick, bursting seam stitched together with fish wire, jagged as a zipper. Her mouth was taped shut around a tube. Alone in my old bedroom, I stared at the dark seam of the closet's shut doors. But why should I feel dread? This was where my Gramma Sophie had stood in the breastplate of a brassiere she wore to go out, a straightjacket with a thousand eye hooks, and shucked it to the floor.

I touched the door handles. The house was dark and quiet. My parents, in their bedroom down the hall, had shut the door behind them. I opened the closet door and pulled on the light.

The closet I had once shared with Gramma Sophie had become, in our absence, my mother's auxiliary, packed wall-to-wall with sheathed dresses, floor-to-ceiling with boxed Italian shoes. I had to push aside the curtain of dry-cleaning bags to find my old Victorian dollhouse, hidden behind the heavy undergrowth of hems. Three stories tall, complete with a widow's walk, it was a fantasy of my mother's that went along with "my" antique doll collection, but had met with rougher use. From seventh grade through our senior year, I'd stuffed it with my high school love letters and padlocked it shut. (My sister Rebecca had a habit of going through my things. It wasn't just the usual little sister stuff. If she found anything revealing, she delivered it straight to my mother. The terms of their intimacy depended, in that way, on me.) Now the lock hung from its slack chain, broken.

A tiny orange armchair upended in the center of the living-room floor, the dollhouse looked like a house someone had fled in haste years before. I pushed my fingers through the torn curtains. I'd once imagined hiding a tiny Stuart Little family in there. Now, ransacked, the dollhouse felt like a preview of things to come on Dunsmuir Drive. It had been stripped bare—except for an old photo stuffed into a corner of the attic: a picture of Liz. She had bared her teeth brightly for the camera, always ready to put on a public face.

Before I knew Liz, Fiona and I called her "Miss Priss." Fiona and I had just started middle school at Ferngrove; we hadn't discovered that our social lives would have little to do with each other. "There goes Miss Priss," Fiona gestured toward the library, whose jutting corner Eliza Beth Williams was just rounding in her blue uniform jumper, her nose tilted up, her blond Peter Pan haircut blowing off her forehead.

Was Eliza Beth really a prig? A goody two-shoes? I knew she spoke with a Southern accent. She was probably the only twelve-year-old who really knew what *irony* meant. She practiced good posture. She wanted to run for student council. She was articulate. Politic. Also, the first girl to suck my nipples, stick her tongue in my mouth, pull my face between her legs. *Irony*.

Tall, blond, smart and Southern, Liz was never quite popular, exactly, but she had ambition, and that took her far. The thing that saved her from real popularity at Ferngrove was a strong Southern sense of propriety without a properly Southern thrill for sin. Maybe because she had only been born there.

Back in the seventh grade, Liz and I quickly began to spend all of our free periods together, wandering down the long steps of the terraced hillside behind Ferngrove's huge, endowed class-room buildings. We walked slowly in our penny loafers, holding hands. It didn't mean anything. We were only twelve years old. Then one day, a senior girl with a hemline, Liz said afterward, "straight up to her pubic bone," saw us coming up the steps.

"Don't get caught *going down* in the fern grove, girls." Her friends sat on the long path beside the grass with their skirts hiked up over shorts, tanning their legs. I turned, baffled, to Liz. The color had risen up in her face, so red that the blond hair on her cheeks stood out white. (Swarthy myself, I found her transparency fascinating.) Liz dropped my hand. Her drawl gathered up like bunched crinoline around the words, "They're *vulgar*." It was her strongest indictment.

We attracted attention, the two of us. We were emitting signals neither one of us could read, a high-frequency Morse code of mutual attraction to which we, ourselves, remained willfully deaf for years, until rumor and innuendo helpfully pointed them out.

Ferngrove was old, by West Coast standards, and the school had elevated its age to a status symbol through the unbroken observance of the fussy and antiquated rites that had been performed there since its inception in 1901. The Junior Gown ceremony commemorated the rising of the first Ferngrove junior class in 1906, in which the senior girls handed down their yellowing antique linen and lace commencement gowns. (I suspected the lace gowns were possibly the real reason my mother had sent me to Ferngrove.) It was a gesture of recognition, continuity and— most of us thought, eyeing the antique linen—grateful casting off. (We thought they looked like our great-grandmothers' nighties.) The ceremony itself took place on Ferngrove's wide lawn in the inevitable, broiling June sun. Fiona gripped the bodice of her gown and fanned it, melodramatically, over her sweating chest. Then, after tea sandwiches on the terrace, the seniors gave us their real present: an unofficial, unchaperoned off-campus party with a DJ to which, in one of those queer, old-fashioned Ferngrove throwbacks, boys were never invited.

The seniors had rented out the Wellbourne Estate, an old mansion up in the Bel Air hills where the streets were wide, white cement patched here and there with dark asphalt veins and canopied with trees. The name didn't have any real provenance;

it was just what the real estate agent (one of my father's professional enemies) had decided to call it.

Liz found me that night at one of the tables near the dance floor in the ballroom, which had been strung overhead with leafy vines and white twinkle lights for a "Girls' Wild Night Out." A DJ was playing Yaz, and I watched while Fiona whooped and shimmied with a knot of seniors, half of them stripped down to their bras. I was staring intently at the bottom of my paper cup, tapping my foot, when Liz's fingers alighted on my shoulder. I looked up, relieved—Liz never danced at these things, either—but Liz's face was grim, pale and knotted. "I need to talk to you." She'd changed from her gown into a white summer dress, long and gauzy and sleeveless. "Not here," she hissed.

I followed Liz out into a long, paneled hall, past girls lounging on leather divans, into a dark parlor whose French doors led into the garden. Liz tested a handle and swung the door out into the night. Trailing her was like trailing a phantom; her white dress and blond hair floated in the gray gloom past tall pruned hedges and huge blooming flowers that looked, in the grainy black and white of the evening, vaguely man-eating. When we had gotten far enough from the house, she stopped to let me catch up. We walked side by side through the lane, turning at a break in the hedge, and then another. Then Liz snatched at my fingertips and pulled me into a little alcove at the base of two trees, closed in by trained vines, a dark bower at the nighttime garden's dark heart. Our rough breath made the only sound.

Liz cleared her throat. Her face was a pale oblong, blurred but aghast. Something tickled my face and I started, beating at the air. A tendril. "I was in the sitting room," she murmured, "with Ginny. And then," the words caught for a second in Liz's throat. I had become aware of a deep, pressing sweetness in the air, thick around us. "Out of absolutely *nowhere*, Ginny said, 'You should probably know, people think something's going on between you and Ellen Margolis.'" Liz perfectly mimicked Ginny's Valley-girl cadence, capriciousness married to deadly gravity. I thought she was done, but she went on in Ginny's voice, "'Sara Masters says a girl saw you two kissing in the bathroom.'" Even in the dark, I could see Liz was trembling. I could feel the heat off her skin as she flushed furiously. Or maybe it was me trembling.

I stumbled back against the base of one of the trees, my head racing. We had never done any of those things. Maybe we were more affectionate than some girls. So what? Inside the bower, it was dark, and cool. Liz started to shiver. I put my arms around her bare arms. We stood like that in the close little bower for a long time, until Liz drew back, her face blurry. All around us, the deep balm of sweet pea soaked our skin like a salve.

"What would I do without you, El?" Liz drawled. Then she leaned in, lightly at first, and kissed me, lightly, on the lips. My heart, which had finally slowed, just about stopped. The green vines and the dark covered us. I hesitated. Then I leaned toward Liz and kissed her back. This time, her mouth opened, and her tongue, sweet and wet and tasting slightly of rum punch, darted in to touch mine. Then she stepped toward me, right under my toes, pressing my back into the base of the tree.

I'd been kissed before, kissed by Mosswood boys with slow rolling tongues the texture of garden snails. But kissing Liz wasn't about tongue, teeth, lips—*parts*. Kissing Liz—from the rising tingle at the roots of my hair to the slow, blooming heat spreading across my chest and thighs—this was the moment I first believed the old stories of wood nymphs, dryads, lovers, their limbs entwined, turned into living trees, could be true.

From a distance, we heard voices. Someone had opened the French doors. "Ginny . . ." Liz started.

"Ginny's an idiot." My words disappeared in the swallowing silence of the thicket.

"We didn't know." Liz held my elbow.

"No," I agreed. "We didn't know."

"This is just between us," I assured her, my arms around her waist.

"Yes," Liz answered.

A peal of laughter from the terrace startled us. Liz dropped my elbow. Even in the bower, I could see her face harden. "We'd better go in. Not—" she added, dropping her voice, "—together."

As we walked back in silence, I twirled a strand of hair over and over in my fist, wondering if she'd only thought I meant we shouldn't tell anyone else, or we shouldn't kiss anyone else, or both.

In the darkness behind the hedge, I was turned around. But Liz knew her way back. She led us to the dark parlor. Then she pointed past the girls smoking outside, their little orange cherries bobbing in the dark. "Go," she mouthed. She passed back quietly through the door we'd come out, alone, only her white dress, luminous as a ghost, appearing for a moment through the garden doors. I walked alone along the back of the house toward the ballroom, my legs shaking so badly I thought I might collapse onto the gravel.

In the ballroom, I found Fiona fanning herself with a napkin at one of the tables by the dance floor and fell into the chair beside her. Sweat beaded Fiona's upper lip; her eyelids hung low. "Hey," she said.

I wondered if Liz was in the bathroom, examining her face in the mirror for signs of change, or if she'd gone back to the parlor and was sitting next to Ginny, her secret all tied up with a bright bow of irony. "Hey," I said.

"Someone's put rum in the punch," she commented, wrinkling her nose at the paper cup she'd picked up.

I shrugged. It was a "wild night out," right? It never got wilder than that—just a little rum in the punch. Then, with a jolt of electricity, I remembered Liz's tongue in my mouth.

"I think I'm an alcoholic," Fiona went on.

"Hmmm." I nodded. "You don't drink," I pointed out.

"Ex-actly." Fiona leaned back against her chair, case closed. She resumed fanning herself with her napkin. Then, lazily plucking at the fabric of her shirt, she leaned over and fanned down into the cleft between her breasts. She had been dancing all night.

To keep myself from thinking about what Liz and I had just done in the trees, I asked, "Why do you think you're an alcoholic?"

Fiona blinked, a momentary eclipse of green. "Hel-lo," she quipped. We were old enough, finally, to have put words to the fact that Fiona's mother Cait Collins's habit of traveling with a tumbler of whisky was not just a distinguishing personal feature, like having a mole or wearing a felt hat.

"You're nothing like her," I told Fiona. "You're not like that."

Fiona leaned in toward the table and grabbed both of my hands. "Ellen," she pleaded—her green gaze nearly pierced me—"don't *ever* let me start drinking." She let her eyelids droop again, regarding me with a blend of sisterly comfort and deep gratitude. Then she squinted at me hard. I felt little pinpricks on my scalp as she tugged at strands behind my left ear. "What's in your hair?"

"Ow!"

"You've got all this—" she freed something, held a piece of bark in my face, "crap in your hair." She deposited the bit of wood on the paper tablecloth. "Oh my god!" she plucked at my head again. "You've got, like, an entire fucking forest in there!" Out came another piece of bark, a leaf and, after an uncomfortable bout of yanking—Fiona, with her wax-shiny black hair didn't know anything about tangles—an entire sweet pea, its petals pale pink, and smelling intoxicatingly of Liz's kisses, came out in her hand. I sniffed it clandestinely between my fingers as Fiona, who had moved around to the back, pulled at my hair. "Where the hell have you been?"

"Nowhere," I choked, pressing the sweet pea deep into my palm, where I kept it, hidden, for the rest of the night.

I stretched my legs on the closet floor, wondering if I would find that flower on my shelf, pressed into a book. I wondered, too, now that Francine and I were "engaged," was I supposed to throw it out?

Francine had never expressed jealousy over Liz, exactly. It was more like skepticism. Tall, blond, political and Southern, Liz was everything Francine was not. "What do you mean?" I'd reassured her. "You're smart, and funnier, too."

But that wasn't what Francine meant. "Your big, blond WASP," Francine called her. How could the same heart, she meant, possibly love them both? (I didn't suppose she'd feel the same skepticism about Jill. But I decided not to think about that.)

On my bookshelf, beneath the faded cover of *A Separate Peace*,

I found the sweet pea, its petals faded the pale brown of old paper, and smelling like first kisses. Liz had always had a hold on me. She was my first love; the *genie* becomes a slave to the person who lets her out of the bottle. But it was more than primacy; our love had been a dangerous secret. That was powerful, too. I put the sweet pea back into the book and tucked the book deep into my bag to take back home.

( )

The next day, I had lunch in the Valley with my cousin Nathan. One of the last times I'd seen him had been at Gramma Sophie's 85th birthday, where Gramma Sophie, literally stricken with surprise, had sunk to the floor before our eyes. Around the table, all of us Margolises, stock-still, almost blacked out from the g-forces required not to cry, while the ice in the glasses at the big, U-shaped table shifted, audibly clinking. Nathan and I met at Jerry's Deli for matzoh ball soup—a pale imitation of Gramma Sophie's, and too salty, but comforting, too—and blintzes smothered in strawberry jam. I told him Francine and I were getting married, relieved to be able to tell *someone* in my family something real, then buckled myself up and drove home to my mother.

"The car keys are on your desk," I called out to my mother when I got back.

Her head popped out of the room I thought of as the Vault, the place where she hid away all her antique lace. My mother's locked room was packed with turn-of-the-century lace skirts, tea gowns, velvet walking suits. It was like that warehouse in the last scene of *Raiders of the Lost Ark*. After Indiana Jones has rescued the Ark from the Nazis, someone asks, "Is it safe?" You see the Ark, sealed in an anonymous wooden box, stamped with a ten-digit bureaucratic filing code; the camera pans back as the crate gets slipped onto a shelf with a thousand other boxes just like it, then pans back again to a thousand other shelves just like them. Just like that.

My mother was holding a piece of yellowed fabric, something my Gramma Sophie might have called a *shmata*. It looked lacy. And old. "This is the Hapsburg Coverlet," my mother announced. "It belonged to Empress Elizabeth during her *accouchement* at the time of the birth of Crown Prince Rudolph. The four crowns," my mother pointed, "are the four High Orders of Austria and Hungary: the Golden Fleece, the Order of Leopold, the Order of St. Stephen, and the Order of the Iron Cross." It was the new acquisition my mother had been telling my father about in the car. I looked more closely at the coverlet, trying to discern in its creamy loops and threads the story my mother had found there. "Empress Elizabeth was your kind of gal." She held the coverlet out like an offering. Did my mother mean that she was a lesbian? My mother often spoke in code. "She was a fitness fanatic. She had a nineteen-inch waist when she was sixty years old." As a matter of fact, she sounded a lot like my mother's kind of gal. (A slow but determined treadmill runner on whom the skin, lately, had begun to seem a little loose, my mother liked to point out that she was still, at nearly sixty, a size four.) My mother held the fabric gingerly in her hands, careful not to distress the stitching. "She was out walking with one of her maids when a young Italian stabbed her under the corset with a needle file. She walked a little further, asked, 'What happened to me?' and died."

In her own way, my mother was also looking for ghosts in the mirror. But she didn't want to let them out. "Are you going to sell it?" I asked her. "To a museum, maybe?" I always wondered what her life might have been like if she had played a less traditional role in her marriage.

My mother made a sour face and whisked the coverlet out of sight. For all I knew, I'd be the last person besides her to see it again. "Did you ask your cousin why we never hear from him?" My mother frowned again. "Is he still seeing that *Amy*?"

Amy and Nathan had been dating even longer than Francine

and I. They'd met at UCLA, where Amy was computer science, Nathan film. Francine and I both liked Amy. In some way that was totally different from Francine's other-ness, Amy was the anti-Margolis. Straightforward, a little wonky, a little literal. She wore little wire-framed glasses and sensible shoes. My mother had never liked Amy because Amy wasn't Jewish. *Scratch a goy, find an anti-Semite* my mother liked to say. (So why didn't I get more credit for being with Francine?) "He's only ever dated the one girl," lamented my mother, who had never dated a man besides my father.

"He loves Amy," I pointed out. It was so much easier than telling her I loved Francine.

My mother shrugged as if that were not a very good reason. "How does he know he can't love a Jewish girl better?" My mother and father hadn't been to synagogue since my sister's bat mitzvah, when my parents might as well have kicked their heels as they fled the building, singing "Free at last! Free at last! Thank God Almighty, we're free at last!" Still, my mother maintained a stubborn, deep tribalism that had nothing to do with religion. Then, as if it weren't a complete contradiction to everything she'd just said, she asked, "Did you ask your cousin why he hasn't gotten married yet?" It was a variation on the question my mother sometimes threw at me like an accusation: "When is your cousin Nathan going to get married?" Of course, she had any number of theories, including the supposed anti-Semitism of Amy's parents, whom my parents had never met. "I don't need to meet them. I know the type." She'd never once asked the same thing of me.

Now, with smug pleasure at the dissonance I knew this would cause in my mother, I announced, "She *won't* marry him." With his thick head of dark hair, his strong nose, square chin, and neat white teeth, Nathan moved through life blithe as a movie star. That any woman wouldn't marry Nathan violated everything my mother had ever told us about how unusually talented, good-looking, and *special* we Margolis children all were (and wasn't Nathan, after all, sort of like her own son?).

My mother actually gasped. "Why not?" Her fingers gripped the door and she started back into her room, like a turtle retreating to its shell. I could see her waiting for me to confirm every suspicion she had ever had about Amy and her parents.

I hesitated. I remembered the look on his face when Nathan told me the real reason Amy wouldn't marry him, or anyone. He had just smeared a glob of Russian dressing under the top layer of rye bread on the second half of his pastrami sandwich, replaced the bread and clamped the whole thing shut with one hand. At his throat, the dark skin at his jaw raised in one spot in the shape of a pale, thin new moon where he had slit his chin jumping off the diving board backwards. "She says she won't marry me until you and Francine can get married." My eyes had welled with tears. But I couldn't say that to my mother. Not yet. So I looked my mother hard in the eye and, out of self-protection and spite, quoting Debbie, I lied: "Why would you want to support a patriarchal, heterosexist institution whose original purpose was the exchange of women as chattel?"

If I'd intended to hurt her, I'd missed the mark. As far as my parents were concerned, the exchange of women for goods was the whole point. In their eyes, Francine and I together had committed not one but two *shandas*: not marrying men *and* not making the kind of money earned by a man. So, when Francine's Volvo stuttered up to 105 Dunsmuir Drive at last to say goodbye to the house and to carry me back home with whatever I had salvaged, my father settled down to his salad and started in with the usual routine. It was the same conversation my father had had with me and Francine since I'd left graduate school, the same conversation he'd had with me the first night I'd arrived. He played it back the millionth time now that Francine was here, as he always did, as if Francine had more sense than I did, and could help me see the error of my ways. "You're still working at the Jewish place?" he asked me. He knew I did. It was almost quaint, his refusal to accept my reality, as if he could truly make it disappear.

"The Foundation."

"That doesn't pay very well, does it?" My father was the son of immigrants, a self-made man. He already knew exactly what the Foundation paid.

Like my father's backup singer, my mother chimed in, "What those people went through was unspeakable. But you don't have to sacrifice your life for them. You can do anything you want."

"*Those people?* Mom, those are your people, my people—they're our people."

"Ellen, our people come from New Jersey. We're *Americans.*"

My father, a forkful of salad stuffed into his cheek, took a more practical view. "All those old people are dying," he reminded me. "And then what?" Then, as he always did, my father turned to Francine, as if she were the one who might save us. (It was sort of touching, really, his confidence in her.) He asked his signature question, as always, with the same fresh innocence as Fiona, aged 7, after her first Sunday school Christmas, asking, "Have you heard about the newborn king?"—"Have you thought about real estate?" Francine had not.

Having Francine with me had always been my bulwark against the vast otherness that was my parents' life. That night, I found Francine in my childhood bedroom, where she had retreated for safety. On the old black and white TV, she was watching her secret vice, *Antiques Roadshow.* She lived for the dissembling. ("And, Mrs. Petroskas, how much do you think your great-grandfather's Civil War-era musket ball collection might be worth?" "Oh!" pleaded Mrs. Petroskas, her small chin tight, set-curls stiff on her shaking head, all protest. "We really never considered it to have any value at all.")

"Are you sure my Dad's not right?" I pointed at the TV, where a *Roadshow* appraiser was announcing the value of a Chippendale desk. "You love that stuff," I ventured, considering Francine's true passion for the *Roadshow.* Here in my parents' house, I felt so small. My father had given my mother everything. Without a fortune, what would I have to give? "Antiques." I mouthed the word with distaste.

"It's fun." Francine shrugged at the TV. "It's history," she added, meaning I should like it, too. It wouldn't have been a sore spot, if my mother weren't always trying to sell me on the provenance of objects.

"But, I mean," I cleared my throat, "you want those kinds of things." Like a *fabulous*, sparkly wedding ring. Things I would never be able to afford.

"You mean, I want nice things?"

I shrugged, self-conscious. "Yeah." I worked at a small nonprofit. Francine was a preschool teacher. Should two people with such limited incomes really get married to each other? Shouldn't we each have found someone rich?

"Don't you want nice things?" Francine asked. When I didn't answer, she added, "Not fancy things. Just a nice house with nice things. Like a real couch." She looked up from my old, iron-framed childhood bed. It wasn't fancy, but it was nicer than anything Francine and I owned.

"I guess." I frowned at Francine, turning off the TV. When had I started scrutinizing Francine not through my eyes, but through the eyes of the world, in which Francine and I could never really be married because one of us wasn't a male-salary-earning man? Since dinner? Since I'd walked into this house?

Francine lifted a corner of the blanket and waited for me to climb into bed with her. (It never occurred to my mother to require us, like Rebecca and Ted before they were married, to sleep in separate bedrooms; she preferred to think of us as "girlfriends" in her generation's sense of the word.) "I'm not the one who grew up in a house full of antiques, remember?"

I hated having my parents' wealth held against me. "Exactly," I pressed her. Wasn't that how it went? I'd had everything, and I didn't care. But Francine, who hadn't, almost certainly wanted more.

Francine chewed at the cuticle around her index finger. She was a preschool teacher; she had the infuriating, natural ability not to get drawn into stupid fights. "Maybe you just assume that you'll eventually have all that stuff, because you grew up with it. Maybe you don't even know you want it. Maybe," Francine looked at me piercingly, "maybe *you'll* be the one who's disappointed."

"Hmph," I grunted, turning off the light.

I thought that was the end of it. But as we lay side by side on the creaking trundle bed in my childhood bedroom on Dunsmuir Drive, Francine spoke into the dark. "Are we taking the dolls?" Silent, mutinous, the dolls' shadowed faces huddled on the shelf beside the bed. The dolls had been my mother's idea ("Every girl should have a collection of something"); the crinolines made my fingers itch; the lace trim sent goose pimples up my arms. "They're probably worth a fortune," Francine mused. I bristled at this, more evidence of her secret love of "nice things." But I made myself behave.

"Would you mind if I leave them?"

"Hell no!" Francine pressed her icy feet against my legs in the creaking trundle bed. "Those things have always given me the creeps!"

Francine didn't want anything fancy. Just a ring. From me.

( )

Los Angeles, seen from the night sky above, is a vast carpet of glittering jewels. It is a city made of glamour and dreams. I figured that, by association alone, L.A. would be the perfect place to get Francine something fabulous. The next afternoon, I took her out to find it.

From where Francine and I stood deep in the hidden recess of the Westwood Jewelry Mart, the shimmering light off the hot sidewalks looked as far away as the light at the mouth of a cave. Francine and I walked into the jeweler's too close together, but not holding hands. We crept from case to case, reverent as museumgoers, resting a finger here and there on the cold glass: *What about that one?* An older man glided toward us, quiet and solicitous. Could he help us? The jeweler whisked out a small palette of black velvet, and set one ring down, gleaming. He watched silently as we took turns slipping it on. Maybe he thought I was the bridesmaid and Francine was the bride, expediting the process by leaving the man at home. We moved on to another stall where a Persian vendor peered at us curiously, a colorful silk scarf tied up around her hair. "Are you sisters?" She looked from my olive features to Francine's fair cheeks, smiling, accusing. "Auntie and niece?" She tried to catch Francine's eye with a conspiratorial smile. Her pointing finger seemed to say, "Gotcha!" Francine smiled a tight smile and shook her head.

Back out in the sunlight of the L.A. afternoon, the Westwood sidewalk glittering with little chips of silica, Francine and I nattered over soft pretzels. "What is it, anyway? We don't look a thing alike."

"They sense there's a connection between us, but they can't quite put their finger on it." Francine popped a big white grain of salt onto her tongue. "It just doesn't occur to most people that girls with ponytails," she swung her hair toward me, catching me on the cheek, "go home and make wild love." Francine held my eye for longer than a second. I looked down at my pretzel, not wanting to talk about what we hadn't gone home to do in a bit too long.

"I spent all my money in that place, once," I confessed, changing the subject—one kind of intimacy exchanged, I hoped, for another. "In high school. I wanted to get Liz something special for her eighteenth birthday. Something she wouldn't forget."

"You didn't want her to forget *you*," Francine corrected me. "You wanted her to wear your ring and be your wife." I stuck out my tongue, but my face felt hot. Francine had been so cavalier before, when I told her that Liz and I had "traded rings." I thought she was joking now, until she said, "Were you really going to buy me a wedding ring from the same place you got Liz an engagement ring?"

As we drove back to my parents' house, I protested. "It wasn't anything like that."

But it was. I'd walked into the Jewelry Mart with all the money I'd ever saved, a thick copper- and dirt-smelling bundle of tens and ones anchored with huge, silver bicentennial dollars. When I walked back out onto Westwood Boulevard, a dark blue velvet box bulged in my pocket where the money had been. Inside glimmered an oval sapphire, the color of the night sky in summertime. I had tucked the box into my drawer for September.

"How on earth did *you* wait three months to reveal a surprise?" Francine and I sat in the Volvo, all its parts creaking as it settled in my parents' driveway. We stayed outside, not ready to assume our inscrutability yet.

"Are you saying I can't keep a secret?" I countered, propping my feet up on the dash. A squirrel perched up in the oak above us, nibbled an acorn, and pelted it down onto the roof of the car. Sitting with Francine in the Volvo at the top of my parents' driveway, I flashed guiltily on my car ride with Jill and then, more guiltily, on what I'd told her about: my meeting with Anya. I didn't realize until Francine answered me that I'd been holding my breath.

Francine squinted up into the tree. "I know you're full of secrets." Francine turned to me; she spread her hand with its sexy, ringless fingers insinuatingly on the knee of my jeans and leaned in to whisper in my ear, "But you're terrible with surprises."

I conceded. "I gave it to her in June."

Francine crossed her arms, satisfied, over her chest.

When Liz opened the box, her face had broken open in joy, her big front teeth shining, her cheeks flushed with embarrassed pleasure. "It's beautiful!" she gasped, as overtaken as the woman in the diamond commercial. "Oh, Ellen!" She had flung her arms around me, buried her face in my neck. "I love it!"

"Diamonds *are* a girl's best friend," Francine reminded me. We'd already decided that we couldn't afford diamonds. Another acorn pelted the windshield and ricocheted off onto the Italian pavers.

A few months later, Liz had given me a ring back. "It's an early birthday present," Liz told me, sitting me on her bed, her door firmly shut. Above us, Liz's certificates of achievement, parchment and gold foil, hung from the same corkboard to which she'd pinned the garland of dried flowers from Junior Gown Ceremony. She pulled the small box from under her sweater. Inside, I found a small gold ring, a sapphire chip flanked by pinprick diamonds. Liz's face glowed with expectation; she'd picked it to match. "That's queer, isn't it?" Gramma Sophie had squinted across the kitchen counter when I came home. "A girl giving another girl a ring?"

"When did you take it off?" Francine glanced at my finger, as if the ring might still be there. "Do you still have it?"

I'd taken the ring off in college, after Liz told me she was fucking a sophomore from the campus Republican Caucus.

(No danger of being called "Lez" anymore.) "It's gone," I told Francine, pretty sure, in fact, that it was right here in my parents' house, inside my father's locked closet.

Why were we even talking about Liz? I had let go of Liz long before I met Francine. But the ghost of our love, Liz's and mine, was an old, implacable ghost, the way ghosts often are, so sensitive, so defensive, so reluctant to be swept away.

Fiona had another theory: "You need to get the *fuck* out of your parents' house. Immediately." Reprising the role of my teenage life, I had called her from my childhood bedroom for what I knew would be the last time. Fiona was living in one of those New York apartments with the bathtub in the kitchen; I could hear the running water in her apartment three thousand miles away. I cradled my old pink SlimLine to my ear, another installment in the three-thousand-year-long conversation we'd been having since we met. Fiona had always hated Liz for insinuating herself between us. She spat into the phone, as reanimated with ancient jealousy as I had been by ancient love, "Francine is ten thousand times better than that bitch Liz—who, *hello!* never even had the guts to acknowledge you were a couple." That was just it. If Liz had still been in my life or at least been an acknowledged part of it, her memory never would have loomed so large. But she was gone. Except for one dried sweet pea blossom, truly gone without a trace. Because no one had ever known we were a couple. I remembered our picture in the senior yearbook, our arms around each other on the wide green Ferngrove lawn, hiding in plain sight.

Suddenly, I remembered Anya's photo, the one of her and her "friend." The girl with raven-black hair. "Shit," I whispered out loud. Anya hadn't said anything to suggest this girl had been her lover. But that was just the thing, wasn't it? If that girl *had been* Anya's lover, Anya wouldn't say. Honestly, as an argument, it made very little sense. But it made perfect sense to me. Awed— I had never met an elderly lesbian, let alone a lesbian Holocaust survivor—I whispered: "No *way*."

Fiona crunched a carrot into my ear. We had been friends all our lives, seen the same movies, listened to the same mix tapes. She had no idea what I was thinking about, but it didn't matter. "Um? *Way!*"

Yes. *Way!* I had come back "home" to get my things, and I had the sudden sensation that I had discovered something huge that belonged to me, something I didn't ever expect to find: Anya was my foremother. She was my "people" and her history was my history, too. If I had been born at a different time, I might have continued to live my life in secrecy. My entire past would have been erased, no record of Liz; probably, no Francine. Anya *had* been born in a different time. And her past was in danger! But not if I could help it.

The next day, as Francine and I pulled away from Dunsmuir Drive for the very last time, I determined to find out who the girl in Anya's photo was. And what had happened to her.

( )

Down in the reading room, Jill's black hair flashed. I ducked out before she could see me leaving the Foundation, glad that Anya had refused to meet at the Foundation. Francine and I were getting married. There was no sense risking a flirtation.

Anya looked skeptical when she met me at the door. "Tennis shoes," she *tsk*ed, glancing down at my feet. It would become a refrain between us. She, herself, was dressed immaculately in gray flannel slacks, a white linen shirt, her hair held back smooth, the deep creases at the sides of her eyes and mouth bracketing her secrets.

If I had thought I was going to plunk myself down on Anya's couch and start in with my questions about the girl in the photo, Foundation-Oral-Historian-style, I didn't know much about Anya's skill at creating a composition. Anya pointed to the white leather couch and sat across from me. She set two slices of cake—Linzer torte, this time—on two bone china plates on the gleaming glass tabletop. The small living room expanded with air and light. Anya picked up her plate. She watched me until I did the same. Without speaking, we ate our cake. Once, I caught her glance at me and, parenthetically, smile.

It's much harder to interrogate someone who doesn't have any intention of speaking to you than it is to listen quietly to someone who has decided to speak. I had never really learned the art of interrogation. I'd learned the opposite. How to sit across from my Gramma Sophie to the flick of playing cards, the click of Rummy Tiles. Even with my clients, I had learned to listen, to be still. So I was hiding behind my teacup, working up enough momentum to initiate a conversation with Anya, when she slid a large, coffee-table art book from the side table at her elbow and opened it in her lap. On the side table, the mysterious photo huddled inside the bower of vines spilling from a potted plant. "Do you like art?" Anya asked me, paging through the book. Big Georgia O'Keeffe flowers slipped through her fingers. I almost laughed. Those huge, labial flowers were the staple of lesbian college dorm rooms the world over. I congratulated myself. She glanced up at my black pants. "Are you going to a funeral? Young people should like color."

"I do," I hurried to reassure her. Most of my work clothes were black, but *I have so many purple T-shirts!* I wanted to protest. *Red, green, blue!* (All the colors except yellow, which my mother always told me looked terrible on me, and which only she could wear.) Already, I was trying to please her. "I had that painting on my wall. In college." I pointed at O'Keeffe's *Red Canna*, the most lady-parts flower ever painted, a print Sam had picked out for me at the Coop to get me up to lesbian speed.

"Mmm." Anya's invisible eyebrows rose up in two invisible arcs. "It's a kind of paradox." I panicked, wondering what she meant that my having this painting on my wall was a paradox. But, of course, she wasn't talking about me. "By looking at it so closely, O'Keeffe turns the most delicate object into something so powerful, it is almost monstrous." Anya's finger tapped the book, but she had looked up at me. "Don't you think so?"

Suddenly, there was no question in my mind that she *was* talking about me. *I* was a person whose job was to look at small things closely. She seemed to be warning me that if I looked too closely at something fragile—like her story, like the girl in the picture—I would make it turn monstrous. Involuntarily, I glanced at the photo hidden in the tangle of vines.

Anya shook her head. "No. Not Sheva," she warned me. I was right. She didn't want me probing. But now it didn't matter.

"No," I reassured her. I picked up my teacup and told Anya I had finished my tea. I didn't need anything else.

When I got back to the Foundation, I made sure Wendy was out and then I called Vicky at the Holocaust and War Victims Tracing Center and placed a request to find a person from Kaunas, Lithuania. Kovno Ghetto. A woman named Sheva.

( )

Not long after Rebecca and Ted got engaged, my mother had called me to tell me she was giving her engagement ring to my future brother-in-law Ted. "If he wants it, fine. If not, fine." Her pronouncement startled me. It hadn't occurred to me that my mother was going to give her engagement ring, which she still wore herself, to anyone, let alone my sister's fiancé.

"Didn't his mother already give him her jade necklace and earrings?" My sister had showed me the set, handed down from Ted's grandmother, saved for the Hsu's oldest son's bride. That the bride had turned out to be a nice Jewish girl instead of a nice Chinese one hadn't disrupted the transmission. Rebecca, it was assumed—wrongly, I might add: my sister had long ago declared her intention to remain childless—would pass the set on to the next generation of Hsus, my sister, in the long lineage of Ted's family that stretched from the Tang dynasty into the future, just a brief moment of static on the line. I was the oldest daughter. Shouldn't my mother be doing the same for me?

"Was she asking your permission?" Francine had wanted to know. "Did you tell her *you* might want it?"

"That's just it," I told Francine. "It's not that I want the ring. I just wanted her to ask me first."

But she hadn't and I would have to move on. When I picked Francine up from work the next Thursday, we headed out to find something that could be ours alone. "Maybe we've been doing it wrong," Francine mused. "Maybe we shouldn't try to find rings we like. Maybe we should have rings made." Fairy tales are full of transformations, magical moments when the princess utters the secret words, and suddenly a door appears in the floor, a hidden forest lit by moonlight. Francine's suggestion was like that: where we had encountered a solid wall, suddenly a door appeared.

We'd walked by it a thousand times. *Byzantium*. It was no more than a closet tucked between a diner and a tiny Provencal chicken and *frites* place with five tables and a wicked draft under the door. The door to Byzantium was an afterthought, a sliver, a hole in the wall. We rang to get in.

Inside Byzantium, potted orchids on thin necks craned from golden pots; a golden bowl held silver-wrapped chocolate kisses. In black velvet-draped jewel cases, hand-wrought gold rings massive enough for the fingers of giants (black pearls, black gold, titanium set with diamonds) sat beside smooth bands of swirling red and yellow golds, delicate as Pompeiian treasure. And behind each case, beckoning, sat a siren.

"How can I help you two ladies today?" A voice like running water. Long hair cast loose over her shoulders. "I'm Sarah."

"We're looking for rings," Francine told her. "Wedding rings," she added.

Sarah arched an eyebrow over one deep brown eye. "Congratulations, you two!" She glowed. "Why don't I show you our collection. And, of course, if you like, I can help you design your own rings."

I noticed Francine's back and shoulders drop an inch; I felt my own neck loosen. We weren't a ready-made couple. Why should the symbol of our relationship be off-the-rack?

Sarah's smile twinkled. She pulled out a set of colored pencils—jewel-toned reds, purples and greens, metallic yellows and grays, chatting gaily as she chose each color. Before our eyes, two solid, bright shapes emerged; the rings, sketched in Sarah's hand, looked real enough to pick up with your fingers.

"That's my ring!" Francine held the sketch as if peering into a magic looking glass. Inside it, I thought, watching Francine's gaze, she was seeing the future in which we were married.

Sarah smiled. She took out a yellow slip and began to fill out our information—name, phone number, price of the rings. *Wow.* The price of the rings. Francine and I both started. "I'll just need a credit card."

I panicked. But Francine pulled her card out of her wallet. It flashed, gold, among the gold and jewels.

Out on College Avenue, sucking chocolate kisses, we took tentative steps. "What just happened in there?" I asked Francine. Little bits of silver foil stuck to the cuticle of her index finger. The receipt from Byzantium, along with Sarah Fine's card, peeked out the top of her pocket.

"I'm not sure," Francine said. Her fingers brushed mine and caught as we headed slowly toward home. "I think we just agreed to get married."

( )

"Lunch?" Jill caught my sleeve and I nearly tripped. I'd been avoiding her. It wasn't just the attraction. Since I'd seen Anya again at her apartment, I wished I hadn't told Jill about Anya at all. Before I'd been resolved about dropping the whole thing, but now called the Red Cross Tracing Center and I felt like I'd somehow cheated on her. I reminded myself I hadn't done anything wrong. How could I cheat on Jill? I hadn't slept with her. Jill was my friend; friends fall into something like love with each other, right?

We took our brown paper sacks out to Chiang Kai-shek Park, where we sat watching an old man in gray pants and a white T-shirt dump crumbs for a thousand cooing, crapping pigeons. Once, we'd had a long, intense conversation in that very spot, our knees nearly touching, about whether or not to have children, without ever mentioning husbands or wives, partners or spouses. I couldn't do that anymore.

Jill started talking first. "An editor from Oxford called me," she said.

"Wow!" I gobbled down my mouthful of greasy noodles. "I can't believe you're going to publish your book before you finish your degree. With Oxford!" My neck flushed. Of course, I was happy for her. Jill's work, her intelligence, was part of what made her so attractive. But I was starting to feel mildly insecure. "Don't people usually wait until they're facing down tenure review before they even start contemplating a book?" Earlier in the summer, Francine and I had gone to see Alvin Ailey at Zellerbach Hall. We'd sat spellbound while dancers flew, suspended, in jewel-toned spandex. I knew, though she loved it, watching dance always made Francine feel wistful. Now, contemplating Jill's meteoric ascent, I felt a pang of it myself. The thing about Jill was, and I could see this myself, all her strengths, all the things I found attractive in her in small doses—her social ease, her intellectual panache, her certain success—were things that, in close proximity, would highlight all of my failures. It was good to remember that. "Shit, Jill," I teased her, "you're a regular child prodigy." I didn't need to compare myself to Jill. We were just friends.

"I think you mean a prodigal child," she corrected me, shoveling noodles into her mouth. We looked up at each other and laughed, our eyes locking. Jill frowned. "There's something I need to tell you."

I stared away toward the pigeon man.

"I've really enjoyed our lunches together." I felt my neck warming. What could I say if Jill confessed an attraction? Or accused me of one? It would be wrong to admit one. It would be a lie to deny it. Bottom line: Jill was hot. Hotter yet: she cared about what I cared about. Jill looked up from our shared lunch and smiled, a warm, sad smile. She spread her hands, taking in us, our lunch, the pigeon man. "When I started doing my research at the Foundation, I didn't have any idea I'd also be meeting someone I liked so much." This wasn't supposed to be happening. My stomach tightened. My hands felt cold, but my cheeks felt hot. I hoped Jill didn't notice.

"That was a huge plus," Jill added, "for me."

I nodded. When I looked up, I caught her looking back at me, a huge wave of self-consciousness rising over my head. "Me too," I managed, my face a raging fire of guilt. It didn't matter what my head knew; my body had its own agenda. Jill's hands, on the blistered green bench, sat very close to mine.

"Ellen," Jill ducked her head to find my eyes, "I've been offered a job at Brandeis. A tenure track position."

My stomach flopped.

"I'm moving to Boston."

Of course. What an idiot I was, thinking Jill wanted me, even when Francine and I were about to get married, even when Jill probably never had!

"I went on the market last year. I'd interviewed but nothing came up. Then, someone in the department at Brandeis died. An old guy. I'm leaving in August." *Next month.*

"Congratulations," I mustered the words. The continent was rearing up between me and Jill. Jill and I didn't have a friendship that was established enough to stand up over that kind of distance, did we? We were sitting as far apart as a take-out container.

I looked hard at Jill's intelligent face. Her teeth were small and white. It hit me now with a pang of real regret: We could have been friends. But now it was too late.

A roar of skateboard wheels filled the park, reverberated off the walls of the buildings. "Yah!" the pigeon man shouted. The pigeons gathered into a single noisy blot and rose up like a cloud of smoke into the sky. The pigeon man shook his fist, alone on the brick in his thin T-shirt, surrounded by a circle of breadcrumbs and pigeon shit.

"I'll email," I offered. But I knew I wouldn't. I was too attracted to Jill to risk a virtual flirtation, too easily seduced by distance to share things that I shouldn't share. And I was too insecure to watch her rise while I stayed here in one place. We watched the pigeon man retreat, a fistful of plastic bags trailing him like a cloud.

"Yeah," Jill smiled. "I will, too." But I knew she wouldn't, either. And I was glad. I knew I would be sad to lose Jill, but I told myself it was better this way, that the sadness was a symptom of the danger I had skirted, that nothing untoward had happened between me and Jill, and, as long as she was far away, it never would. It was as if, by vanquishing the danger of Jill, I could avoid, by association, the danger of Anya.

Back at the office, I had a message from Vicky at the Holocaust and War Victims Tracing Center. "Sorry," Vicky apologized. "I'm having trouble with the name Sheva. Is it possible that's short for something else? Batsheva? Sorry, Ellen," Vicky told me. "It's just not much to go on."

If I really wanted to find out what happened to Sheva, I was going to have to ask Anya some questions.

Francine had warned me early on in my job, "You're going to get into trouble if you think these people are saints."

"I don't think they're saints," I'd countered.

"You do. Because you loved your grandmother more than anyone else, and, in some strange way, all old Jewish ladies remind you of her."

That was an oversimplification, I told myself, as I picked up the phone and dialed Anya's now-familiar number. And even if it wasn't, I conceded, what harm could *really* come of it? Jill, in whom I might have confided inappropriately, was leaving. And I wouldn't let it become a concern for Wendy or Francine.

Elizabeth Landau and her husband had never talked about the Holocaust they'd both survived. *Dignity,* she had said. So why tell Francine about Anya? Wasn't that Mrs. Landau's point? That, like so many women of my generation—like so many women I knew—I often confused intimacy with telling the truth?

We all have compartments inside ourselves, I reminded myself. I guessed my father was right about that.

( )

It was cold. Another Bay Area August. Francine lay upstairs in the blood-red bathroom, soaking in a hot, hot tub. I sat on the floor, sponging sudsy water over her flushed pink nipples. Her auburn curls floated on the surface of the steaming water like kelp and she lay, sweltering, in a steaming brew of cedar and cinnamon, warm smells, red smells that matched the tiles, matched her hair. And, come to think of it, O'Keeffe's *Red Canna.*

Francine panted. "I could use a roll in the snow. Like the Norwegians. Or is it the Swedes? Hot sauna, cold snow."

"You'd never make it as a Swede," I told her.

"Are you calling me a wimp?" Francine released a long, hot

gasp, the only other sound between our words, the *drip drip drip* of the leaking faucet. Her face was young, and beautiful, and I planned, despite all my failings, to love her even when it no longer was.

"No," I said. But I let uncertainty hang in my voice. I just felt like teasing her, a vestige of having a little sister. "Not exactly."

Francine's sweaty eyebrows arched up.

"If I gave you a hundred bucks, would you run into the garden naked and let me spray you with the hose?" Our yard lay under a damp gray blanket of mist.

"One hundred. That's not very much."

"Forget the money." I changed tack. "I *dare* you."

If the neighbors had cared to look, they would have spied Francine's pale flesh glowing against the camellia leaves. "You're a cheap thrill," I told her as I led her, shivering, back up the path.

"That's what all the girls say."

The phone was ringing when we got in. "That bitch!" Fiona's words were sticky with tears. I'd seen Fiona cry a thousand times. I knew her eyes, rimmed with red, turned into sparkling emeralds of righteous fury. I wasn't sure if she was talking about her mother or her girlfriend Chandra. "I was going to meet her at her apartment. After work. Except, I left early." Fiona took a punctured breath. I could hear the edges of her teeth meeting. "I saw her truck parked in front of her building. Except, it couldn't be hers—" Fiona sounded truly confounded "—because there were two people inside it making out—" Fiona's voice rose dangerously high. She took a breath, descended. "After about a million hours, the two of them finally stopped kissing long enough for me to see her face." Fiona paused dramatically. "It was Chandra and that *bitch* ex-girlfriend of hers!" All Fiona's hardened private-eye cool fell away. She broke into rhythmic sobs, and I didn't know what to say. *I can't believe it*? From what I'd heard—graduate student, baby dyke—the drama didn't surprise me. What surprised me was this: Fiona sobbing her heart out over a girl.

Later, when I called to check on her, Fiona's line was busy forever. I told myself she was in the middle of a hideous drama with Chandra, though a tiny, cold chunk of me suspected she had called up her old boyfriend David Charles.

Francine and I lay in bed. Francine was reading something she'd pulled from the sci-fi collection in Jigme's bedroom. I was reading *Aimee & Jaguar* for the second time, thick in the history of the two German women—one Gentile, one Jewish—who had become lovers in Berlin during the War. Felice, the Jewish partner, had tried to remain undercover in Berlin, a "U-boat," moving through the city under the noses of the Nazis. In the glossy black and white photos at the center of the book, the young Felice, her hips wide in her black bathing suit, could have been my Gramma Sophie. I was rooting for Felice, the bold young lover who stayed in Berlin despite the danger. But I'd already read the book.

"Fiona's lovers come and go." Francine looked up behind reading glasses. "You're the one who'll always be the constant." Then she tucked my hair behind my ears and kissed me, just to remind me that I would always be her constant, and she would be mine.

The phone rang again. It was Fiona. Not sobbing, but subdued. "Oh my god," she breathed. "You're not going to believe this." I was prepared for Chandra's miraculous explanation, the reconciliation, the love-fest. I was even prepared for David Charles.

Fiona breathed disbelief into the space between us: "Princess Diana is dead."

( )

If we'd needed any further reminder that life was short, that what seemed immutable could change in a moment, there it was. As the doors of the BART train opened on the yeasty breeze of West Oakland station on a clear night in late September, I realized no one was going to give us permission to get married. Not Debbie, not my parents. If we'd been waiting, like Debbie suggested, for the world to change, well, you couldn't wait for that. When I got home, I called Sarah from Byzantium. I told her we wanted her to cast our rings.

Sarah had told us that, before Byzantium's goldsmith makes a ring, he carves a prototype in wax, a perfect replica. Then the jeweler pours plaster around it to make a mold and then bakes the mold, allowing the wax to run out. The plaster mold remains, ready to receive molten metal. Which is how something solid gets shaped in the place of an emptiness left behind.

( )

Francine stood at the counter, prepping vegetable *momos* for dinner with her brother Jigme and his new girlfriend while I mulled the book review for *Paneriu Street: Tales of Kovno*. I was still trying to find out more about Anya's story without asking her directly. The book, an anthology, included essays by survivors who had made it into the forest and conducted forays with the

Soviet partisans. Survivors like Anya. *Paneriu Street* included a short essay by a woman named Alina Sapozhnik, also of Kaunas. Alina, like Anya, was one of those Jewish women whose so-called "Aryan" looks—blond hair, blue eyes—allowed her to pass between the ghetto walls and the outside world. I wondered if Anya knew her.

Sapozhnik had provided information that led to the bombing of several rail lines. "Before I escaped to the forest—the Germans were looking for me then; they suspected me—I returned to the ghetto wall one last time, looking for my cousin. But Pasha and his wife, his wife's family, had all been deported. This, for the terrible crime of stealing a rotten potato."

The words to an old Yiddish tune wound their way through my brain—"*Zuntig bulbes, muntig bulbes . . .*"—as I got up and slid a tray of hot cookies out of the oven.

Francine swung her hip toward the oven door. "My brother loves your cookies." I smiled. I liked knowing that in spite of all his groomed Buddhist inner peace, Jigme hadn't tamed a sweet tooth I shared.

"Speaking of dessert . . . ," I started, "we're going to have a wedding cake, right?" I nipped a piece of broken cookie off the tray and tucked it into Francine's mouth. Now that our rings were underway, cake seemed like the obvious next step.

Francine licked a smudge of chocolate from her upper lip. "Some big, dry white thing covered in brides?"

"No brides," I said. "Not dry. But, what's wrong with white?" For someone who had never had a single girlhood fantasy about a white cake or a white dress, I found myself oddly attached to the big white cake. What was the point of getting married, if you got rid of all of the symbols?

Francine looked at me indulgently. "Nothing. As long as it's chocolate."

She bent into the fridge to root through the vegetable drawer, pulling out carrots, garlic, little yellow butter potatoes. She held out a potato on her open palm. "Too starchy for a dumpling?"

She glanced at the potato, which was a little dusty, and tucked it against her shirt, wiping it, and brought it out again into her palm. As if it had disappeared. *Bulbes!*

The world is full of connections, these crazy coincidences that mean nothing unless we choose to see them. Sheva, Anya's "friend," had been deported for stealing a rotten potato. Just like Alina Sapozhnik's family. The coincidence was just too great. Hell, it wasn't even a coincidence. I tore out the book review and folded it into my pocket.

Francine and I were still talking cake when Jigme and his girl-friend Suzanne arrived. "Do you just tell them you're getting married?"

Jigme opened the fridge. "Who's getting married?" Despite his impassive face, Jigme looked nervous for a second, as if it might be him.

"Hello." Francine kissed him, exchanged an air hug with Suzanne. Suzanne was friendly and smart, but something about their match seemed improbable, and not just because they'd met in the campus computer lab.

"Cookies?" Jigme observed, hopefully.

"Ellen and I are getting married," Francine announced. Just like that.

Jigme poked his glasses up his nose with an index finger, blinking. "Cool," he said. He bit into a cookie.

Suzanne murmured, "I didn't realize two women could do that." Then she excused herself to the bathroom.

The only way to the bathroom was through our bedroom. "If Suzanne's uncomfortable with two women getting married," Francine quipped, "I'm not sure our queen-sized bed is going to help her forget about it."

Jigme gave her a warning glance. "She's cool," he said.

"What do you do?" I went on, preoccupied with baked goods. "Just call up and say you want to taste cake?"

"You must need proof," Jigme countered. Fizzy water sputtered in his glass like champagne. "Otherwise, people would just show up, posing as fiancés, asking for cake." The fact that Jigme imagined cake-inspired crime sprees was one of the reasons I liked him so much.

"Like Bonnie and Clyde," Francine cracked. "Culinary crime couples moving from bakery to bakery, making off with tiny squares of cappuccino truffle torte!"

"Actually," Suzanne appeared in the doorway, "I think you need an appointment." When Jigme raised his eyebrows, she added, "My sister just got married." She looked from Jigme to me and Francine. "You weren't being serious, were you?" The kitchen went quiet.

A flicker of worry passed over Jigme's face. Suzanne turned to him, as if seeking confirmation that she'd been pranked. "They know they can't get married, right?" and then she smiled, as if it was all one big joke, and punched him in the arm.

( )

By the time I called the fifth bakery in the phone book, I realized I was going to have to stop answering the question, "Wedding date?" with the word, "No." When I wised up and told the little bakery right next to our bagel place, "December 15th," they found a spot for us the following Saturday. Jigme met us there. Alone. "It wasn't a cake-tasting kind of relationship," he conceded.

The three of us flipped through glossy shots of sheet cakes topped with baby booties and Torah scrolls, triple-tiered wedding cakes garnished with curlicues and dots, until the server appeared, bearing three glasses of water and a platter of samples: permutations of chocolate and vanilla cake and frosting, some with mocha cream spread between the layers. We sipped water between bites while the server took our names and our made-up wedding facts. We were really doing this; still, I couldn't shake the uncomfortable sense that we were faking.

Jigme scraped a smear of chocolate frosting up off the plate with the side of his fork, hopped up to the refrigerator case, and downed a pint of milk in three chugs. (We had asked him not to say anything, yet, to Betty and Sol; he didn't need any persuasion to let us take that one on ourselves.) "Thanks for the cake."

Outside, I complained to Francine, "I can't keep lying to bakery ladies about when and where we're getting married. I feel like I'm making the whole thing up."

"You *are* making that part up." I stared at Francine. "Okay," she said. We walked along under the BART tracks. "So, let's get a date."

( )

On Wednesday night, just before the first *Ellen* episode of the season, my mother called. They were back in L.A. Not just for the season. Forever. My father, it turned out, hadn't proved as peripatetic as his people. After a single summer knocking around quaint little towns in Southern Italy, he bought a small condo complex ("Would you buy an egg? Or would you buy a dozen?"), a place big enough to secrete my mother's antique costume collection, but too small for us to visit, and decided he didn't need to travel more than two months a year, and that he wanted "to work the other twelve." My mother, who had waited her entire married life for time alone with my father, found herself, once again, simply alone.

"Are we watching *Ellen*?" I recognized her tone, all chummy confidence, from those nights when my father's competitors came over for collegial cocktails with their wives, to whom my mother sidled up with her terrible, formal intimacy.

"Yes," I said, "we are."

Ever since they'd washed up back in L.A., my mother had been finding reasons to call daily. Had I spoken to Fiona, because Fiona's old neighbor had been struck by a car on Sunset Boulevard. Had Fiona heard? I knew my mother just wanted to be close. But I'd spent all my life being the daughter my mother hadn't liked or understood. Indulging her need for contact never ended well.

"You're a lot like Ellen, Ellen." My mother's voice, echoing off the high ceilings of the new condo, assumed a philosophic tone.

I wasn't in the mood to be summed up. "I don't own a bookstore. I don't live in L.A. I'm not blond." I wasn't wholesome, either, or daftly affable.

My mother remained impassive; she drew the cloak of her maternal power—all-knowing, all-seeing—around her like a royal robe. "There's just something about her that reminds me a lot of you."

Honestly. Was there really only the one thing she knew about me? "You mean, I'm gay."

Across the line, a bell rang, formal and hollow. "The carpet man is here. I love you. Bye bye."

I picked up the phone, pressed in Gramma Sophie's number, put down the phone. Then I dialed Anya.

( )

Anya was wearing a simple black linen dress when she came to the door. She'd tied her blond hair back in a black ribbon. "Opening at the Museum," she commented. I hadn't seen her since I'd started snooping around, trying to find Sheva. I felt a little guilty. But Anya looked down at my feet. "Tennis shoes." She was shaking her head. "So, are you going to play tennis?"

Anya felt like family. I stopped feeling guilty about digging around in her past. These were the small, calculated liberties that we took with people we cared about when we knew they would be justified in the end. I made a point of sitting in Anya's seat, next to the table with the picture on it.

We sat, like before, at opposite sides of the coffee table. If the glass had ever held so much as a fingerprint, it had been wiped, impeccably, away. Before, she had had the photo at her elbow. Before, when we had talked about her past, Anya gazed out the large windows of her apartment, framing the sky. Today her gaze shifted to my right, toward the end table twined with passion-flower vines. Anya told me that the plants flower. "In the spring.

They're quite grotesquely beautiful," she assured me, with her enigmatic smile, half-Mona Lisa, half-misery.

I turned to look at the vines. There, nested among them in a simple leather frame, so close, sat the photo of Sheva. I wanted to pick it up; I rued the frame, imagining all of its secrets inscribed on the back. I wouldn't dare to pick it up. But I managed the courage to ask. "Did you ever know a woman named Alina Sapozhnik? From Kovno?" Alina's cousins had been deported from the ghetto for stealing a rotten potato. Like Sheva. I pulled *Paneriu Street* out of my bag, as if the question were not about Sheva, but about my research.

Anya's gaze shifted to the window. "You don't have large birds here," she commented. "In Lithuania, we have large birds. *Gandras.*" Anya nodded, as if she had just discovered an envelope, lost for many years, with money inside it. She turned to me. "You've been to Kaunas?"

I shook my head.

"My father used to say the *gandras* bring luck." I wasn't sure which bird Anya meant. "He told me, 'They can never live on the house of a bad man.'" Anya smiled, a small rueful smile that crinkled the corners of her eyes. They used to call Vilnus, a hundred kilometers from Kaunas, "the Jerusalem of the West." There were more Jews living in Vilnus—a thriving cultural center— than anywhere else in Europe. Most of them were executed before the war even got into full swing. Where had the birds of good fortune roosted then?

"*Such* large nests. You can see them on the towers of Kaunas castle." Storks. That's what she meant. My Uncle Irvin had told me about the nests, bursting like handfuls of stuffing from the turrets of the castles, tucked behind the church spires. The city had set up huge nesting boxes on poles along the highway to encourage the storks to return.

Anya and I looked out the windows, both of us. "In Kovno, parents pretended these birds would bring things for the children. Candy, oranges, painted eggs. Like the Tooth Fairy. The parents would tie goodies up in the trees for the children to find."

Anya stroked her chin. "*Gandras,*" Anya murmured. She turned to me. "She brought things. Butter. Bread."

Anya had told me that, as a partisan, she had brought things back to the Ghetto. "*You* brought things back," I reminded her.

Anya closed her eyes, an acknowledgement. Then she said, "Not only me."

"Alina Sapozhnik?"

"We never used real names." Anya blinked, as if we couldn't say these things out loud, as if it were still necessary to speak in code.

Gandras. That must have been Sapozhnik's code name. She had come to the ghetto as *the Gandras* to bring supplies in, and to smuggle people away. Anya frowned, her mouth an upside-down parenthesis.

"Did you work with her, then?" Anya had been a partisan, too. But she had been in the ghetto with Sheva when Alina Sapozhnik came for the last time. Hadn't she?

Anya stared out the window at the sky. She murmured "Mmmmm . . ."

According to *Paneriu Street*, Alina Sapozhnik had returned one last time to help her family escape, but found that they had already been deported. Had she taken Anya in their place? "You left with her?" Anya stood up, frowned minutely. She returned with two plates balanced in her hands, and set down two equal slices of cake. "She helped you escape the ghetto?"

Anya shook her head once as she sat. "Not me. Batsheva." The leather sighed under her body. Batsheva—Sheva. As if it were obvious. As one piece of the puzzle clicked into place, another lacuna appeared.

"But Batsheva was deported. With her sister." Wasn't she? I was almost certain that was what Anya had told me. Or was it just what Anya had led me to believe? I hadn't recorded that conversation. I had never even taken my camera out of the bag.

Anya shrugged. She held her palms up, open. She shook her head. "No. Batsheva was hidden." *Hidden?* I was certain Anya had never told me this. Almost absolutely certain. I leaned in over the table. "Hidden? How?"

"I hid her. Until the *Gandras* came." Satisfied, she sunk the side of her fork into the cake.

"You hid her?" Never mind where or how. Why hadn't Anya told me the truth? "Why didn't you tell me that before?"

She dabbed her lips lightly with a napkin. "Why speak of things that never happened?"

I still didn't understand. It *had* happened. She'd just told me so.

Anya leaned in. She spoke very softly, very slowly. "If it never happened, then she cannot be found."

I leaned back heavily in my chair and stared with perfect understanding at the wide, blank canvas of sky. *Who could be forced to reveal what she doesn't know?* Anya had resolved to keep this secret even from herself. Lies of omission—they were a tic, a habit of self-preservation, a way to protect not just yourself, but the person you loved the most.

But if Sheva had been hidden, and not been deported, that meant she could still be alive. I had been looking for a death record. I stared at Anya, the soft, worn lines of her mouth, the hands with which she'd brought me cake. My grandfather had died before I was born. My grandmother never talked about him. It wasn't until I was an adult that I realized she had been lonely for half of her life. When I got home, I called Vicky back. If Sheva had escaped, she might still be alive, and, if she was alive, she could still be found. A new sense of righteousness blazed inside me, a renewed sense of innocence. I would restore Sheva to Anya. By the time it was too late to deny my role, I would be her hero.

( )

There was more than one kind of hunt going on in my life those days. "How about the Women's Cultural Arts Building?" I was leafing, once again, through *Here Comes the Guide*, thumbing through its crisp, white pages. Getting married, I realized, was sort of like a huge research project. I'd always loved black words on a smooth, polished page, the dates, the postscripts: *See also.* It was one of the things I had lost along with Annie Talbot. "The Fireside Salon glows with a whimsical interpretation of the Garden of Eden painted on persimmon-red walls: trees laden with golden fruit and a mermaid disappearing into the sea . . ."

Getting a wedding date, it turned out, was all about getting a wedding place.

Francine, who was picking fleas off Bear with her fingers, laughed, a single, punctuating "Ha!" She dropped the flea she was holding into a glass of water. She was drowning them, pushing their buoyant little bodies, tiny as flakes of pepper, down with the tip of her finger. "Here." I passed the book to Francine. On the cover, a bride with something gauzy on her head and a groom who looked a lot like Art Garfunkel squinted against a rain of white rice. They were half-smiling, half-grimacing.

"How about the Brazil Room? Up in Tilden Park. I went to a wedding there once." Francine turned to the window; she was staring down the yard, into the shadows of the redwood tree. "As the couple said their vows, you could hear a hawk screeching. It felt like it came from out of the sky, somewhere so far away you just couldn't see, but close, too." Francine turned to me. "Sort of like God." She dipped her head self-consciously. We talked about Jewish holidays, and Jewish history; we never talked about God.

I considered Francine's profile, the way her nose ran down into that little channel that connects your nose to the top of your lip. Once Annie Talbot had told me, "Before we're born, we know everything there is to know. An angel shows us all of these things while we're still in the womb." I had imagined the entire world, and all of history, seen, spread out, as if from a very great height. "But then, right before we're born, the angel touches its finger to our lips—" Here, Annie fitted her finger neatly into the groove above her upper lip. "Shh . . . ," she said. "And we forget everything."

Annie had told me about the Brazil Room, too. Not long before she died. It was one of the few times she'd talked to me about her own life. The building had originally been part of the 1939 Golden Gate Exposition on Treasure Island; the World's Fair on the Pacific, she'd called it. "*We were no longer young.*" Annie gazed out the window of her study toward the Bay; through her windows, in the distance, you could see the towers of the Golden Gate. "It was still the Depression. The world on the brink of war. Franklin Roosevelt opened the Fair himself, over the radio." ("*Ms. Talbot, nee Anne Marie Giamartino, native of San Francisco, daughter of Anna and Frank Giamartino, also native of San Francisco . . .*") "My mother went on the ferry to watch the hula girls dance. It was the first time she had ever eaten a *crepe*." Annie Talbot smiled. "She met her husband there, walking through those magical places: The Tower of the Sun. The Court of the Moon. I imagined they were on another planet.

"Just a few months later, war broke out. Treasure Island became the Naval base. My mother's husband left for the Pacific Theater." ("*Ms. Talbot is pre-deceased by her mother Anna Giamartino and by her stepfather, World War II Lance Corporal Jackson Ames.*") She gestured with her palm toward the big picture window facing the Bay and out beyond it, toward the Western rim of the world.

"The luminous city," Annie Talbot mused. (*Ms. Talbot is survived by her daughter Camille, by her brothers Peter and Douglas Ames, and by her former husband Thomas Talbot.*) Her eyes were far away. Her face was bronze, the golden hairs above her lip dusted with golden light. (*"She was renowned for her generosity and for her high standards. For many of her graduate students, she was an inspiring professional model, a strong advocate, and a friend."*)

I wished Annie Talbot were still alive. I wanted to touch my finger to her lip.

"Whose wedding?" I asked Francine.

Francine shook her head dismissively. "A cousin of Jordan's."

I could feel my eyebrows lifting my forehead into my scalp. "You went to a wedding there with your high school boyfriend?" Why would I want to celebrate our love in a place she'd already consecrated with some guy she'd managed to fake straight with? Yet, almost every lesbian I'd ever met had a story like that, each woman who seemed so often to know just what she wanted had remained untrue to herself for so long.

Francine pulled her legs up and hugged her knees. "I always thought, when I got married"—I blinked; I had never heard Francine suggest that she had ever spent a moment thinking about marriage—"I wanted to be under that huge sky right next to the person who would be my forever." I could see us there, then, two tiny figures, white dresses fluttering, under a fluttering *chuppah*, against the endless, unfurling golden grass of late summer, minuscule but together, side by side under the huge, unwavering canopy of sky.

"Okay," I said.

( )

On a Tuesday afternoon in October, Francine and I drove up into the Berkeley hills, pulled into the little parking lot off Wildcat Canyon and, without a clue whether we needed sitting room for fifty or a hundred, went in to reserve a wedding date at the Brazil Room.

I'd seen pictures of the building, its stonework walls and leaded glass doors, in *The Guide*. What you couldn't see in the pictures was the space around the Brazil room—not the thick roadside border of forest, not the high green slope over which the patio perched, rolling down into the park, but the huge scoop of blue carved out above the slope, the living air, ascending and extending out over all two thousand acres of eucalyptus, oak and pine. Standing out on the patio, I understood what Francine meant. I wanted to get married under that sky.

Francine and I made our way into the little foyer. Several straight couples stood in the dark, wood-paneled entry, pressed close along the wall where a printout listing every weekend for the next twenty-four months stretched from one end of the room to the other. We edged our way uncertainly toward it. Several of the men consulted glowing PalmPilots, the small cold flames cupped in their huge hands; the women hefted tabbed binders. "Come on." Francine stepped forward, pulling me after her.

Time unfurled in front of us, slot after slot, like entries in the Book of Life; almost every one, we discovered with shock, was already penned with the name of another couple, two per day, like litigants' outside a courtroom, except that an ampersand, instead of a *v.*, linked them: Phillips & Sanders, Roth & Kaplan, Chavez & Hirsch. "Well," Francine frowned, "it looks like we'll need to wait until . . ." she trailed her finger along the wall, "February 18, 2001."

Just then, a park ranger, the person in charge of the events calendar for the building, grabbed the black Sharpie that dangled from a piece of yarn and crossed out a name. Francine stepped over lightly, a dancer's neat, sideways step. "Unless," she said, frowning, "you want October 11, 1998."

Sunday, October 11. National Coming Out Day. The eleventh of October, the leaf-strewn, pumpkin-porched, three-day weekend when the last surge of equinoctial heat pulses into the brilliant sky-vaulted blues and molten-golds of fall. It was Columbus Day, or, in Berkeley: Indigenous Peoples' Day. Both of those seemed right. We wouldn't be the first two women to marry each other, but we would be among the first to call it that in front of others, and that was to sail toward a horizon with no assurance of not falling off the flat edge of the mapped world. But this was aboriginal ground, too. We are who we are, indigenously: each the whole world to each other.

I grabbed the black Sharpie hanging on its tattered string. Francine rested her hand on my shoulder, her breath hot in my ear as I marked our names in jagged capitals on the calendar, Margolis & Jaffe. "Call Fiona," Francine said. "She'll probably buy her ticket today." We'd just inscribed our names in the Book of the Future.

When I did call Fiona, she surprised me. "Well, it's about time." Fiona, whom I'd expected to be excited to the point of overbearing sounded, instead, unaccountably sober. She was back to balancing David Charles and Chris. "We're about to turn thirty. You don't really understand yet," Fiona advised me. She was six months older. "But we're about to hit a decision point in our lives."

I was standing in the kitchen, holding the phone in one hand and paging through the calendar. The rest of the year unfurled under my fingers, sectioned out in perfect white squares. Francine and I had chosen ours. But what about Fiona?

"We're at the turning point," Fiona went on, a little heavily, I thought. I was getting married. Fiona wasn't. I didn't know what to say. As I turned toward the sink, I noticed a stray chocolate jimmy on the counter near the toaster, a remnant, I guessed, from the box of See's candy Francine had brought home from school. Reflexively, I blotted up the loose jimmy on the tip of my index finger and popped it into my mouth. Fiona was carrying on with her gloomy tirade. "Either we make our major life choices now, or we don't." The jimmy tasted dry, hard and old as the earth. Spitting as I said goodbye quickly to Fiona, I had the distinct feeling that I'd just eaten shit.

( )

On Sunday night, I found myself, as I often did, watching my future mother-in-law stitch a quilt at her machine. She was making something covered with the little purple and yellow flowers Francine had told me once were called Johnny Jump Ups. "Damn." Betty tugged the fabric away from the machine and snipped at loose threads with her sewing scissors. Little bits of the satin border kept unraveling at the cut edge. I watched her reseat the fabric. We still hadn't told Betty and Sol because I hadn't told my parents. There was something else I wanted to broach with Betty, something Betty knew a lot about.

"Who's it for?" I asked her.

"Hmmm?" Betty drew her lips together like the strings of a purse. "A woman I used to know." Betty was always tight-lipped about her work, which was for a battered women's shelter. There were significant parts of *her* life, too, I reassured myself, she couldn't share with Sol. Outside, Francine and Sol were dragging trash cans together from behind the house down the long drive-way, their plastic wheels rumbling against the rough cement.

Betty looked up. "Hand me the chalk?" She nodded toward an old wooden matchbox filled with hard, flat lozenges the shape of guitar picks. "Thank you." I watched her fingers as she fished through the box, looking, as I often did, for clues, faint foreshadowings of the person Francine might become. Betty gripped the slim, blue triangle between her thumb and her fingers, marking out a swift, clean line. "She got away from one of those tough guys who spells everything out with his fists." So, the blanket was for one of her former clients, a woman Betty and her shelter had helped escape from an abusive husband. Betty frowned, blew at the chalk line and dropped the little tab with a *plik* into the matchbox. "I like it when stories end this way. She managed to get away, put herself through school. And now," Betty looked up, her eyebrows rising to telegraph contented surprise, "she's having a baby."

"Do you see her often?" I wondered if this woman thought of Betty as a model, an advocate, a friend.

Betty's face contracted. "Never." She engaged the pedal, and the needle began to bob, slowly at first, then faster. "If they start out here, they can never end here. Not if they're going to survive." The women at the shelter had to relocate to other cities or towns, places their batterers would never think to look for them. They had to disappear. Betty fed the fabric through the machine with both hands.

Francine's and Sol's voices got louder as they meandered up the driveway. *They won't be able to call her the Gray Lady anymore,* Sol intoned. The low rumble of trash cans started up again like the roar of jet engines as Francine and Sol pulled another pair down toward the street.

"So, how do you find out about people after they've . . . moved on."

"Oh." Betty canted her head lightly to the side. I'd seen Francine do the same—a tilt of thought. "They know how to find me."

I watched the fabric disappear as Betty fed it under the needle, a thin, shining stitch of pale violet appearing like the center line on a long, long highway. "I'm trying to help a survivor find someone," I said. It wasn't exactly the truth. I was the one trying to find Batsheva, and Anya didn't know about it. But that didn't mean I wasn't helping Anya, either. "They haven't seen each other since the War."

"I imagine you've got all sorts of resources for doing that,"

Betty said. She'd picked a pin out of the fabric and tucked it now between her closed lips.

"Mmmm," I murmured, as if I were the one with the pin between my lips. There hadn't been any information yet from Vicky since I'd called her again. But it was still early on that front; at least finding a survivor would be much easier than finding someone who had died.

Betty and I watched as she turned the corner of the blanket carefully with both hands, like someone turning the steering wheel of a large truck. "Of course," Betty murmured, "it's a lot harder to find someone who doesn't want to be found."

I squinted at the woman who didn't realize she was my not-yet-mother-not-quite-in-law, thrown off guard, once again, at one of her tossed-off remarks. I considered what little I knew about the person whose photo Anya had managed to smuggle out of Europe, whose photo she brandished like a charm, whose photo she had installed like a memorial under the leaves of her passion flower, the woman with whom Anya's own story finally ended, the woman whom she had called, simply, "my friend." "I don't think that's true here," I told Betty.

"Maybe," Betty raised her eyebrows without lifting her gaze from the quilt.

The next day, I sent a letter to the publisher of *Paneriu Street*, asking how to find Alina Sapozhnik, the *Gandras*.

( )

Heading up Broadway in the detail-erasing fog, the first Monday of November, the only thing I could see as I moved toward home was the string of traffic signals, blinking green and red against the milky white of the enveloping sky, looking like nothing more, even to my Jewish eyes, than the coming of Christmas. I panted through the front door, sweaty and chilled, and cursed the pain under the ball of my foot: Spread by the slips of my scraping knife, my plantars wart had become its own little colony of warts, a small constellation around the mother wart, thick and deep, translucent yellow. Fuck if I was going to step on a glass with a big ugly wart on my foot. I peeled off my socks in the shoe corner and, trying to remember not to leave them there for Francine to pick up after me, thumped heavily up the stairs.

The letter from the publisher of *Paneriu Street* sat open on my desk. Prompt and polite, it had directed me to the administrator of Alina Sapozhnik's estate. She had died last summer. If Anya had told me about her when we first met, I might have found the last known witness to Batsheva's whereabouts after the ghetto. But now it was too late.

I chucked my socks into the laundry bin and sighed. The fog had started to burn off. Outside, like a new day unwrapped from inside the old one, the sky blazed blue. I hauled myself into the dark red womb of our bathroom, sat heavily on the floor, and curled in an apostrophe over my bare foot. "'Marriage is as irrevocable,'" Francine had read to me, "'as it is to mend the shattered glass.' Ellen, you'd better smash it *hard*."

"Shit!" I nicked my foot again. Disgusted, I threw the scalpel—was that rust on the blade, or blood?—wrapped in the letter, into the trash, and headed downstairs to find the Kaiser magnet stuck on the refrigerator door.

( )

"Do you think we should start taking the pill?"

Francine, finally home, had fallen, exhausted, onto the bed. She spoke to me through her arms. "You do know how this baby-making thing happens, right?"

"Shut up." I lay down next to her on the bed. "So we don't have our periods on our wedding night."

Francine sat up; she leaned her head on her elbow. "You *do* know how this baby-making thing happens, right?"

"Ugh." I pushed her over.

"On the other hand," she murmured, slipping my hand up under her shirt, "it might be worth a try."

"You know what I mean." I slipped my hand farther until I could feel her nipple harden in the palm of my hand. "So we won't be crazy, premenstrual bitches on our wedding day." I whispered it like a seduction.

"This may come as a surprise," Francine murmured into my hair. She reached for my hand and slid it down, pulling her belly in, "but I'm a lesbian." Francine pulled at the buttons on her jeans. "That's one of the things I like about being a lesbian." She bit my ear; her breath rushed into me like the sea. "Not worrying about things like birth control."

"Oh."

"You know what else I like about being a lesbian?" Francine went on.

134

I sucked at the side of her mouth.

"This," she said, as she slid her hand down into my jeans.

"I think you need to go into the office more often," Francine commented, lying naked on top of the bed. She had come so loudly, the dogs had run in, barking. "You're spending too much time reading bridal porn on the internet." She slapped my belly gently with her open palm. I was surprised to hear that Francine knew I'd been stepping out of the office, and I was glad to hear she ascribed it to wedding planning, and not to digging up the details of an old woman's life. "By the way," Francine was pulling on a pair of sweatpants. Lying on my back, I watched two Francines—the Francine looking into the closet, and the Francine in the mirror, the side of her face to me. "Laura gave me the name of a rabbi." Congregation Sha'ar Zahav, the City's gay and lesbian synagogue, was currently between rabbis and, lacking the power of the State of California and feeling the need for a higher authority, we really wanted one.

"You told Laura we're getting married?" Laura was Francine's director at the preschool, her boss. Weren't you supposed to keep that kind of thing—getting married, getting pregnant—to yourself for as long as possible? Francine pulled a sweatshirt over her head. The hood buoyed up her hair like an Elizabethan ruff. "Anyway, I thought we were going to this thing," I said, lifting a flyer from the corner of my desk: *Congregation Ir Ilan invites our friends in the Gay, Lesbian and Bisexual Community to Meet the Rabbis: A Forum on Same-Sex Partnerships and Jewish Life.* "Think of it like a one-stop shop."

"They're really trying to get our vote, aren't they?" Francine examined the flyer, the first official sign we'd ever seen that the East Bay's reform synagogues knew that we existed. Clearly, other couples were out there, doing what we were doing, and the rabbis, in their own way, wanted to play a part. Or maybe they just wanted to hawk a few more synagogue memberships.

"It's this Saturday. After our cake-tasting appointment."

Francine eyed me appreciatively. She took my hand in both of hers and looked at my palm, dark and square against her light, tapered fingers, as if she could read my future there. "You *have* been busy today, haven't you?" If only she knew the half of it.

( )

At the "Meet the Rabbis" event at Ir Ilan, Rabbi Sokol, a robust man with a receding hairline and prominent red lips, stood up and cleared his throat. "I have worked with several gay and lesbian couples," he started, his voice baronial, "to create a new tradition out of an old one, something quite lovely"—here Rabbi Sokol shaped an hourglass between his blunt fingers—"called a *brit ahava*. A covenant of love."

One by one, the rabbis went around the circle talking about how they had cadged together Jewish rituals around their own version of a new thing meant for gay and lesbian couples. Earnest and well-meaning to a one, each of them, it seemed, had worked out something that was, as far as I could tell, not quite a wedding.

"Right. Well," Francine said, as the Volvo stuttered, then exploded into life in the Ir Ilan parking lot, "Rabbi Loew wasn't there."

"Rabbi Loew?" What did the legendary sixteenth-century Rabbi of Prague have to do with same-sex partnerships and contemporary Jewish life?

"The one Laura recommended." Francine made a quick turn, and we were back out on Broadway, speeding past car dealership after car dealership, heading home. I stared at her. Here we were, shopping for rabbis at Ir Ilan, when Francine had managed, through sheer dumb luck, to come up with a living descendant of the Maharal of Prague, Judah Loew ben Bezalel, father of the Golem.

Though the story of the Golem did not appear in print until two hundred years after his death, Rabbi Loew, whose gravestone you can still visit in the old Jewish Cemetery in Prague, has long been credited as creator of the man of clay, formed out of Vlatva River mud and the mystical words of *kabbalah*, to protect the Jews of

Prague. Legend held that the man of clay could be called upon to rise again whenever the Jews of Prague needed help. Instead, the story of the Golem had entered popular culture, and through the inevitable forces of dejudafication, become a simple Frankenstein's monster; we prefer our cautions against *hubris* to the awkward monster of genocide. But here we were, and we needed help. "Rabbi Loew?" I was amazed at Francine's nonchalance: the opportunity of having our wedding officiated by a real, living blood relative of one of the most famous figures of European Jewish folklore, ever!

Our freshman year of college, Debbie and I went to Hillel's Yom Kippur services together, all the campus's observant and semi-observant Jews packed together in dark coats and *kippot* under the towering steeple of Memorial Church, *davening* in hard pews under the lectern's gleaming eagles, surrounded on all the church's white walls by the inscribed rolls of the college's war dead. Afterward, trying not to think about food, we walked along the angled paths of the Tercentenary Theatre, talking about synagogue architecture. Debbie's maternal grandfather came from an Orthodox Jewish family in New York; her father's parents published the literary magazine *Shadows* during the Harlem Renaissance. "I suspect that the driving principle in twentieth-century synagogue architecture," she mused, turning away from a sophomore cradling a burrito, "is that synagogues never, ever look like churches."

"Meaning . . ." It was late in the afternoon. We felt slight with hunger, drinking in the last of the evening light, looking forward, even, to the Union's hard rolls.

"Meaning they look like something completely different. Like, say, spaceships."

Rabbi Loew's Congregation Tzi-Li, a big, low, round building with a dark, sloping cone of a roof and a windshield of purply-red stained glass, looked quite a bit like a spaceship, poised to lift off from the Palo Alto hills into the great cosmological unknown. Smaller surrounding buildings, squat and round as native huts, made up the Tzi-Li campus, one of them Rabbi Loew's office.

Inside the doorpost hung not one, but two *mezuzot*: the first, made of tiny stone bricks, looked like a section of the Western Wall; below it, sculpted from colorful plastic clay, hung a second, shaped like R2-D2. I shot a worried look at Francine, who whispered, "He probably spends a lot of time with the religious school kids," just as Rabbi Loew opened the door.

"I do," he said, glancing at the *mezzuzah*, "and I'm a huge *Star Wars* fan." A small, unassuming man with glossy black hair that hung into his eyes, Rabbi Loew wore a crooked smile and tan khakis. Francine and I smiled, caught. "I'll make sure not to mention the Force in your ceremony." Rabbi Loew laughed. Instantly, I thought of Rabbi Loew's ancestor, the famous *kabbalist*, incanting the spell of life by the banks of the Vlatva.

"I'm Rabbi Loew. Allan." Rabbi Loew had a round, boyish face, and a small, freckled nose. He smiled as he showed us to two folding chairs set against the wall. On the other side of the room, his desk loomed, cluttered with picture frames, Jedi figurines, and large books with gilded Hebrew letters on the spines. With the alacrity of a leprechaun, he pulled out his rolling chair and glided over to us, eager, his straight black hair flopping, as if he'd been waiting to meet us for a long, long time.

I let my eyes wander Rabbi Loew's office, taking in the warm sloped planks of the ceiling, the huge window on the courtyard, the long shelves of books, dark-spined volumes of *Mishnah*, *Talmud*, *Tenach*. Tucked beside his diploma from Hebrew Union College sat *The Kabbalah of Kenobi*. "You don't have any books about the Golem," I commented.

Rabbi Loew cocked his head quizzically. "The Golem?" He glanced at Francine, trying to ascertain whether she, too, considered the Golem an important component of Jewish wedding liturgy. Francine shook her head minutely.

Francine and Rabbi Loew waited. Was that a tiny Yoda on the collar of his Oxford? "You know," I laughed, "not many rabbis can claim descent from the Great Rabbi of Prague." Rabbi Loew's faint eyebrows—nearly invisible, I noticed, more like the placeholders for eyebrows than eyebrows themselves—shot up in surprise. His two index fingers popped into the air—*a moment, please*—and he twirled his chair toward his desk, swiveled back, and handed me his card. "Associate Rabbi," it read, "Allan Loh."

I glanced up at Rabbi Loh, his straight, black hair, his dark, narrow eyes, the low-bridged, freckled nose. At Ellis Island, I knew, they frequently changed the spellings of names. Rabbi Loh shook his head slowly, holding my eyes with his own. "My father's parents came from Vienna. My other grandfather was Chinese."

"In Kaifeng," Jill had told me once, "in Henan Province, there's been a Jewish community for at least seven hundred years." But Jill was not a descendant of the Kaifeng Jews and neither, it turned out, was Rabbi Loh, who also wasn't related to the father of the Golem. He was a descendant of *shtetl* Jews, like my own great-grandparents. "I hope I can still provide you with what you need," Rabbi Loh apologized; I wasn't sure if he was joking.

I looked at Rabbi Loh, a *shtetl* Jew, an outsider/insider, a Jew like us. The original Rabbi Loew had summoned protection with a word—*Truth*—inscribed upon the Golem's forehead. And with a word, he had extinguished the Golem, too. "That depends," I cocked my head at his little Star Wars pin. "What, exactly, would you be calling our ceremony?"

( )

We were getting ready for Sunday dinner at Betty and Sol's—*the* dinner at Betty and Sol's; Francine's desire to tell her parents had finally outweighed her insistence on waiting for me to tell mine—when my mother called. "Your father took me out for a really fantastic meal last night." My parents, who didn't even stock butter in the fridge, went out every weekend to fancy French restaurants and stuffed themselves with mussels and *pommes frites*, for which they compensated by not eating dinner the rest of the week. I spaced out while she went over the menu, thinking about what I was going to wear to dinner—normally not a concern, except that Francine had decided: Tonight was going to be the night we told Betty and Sol. "And then, in our quiet little house, without either of our *children* in it, he made passionate love to me." *What?* My ears folded inward like bewitched cockle shells; my eyes, in the flash of the Medusa's grin, shrunk to slits. This was the same woman who, when I mentioned Gay Pride, protested, "What you do in your own bedroom is your business." Why was she *telling* me this?

When I got off the phone, Francine was dressing. "Aren't you being a little bit prudish?" she asked. "After all, how do you think you got here?"

"Please!" I protested. "You're talking about my mother. What's *that?*"

Francine was standing in front of the mirror, dressed like a

140

Hasid. "It's called a skirt," Francine answered, her gaze fixed on the mirror. She brushed a stray thread from the fabric, which was kind of a stretchy crepe, too sexy for a *Hasid* probably. A little more like a mermaid. "You've seen one before?"

"Not on you," I pointed out. Francine turned, her hands on her hips, to show me. Francine dressed up well, but she spent most of her days with five-year-olds in T-shirts and jeans. I liked her that way. "Are you hoping that if you dress up like a lady, they'll forget you're marrying one, too?" Francine rolled her eyes. She did look lovely, in a cute little dyke-in-drag kind of way.

"You're not worried, are you?" I pressed her. Compared to my parents, I thought Betty and Sol were pretty cool, a prejudice Francine attributed to my "philogeriatrica." Though Betty and Sol weren't exactly the PFLAG-types, they were still our ace in the hole. They loved Francine and accepted her choices (my parents had just one out of two here); they accepted me as part of the family, at least as far as Sunday dinner—and what, beyond that, would our marriage really require of them? If Francine was worried about Betty and Sol, we were in more trouble than I realized.

"A little." Francine sat down on the bed, carefully, so as not to wrinkle her skirt. "I just want them to take us seriously."

"Won't they?" I'd started rooting hopelessly through my dresser.

"I just want them to know it's real." Real, she meant, despite the fact that no state in the United States, and no country in the world, except Denmark, recognized same-sex unions. Rabbi Loh would officiate our *wedding*, he promised us, but the State would not approve. Such distinctions matter. Francine tugged at the toe of her sock. Under her long brown skirt, she was wearing the fuzzy pink, green and orange-striped knee-highs I had given her for Chanukkah. "I don't want them to think we're just playing house."

"Then don't wear a costume," I pleaded, stripping off my third pair of pants.

"Just wear what makes you comfortable," Francine advised. As if it were as simple as that. (I still wasn't sure which thing my mother resented more: my being a lesbian, or my wearing shirts from The Gap.)

My mother's chastisements rang in my ears. "I can't," I complained. "I don't want your parents to look at us and think that their beautiful, sexy daughter is planning to marry some *'ragpicker's daughter.'*"

Nervous, we got to Betty and Sol's early. Francine's parents were still mucking around in the garden, Betty in her faded work shirt, Sol in his worn gray corduroys, their faithfulness to their Sunday routine a picture of all we meant, in our own way, to become. "But don't you two girls look fancy." Betty nodded at Francine's long skirt. Sol kissed Francine. His face was pink with January cold, stubbled white, like a winter field. Out in the garden, Francine and I looked ridiculously overdressed, like penguins at the city park. I wished I'd worn jeans, and I wished Francine had, too. I wanted to blend in with Betty and Sol, a Sunday like any other Sunday. Wasn't an endless line of these ultimately the point? "We're putting the garden to bed." Sol turned the ground into itself with the tip of his spade.

I know for some people—people who get married before they know the other person's annoying habits—pushing their toothbrush directly up against the tube, leaving the cereal bowl on the counter—marriage is an adventure, a big crazy leap into the unknown with someone else, someone they hope is the perfect match. I didn't want that kind of adventure. My parents, who'd met when they were kids, hadn't done it; my sister and brother-in-law, who'd met when they were twenty, hadn't done it; and I didn't want to do it, either: pledge myself forever to someone whose socks I hadn't washed.

I wanted to hold on tightly and never let go of the body that was already imprinted on my body, her dreams half-woven with my dreams. I wanted to be sure. And, sure, I wanted a lifetime of Sunday dinners, and Sunday pancakes, and Sunday dog walks, the certain, familiar pace of a life plotted out together. It's not that I didn't want anything to change—adventures, surprises. It's more that life seemed to me like nothing but an endless string of surprises, uncertainties all piled up, waiting to happen, and some of them bad.

But marriage could be the certainty, the thing you could count on, the frame through which you took all those disparate threads and wove them into something whole, something you could show people, and call a life. Whatever their shortcomings, my parents had it in their marriage, and I thought Betty and Sol, dirty in the knees, did too.

"Ellen and I were hoping we could talk to you." Francine's cheeks flushed a little; her lips went white.

Betty pulled herself up on Sol's arm and tugged at the fingers of her gardening glove, its tips blackened with moisture, earth, and age. "Are you okay?" She touched her bare fingertips to the back of Francine's hand.

"I'm fine, mom. Really," Francine reassured her. Betty eyed us both curiously. "We'll be inside when you're done."

Francine and I, nervous as mice, decided to wait in the living room. We wanted to be right there when they came in; we wanted to get it over with. We perched on the overstuffed floral-print sofa and fidgeted with our socks. "Are you sure we shouldn't have just told them out there?" I asked Francine. I imagined a quick, "We're getting married!" exchanged between *Hello*s. I'd realized as soon as we sat down: We'd set ourselves up.

When I had come out to my parents, back in college, Sam had advised me: "Tell your parents on April Fool's Day. That way, if they threaten to disown you, you can tell them it was just a joke." *As if.* Actually, my mother moved through all the phases of grief—anger, denial, all but acceptance—within about an hour. After the predictable lament ("What about grandchildren?") she announced, "I've called your father. He'll speak to you when he gets home." Then she wouldn't say another word (except for "What do you want me to do, kill myself!?"). Five hours later, when my father finally pulled up in his gold Beemer, the two of them left immediately for a long walk. An hour like pulled taffy stretched endlessly from an already endless day. When they came back, the three of us ate dinner in silence.

Finally, over the remains of the salad and the Dover sole and the little apricot tartlets, my father demanded, "Have you ever slept with a man?" His tone, clinically prurient, made my skin crawl. Did he want me to say yes, or no? How much was I expected to prove?

I remembered Sam's coaching. "This isn't a phase," I answered, my face blank.

"You have a choice," my father explained. Which choice was that? To lie to myself and some poor *schmuck*, to make both of our lives miserable? "And you're making the wrong one. But we support you." The last little bit was critical—for them. What he meant was, "We're disappointed, disgusted even. But we're not willing to lose a child over it." Because in some Jewish families *You're dead to us* was an option.

Then my parents were finished with me. They went off to watch the news. I called Fiona. She pulled down my parents' steep drive-way in her father's classic green Mini Cooper, smiled with exaggerated politeness at my parents, and whisked me away. "Let's get the fuck out of here," she said, shifting quickly into second. We sat clutching hands through three endless hours of *The Unbearable Lightness of Being*. When she brought me back home, Fiona announced, "I'm staying." She was whispering "my li'l *segotia*" in my ear when my mother popped in without knocking, recoiled, and backed out again. "Jesus," I groaned. It had been the longest day of my life.

Now here we were, Francine and I, waiting for Betty and Sol, painted into a corner. Their house smelled of redwood beams and black tea: dark, warm, ancient smells. I glanced at the grandfather clock that stood between the French doors; mer-cifully, the pendulum hung still. Then I looked at Francine, whose pale skin had gone a little paler, and tried to get a hold of myself. They were *her* parents, after all. And I wasn't nine-teen, coming out to my father, who paid my college tuition. I was twenty-eight, declaring my intentions to people who had already, for all practical purposes, accepted me into their lives. Of course, I wanted their support. More than that. Their joy. But I had already learned to accept less. Francine and I would get married, our own joy, if necessary, enough to get us by. "It'll be okay," I mustered, "either way."

Francine nodded one too many times. Her moist eyelids shone in the light of the lamp. "My family doesn't do this either, you know," she said, her hazel eyes burning pure rust in the last of the afternoon light. It was winter; suddenly, it was nearly dark. "Emote."

It was true. I hadn't really thought about it, but Francine was right. Betty and Sol talked about ideas—discussed, inquired, debated—and they showed affection for each other—teased, hugged, fed—but the Jaffes didn't have conversations about feelings. In that way, they were like my own family, but milder: no scathing attacks, no white flashes of teeth on bone, no suffocating, impermeable silences. But no feelings talk, no big self-revelations, either. What had Betty said when I'd gushed about their family? *You've grown too fond of us, dear.*

Which is why it shouldn't have surprised me that when Francine, finally, stood up in her straight skirt, pulled in a deep breath, looked her dirt-smeared parents both in the eye and announced, "Mom. Dad. Ellen and I are getting married," Sol settled his hands on the knees of his corduroys and asked, "Is that possible?"

"Yes," Francine retorted, abrupt with determination. Then, "Do you mean, is it legal?" Sol nodded. "No. But we are anyway."

Betty was smoothing the hem of her work shirt absently with her fingers. She fixed Francine in an intense stare, her lips tight. Despite my anxieties, this was actually going worse than I'd allowed myself to imagine. I wished desperately—and I got the feeling that Betty did, too—that I had stayed at home. "Marriage is a lifelong commitment. The price of a mistake," Betty gazed intently at Francine, "is very high." *A mistake.* Is that what Betty thought of Francine choosing me?

Francine colored—with embarrassment, or anger? "Mom. Dad. Ellen and I are getting married." Francine didn't smile. "Just be happy for us."

After a long silence, Sol spoke. "You feel strongly about this."

"Yes," she answered, "we do."

Betty looked at Francine. The skin on her face had been softened, worn from use, lined with a lifetime of Sunday gardening, creased with maternal concern. In that moment, she looked even more deeply worn, wizened, like she could see something that we could not. She turned to Sol. "This is what they need to do."

Francine and I retreated to her childhood bedroom; we sat on the floor, debriefing in whispers. "And these are the supportive parents," I marveled. "It's definitely not like this for straight people."

Francine gazed across the room, unfocused. She'd pulled her skirt up to her knees. On her left kneecap, a little white lozenge of flesh marked the place where she had fallen onto a sprinkler and cut out a perfect cube of flesh; Betty had lifted her out of the grass like a bride. "Except Romeo and Juliet." She bunched her skirt in her fists.

"And Rebecca and Ted," I considered.

Francine shook her head. "Your mom got into it. The whole idea of a lace-covered, heterosexual wedding totally outweighed your sister marrying the wrong man."

"The wrong idea of a man," I corrected her. It had nothing to do with Ted, personally; his history was the wrong history, his continent the wrong continent, overflowing with the wrong peasants eager for escape—not our people, not our past. Well, my sister hadn't found it. But I had. I settled my hand on Francine's bare knee. "You did great," I told her.

"Thanks," she answered, sliding her hand over mine.

At a sudden terse knock at the door, Francine and I instinctively startled. Our adolescence had turned us as timid as Bambis, alone in our room with a girl on the bed, listening at each second for the hand on the door, the gunshot cry of "Girls!" Francine drew her skirt down over her legs.

Betty and Sol were standing in the hall in their coats. "We're having dinner out. To celebrate. Go get your coats." Francine and I looked at each other. "Don't look so surprised," Betty chided us. "We're slow, but we're not stupid."

Betty embraced Francine warmly. I got up and she kissed me. I guessed it was good enough. Then I looked at Francine, all dressed up in her skirt; her cheeks were glowing, her eyes bright. Her parents had accepted her; it still mattered; at that moment, it was all that mattered.

I hesitated. "What about what's in the kitchen?" I was waiting for the daily routines—chopping, washing, cooking—to reassert their primacy.

Betty stopped in the front hall. The locket she always wore in the hollow of her neck caught on the collar of her blouse. It clung, half in, half out, like a kite caught on a fence. I'd never seen her open it. "Unless you have any other announcements for us," she settled her gaze on me, "I expect Sol and I will be around to eat dinner tomorrow night."

( )

Now the house was quiet, except for the rain. My mother had finally stopped calling daily. Trumping her loneliness, the unspoken rule in our family: Nobody called anybody around this time of year. That's what you do, isn't it, to commemorate an unspeakable event?

Rain drummed steadily against the drainpipe outside our bedroom window. Inside, Francine and I lay on the bed, littered with remnants of the Sunday paper. I was daydreaming about Gramma Sophie, a faded blue beach towel wrapped tight around her middle. An orange towel hung around her shoulders, clasped in one hand like a bishop's cassock. As she bent to pick up her flip-flops, she let out a voiceless "oh." The sky echoed back a low, thickening thunder. My sister and I had spent the summer watching jets pass. "Aer Lingus!" Rebecca called out. We thought we could master them, every color a country, a starting point left miles behind. My sister's pale legs cycled wildly. Then she slipped under the water. Silver bubbles trailed from her nose.

"Can I get you something, doll?" Gramma Sophie asked me.

"Why do you have to go inside?"

"Your father will be home soon," she said. Her towel clasped in her hand, she flip-flopped to the back door in her Sav-On sandals.

Why did she have to go?

( )

"Take my car." Wendy, ever trusting, handed me directions to the Western Home for the Aged. I had an interview that day at two with a Mrs. Klein. It was only eleven, but Wendy had spread out her lunch on her blotter: an apple, a bag of corn chips, and a green bag of sour Skittles. It was a very strange lunch for an adult human. "Honestly, I'm not sure how much you'll get," she offered. Mrs. Klein, her daughter Carolyn had told Wendy, suffered from senile dementia. Today was Mrs. Klein's birthday. Her family would be there; they thought that might make the interview easier.

At one o'clock, I drove out to the outer Sunset, where the city-scape of downtown gives way to a carpet of little pink, blue, and yellow bungalows. Farther along, the streets flattened, and, though the ocean was still too far to see, the wide, unobstructed Western sky reached out toward it, worn thin with longing. At one time, this neighborhood had been nothing but sand dunes, stretching out to the Pacific. In the nineteenth century, San Franciscans called it "the Outside lands."

Piloting Wendy's Volvo through the Avenues, I felt like an out-sider in the Outside lands. I had driven out past the tideline of internet money, past the high-water mark traced by internet cafes, little storefronts advertising Bubble Tea, where the crumbling stucco facades of Thai and Italian and Russian restaurants announced the cultural pluralism of the Thirties and Forties.

In the middle of the next block, an ancient movie theater managed with aching joists still to lift its forlorn marquee: "Welcome to the Western Home Availability NOW!! Wed. Night Bingo." Inside the lobby, half a dozen residents lolled in wheelchairs on the faded red carpet; their heads, hanging on the frail stems of their necks, bobbed low, clouded eyes settled on their laps, on their tremulous clasped hands, on the unmoving front door. Behind the old concession stand, two attendants in floral nurses' scrubs stood talking in rapid Spanish.

"Excuse me." I stepped toward the nurses' station. A man in a brown suit didn't move his head, but his marble-blue eyes followed me like the eyes of a painting. "I'm looking for Ruth Klein." Without breaking her rapid-fire stream of Spanish, one of the nurses pointed a lacquered pink nail to the double doors on the right.

I walked into a large, bright room where old people sat in scattered pairs, or alone on faded couches. One pair of women actually sat talking to each other; another woman played solitaire on a tray. An attendant in white pants and a white tunic approached her. "Would you like some cake?" he asked. He set the cake in front of her without waiting for an answer.

At the far end of the room, a middle-aged woman in a silk blouse stood assiduously slicing piece after piece from a large sheet cake. "Ms. Klein?" I asked. "Carolyn?"

"Ms. Margolis." She wiped her hand on a napkin before offering to take mine. "I'm so glad you could come." Ruth Klein's daughter and I exchanged introductions. "My mother has never spoken much about her experiences during the War," she told me. "But, lately, she's become," Carolyn hesitated, "a little looser. We were hoping," she smiled a large, eye-wrinkling smile of polite grief, "you could capture some of that before it's too late. To leave behind some good. And for my son Jason." She gestured toward a couch near the window, where a young man about my age with dark hair and khaki pants sat playing a game of Rummy Tiles with the hunched, white-haired woman who I thought must be Ruth Klein. They sat quietly, kitty-corner, brown plastic trays set up in front of them filled with numbered tiles, red, blue, yellow and black.

Rummikub. Gramma Sophie and I had played it endlessly, perched on the stools at the turquoise-tiled kitchen counter, long hours unspeaking, surveying the runs and sets laid out before us. I'd tried to explain it to Francine once. It's a lot like gin rummy. Except that, once a set or a run goes down on the table, any player can add to or subtract from them, reorganize them, realign them in order to use as many possible tiles from their own tray. (Woe to the player, like Rebecca, who moved around half the pieces on the table, realized she had nowhere to put a yellow eleven, and got stuck putting all the other tiles back where they'd started.) Gramma Sophie and I spent the bulk of our turns silently working through our strategy in our heads, like chess masters, without touching a thing. It was a very slow game. "Just one more," Gramma Sophie would beg, already starting to flip the tiles over on the counter, blank side up. She'd sweep the blank tiles together into a pile Rebecca and I swirled. "Mix 'em up good."

The very last game we played, Gramma Sophie won. "How many rooms does it have?" she was asking me, picking from the pile on the counter with the click of her fingernails; she wanted to know about the house I'd just moved into with my "friend" Francine. "How many bedrooms?" I kept my eyes fixed on the tiles. "You have your own bedroom?" Gramma Sophie pressed me, looking up from behind her tiles.

"Mmm," I answered, pretending to consider the joker I held, secreted in my hand.

Jason looked up from his tray. Straight, dark hair flopped over his pale, upturned nose. "It's still your turn, Gram," he reminded Ruth Klein.

"Where can the one go?" she asked him, waving a red one in her gnarled hand.

"Before the two," he pointed. "Or after the thirteen. Like an ace."

"An ace. An ace. All over the place," she muttered.

Jason slid the one onto a run. "Good move," he said. "Do you have any more?"

She looked uncertain. He slid her tray toward him. "I think that's it," he concluded. "Pick three tiles," he said, pointing to the pile of down-turned pieces beside Ruth Klein. On his right hand, I noticed, Jason wore a thick college ring carved with insignia; nevertheless, I liked him.

"Would you like a piece of cake?" Ruth's daughter Carolyn held out a perfect square of golden layer cake frosted in white; between the layers glowed a single golden stripe.

"*I* would like a piece of cake," Ruth Klein answered. Still pretty sharp, I thought. And her hearing was good, too.

Taking the plate from Barbara, I set it down at Mrs. Klein's elbow, directly on top of a second plate streaked with white frosting. I introduced myself. "I'm from the Foundation for the Preservation of Memory," I told her.

Carolyn Klein added, "Ms. Margolis came to talk to you about your experiences during the War."

Mrs. Klein squinted up at me suspiciously. She'd already set to work on the cake, which was nearly gone. When she finished, she took my hand and turned it over in both of hers, exposing the small, blue tattoo on the inside of her forearm, the six digits she had never been able to reorder, flip to white, sweep away. "Are you the second wife?"

Jason scolded her harmlessly. "You know I'm not married, Gram."

"I liked the first wife better." She shook her head, and returned to the tile tray.

"Mrs. Klein," I started, "would you prefer to speak in English or German?" My own German was only strong enough to have passed the graduate proficiency exam, but, typically, these narratives had a way of unfolding without prompting.

Ruth Klein looked up sharply. Her wet lips trembled slightly as she spoke. "In *that* language," she poked a finger hard into the air, "I never speak." The cake caught her eye, and she asked for a piece, a little peevish. But, when Carolyn Klein delivered it, she began to eat again with evident delight. "This is *very* good cake," she said. She looked up hopefully. "Did my mother make this cake?"

( )

"Do we have any more cake tasting on the docket?" I asked Francine. I pulled a receipt from my pocket and tore it up; it was February; I'd brought Anya French tulips. "I've got a wicked *yen* for some lemon layer cake."

Francine grunted. She was glued to the TV, to women's giant slalom. Ever since the Olympics had started, she'd been coming home, flipping on the tube and parking in front of it. If she had work to do, she did it right there at the little coffee table, watching CBS.

"Bring me some chips, will you?" Francine called out as I headed into the kitchen to check the calendar. It was less than a week from Valentine's Day, a day we never celebrate as a couple because it's already been claimed by grief. The day was already dark. As I stepped through the kitchen door, reaching for the dimmer switch, a pale shape scuttled from the dogs' kibble dish to the bottom of the fridge like a hurried ghost. "Whoa!" I flicked on the light.

"What?" Francine called out. It was good to know she could still make out voices other than Jim Nantz's.

"There's something in the kitchen. Alive."

Francine was beside me in an instant—possibly a new linoleum-speed-skating record, set in her blue wool socks. "Let's see," she said. Bracing ourselves against the kitchen cupboards, we shoved the refrigerator aside and set our small, terrified poltergeist flying under the stove.

"There!" we yelled, hopping and pointing. Lola shoved her snout under the stove, face scrunched in ancestral fury, and barked like a maniac. The cornered mouse made a break for it; it shot out from behind the stove straight into the living room, Lola, all fur and teeth, in hot pursuit. Lola skidded across the pine planks, crashing against the coffee table as the mouse darted past the icy slopes of Nagano, and then disappeared, a quick gray smudge, between the two bricks at the back of the fireplace where the mortar had fallen out. Lola pushed her nose to the crack, snuffling hungrily.

Francine walked toward the fireplace, working something small and black in her palm, which she pushed into the crack. "It's okay," she told me. "It's Fimo. It bakes dry."

Back in the kitchen, we pushed the refrigerator farther from the wall to reveal an enormous pile of dog kibble. My eyes traced the short path from the dog bowl to the fridge. Each kibble probably weighed at least a tenth of the mouse, and there were at least two hundred pieces under there.

I held the dustpan as Francine swept. Together, we pushed the refrigerator back into place. Suddenly, I recalled the nasty "jimmy" I'd found on the counter. "I think I ate mouse shit," I told Francine.

"And you're usually so picky about your food." She raised her eyebrows and handed me a bowl of hot salsa and a bag of chips. "Salt and jalapeno are very cleansing."

We sat side by side on the couch, casting an occasional glance at the fireplace. It was raining hard outside. Night had fallen. "Do you think it will come back?"

Francine shrugged. "We'll see."

By Friday night, there was still no sign of the exiled mouse. No "jimmies" on the counter. No stench of death in the living room walls. I let myself think about its small, gray form, safe somewhere, out of sight, while I took down the matches, set the candle on the stove. Francine was in the living room, watching athletes fold themselves mummy-style into colored tubes and shoot noiselessly through the mountains. It was late Friday night, almost the fourteenth of February. The anniversary of the day that had crushed my heart to a fine, dry powder. In a minute or two, I'd go in and sit with her, watch the end of the day's competitions and we'd go up together to bed, while, in the kitchen, on the stove, this light continued to flicker, casting shadows through the house.

The light was off in the kitchen. The sounds of the living room—television, doggy snores—were far away. I held tight to my *New Union Home Prayer* book. *A woman of valor—seek her out/for she is to be valued above rubies.* The match whispered. *Give her honor for her work; her life proclaims her praise.* The fire took hold without a sound. My eyes burned. The darkness of the room, growing darker, cupped the flame. I rocked back and forth on the heels of my feet; standing alone in front of the stove, I whispered my grandmother's name.

( )

Behind the counter at Bacardi's, tiny mousse cakes—lemon, chocolate, pistachio, mango—floated, perfect as Anya's little Thiebauds. She'd been trying to get more modern art into me. Like playing Rummikub, looking at paintings was companionable, safe. We could sit next to each other without talking about anything personal. I took in the pale pastels of a dozen mousse cakes and imagined the impossible: Anya tasting one at my wedding.

"Can I help you?" a woman asked as we approached the counter. With her close-cropped auburn hair, light brown eyes and freckles, she seemed cocoa-dusted.

"We have an appointment," I answered. "Margolis and Jaffe."

She popped out from behind the pastry case and thrust out her hand. "Barbara Bacardi," she said. "My husband Anthony is the pastry chef."

We looked through Anthony's album while Barbara brought us glasses of water and slices of cake on a shiny tray. There was the obligatory Torah scroll, the three-tiered wedding cakes. And then—what was that?—a pink cake in the shape of a pig. "Anthony made that for a fiftieth-anniversary party; it was a vegetarian *luau*." Barbara sat down at the third chair. "Anthony can do anything you want." She stayed with us as we tasted the chocolate, lemon, and mango mousse.

A look of rapture passed Francine's face. She had tried the chocolate. "Barbara," she breathed. "This is incredible."

Barbara smiled, unsurprised. "We can do that with a very light buttercream and some fresh flowers. And maybe a tray of *petit fours*."

Francine and I exchanged hopefull glances. "*Petit fours?*" I remembered Anya's delicate square of raspberry-filled cake. "Yes."

Barbara's face lit up. "We could do some pastry puffs," she nodded. "Or little tarts." She made quick notes on her clipboard.

I was nodding vigorously toward Francine. This was really starting to be fun!

Before we left, Francine and I put down a deposit on a two-tiered wedding cake finished with white buttercream and fresh pansies (Francine's little joke) and a tray of lemon meringue tartlets. We walked out of the shop giddy, clinging to each other like drunks. "It's like we're stoned!" Francine giggled.

"No," I corrected her. "It's like we're brides!"

We looked at each other, startled, then burst out laughing.

When we'd calmed down, Francine whispered, "So this is what it's all about." One of those moments all that bridal porn was about, all the anticipation of the girly girlhoods we hadn't had—all the sweeter, I guessed, because we hadn't expected it at all.

Then I went home and recorded the check.

It was that time of the month. I sat at the coffee table, studying the phone bill with a double-sided highlighter in my hand, the big-button calculator from Margolis & Margolis on my knee, and striped all of Francine's phone calls orange, all of mine green. Forty-three sixty-eight. Forty-three, I thought reflexively, the year Hitler declared total war; sixty-eight, the year Francine was born. Who took the extra penny last time? I couldn't remember.

"Francine!" She didn't answer. "Francine!" I yelled. The hair-

156

dryer drone of the popcorn popper blotted out my voice. I sighed, gathered the detritus of our joint expenses, and marched my fistful into the kitchen.

"Ow!" A scalding pellet glanced off my forearm, so hot I couldn't tell if I'd been burned or frozen. It ricocheted to the linoleum with a skitter that multiplied like hail. Popcorn kernels were flying everywhere. Francine's head emerged from the cabinet below, where she'd been rooting for the popcorn bowl, just in time to catch a flying kernel to the scalp.

"Ow!" She flung the bowl up in front of her face like a shield. A kernel hit it with a *ping!* "Ellen!" Francine shouted from inside the bowl. "Help!" I stepped into the kitchen with the bills fanned out protectively in front of me. By the time I reached the popper, popped corn was rising out of the machine like a head of beer. "Turn it—" Francine yanked the plug, "off." The kitchen went silent. From deep in the popper's metal cylinder came the thud of a single, emphatic pop. Francine took the broom from the side of the refrigerator.

"Jesus!" A little red welt had risen on my arm. I clutched the phone bill, crushed, in my hand. "Do you think you can write a check today?"

"Are we ever going to stop doing this?" Francine asked, tipping the dustpan into the trash.

"Popping without the lid on?"

"Keeping all our money separate." She gathered popcorn from the counter in both hands. "Nickel and diming each other over every bill."

"We're not nickel and diming," I protested, my heart suddenly clenched fiercely around my bank account. "We're splitting things. Evenly. That's just fair." We'd already paid the deposit on the rings and on the Brazilian room, but there were plenty more bills to share.

Francine popped a piece of unbuttered corn into her mouth. "It's not about being fair, Ellen. We're supposed to be a team."

"We are a team." Why did that mean we had to share everything? I absently picked up a dry puff of corn, then noticed a

157

strand of my own hair curled around it. I changed tack. "What if I wanted to buy you a present?"

Francine was measuring out a new scoop of kernels into the canister of the popper. She looked up encouragingly.

"If I wanted to buy you a present, it's just like you're buying it for yourself, right, if our money is all," I swirled my hands in a confused circle to illustrate the hopelessness of it, "merged together." *Merged*—that seemed like just the right word to scare a self-respecting lesbian. Isn't that what the self-help books try to warn us against? Letting our identities merge. Losing our selves. Wasn't it Francine who had announced, right from the start, "I don't ever want us to wear each other's underwear"?

Kernels began to explode one at a time. "Ellen," she said over the whine of the popper, "it's not like I want to quit working and become dependent on you. Couples share their resources. Honestly, I think keeping everything separate is a little weird." I bristled. "Especially at this point," she added.

Just because we're getting married, we should marry our bank accounts, too?

"When are we going to stop handling our money like it's every woman for herself?"

Behind Francine, the pops suddenly slowed. A crowd of popped corn huddled together under the clear plastic dome, jammed together, unable to come out. Francine tapped the dome a few times with her finger. A few pieces fell into the bowl. Then, suddenly, the entire mass released and a great whirlwind of popcorn swirled once around the dome of the popper, down the spout, and was gone.

( )

I was still reciting bank balances like a mantra as I walked into my office and discovered Wendy vomiting into her wastebasket. The pale blue cotton of her blouse stretched tightly between her shoulder blades, outlining her bra straps. "Are you okay?" I managed. I tried not to breathe through my nose.

Wendy looked up, pale and sweaty, a few strands of loose hair stuck to her forehead. "Sorry," she panted, wiping her mouth with her sleeve. Grabbing the trash basket, she lurched out of her seat and hurried down the hall. She was having hot and cold nauseous flashes every afternoon. "I knew it wasn't going to be glamorous," Wendy had panted, gripping the side of her desk, "but I never expected menopause to be so damn chemotherapeutic."

Wendy's mother had gone through breast cancer. Every three weeks, Wendy had taken the afternoon off to drive her mother to the treatment and, the next week, to hold her mother's head while she vomited into a plastic bucket. I secretly feared that Wendy, whom I could hear retching down the hall, had cancer herself and was going to die.

I shivered. Was it the thought of Wendy's death or the lingering smell of vomit I needed to escape? I dropped my bag on my chair and fled to the reading room, which was closed to the public on Mondays. A little nauseated myself, I drifted toward the wide window and looked out at the dark, choppy blue of the Bay, toward home. What was it that made Francine so open about money and

159

me so jealous with it? *You have to hold on to what you've got*, my guts urged me, *or you'll have nothing!*

It's impossible to have a solitary thought in the reading room. Behind me, beside me, surrounding me on every side: the uttered testimony of a thousand voices. I moved toward the shelf, toward any voice whose solid timbre would cover the high relentless whine of my own compulsive brain, and reached for Jerry K.

Jerry K. himself had come to my undergraduate History 1B class once. His tan face framed by a full head of white hair, Jerry had stood in front of the classroom in a butter-yellow sweater, talking quietly about his childhood in Prague:

> *My father was a piano tuner. My mother, a cellist who gave lessons in the little parlor at our house. We were just kids. Even after the anti-Jewish laws, the noose was getting tighter, but we had no idea. My brother Josef—he was older. He understood first that we would have to grow up too soon.*
>
> *It was my father who came to tell us, after the others were asleep, that we were to leave. Josef and I. They would tell the neighbors we had been sent to relatives in Holland, when, in fact, it was a student of my mother's who took us.*
> *That night, my father came to us with his watch. It was the only thing, beside his tools, he ever prized. He gave the watch to Josef. Josef didn't want to take it. But my father, Josef discovered later, hid the watch in the lining of Josef's coat, and it was too late. We never saw our father again.*

I remember thinking, as he stood in my class, touching his fingertips together as if in prayer, *He's going to pull it out. Right now. His father's watch.* Like a rabbit from a hat. But he didn't. He pulled his hands apart, empty.

I slid Jerry's testimony back in its folder, and the folder back into its file. I rubbed my eyes. The sun had shifted, throwing big squares of light onto the tables. I shrugged my shoulders, checked my own watch, and felt suddenly remorseful about my argument with Francine. All the voices in the reading room repudiated me: *Everything you think you have is nothing!*

But that wasn't what my family believed. My grandparents sewed on buttons in a women's garment factory for twenty years to send my father and my uncle to school. And my father became a tycoon. I was supposed to build something bigger than myself.

But wasn't that what the archive was? Something bigger than me?

When I'd declared my major in Folklore & History, my father had reacted as if I'd declared Penury & Hardship. *And yet.* My father hadn't done it alone—he had my mother. And my mother counted on him for financial support. Even my grandparents were a team. What about me and Francine? Was I being homophobic? Not treating Francine the way all those married heterosexuals treated their partners?

Doesn't everyone have a secret, parsimonious heart? *Everyone* withholds *something*: time, sex, love. The past—which most of my survivors kept hidden. Certain delicate facts. I thought, gingerly, of Anya, arranging her French tulips in a crystal vase. I sat quietly justifying myself, and tried to think of the thing Francine withheld from me. Right then, I couldn't think of anything.

( )

Whether or not we merged our money, we still had plenty of spending to do. Some of it not as nice as cake and rings.

"I told you this was a bad idea."

Francine pushed a piece of cheese pizza across the smeary brown Formica at Sbarro's in the Stoneridge Mall. "Eat." She took a swig from the tankard of Diet Pepsi sweating on the table, "You'll feel better."

Eight years ago, I'd marched up the escalators of this mall hand-in-hand with Debbie in our *Queer Nation* T-shirts, chanting "We're here; we're queer; get used to it!" while frightened mothers yanked their children away, hard, by the hand. Now, Francine and

I sat defeated in a greasy vinyl booth, sucking up Diet Pepsi, two American consumer brides, out on the prowl for wedding dresses.

In the wedding shop, I had blanched at the bolts of lace that smelled like the inside of my mother's secret room; I crouched, catching my breath, in the corner.

"Shopping malls make me sick."

"Shopping makes you sick," Francine corrected me. "Mentally ill."

But Francine was not one to give up when it came to shopping for clothes. "I think we should look for dresses in New York," she announced. "We have to go anyway, right?" She meant Fiona's big fundraiser for GMHC. Fiona, at that moment, was sitting in our living room.

"It's my biggest event of the year," she confirmed. "Now that everyone's on the cocktail the mood is actually festive again. You *have to* come." Fiona had been parked on our couch for several days, and she was parked there now, waiting for *ER* to start when my mother called.

"Wasn't Fiona just there?" My mother wasn't going to be satisfied. "What is it? Boy trouble?" I hadn't bothered to mention that Fiona's last major relationship had been with a woman. Now didn't seem like the right time to overthrow Fiona as the patron saint of heterosexuality. "Family trouble?" Fiona wasn't speaking to either of her parents. But that wasn't news. She kept coming, I thought, because her best friend was getting married.

"Actually, Mom, Francine and I are getting married." Woops. Stunned silence. "This weekend?" my mother finally managed.

"Of course not," I told her. "This fall. October." I slid, shaking, to the amber linoleum, and pressed my back against the cabinets.

"I see," my mother answered crisply. "Ellen, please hold on. I'm going to get your father. You can tell him what you just told me."

My father picked up the phone in his office. I could hear my mother's muffled breathing on the other line. "Ellen," my father started, all calm naiveté, "Your mother says you have something you'd like to tell us."

I had moved away from home, established a life for myself away from them, lived with an emotional distance that kept me safe. And yet here I was, coming out to my parents all over again. Would it never end? I took a deep, silent breath. "Francine and I are getting married."

My father cleared his throat. "Will this be a legal marriage?"

I tried to remain calm myself. Sol, I reminded myself, had asked essentially the same thing. "It means we'll have a ceremony officiated by a rabbi—" Just thinking of Rabbi Loh made me feel more sure. "But, no, we can't get married legally. Yet," I added.

"Well," my father considered this. "There won't be any negative tax consequences." Was this his blessing? "Are you sure this is what you want to do?"

"Yes, Dad, it is."

My mother couldn't stand it another second. "How do you know that?" she broke in. "You were in love with that other girl. Samantha. And now you're not. How do you know this isn't the same thing?"

My father's level voice cut in. "If you want to do this"—he sounded preternaturally calm, practically medicated, but why not? There were no negative tax consequences—"of course, we'll be there."

I picked myself up and walked back into the living room, where I found Fiona and Francine, rapt, in front of the muted television, staring at me. Fiona looked stunned. Francine's mouth formed a silent whistle of admiration.

"Ellen!" Francine exclaimed. "I don't think I've ever heard you speak to your parents like that." She looked at me as if I'd just emerged from the kitchen with a dragon's head in my hand.

Fiona raised her eyebrows knowingly. "I've known her practically since she was born," she said. "*Believe me*. She never has."

( )

"It wasn't so good. In the end." Sitting across from me, Rose Kantor, née Bloch, had survived Auschwitz thanks to the scrupulous vigilance of her then twenty-four-year-old sister, Theresia. Theresia had married and lived in New York. Rose had married and moved to California, but the sisters, six children and twelve grandchildren between them, had remained close.

"We're old women. My sister, she's nearly eighty years old.
"'How did this happen to me?' she asks.
"'I don't know.'
"'Don't forget me,' she says.
"'I won't,' I tell her. The next time we were together, I was throwing dirt into her grave."

( )

When I got home from Mrs. Kantor's interview, there were not one, but two messages from Fiona. When I called her back, she sounded both excited and cagey.

"How's the big fundraiser coming along?" I closed my eyes, expecting a Fiona-length answer.

Instead, she said, "It's fine."

"What's going on?"

Fiona took a deep breath. "I've just had—" She paused, "the most incredible night of my *life*." She exhaled theatrically. "With

164

the most incredible person I've ever met." Usually, Fiona qualified a statement like that with "except you." "Do you remember Duncan Black?" Fiona had gushed a few months ago about a volunteer who had revolutionized her databases.

"The one with the great-granduncle the Ulster Unionist?" When she'd first told me about Duncan Black, Fiona had also mentioned that he was researching his Irish roots. He had an ancestor who had fought in the Battle of the Boyne. "He's not gay?"

"*Not* gay," Fiona warmed up a little. "He's very polite. Charming. But I never really looked at him *that way*, you know?"

"Hmm." Francine was downstairs, listening to Ella Fitzgerald and, from the smell of the wood smoke filtering up through the floorboards, starting a fire; it had rained all day, and now the wind shook big drops from the trees that spattered the windows in bursts.

"Last week he started working with me on our contingent for Pride—there are about a thousand marchers to coordinate; and last night we went out and—" Fiona hesitated; a thin fiber of excitement vibrated through each word. "Ellen, it was the most intense night of my life." She stopped for effect. "We talked and talked. We went out for drinks afterwards—"

"Drinks?" Fiona had renounced drinking back in high school. "I thought you were an alcoholic."

"That was just some dumb thing I said. You weren't supposed to take it *literally*." That was the problem with having a friend you'd known forever. You remembered too much about each other. You held each other to your own forgotten words.

Fiona cleared her throat. "He walked me back to my apartment and we talked, Ellen, *all night long*. About everything—his family, my family, our work, our dreams. He wants to write this book about his family history. He's an incredibly sensitive and perceptive man. More like a woman than any man I've ever met."

My eyes strayed to the pile of *ketubot* on my desk. The Jewish wedding contract has undergone a few changes since Jacob took Rachel in exchange for 200 *zuzim* and a herd of sheep. *They vow to remain friends*, I read. *To talk and listen to one another openly, remembering apology and patience.* Fiona swallowed. I could hear her spoon clinking against her mug and tried to imagine the thousands of miles of desert and farmland and mountains that lay between us.

"Ellen," Fiona whispered, confiding something fragile. "I'm so into him."

"That's great," I told her. Then I added, "Hey, you've officially moved on to the letter *D*." I'd teased Fiona about how she only dated people whose names began with the letter *C*—Chris, Chandra, and David Charles, who I always pretended to think was Charles David.

Fiona didn't laugh.

"We spent the entire night together," she went on. "We stared into each other's eyes, Ellen, and talked about how we want to have beautiful babies together." I pictured the two of them stretched out next to the tub, Fiona's Babar and Celeste gazing down at them from the hot air balloon suspended over Fiona's bed.

I rubbed my knuckles across my face. Francine and I were going to have to get our *ketubah* custom calligraphed. All the preprinted ones said *bride* and *groom*. "Wow," I told her. "Babies? Don't you think you might be moving a little fast?"

That was not the response Fiona wanted to hear. "I was happy for you when you told me you were getting married."

"Are you telling me you're getting *married*?" Hadn't she just met this guy? What was going on?

Fiona had disowned her own parents for their various acts of disapproval. This tone was not what she wanted in her best friend. "Call me when you can be happy for me," Fiona retorted. Then she hung up.

A week later, I got home to a terse message from Fiona. "We need to talk." Probably, I thought, she wanted to apologize.

But when I reached her, Fiona sounded hedgy, defensive. "I've been thinking about your trip," she started. "You know my apartment is really small, and it's going to be crazy for me that weekend." Fiona paused. Her apartment, a studio, *was* small. But Francine and I had stayed there before, regardless of who was sharing it with her. "Duncan and I think it would be better if you find a different place to stay." *Duncan and I.* "It *is* New York," Fiona added. "There are a million hotels."

"You do realize that we're planning a wedding?" I stared at the receipts spilling from my desk. "We don't exactly have money to spend on hotels in New York City."

"I'm sure you can find something cheap." Fiona's voice had resolved to the icily professional tone I'd heard her use with her mother. "Duncan and I are starting a new relationship. I just can't handle four people in my apartment."

"Your new relationship doesn't seem to leave much space for your old relationships," I pointed out.

Fiona simmered. "I'd appreciate you not bringing Duncan into this."

That night, while Francine sat down in front of *ER*, I stayed upstairs in front of the computer and did two things, which, in combination, a person in a state of mental distress should never do: I wrote Fiona an angry email and I hit "send." And then, full of second thoughts, I did it again. *If you really wanted me to come to your event, you'd have come up with some real alternatives*, I charged. Then I got a little closer to the heart of it. *I don't know why*, I wrote, *but I feel like you're pushing me away.*

We had never had an electronic relationship before, and it wasn't starting out well.

Francine's attempts to talk me down only made it worse. "Fiona's being incredibly insensitive," she reassured me, "which, honestly, is not that surprising. She's a drama queen and you're her perfect audience."

( )

Fiona or not, our wedding train had left the station. We were talking with a caterer about menus. So Francine and I went to Betty and Sol's late on a Friday afternoon to tackle Betty's *Gourmet* collection. "My mother has a ton of cooking magazines; maybe we'll find lemon ricotta ravioli in one of them." It seemed to me that caterers should have the recipe for everything, but the one we wanted to work with hadn't heard of the pasta dish Francine and I had fallen in love with at a Los Angeles restaurant with my parents, and they wanted us to do the legwork. I guessed that's what you get from going discount.

In eight years of Sunday dinners, I had never been in Betty and Sol's bedroom. Francine herself seemed to hush as she leaned against the double doors of the *sanctum sanctorum*. The bedroom was dark and quiet, the curtains drawn. Betty had decorated the room in a tasteful, feminine style, country French, dark wood, floral spread. Opposite the curtained French doors, a long, high dresser stood against the wall under a Cassatt print.

Francine disappeared into the closet, where she slouched on the rug, sorting through piles of magazines. I'd stopped at the dresser, drawn to the gleaming row of silver frames, the Jaffe family history. There, in black and white, stood a dashing young soldier with jet-black hair, clutching his cap under his arm: Sol. In the next frame, the same young rake wrapped one arm around a slender, pixie-haired girl in white; together, they piloted a knife into the top tier of a white cake: Betty and Sol. Their lips and cheeks had been hand-tinted pink. I held the frames by the edges, careful not to leave prints.

Francine had turned on the light inside the closet, but the dark still wrapped around us, like a cave. "There's a lemon spaghetti," Francine wrinkled her nose.

A shining object on top of the second dresser caught my eye, another photo. Pulling it out into the light, I made out Francine and a small, bald creature that must have been Jigme, propped together on the flowered couch that still sat in the living room. Francine wore a smocked white dress and scuffed white shoes; she gripped an enormous bundle of brother, his triple chins luxuriant as a centerfold. I set the photo carefully back on the dresser and lifted out the only other picture next to it. This one was framed in ceramic with pink alphabet blocks tumbling down along the side. It was a photo of Francine, a toddler with elfin hazel eyes set in a toddler's chubby face. I held the photo, disconcerted. "Was your hair straight when you were a baby?"

"Huh?" Francine had begun to flip pages so quickly, they sounded caught up in the wind. "No," she said. "My mother had to pull my curls out of my face with a tiny barrette before I left the hospital." Francine looked up.

I held up the photo in the ceramic frame.

"That's Julia," she said. Then she went back to flipping pages.

Julia? A cousin, I guessed. Francine had never mentioned her. "Julia?"

"My parents' first child." She said it without looking up, flipping through the July 1991 issue of *Gourmet*.

Her parents' first child? "Your *sister*?" Instantly, I imagined another Francine out there, an older woman named Julia, living abroad—back in South Africa, maybe?—the family black sheep. But Francine was a lesbian. What could Julia have done?

"She died." Francine turned the page. "When she was a baby."

"Oh." I looked more closely at the picture. Julia looked older than a baby. She was eating a cookie. She was walking. "How?"

"Choked on a button."

169

Francine threw the magazine behind her and pulled another from the pile. It sounded like a phrase Francine had memorized from a foreign language. It sounded like an epithet. "Julia, who choked on a button." She'd tossed it off with the kind of nonchalance you could only pull off if you'd grown up with it.

"That's . . . sad."

"I know." She said it without feeling.

I set the photo back on the dresser. "I can't believe you never told me you had a sister."

"I've told you about her." Francine flung the next magazine down and picked up a third. "You probably just don't remember."

"You did *not*," I insisted.

"Well," Francine murmured, "I probably never told you about my grandfather, either."

"Didn't he die before you were born?"

"Exactly."

I stared into the gloom of the back of Betty's closet, then back at Francine, her hair glowing like a flame. "Did your parents ever talk about her?"

"Hey!" Francine looked up, eager. "Here's a ricotta ravioli with brown butter and sage." She turned down the corner of the page.

A sister. The world tilted. Francine had had a sister and never, in eight years, told me about her. What else, I wondered, was she capable of not telling me? "Did your parents ever talk about Julia?"

Francine shrugged. "I don't think so." And yet, Julia had had a birthday. Julia had a *yahrzeit*. Dates that came back, like stubborn weeds, every year.

"What did they tell *you* about Julia?"

Francine looked like she was getting annoyed. "How much can you say about someone who died as a baby?" Francine handed me a magazine and I took it. I recognized her detachment. Francine, I thought, was like a child of Survivors, a child whose birth had in some way answered the deep, resounding echo of tremendous grief; a child insulated from her parents' ancient loss, for whom the story of that prehistoric, antenatal loss can only ever be a story. (But how many of my subjects, when they came to the Foundation, came to speak, finally, not for their own sake, but for the sake of their children, for their children's children?) To Francine, Julia came from a time before time. I was shocked she had never thought to mention this piece of her family history, but I guessed it made a certain kind of sense.

But I wondered in a new way about Betty and Sol; I wondered whose picture graced Betty's locket. I wondered about where they kept this loss, and why they had never talked about it. What might you say about a person who died so young—if the pain weren't too much to bear? That the day she was born, whole peaches clung to the trees? That they held her little body in their arms while she slept, and watched her dream? I had known these people, whom I loved as parents, for over eight years, and they had never mentioned another daughter. They kept her photo in a closet. It troubled me, this utter silence, smoothed over Julia's life like water over a stone. Julia wasn't a secret exactly. She was one of those big things everyone knew but no one talked about, either a screaming absence or a fantastic erasure, a big white spot. I had thought of Betty and Sol as the opposite of my parents. They weren't, and it troubled me. But then I remembered Hannah Weiner, who couldn't remember her four-year-old daughter's name. I knew too much about terrible things to blame Sol and Betty for their silence. They had watched their daughter die. At that moment, I forgave them. Maybe the best you could do was survive.

( )

I didn't hear from Fiona again until well after St. Patrick's Day. I'd set a pan of blackberry *hamentaschen*, cooling, on the stove. Her announcement was terse. "I just wanted to let you know, Duncan has proposed to me. We're going to get married."

"Wow," I said, trying to sound encouraging, rather than stunned. I'd resolved, since my email, to try harder. But my follow-up fell through, "That's so—fast."

"Duncan and I are soul mates," Fiona answered. Then she added, "I'm not like you; I don't need eight years to make up my mind."

Soul mates. So, what did that make me and Francine? Play-mates? Check-mates? Stale-mates? Fiona and Duncan had fallen in love and decided to get married in a single motion, a smooth, graceful arc that looked like the beginning of a perfect circle. Francine and I had fallen in love so long ago I could hardly remember it now. Yes—I'd fallen in love, madly, wildly, for the girl who danced with no bones. But we'd also nearly broken up after a stupid fight about shrimp. Nothing in our past was perfect.

Francine didn't see it that way. At all. "The thing that really pisses me off," admitted Francine, "is that you and I can't get married anywhere, but she can meet some guy off the street and, six weeks later, be married with all of society behind them. It makes me sick."

"But don't you wonder," I ventured, sitting next to Francine on the couch, "if they have something—some soul connection . . ." I didn't say *that we don't.*

"Are you kidding?" Francine turned to me. "They don't even *know* each other."

"But," I mumbled. "We didn't even propose, did we? Isn't that unromantic?"

"He probably proposed to her on the top of the Empire State Building on St. Patrick's Day," Francine answered. "That's not romantic; it's a cliché. It's like people playacting at love."

"But what about us?" I persisted. "Are we wildly in love?"

"Don't be so insecure," Francine chided me. She took my hands. "You're just not an impulsive person. Do you want to marry me?" she asked me now, her gaze shifting from my left eye to my right. "Do you want to stand up in front of everyone we love, everyone in our lives, and say that you choose me?" The glow of the evening firelight in our cozy living room haloed her whole face, which looked a little flushed, her eyes a little wet.

"Yes." I touched Francine's warm cheek with the back of my hand. "I do."

Fiona called one last time. "We're moving to Dublin," she told me, "next month."

"You're quitting your job?" I asked, incredulous, "to follow a man?" Fiona was the one who'd petitioned to start a Women's Studies class at Ferngrove. We were members of NOW! After school, Fiona had driven us down to the Westside Pavilion, where we cruised the parking lot with a green Sharpie, blacking out the word "Life" in the "Right to Life" bumper stickers, and penning in "Choose." It had been one of our most thrilling acts of delinquency. Now she was quitting the only job she'd held for more than a year, and moving to a country she hadn't visited since childhood, to follow a man she'd been in love with for all of five minutes. "Duncan's going to write his book," she said, as if that explained everything.

"What about you?" I protested.

"It'll be like going home."

I couldn't see how Ireland would be much like L.A. *That* was our ancestral home, Fiona's and mine—the land of the palm tree and the Galleria, the beach and Beverly Hills, the chaparral and the coastal mountains, brown on brown. What did misty green hills and tiny ponies, acres and acres of cold, rocky shore, and thousands of years of history have to do with that? *Going home.* That must have been a line he had used, Duncan Black, descendant of the Ulster Unionists. What a load of crap.

"You, of all people," she added, "should understand."

"What does that mean?"

"Everything you do is about the Jewish people. Your people."

I thought of Elizabeth Landau and her return trip to Poland: *There are no Jews in Lodz.* "My people," I answered, "and your people, too, will tell you that home—if you mean Europe—stinks. Home is the place you flee from, and put behind you, and spend your life trying to forget." I gasped for breath. "No one goes back to Europe. Only Americans so American they can't remember anything about why their ancestors *left* expatriate to Europe. And it's not to go home, either; it's to run away."

Fiona didn't answer.

"I can't believe you're moving halfway around the world with someone I've never even *met*." I started to have the feeling that was the point.

"I just called to say goodbye."

"Do you think they'll really stay together?" I asked Francine for the hundredth time.

"Read *Angela's Ashes* again; it'll make you feel better." She patted the pearlescent pink cover of *The Essential Guide to Gay and Lesbian Weddings.* "Invitations need to be *mailed* two months ahead. Time to get cracking."

( )

Francine and I sanded our fingertips smooth on 100 percent cotton ivory card stock, beefed up our biceps hefting sample books bulging with starchy invitations, all announcing with joy the marriage of a putative "Diane Helene to Mark Charles Cadwallader." Finally, we decided to make our invitations ourselves: a crimson pomegranate tree crowning a square, cream-colored card. The fruit of fertility and marriage. At synagogue, silver pomegranates, little bells swinging from their crests, crowned each wooden handle of the Torah scrolls.

"Nigel and I just chose an invitation out of a book," Wendy admitted, crunching a potato chip out of a can. "We were lucky," she added. Were those Pringles? Wendy never even ate white bread. "We had it all set out for us. You and Francine have to make it up as you go along." Wendy had always been so, so generous. I felt a flush of luck at having wound up working for her.

Wendy's curls fell into her face, framing full, flushed cheeks. "Ellen," she started. Her face looked strange, like she was about to either laugh or cry. "We need to talk." For a second, my heart raced with panic: Wendy had been throwing up at work. Maybe it really *was* cancer. "You may have noticed I haven't been feeling my best." I glanced at the trash can beside her desk. "I've been a little tired," she added, "a little run-down." *Oh. Shit.* This, I knew, taking in the red Pringles can, the little gold watch that dug gently into Wendy's wrist, was the moment *before* I knew.

"I thought it was menopause. I'm almost forty-four," Wendy said. We both knew what was coming. Wendy was sick; Wendy had cancer; like her mother, Wendy was going to die. It was written in her genes, history becoming the future, inevitable. "I didn't think it was possible."

Of course it was possible. Was it possible that Wendy— Wendy Rosenberg, inscrutable witness to one of humanity's ugliest moments—was flinching from the truth? Immediately, I chastised myself: *Wendy has cancer.*

"Ellen?" Wendy peered curiously into my face. "Did you hear me?"

Jesus Christ. She'd told me she was dying and I hadn't responded.

"Ellen?" she said. "I'm *pregnant.*"

Tears sprung to my eyes. "Oh my god! Wendy! Sorry, I—" I was sobbing. *I thought you were dying.* "You're pregnant," I said. "You're going to have a baby."

"I know," she said. "I can hardly believe it. Can you?" Far away, somewhere else in the building, you could hear a woman's voice, laughing.

That was it. Wendy was a wonderful person and I had been lying to her. I decided I had to tell Wendy the truth about Anya. After all, wasn't the truth what Wendy had always given to me? I promised myself I would tell her before she had the baby.

But, then, I ran into Barbara, one of the ladies from the Post-Soviet Jewish Diaspora Project upstairs, heading back to the building after lunch. She had always been friendly towards me, but only because I worked with Wendy. "Do you know I've been in that office since it opened, three, almost four years, and *every* year on my Marty's *yahrzeit,* may he rest in peace, your Wendy brings me a tin of cookies—good ones, too, cinnamon *rugelah* from Norman's. Not that I need it," she added. Barbara gripped my shoulder for support, tight enough to make me regret the buckle on my shoulder bag. "You know she's pregnant, right?" She eyed me, as if I were responsible for something very serious, as if I were the one who had done this to Wendy, as if she were chastising me. I didn't understand it until Barbara told me something that Wendy herself had never told me: The last time Wendy was pregnant, her husband died.

"Such a tragedy," Barbara clopped along. "She was expecting Jenny." Jenny was Wendy's fourteen-year-old daughter, the daughter I'd always assumed she'd had with her husband, Nigel. "You didn't hear?" I *hadn't* heard. Barbara's left leg, a bit shorter than the right, struck the pavement with each step a half-beat late. Walking with Barbara felt a little like being hitched to a pony. "His name was Moshe. Young Israeli fella. He was walking on the beach with his brother, talking—then—" Barbara gripped my shoulder hard and stopped walking. The pavement, which had echoed her clip-clopping, fell silent. Barbara released my shoulder and held up her hand. "'Wait a minute.' He just held up his hand, like that. 'Wait a minute,' he said. And then he fell down dead." Barbara's face searched my own. "Electrical storm, they said. Electrical storm of the heart." Wendy had never told me about Moshe. And that was how I understood, Wendy, too, had mastered it: the silence after a heartbeat.

( )

I didn't begrudge Wendy her secrets. Wendy's life was filling with a precarious joy I dared not shatter. And mine, too. My wedding, of course. And a sly and careful little friendship with a kind of person I could never have imagined I would meet. Anya must have felt that way, too, because, for the first time since we first sat down in her apartment, she brought up the past.

It was a Thursday afternoon. For the first time, Anya led me into her bedroom, which I'd only glimpsed, and pulled out a small, battered cardboard box. Tossed in along with her expired passport: a few letters, and one loose piece of metal type—the Hebrew letter *bet*. From the box, she extracted a life-sized egg, which I took in my two fingers. "From Ukraine," she explained. "After." After she was liberated from the Soviet hard-labor camp in which I felt sure she had survived on the hope of finding

Sheva again, Sheva whom she had rescued, Sheva whom she had given her own escape. "An Easter egg?" I asked her.

Anya frowned. "*Pysanka*. A gift of friendship." A harlequin pattern in red and antique umber covered the shell, diamonds of various patinas intersecting across its shining circumference, a thousand little lines of tracery woven through the design. It was a real, hand-blown egg, onto which an intricate design, fragile as lace, had been traced in wax; after the egg had been dipped into dyes, a warm bath removed the wax, exposing the brilliant white filigree; it was a perfect negative, an intricate network of shining bones.

I felt aware, as I held it in my hand, of the space inside it, the careful hollow its curved walls cupped, smooth as a skull. I examined the fine webbing of white lines—wax resist. That's what it was called: *resistance*.

"The woman who gave this to me," Anya told me, "was a farmer's wife." She had let Anya sleep in the hayloft, and hadn't told her husband because, after the war, in the villages from which the Jews had been deported, the neighbors greeted the few who had had the audacity to come back with swords and guns. "Before I left, my protector told me, 'A *pysanka* egg given from the heart will never spoil.'" Maybe that's why Anya kept her egg tucked away in the dark, in the box, so that the color would never blanch.

I took the egg on the tips of my fingers and held it up to the light. Negative images danced across its surface. The world is fundamentally a place of loss, and our ghosts are everywhere, taunting us to dare to try to make even one thing last. But if it was possible for something as tenuous as an eggshell to hold its shape, hold its color, then perhaps other things, ineffable things, dyed true, could hold true, also. Anya watched my eyes as I handed the egg back. Sharing the egg was a sign, I thought, that *we* were friends. What was less obvious: Our connection was a thin shell cradling the potent absence of those who had left us.

( )

"Ellen?" It was Vicky from the Red Cross. "I've got a few names for you. Bat Shewa Lewinas," she said, "born Kaunas, 1935 to Yitzhak and Tziporah. Perished in the Kaunas ghetto." Vicky read me her notes. All of the Batshevas and Bat Shewas were either too young or too old. And Anya's Batsheva hadn't perished in the Kaunas ghetto after all. She'd been rescued, at least temporarily, by the *Gandras*. I didn't want a death record, I thought, hoping against hope; I wanted to find her.

"A last name would help," Vicky said. "Who did you say is looking for her?"

I sucked my teeth, a betrayer. "Anya Kamenets," I answered, spelling her name.

( )

At the beginning of April, Francine went to New York on the wedding dress expedition we'd planned weeks before. Alone. "New York City is the best place to shop for clothes," Francine repeated, unable to suppress her excitement about going back to a city that was, for her, mostly unruined by Fiona's absence. "I'll find something for you," she promised.

Though I hated to have Francine leave me for a week, I hated the thought of shopping even more, so I kissed her at the gate and went home, unable to shake the feeling that Francine had left and (plane crash, taxi crash, mugging, murder) wasn't coming back.

I was at work, down in the media room, my head deep in the gloom of a viewing carrel, ghost worlds racing by, when a white shape flickered in the corner of my eye. "Jesus! You scared me."

Wendy hovered at the edge of the carrel in a loose white blouse. "Call for you," she said. "It's Francine."

I took the carpeted steps two at a time.

"Ellen?" Francine yelled. Beyond her voice, I could hear the thousand voices of New York, the dull throb and roar of it.

"Where are you?"

"I'm outside Century 21," Francine hollered. I pictured yellow cabs zipping by, huge buildings blotting out the spring sun. "Ellen," she called across all the miles that stood between us, "I think I've found our dresses!"

I hardly knew what to imagine. We'd already agreed: "No meringues." But what else could a wedding dress look like?

Francine started. "Mine is floor-length, kind of a shimmery rust and green. It's kind of hard to describe." I heard a click.

"Francine!?"

"Hold on." I heard a series of clicks as the coins dropped into the phone. "Okay," Francine continued, "so, on the top layer—it's all lacy, kind of antique, with shimmery beads." I could already hear my mother's voice drawling *machine-made lace*. "It's very elegant. And, it's only three hundred dollars." She let that sink in. "I'm getting it."

"Okay," I said. "Great."

The sound at the other end went muffled for a second, then Francine's voice returned more clearly. "Now *your* dress," she went on, more tentatively. "It's not the same, but it's in the same style, so they go together without being, you know . . ."

"Twins-y."

"It's an ivory silk sheath covered with bone-colored antique lace—" if only she could stop using that word—"with some shimmery sequin things. I think you would look incredible in it."

"Okay," I said. "I guess so."

"Oh—and they're both sleeveless. And they only have yours in a size six."

I hesitated. I pulled up the sleeves of my T-shirt and fingered the tops of my arms. "I don't know." I didn't have my Gramma Sophie's pizza-dough arms, but I wasn't Linda Hamilton in *Terminator 2*, either.

A taxi blared impatiently. If I said *Yes*, I'd be done. If not, I was on my own.

"I don't know," I told Francine. "Six sounds sort of small."

There was a long pause. "It might be small," Francine conceded. "But it's the only one they have." The taxi driver leaned on his horn long and hard.

I stared absently at my desk phone. "I don't think so," I said, finally, wincing.

"Okay," Francine said. "It's okay," she reassured me, reassuring as a Lamaze coach. "We'll keep looking for you."

In Francine's absence, my mother called to check on me. "Have you thought about writing a book?" Recent publications had rekindled in my mother the hope that, even if I would never become rich studying the Holocaust, I might at least become famous. "Just do that. Be the next Daniel Jonah Goldhagen."

"I'm not sure the world wants another one."

In her own way, she really did try. "How's the *planning*?" My mother handled the word at the edges, like a tissue picked up off the ground, the way she usually said the word, *gay*.

"Fine," I said. "We're having the invitations designed."

"I see." What did she see? We still hadn't figured out how to word them. Traditionally, wedding invitations announce that the parents of the bride cordially invite you to the wedding of their daughter. No one's parents were cordially inviting anyone to this wedding. Though my parents, my mother had informed me, were going to pay for the flowers. It was the same gift they had made to my successful entrepreneur West L.A. sister. That was something. I finished spooning yogurt on top of my cereal and took a bite.

"What's that you're eating?"

"Granola and yogurt."

"Wow. That's enough calories to run a marathon. You'd better knock off the chow if you're going to fit into a wedding dress."

I'd spent my whole life fending off the dresses my mother had tried to costume me in. She no longer got an official say in what I'd be wearing. So was I really going to start my married life by letting Francine take over the mommy role? I decided to surprise Francine by getting over my shop-o-phobia and getting my dress myself. It was a very bad idea.

Bicycle messengers zipped by as I hustled up Market through the cigarette smoke trailing the downtown office workers who had begun to look suspiciously young to me. The day had warmed oppressively. The smell of food filled Union Square; men in Oxfords and ties cradled silver-lined boats of *schwarma*; women, starved for the sun, sat out on the steps sipping Calistoga and Diet Coke. I could use a Diet Coke, I thought longingly, as I fanned my face. *Focus.* I needed a store with loads of dresses. Racks and racks of dresses. The idea made me hyperventilate a little. The irony: Francine, who could have happily continued browsing the racks from now through September, had already found her perfect dress, while I, for whom fabric induced anaphylaxis, had nothing. But I could do this. And when Francine came home and saw that I, too, had a dress, it would be like an early wedding present, a proof that I wasn't too scarred by my childhood to make a decent wife.

A little light-headed, I pulled open the big, silent glass doors of Saks Fifth Avenue. The glittering buzz around my head felt cool, perfumed and bright, hard and hollow as a seashell. Well-dressed women moved past the glass cases, purposeful as nurses. White-smocked women leaned close over acquiescent, upturned faces, applying unguents through thick, magnifying lenses. And all around, the murmur of voices mingled tonelessly with the susurration of leather soles across the shining marble floor. The exit disappeared behind me like a dream.

"May I help you?" A man in a dove-gray suit lingered above me.

I squinted at him, my sweat-damp hair springing in bunches behind my ears. After the street, the cool, filtered air chilled me. My skin rose in bumps. "Dresses?" I croaked. I took a few steps forward.

He nodded, a simple nod over the knot of his periwinkle tie. *Of course.* And swept his hand up behind him, half-turning as he appealed to the escalating floors of *couture* layered high above us. Up, up, up. I craned my neck: floor after receding floor of evening gowns, delicate laces, little black dresses; archeologically exposed strata of costume, class and correctness. Between the bands of social situation—black tie, semiformal, cocktail, tea—a huge, winding escalator rose like the spine of a nautilus, twisting end-lessly up. The dresses pressed hugely down. I tilted my head so

183

far up, my eyes rolled back. Inside my head, a confetti of sparks began to shower down, dissolving the glass, the escalator, the gowns.

"Occasion?" the man asked. I tried to fake normalcy even as the irresistible force of hundreds, probably thousands of dresses, pressed down against the top of my head. A thousand wings—skirts and bodices, flaps and zips—thundered in my ears. His face dissolved over the periwinkle tie.

I was already out before I hit the floor.

"They were awfully solicitous." I told Wendy, afterward, about the cream-colored couch to which the man in the periwinkle tie had led me, the crystal decanter of orange juice he had offered. Fresh-squeezed.

"They don't want you to sue them," Wendy pointed out. "What happened to you?"

"I didn't eat," I answered. "I was trying to find a dress."

Wendy nodded, as if buying a dress were a perfectly normal thing for me to do. I was still marveling at the fact that she had not once, in all these years, mentioned her first husband Moshe. I wondered if she would mention him now that she was pregnant. Or, if that was a reason she definitely would not.

Wendy stood up. She'd been to the bathroom about ten times already this afternoon. "Time to go to Arachnid." I glanced at my desk calendar, where I'd doodled in a tiny sketch of a spider in its web. *Arachnid.* Was that a person? An exterminator? "Sorry," I shrugged. "I wrote it down." I pointed to the cartoon, "sort of."

"I thought I was the one with baby brain," she clucked. "It's the wedding," she added. "You're preoccupied." I *was* preoccupied. Francine was coming home today—without a dress for me.

"The website," Wendy reminded me. "We need to be ready to leave in fifteen."

Barbara from the Jewish Diaspora Project upstairs was already in the elevator when we got in. "Ellen," she nodded to me. Then she cast only a sideways glance at Wendy. "Hello, doll."

She reached out with one plump hand and squeezed Wendy's arm. She seemed to make a deliberate effort not to look at Wendy straight on, but I caught her glancing at Wendy as the car descended, a look of secret pleasure on her heavily powdered face. Wendy had Barbara, I told myself, so why shouldn't I have Anya?

( )

Wendy and I didn't have far to go. Arachnid's office sat at the top floor of the old Barbary Coast Coffee Building, a seven-story brick building—unreinforced masonry. I thought, immediately, of The Big One. (On the other hand, that would solve the wedding dress problem.) The lunchtime courtyard swarmed with khaki-clad men and women in black knit shirts, sipping green super-food smoothies from plastic bottles. Wendy and I got into the elevator with two tall, thin women carrying shopping bags. One hefted an armful of pink spaghetti-strap T-shirts. "Corduroy is going to be very, very hot again." We kept our eyes on our unfashionable shoes.

The doors opened on Arachnid, a foyer of exposed brick and glazed, industrial cement. Across from the elevator, an iron spider-web, backlit with red neon, graced the wall. While Wendy made her way to the reception desk, I studied the rows of open cubicles ranged throughout the big, open room, and the Bay views visible through the glassed-in offices banked along the eastern wall. A moment later, Eric Northpoint, tall and muscular in a tight black T-shirt, his head stubbled salt and pepper, pressed business cards embossed with spiderwebs into our palms and led us down the concrete hall to a large glassed-in room as he called out to the receptionist, "Tell the rest of the team we're in the Box." I glanced down at the card, black, the web, silver. Beneath it, in silver type: "We spin the Web. ™"

During the meeting—which was accompanied by a huge tray of Specialty's chocolate chip cookies—Eric and his team darkened the room for a PowerPoint slideshow in which they talked about "eyeballs" and "click-throughs," and the importance of creating a "branded presence" on the web. "In the next five years," Eric spread out his large fingers, "the web will be the site of 80 percent of all business and personal transactions and interactions." Five years ago, I thought, the archive had been a few cardboard cartons collecting mold in a dank basement. But when an art guy showed us mock-ups of a bunch of interactive tools, Wendy looked impressed. "How much would something like that cost?"

Shocking numbers were spoken. Wendy's eyes bugged behind her glasses.

Eric Northpoint assured Wendy that an online "storefront" would give us the edge we needed. Had the Holocaust needed an edge?

The meeting dissolved into a white noise of voices as Wendy conferred privately with Eric Northpoint, and the rest of the team drifted back through the big glass doors. I followed them out to the restroom and, there in the big cement corridor, found myself nose-to-chest with six-foot-tall Charlie May.

Charlie May had been my best friend in graduate school. A classicist studying ancient Greece, Charlie's big blue eyes with their sleepy lids seldom opened wide, but his nostrils used to flare like a horse when he started comparing the city-states of classical antiquity to the birth of the nation in early modern Europe. Charlie had been the one to whom I'd confided about Francine when I'd first fallen for her, my careful and slowly worked-out plan to get to know her, the annoyingly platonic goodbyes in the parking lot. A self-professed expert with women, Charlie had shaken his head knowingly. "Maybe it's different with you girls," his nostrils quivered slightly, "but do you want to date her, or just be her friend? Because if you spend too much time just hanging out," Charlie drew a thick finger across his throat, "it's the kiss of death for sex." Those days Charlie and I sat for hours in Café Milano at a table near the wall, where afternoon light filtered in through the huge windows like the dappled cubes of light at the surface of the ocean. Charlie's eyes had looked bluer than blue, his skin tanner than tan against the white, mandarin collar of a sky-blue dress shirt. His J. Peterman look, he'd told me, a ploy to be taken more seriously by our professors. Charlie had gazed at me sleepily, the wisdom of the senior faculty painted across his brow. He'd leaned back against the booth, his long legs stretched out. "Don't be such a pussy, Ellen. You like her. So, do something about it. Maybe you'll make a total ass of yourself. But maybe you won't."

Charlie May had been right. Now here he was, larger than life, in the polished-cement halls of an internet design company. "Ellen Margolis!" He smiled his big, toothy grin while I told him about my job at the Foundation and the website meeting.

"What about you?" I asked Charlie. "What are you doing here? I guess you finished your degree?" I tried to sound neutral. Why wouldn't Charlie have gotten his Ph.D., an associate professorship in some department of history or classics? He'd always had the face for it.

Charlie shook his head. "Degrees are for pansies." He winked. "I work here." He smiled. "Can you believe it? I love it here," he whispered, conspiratorially. "I make *way* more than any professor ever made."

"That's great," I said.

"I'm sure it's not as important as what you do," Charlie offered, composing his face into a mask of classical *gravitas*.

"Hey, Charlie!" A short guy with a ZZ Top beard and a long, frizzy ponytail was passing us in the hall, a sheaf of papers clutched in his hands. "If you ever doubt whether what you're doing here is important," his slow voice cracked as he began to laugh, "just take a look in your bank account!" He walked away, still chuckling.

Charlie May smiled. Then he asked me, "Whatever happened with the red-haired girl?"

"Francine," I brightened. She was coming home today from

New York. I may not be making the big bucks like Charlie May, but I had Francine. "Actually," I added, smiling for the first time since I'd walked into Arachnid, "we're getting married."

Charlie looked at me down his long, equine nose. His eyebrows hunched together. "Can you do that?" He gazed at me for a moment, then cocked his head like a dog when it hears a squirrel in a high branch. "It was really great to see you, man," he said. "I'll call you." Charlie May pantomimed phone-to-ear and disappeared down the hall.

( )

"You should have invited him," Francine teased me, folding a pair of jeans into her drawer. Her black garment bag hung like a flag over the closet door: Francine's wedding dress. "He might need an excuse to spend some of that career-boy cash." Francine shook a sweater out of her suitcase. "You know, a bread machine, an electric mixer ..."

"Oh, he'd never come." I watched Francine lift a camisole out of her bag, sniff it, then tuck it into her drawer. I lay at the foot of our bed on my stomach, the way I used to lie watching Gramma Sophie unpack her nightie and slippers from her overnight bag, sedated by the smooth movement of her softest things back into their place in our closet.

"He's still not over you," Francine said, pulling out a plastic bag of underwear and dumping it onto the floor.

"What?"

"Oh, it's just because you're unattainable," she answered breezily, adding a pair of jeans to the pile of dirties.

"Thanks," I muttered, throwing myself back against the pillows. Outside, the trumpet vine that crept to the top of the redwood tree thrust its long, red blooms against the bedroom window.

The bed rocked as Francine threw herself down beside me. "Come here."

I didn't really believe Charlie May had anything to "get over" with me. I wasn't the girl he'd never gotten. It was the other way

189

around: His was the life I hadn't picked. "Don't you wish *I*'d become a career girl instead of a . . . sad old story solicitor?"

Francine's eyebrows shot up. "Don't *you* wish I was a psychotherapist serving the troubled spawn of the wealthy?" Well, my father did. I fidgeted my feet. "Ellen," Francine sat up. "What do we really need?" she asked, lifting her hands to our bedroom, ourselves, our life. "Oh! That reminds me!" She hopped off the bed. "Here," she said, "Live, from New York." She handed me a wrinkled white wax bag. "Krispy Kreme!"

Careful not to smear the frosting, I lifted a chocolate doughnut out of the bag, igniting a gentle shower of rainbow sprinkles, and sank my teeth in. I'd read about these in *The New Yorker*. "Mmmm," I murmured. What had we been talking about, anyway? "Bite?"

"No thanks," Francine said, disappearing into the bathroom. "I had two in New York. Don't look in that garment bag!" she called out before the shower rushed on.

The water was still running when the phone rang. It was Fiona's old boyfriend David Charles. "I can't seem to reach her," David Charles drawled, "and I'm worried."

Touching. "She's fine," I answered. I didn't need to protect her anymore. "She's gone," I told him. "She's getting married."

David Charles went silent for a minute. "Isn't that something," he said. But he didn't really seem surprised. Come to think of it, neither was I. Inside my chest, something shifted, the way a safe deposit box slides into its snug and silent vault, and you turn the key, and lock it away.

( )

It was May, but because of the rain, everything had bloomed late this year. Francine and I woke to the shameless cacophony of birds, piercing and clear after the insistent monotony of the rain, the sickening hush of the rain, the thick, gray batting of the rain. Now that the winter had broken, everything felt nearer, more pressing, more real. *The flowers appear on the earth, the time of singing has come, and the voice of the turtledove is heard in our land.* It was nearly the beginning of the summer and, after the summer's end, we'd be getting married. Petals littered the sidewalk like scattered rice.

I drifted down Shattuck Avenue, the women in summer skirts, the bubbling notes of clarinet floating out onto the sidewalk as I drove by to go pick up Francine for lunch, confident, self-possessed, young. Surely, our lives had always been just like this.

But when I pulled around the corner, two black-and-whites loomed outside the Jewish Community Center doors. At the sight of the police cars, my exuberance shifted gears directly into panic: Of course, it was only a matter of time before some crazy bastard came to extract his "price" against the Jews. An image of preschool children holding hands like paper dolls across four lanes of traffic unfolded inside my brain.

Trembling, I dropped the keys. Francine was in there. If she hadn't already been shot. What was I doing, locking the car? It was something I'd never forgive myself for, I realized, *after*. I turned and ran, nearly tripping, to the big black doors of the Jewish Community Center, which burst open in my face. Andy Stein, the mother of a little girl named Emma, flew out of the building, sobbing, her tears splashing into the dark, mussed hair of the chubby baby dangling from the carrier on her chest.

"Andy!" I shrieked, eyeing the baby for blood. I knew, already, that little Emma lay inside, her little pink legs akimbo.

Andy's chest heaved with grief. "I dropped the cupcakes!"

I stared at her lips, trying to make sense of her shock-garbled words. Andy reached around the baby to palm tears from her face. "I put the container"—she pointed out toward the street; two police officers, pizza slices in hand, leaned against the hood of a patrol car, chatting—"on top of the trunk." Purple frosting spattered the road like a bruise.

"Wow," I muttered, my limbic system scrambling to catch up with my mind, my chest and palms cool with sweat. *Cupcakes. Jesus.*

I wasn't the only one freaking out. Wendy had confessed that, as the baby's limbs fitted themselves to her ribs, as the head—that familiar, solid globe—revolved, she found herself doubled over with pangs of certainty that Nigel would suddenly die. At long last, as if it weren't something she'd withheld all this time, she told me about Moshe. "It's not that I'm thinking about Moshe, exactly," she tried to explain, "it's more like my body remembers."

That was our tradition, wasn't it? The glint of future happiness draws *dybbuks*, greedy spirits who will claim whatever they can see. The old, culturally inherited fear. So, for every compliment, a *kine hora*—the charm uttered to ward off the ever-roving evil eye. And it wasn't just the Jews, either. Look at Orpheus, the musician, alone along the lanes of the dead, dust rough beneath the soles of his lime-white feet; the forbidden backward glance that catches one pale shoulder, before it disappears, forever. If you promise 'til death,' doesn't it follow that the person you love most in the world is going to die? *That*, I reminded myself, was why we didn't tell each other everything—as a charm to ward off disaster.

"Ellen, this is Vicky. I think I've found the record you're looking for." *Batsheva.*

My mind flashed on Anya's apartment, the photo framed behind the glass; when I'd visited last week, the twining plant that trailed along the tabletop had been in bloom, a dense forest crawling with blossoms more animal than plant: wide, petaled mouths burst open; long, sticky, tongues thrust out into the air, toward the photo, toward the blank, wide sky, toward anything within their grasp. Anya had been telling me about the upcoming Calder exhibit at SFMOMA. "To stand still, and yet to move; Calder is the genius of this paradox," Anya said, tracing a finger through the air; she leaned in confidentially. "*We* are the geniuses of the other paradox." She lifted her chin. "To move and yet remain firm—this is our story." It was the first time I'd heard her even suggest a kinship with the Jews.

Vicky cleared her throat. "Yad Vashem has a page of testimony submitted by Betsheva Singer . . ." my heart leapt—*submitted by*; she'd survived. I heard Vicky riffle through sheets of paper. ". . . recording the life of Anya Kamenets . . ." Vicky paused. "Here we go. Born 1923, Kaunas. Daughter of Rafael and Dina. Lived, Kaunas, Lithuania. Died 1944, Kaunas Ghetto."

I was confused. "The death of Anya Kamenets?" Something in my brain didn't seem to be working. *Anya dead? Batsheva living?* Batsheva must have survived and assumed, because Anya had stayed behind, that Anya hadn't. By finding Sheva—alive!—that was a tragic misunderstanding that I could clear up. "Would you mind sending that to me?"

( )

I went to find Anya at the Museum of Modern Art. Before she'd retired, she told me, she'd owned a small gallery, "specializing," she said, "in masterworks out of Europe." She didn't like to talk about that, but she did like to talk about painting, and, in the course of our recent visits, she'd set me a rigorous course of study. A course of study that I supposed was meant to keep me from asking more about Betsheva. She could think what she liked.

SFMOMA's great striped oculus shone back the sky. I moved through the big, open lobby, the shifting forms overhead like spirits on the bridge to the World to Come, and found Anya upstairs in a second-floor gallery.

When she saw me, Anya held up her hands in surrender. "Ellen," she pronounced my name like the pleading part of a prayer before looking me up and down. "Tennis shoes!" she tapped her hand against her temple in dismay. Behind her, a blue painting, divided up into rectangles and squares, windows of blue through which light seemed to shine, reminded me of Anya's apartment. "You like Diebenkorn?" Anya turned to the painting, looking at me sideways, eyes asquint. It was an expression I recognized: her eyebrows down-turned arcs, her cheeks parentheses, everything curved, everything hidden.

Did I like it? I liked the color blue. I liked the layers of light. Anya knew I had grown up by the ocean. "My father used to take us to Santa Monica on New Year's Eve, me and my sister," I told her. We'd plodded along in the crisp, end-of-December air, the postcard-wide beach empty, the waves drawing back, our fists in our pockets. It still felt strange, telling Anya something so personal. I wasn't used to talking to anyone this way, anyone beside Francine. But it felt good, too.

"You recognize the light," Anya smiled mysteriously. She turned to the painting and pointed to the label. "Ocean Park #54," it read, "Santa Monica." Anya seemed pleased to know the little details about me, the facts that connected this painting to my life. It gave me courage. Maybe she would be happy that I had discovered something about her, too?

"It's pretty. But a little flat," I protested, gesturing to the blues of *Ocean Park*. It wasn't how the world looked to me, the world always, it seemed, composed of so many layers—so many of them, I thought, glancing at Anya's parenthetical features, hidden. I hoped she understood what I was trying to say: that it was time for us to move beyond the surface.

"The lines that look to you so flat," she opened her palms, "reveal something else, out of sight." I searched Anya's closed face. Was she telling me that she agreed? "There is a painting," she gestured toward the Diebenkorn—"behind this painting."

I glanced at the canvas for a clue. The paint looked so pale, the blue scraped so thin that it looked like the light actually shone through it. Did she mean that there was a painting hidden on the canvas, behind this one? A hidden painting you could only see with x-rays? Famous paintings had been hidden this way, smuggled out of Europe. I thought of Anya's gallery, and I remembered the *Gandras*.

"Not in space. In time. Come." We wound through a narrow passage, back toward a private office where Anya found the book she wanted. As she shuffled through its pages, I noticed that here Anya had no photos on her desk.

Anya pointed to a glossy photo of a blue painting by Matisse, a field of blue intersected with lines, something more solid in it than the pure light of Diebenkorn, sort of like a castle floating there. "A painting behind the painting," Anya repeated. "You think paint is flat," Anya accused me, "but the visual world speaks a language that has been spoken for tens of thousands of years." She touched the picture. "Entire worlds before your very eyes,"— she reached out to touch my cheek; it was the first time she had ever touched me affectionately—"that you cannot see."

"Anya," I said, as she looked, frowning, into my face, "have you ever thought about looking for Batsheva . . . ?" I started, looking for a place to begin, a rationale to explain what I'd done.

Anya shut the book. "Whatever happened to your friend from the Foundation? The dark-haired one. The student." *Jill?* It was just like Anya to deflect a direct question with another question, but this one was a doozy, something she must have been hiding up her sleeve for just the right moment, a moment when she felt I'd gotten too close to something. I had never told Anya about

Jill. I had told *Jill* about *Anya*. And that had felt inappropriate enough. Had Anya been spying on me?

"Someone you saw me with at the Foundation?" I asked, as if I didn't know who she meant.

Anya nodded. "Your friend." *My friend.* That was what Anya had called Batsheva. Batsheva, the dark-haired beauty. *Friend.* A word overburdened with hidden meanings, from a past in which so much had remained hidden. Maybe I was wrong about Batsheva. Could I have been?

"Jill went to Boston," I told Anya. "We were just friends," I insisted, aware, even as I said it, that I sounded too defensive, that there were so many things that word could mean.

Anya assessed me from the corner of her eyes. "I see," she said.

( )

"You should write to her."

"I'm not going to write to her." Sol shook his head.

"Your father got a letter today from his old flame," Betty reported.

She was working the puzzle in the Sunday *Times*.

Sol sat kitty-corner, the latest issue of *Wired* folded back in his lap. "That was before the War. Marion Silver." He waved Marion Silver away with his hand. "Listen to this." Sol wore glasses when he read, half-moons he bought from the rack at Long's. "A clock that will tell time from January 1, 2001, to the year 12,000. Twelve thousand!" Sol put his finger under the digits and studied them. "Stonehenge is only five thousand years old."

"That's a sturdy clock," I said.

"Forget about the clock," Sol said. "How would you communicate our understanding of Time to people for whom our fundamental concepts might no longer have any meaning?"

It didn't seem so far-fetched to me. Wasn't that the same problem the Foundation sets out to solve, Yad Vashem, all of them? To preserve forever a truth away from which Time has shifted so far as to find it inconceivable? Would it be the same for me and Francine, I wondered: Would there ever be a time when people found it unremarkable that Francine and I had gotten married, that they would have to have it explained to them that in 1998 we were living in a different world? It seemed impossible.

Betty cleared her throat. "Your father almost married her." She gripped the gold lozenge that hung around her neck between her thumb and fingers, rubbing it like a talisman as she kept her eyes on her puzzle. "Marion Silver."

Betty was making me uncomfortable and, as I often did when I was uncomfortable, I didn't change the subject, but I pivoted it. "I interviewed a woman recently," I told Francine, turning the present into the past, "whose old flame was another girl." There was an entire group devoted to the Lesbian Daughters of Holocaust Survivors, but Francine knew I had never encountered a lesbian survivor. I watched Francine chew another almond. Her brow wrinkled, clearly puzzled that I had never mentioned this before.

"They were lovers?" Francine licked salt from her fingertips. "Did she tell you that?"

"Not exactly. After we talked, I sort of figured it out."

Francine's head tilted. "You figured it out?"

I hadn't seen the photograph in months, but, in my memory, Sheva's eyes smoldered for Anya. "I sensed a spark."

Betty, still working her puzzle, cleared her throat. "Ellen, I think you're leaking." *Leaking?* "Letting your work affect you." How couldn't it? "Failing to hold up the boundaries between your work and your private life." I imagined my dark thoughts seeping out, the slow hiss of gas.

Betty worked with battered women. She knew something about leaking, I guessed, but I didn't think that was what this was. "Maybe it wouldn't hurt to think about moving on?"

"From this client?" As I said it, I felt how jarring it was to think of Anya as a "client," let alone to think about "moving on."

"From the Foundation." Betty's pencil hung, sharp, above her page. "Leaving this job."

Betty could be hard, I knew, but her comment stunned me. It was so hard-line. Maybe it was the line Wendy would take, when she found out what was going on between me and Anya, but it surprised me to hear it coming from Betty, who didn't even know about the secret visits; it was such an extraordinary reaction to a manageable problem—to up and disappear just because you had some complicated feelings, when there were so many reasons to stay. Many more reasons than Anya. Was it possible that Betty didn't understand the magnitude of my sense of responsibility for what I did? I bristled thinking it.

"When I was fourteen," I told Betty, "my parents went on a trip to Europe. France, Italy, Spain. Before they left, my father took me into his closet." My father's locked closet, where he kept his file cabinets full of deeds, tax returns, personal papers. "He pulled out an envelope with three safe deposit keys in it. 'If something happens,' he told me, 'go to the bank right away.' He pointed to the address. 'Once they get notified of a death, they have to seal the boxes, and they can get tied up in probate for months.'"

"That's pretty morbid," Francine murmured, with the mild contempt a woman can only have for her future in-laws.

I shook my head again. "That was the first time I realized: They're going to be gone and all of it—all this stuff my father kept in his closet—whether or not I knew what it was, whether it was then or thirty years from then; all of it was going to be up to me. To us." Because it wasn't just me. A thousand voices, the voices of our generation, were rising up, one by one, thin as sacrifice, twining wreaths of memory.

"That's right," Betty quietly consented. "You're *not* the only one." In her words, I thought I heard that faint, parental whiff of dismay, the dismay of my parents, of an entire generation of parents, the ones who'd carpooled us to religious school, who felt real shock when we showed signs of believing in God. But unlike my parents, Betty was a person to whom I could give an honest answer. That was part of marrying Francine.

"Me. Me and my generation," I told Betty—because it was Betty's generation, and my parents', who could afford to be complacent, who could choose to believe that, when it came to the big things, silence was best. "We know that, after they die, after *you* die, *we* will be the only ones left in the world to have seen *them*."

"Do you think it's really possible," Betty narrowed her eyes behind her magnifying glasses, but she wasn't looking up at me as she penciled an answer into her crossword, "for people to tell the truth about their lives?"

The conversation had taken a rather pointed turn. "I hope so," I answered, a little shocked, a little offended.

"Oh. Not to you, dear." Betty brandished her pencil, erasing. "To themselves."

When we got ready to go, Francine picked something off the hem of my jacket. It was a pale green sticker from SFMOMA. I was sure, this time, I had peeled it off and thrown it away, but like my bad conscience it had followed me home. "You went to the museum? Again?" Francine frowned.

"Huh?" I shrugged, scrunching my nose at the sticker as if I had no idea how it happened to be stuck to my clothing. "That's weird." It wasn't, technically, a lie.

( )

"I understand, Ms. Janowicz." Wendy tucked the phone between her chin and her chest. "I'll come out myself this evening." She jotted down a note on her big desk calendar in green: "Mr. Kaye, Rose of Sharon, 6 p.m., 8th Floor West."

A frozen yogurt, spun ornately as a conch, going slick and blurry at her elbow, Wendy pecked frantically at her keyboard. As her pregnancy advanced, all of her tasks seemed to take on an increasing sense of urgency, her due date like a D-Day, beyond which the future fate of the world seemed wholly unknown.

"I can take that," I offered. "The interview. Today. At the Rose of Sharon." An opportunity to see Anya that I didn't have to cook up or cover up. I still planned to tell Wendy about Anya before the baby came. But not too much before. Just before she went on maternity leave with a distracting new baby.

Wendy studied me, hesitating. She'd told me that, since she'd gotten pregnant, she could scent a slice of Chicago pizza three blocks away. I wondered if she could smell a fishy reason, too. "All right." She shrugged. "Thanks."

I found Mr. Kaye on the eighth floor of the West tower of the Rose of Sharon. As retirement communities go—and I'd seen a few—the Rose of Sharon seemed fairly benign: a whole community of old people, living in their own apartments, eating together in the big dining hall, wandering past trailing ficus leaves and burbling fish tanks. But, go up into the West tower, I discovered, stepping off the elevator into a hospital wing—walls, desks and floors variations on a single shade of maroon—and you enter the waiting room of the Angel of Death. Room after curtained room of bodies, lumpen in front of dark TVs, lined the hall. In a fluorescent-lit communal room, gowned figures slouched in wheelchairs around a Formica table. Brown eyes, filmed blue, stared, vacant. I blinked hard and moved past. Wendy had warned me: *There may not be much time left.*

But, when I saw Mr. Kaye, I realized quickly that there was no time left at all. "Mr. Kaye?" From the bed, the rail-thin figure stirred under the blanket just enough to show that it heard. But Mr. Kaye's eyes, open without seeing, didn't shift to my face. "Mr. Kaye?" He groaned, a faint, guttural cry, like the moan of an animal.

"Oh." I turned to the wall. What did they want me to do—Ms. Janowicz?—extract some nugget of truth, like a gold filling, before the body was gone?

I collected myself, turned back, leaned down.

"Mr. Kaye," I said. I wanted to whisper, but I doubted he would hear me, so I said it loudly. "Is there anything I can do for you, Mr. Kaye?"

Mr. Kaye's hands had been tucked neatly into the closely tucked blanket, but his mouth fell open. "Unhh."

"I'm sorry, Mr. Kaye," I told him. "I don't understand." Ms. Janowicz had told Wendy that Mr. Kaye had survived the medical experiments. He'd had severe TB. I considered Mr. Kaye, immobile in his bed, and wondered how much of those horrific moments came alive with each rattling breath.

Mr. Kaye's tongue heaved in his mouth. The ground, yellowed teeth parted, revealing something soft, gray, some unrecognizable pap. Mr. Kaye's tongue pushed the mass into his cheek.

I dashed into the hall, intercepted a woman in clogs with a cart full of pills. "Mr. Kaye, in here. There's something in his mouth."

The woman looked up, unhurried. "Who are you?"

"I'm visiting Mr. Kaye. He's got something in his mouth. Can you take it out?"

"Who are *you*?" the nurse pressed me. "Are you his daughter?"

I'd stepped back into the room, trying to lead her behind me. "Look."

"Are you family?"

I stood by Mr. Kaye's bed, gestured toward his rolling lips.

Despite herself, she glanced at Mr. Kaye. "Pouching," she commented. "It's one of the signs." The signs? Mr. Kaye's chest rattled with each breath.

"Can you get it out?" Was this woman a nurse, or a spectator?

"I'm sorry," she said, not sorry at all. "Who did you say you are?"

"I'm Ellen Margolis," I said, loud enough for Mr. Kaye to hear. "I'm here from the Foundation for the Preservation of Memory. I'm here, Mr. Kaye," I knelt by the bed, "so that the world will remember your name."

"Miss, unless you're family or social services, you're going to have to leave." No amount of explaining satisfied her. (If Francine were ever hospitalized, I realized with dread, it would be the same; I'd have no legal status as her spouse. The idea gave me the chills.) "I'm going to have to get a supervisor in here," the nurse warned me. When she disappeared down the hall, I slipped my hand over Mr. Kaye's blankets. There was nothing I could do here; I'd come too late. "I'm sorry, Mr. Kaye," I told him. "I'm so sorry."

I reached the South tower in a state, eager to see Anya. The doors opened on the eleventh floor. Even before I passed Mrs. Linde's door, halfway down the hall, the sickening smell surrounded me. Burned food—burned flesh. I covered my nose with my hands as I pressed toward Anya's door. No one answered. But the knob turned easily in my hand.

The acrid reek of smoke nearly choked me as I walked in. Someone had left the big slider open to the patio, but the thick odor clung to the carpets, the curtains, hung like an invisible fog over the glass table. "Anya?" I'd never been in Anya's apartment without Anya before. Aside from the smell, and the open window, everything appeared as it always did: immaculate, orderly, contained. Glancing at the window, my first thought was: She's finally flown. (Was this horrid stench of flesh, metal, flame, the smell of the Phoenix, self-immolated, risen and flown?) Then I looked around the tiny kitchen, and found the burnt pot, and wondered where Anya had gone.

Mrs. Linde, trailing a rolling oxygen tank on a line like a small, obedient dog, lingered near her door, watching me closely as I backed out of the apartment. "She fell." She nodded her head toward Anya's apartment; a clear tube trailed from her nose.

Anya fell. Anya fell. Anya fell.

"Where is she?"

Mrs. Linde sucked breath through her nose. "Where?" She seemed unable to get words out of her mouth. "West tower?"

I raced back to the West tower. "Yes. I'm her daughter," I repeated to myself as the elevator ascended to the tenth floor. "Her daughter." But, when I got out on the tenth floor, indistinguishable from the antiseptic, mauve halls of the eighth, no one asked.

An old woman in a blue cardigan sat up in the bed near the door, flipping cards out onto the bed tray. "Hello," she greeted me warmly. "Are you from Social Services?" I shook my head. "Here for *her*?" she tried. I nodded, glancing toward the curtain that divided the room, behind which, I assumed, Anya lay in God-knew-what state. "They say she got dizzy. But she's not talking. Maybe she'll talk to you." She studied me for a minute, as if looking for a resemblance. Then she turned back to her game of solitaire.

I stepped behind the pale mauve curtain. The bed was empty. Anya, intact as far as I could see, sat up in a maroon chair in a white "Golden Gate National Parks" T-shirt I had never seen before, a blanket draped across her lap, her back to the window. "Anya." Behind her, the window reflected me back to myself against the blank canvas of the darkening sky.

Anya looked straight through me, hollow, dark, simmering with anger. Her small shoulders hunched under the T-shirt. She ground her jaw. When she glanced at me, it was with wild, animal hatred. She wasn't herself. Staring back at her, I didn't know what to say. I wasn't her daughter. I wasn't her granddaughter. We had no ties of blood, or love. I didn't even know her.

I tried to keep my voice light. I could hear my sister, murmuring to Gramma Sophie in the cardiac unit. "You've had a shock," I said. "But you're going to be okay." Anya didn't say anything; she just glared. "I've got to go now," I told her. "But I'll come back." Then I fled, once again, from the West tower back to Anya's apartment, where I stood at the sink, scrubbing and scrubbing and scrubbing the pot.

( )

When I came back the next day, I brought *hamentaschen*, raspberry ones. The raspberry jam didn't bleed as much as the strawberry, but I'd committed my usual sin, and so I just tried to choose the ones that looked the neatest, their golden corners pinched hard together, clean lines, which I knew—or thought I knew—Anya would prefer.

The bed near the door was empty, the cards stacked neatly on the table. Anya sat up in the chair facing the window. She nodded. "So," she said, "you heard." The stranger who had hunched in last night's crouch of fear and anger had disappeared.

"You fell."

She waved her hands, a dismissal of the whole, overblown establishment.

Someone—*who?*—had brought in a pile of Anya's books, and the photo of Batsheva from Anya's apartment.

"You were cooking." When I'd gotten home, the tang of smoke in my hair and clothes, Francine had turned me around and around, sure I'd escaped from a fire. (I told her there'd been a small chemical plant explosion downtown, a not-very-credible lie.)

Anya shrugged, her gaze on the sky. "I can make more soup."

What was the point of arguing? They'd keep her here or not keep her here. She'd cook or stop cooking. Maybe she'd burn

205

down the place. I wasn't her daughter. I wasn't her granddaughter. What had I been telling myself all this time?

I pulled up a chair and sat next to Anya; out the window, the cars in the street looked like toys. The June light scooped the sky into a hollow, blue shell.

I glanced over to the stack of coffee-table art books. Idly, I slid out *The San Francisco Expressionists*. This is what I knew how to do. I didn't know what to say to Anya, didn't know how to help her, didn't know how to claim her, didn't know if I wanted to. But I knew how to sit, to be still, to stay beside her. I flipped through the big glossy paintings, the chunky gold and ochre hills; I liked the landscapes the best. Then I turned the page. "*Ocean Park*," I said.

Anya settled a crooked finger on the page. Dressed in her own clothes, in her own apartment, her lines never seemed crooked. Here, she was stripped, an old lady.

Anya drew her finger down along the page. "*Pentimenti.* These are the half-hidden, underneath marks—the paths the painter explored and rejected, in search of . . . something else." It was a relief to hear her sound like herself. Anya's fingers stroked the book; even in the photo, I could make out the striations of the brush, the darker strokes overlapping the lighter wash. Anya cleared her throat. Her words, emerging, seemed to reorganize her whole face from the Cubist fragment of pain and rage she'd been last night. "How do you paint the watery air that envelopes you in your studio?" Her head inclined toward the window. Then she turned to me; as she spoke, her face composed itself back into the inscrutable one I knew. "In the Renaissance, these marks, these *pentimenti*, would sometimes appear as a painting aged, but the celebration of them as something—this is a modern idea."

Anya and I stared together at *Ocean Park No. 54*, glancing, now and then, out the window, not down at the city and the cars, but up at the sky. "Anya," I said, "there's a record for you at Yad Vashem." Anya stared closely at the painting, her lips pressed together. She pressed them tighter. It was easier to look at her this way, in profile. But I found I had to turn away, because my eyes smarted. "A death record." It was all I could do not to glance at the photo of Batsheva. But I didn't. I stared straight ahead, out the window, at the watery light in the sky. "Submitted by Batsheva Singer." Anya's fingers curled over the print.

She must have glanced over at the photo herself. "Cookies?" she asked. I handed her the plate. Anya picked up the neatest triangle. "You made this?" she asked with grave suspicion. She held the *hamentaschen* up to the slit of her mouth, opened it just wide enough and took a bite. I watched while she chewed. "A little dry," she commented, crumbs blowing from her lips. "We need tea."

When I came back with the tea, Anya helped herself to a second. "You." She pointed to the plate. When we'd eaten *hamentaschen* and drunk tea for a while, I told her I needed to go. There were things Anya would never tell me. No point in drawing it out.

Anya nodded, grave. "I'm going home tomorrow."

"Home?"

"To my apartment."

"Good."

"You have to prove everything to these people," she spat, dismissing the Rose of Sharon with a wave of her hand.

"I'm glad you're going home. I'll come back then."

Anya nodded like she didn't care either way, a brusque little nod, and turned back to the window.

"Would you like your book?" I offered.

She dismissed me.

As I was walking out, though, she called after me, "Repentance."

"What's that?"

"*Pentimento*," Anya said. "That's what it means, you know."

On the way out of the West tower, so that my alibi to Wendy wouldn't be a complete lie, I stopped back on the eighth floor to check on Mr. Kaye. I stepped out of the elevator, watchful for the suspicious nurse. But the people at the nurses' station were all different, and I made my way, unchallenged, to Mr. Kaye's room. It was empty, the bed stripped. Through the curtains, the filtered sun submerged the room in watery light.

( )

"How did those invitations come out?" Mi'Chelle asked, handing me a pile of mail, an envelope, battered and half-torn, at the top of the stack.

"Perfect, Mi'Chelle. Thank you so much."

Mi'Chelle closed her eyes, perfection acknowledged. She had done the graphic design for us at a very reasonable price. "Then why haven't I got mine?" she pouted.

"We screwed up the envelopes." Mi'Chelle looked alarmed. "But we've figured out a solution." ("We'll make them ourselves," Francine had told me. "How hard can it be?") Relief smoothed Mi'Chelle's features.

"Hand-folded? Well, that *is* nice," she murmured. "But don't you wait too long. I need an excuse for those shoes I saw at Macy's."

I laughed and headed up the stairs, where I found Wendy at her desk, uncharacteristically silent, staring at the *bat mitzvah* photo of her, Nigel, and her daughter Jenny. "Jenny's angry with me," Wendy sighed. "'You're always lecturing me about birth control. You should have known better.'" Underneath her shirt, I saw something solid shift, then disappear. Right then, even I wanted to touch it—the robust talisman.

"She'll change her mind. You know that."

"I know. I know she'll love the baby. It's just that she's so mad at me." Wendy's chin dimpled.

We didn't usually talk like this. "I'll get you some tea," I offered. I made my way to the kitchen slowly, sliding the battered envelope Mi'Chelle had handed me out of my pocket.

Damaged in transit by the U.S. Postal Service. The half-torn piece of mail, which had been fixed crookedly with a real stamp, looked like it had been circulating since World War I. In the upper corner, the return address read "American Red Cross: Tracing." Vicky had included a short, handwritten note, along with a Xeroxed copy of a phone book listing, printed in Hebrew and translated, in another hand, into English: *Batsheva Singer, Rose of Sharon Home, Tel Aviv.* I looked at the twining black letters again, carefully, trying to decipher the hidden meaning there. This is what I saw:

Precociously sad, defiant eyes, eyes dark as the edge of the forest in which they stand, two girls contemplate each other's shadowed places in the shadows of shedding pines. They've been running, their book sacks thumping, damp with sweat under their white blouses, to escape the brutality of their mothers' holiday cleaning, the dusty beating of the rugs, the merciless screech of Batsheva's father's chickens; free, like boys, past the castle, into the woods. The blond, the one with the laughing eyes, falls, laughing, under a pine, lies, laughing, up at the cool September sky, and the dark-haired girl seals her mouth on the laughing mouth, as if she could catch that laughing breath in her own mouth. Then the laughing eyes and the dark eyes change; the paisley-shaped eyes open and melt into the dark eyes, and see whole universes there. That's how it starts. With pine needles in the hair. In the shadow of the forest, in the shadow of the old monastery. They are sixteen. After that,

they find ways to be alone. The dark girl discovers a taste
for salt; the fair-haired girl discovers the love of shape:
curve, angle; breast, bone. They learn the rhythms of
breath. They learn what it means to be breathless. When
they rise, their smooth, white backs come away rough with
the weight of the earth.

I hovered in the hall, stunned with disbelief. The Rose of Sharon
Home. And yet halfway around the world. What kind of coincidence was that?

( )

"A false intimacy," Debbie yelled over the wind. "How many people have gotten married out of the urgency spurred by a fear of death?" She was talking about her twin brother, who had just proposed to his girlfriend. We were out at the Berkeley Marina, Debbie and Francine and I, bracing bags of kettle corn against the wind as we watched the sky. The huge, open fields, carpeted in April with crimson and clover, had given way to green and gold stubble, covered, this festival weekend in July, with people flying kites and watching kites fly. From across the highway, the wide field looked like a small patch of a tropical green sea, colorful kites swaying in one spot like pensive fish. "Anika had surgery for a heart murmur. A week later, he bought her a ring." When I had finally told her Francine and I were getting married—on the phone—she'd exhaled, "Thank you! Finally!" But now she sounded extremely skeptical. On the field, two stunt kites soared up to an Asian-sounding instrumental, something with flutes, a cherry-blossom dance. Debbie mused, "I wonder if seeing her so mortal gave him that pang—how much he's in love with, just, life—and he's confused it with being in love with her." We stared at the twining kites, which revolved around each other—a tangle seemed inevitable—then separated. "Like Ben," Debbie reminded me.

One late spring day of our senior year, Ben, a visiting junior, had been killed in a car crash. None of us really knew him. That night in the Co-op kitchen, I stood slicing asparagus, the big orange

211

kitchen door open onto the empty alley where the lilacs had just started to bloom. Sam was washing bowls, clattering over the rush of the sink. Dusk—glowing, particulate, palpable dusk—filtered in. Sudden and pungent as the slice of an onion, I'd felt it: *I am alive.*

Who wouldn't want to marry that feeling?

Francine licked popcorn salt off her fingers. "Taking care of someone who's totally dependent. I think that can create a sense of intimacy that's not really there."

"I took care of you once," I reminded her.

Just three months into our relationship, Francine got the flu. For days, I rotated her from the bed to the couch and back again, each day a blur of grainy images of night-fired SCUDs, in front of the TV. Four months before, I'd been the person Francine wasn't sure about. Suddenly I was her lifeline to the world.

The wind held up, brisk and constant.

"I should have asked you to marry me then," I joked quietly.

"I was vulnerable," Francine answered. "I might have said yes."

The *Star Wars* theme thundered out over the field, where a black kite chased a white one. Even with the music blasting, you could hear the zips of wind ripping against the nylon as the kites sliced the sky.

Actually, Francine *had* asked me to marry her, not long after that. It was a slip, a fluke. One of those impulsive things women said to each other sometimes, because it didn't really mean anything. It wasn't something we ever talked about.

The sky that day had been gray; big magnolia petals lay bruised and rotting on the sidewalks as I pedaled toward home with a pile of student blue books and a fifty-nine-cent, felt-tipped, red pen. When I opened the front door, I found Francine, head in her hands, on the steps leading up to the flat I shared with Debbie. She grabbed me by the shoulders. Her face looked pale. "Ellen, marry me," she said.

I pulled away. "Don't you have a seminar?" I led her up the stairs to my bedroom.

Francine related a long preschool tale. She slumped on the

bed, bunching the comforter in her hands. "Then he stomped off, the little bastard."

"That sucks," I commiserated. I'd never heard Francine talk this way about a child before. I wondered why something so infantile had set her off. I sat down next to her on the bed and let my hand fall on her thigh.

"Then, during my break, I ran into my friend Jeanette's mother, Joyce." Jeanette had been a high school friend of Francine's. Joyce Babcock was her mother. Francine pronounced the name heavily, like the slice of a knife. Her face collapsed. "All decked out in her Stepford drag." Francine traced a pattern along the leg of her jeans.

I drew up my legs and leaned back against the charcoal wall of my bedroom.

"Joyce Babcock was everything my mother wasn't: really young, really pretty, really, really rich. They lived in a Maybeck with art deco lamps with pink glass shades. My parents love their garden—they work on it all the time—but Joyce's garden looked like something out of *Sunset* magazine. Actually, it was in *Sunset* magazine. She'd landscaped it herself.

"I spent every weekend over there, even when Jeanette was away at her dad's. I even dieted with her."

My neck pricked with alarm. "Dieted?"

"Oh, you know." Francine flicked her knee with her fingernails. "Eight bottles of water a day and rice crackers. Jeanette refused to do them, so I did them with Joyce, for company."

"For company?"

Francine's face reddened. "She was interested in me. In my body."

Not Jeanette. Joyce. I felt anger rising.

"Joyce would say things like, 'Doesn't Francine look amazing? Can you believe she's lost ten pounds?'"

"Ten pounds, Francine. Jesus." I looked over at my lover, her small shoulders hunched over her small, curvy hips and thighs, and wondered how anyone could wish for any less of her. "Francine," I whispered. "This is very, very fucked up."

"I know," she agreed. "It is."

But I could no more stop her confession now than I could stop the clouds from massing, stop Orpheus from turning back, stop Lot's wife turning to salt. What is it about the backwards glance we can't resist, no matter what the price? The inexorable pull, the terrible tide of the truth pulling us out to sea.

We sat quietly and listened to the pock of Francine's tears as they hit the bed. When Francine had gone off to college, Joyce had lost interest, and Francine had developed a full-blown eating disorder.

"I was cold." Francine told me. "All the time."

I considered her sadly. Francine had shrunk into her shoulders. The woman who had electrified me with her dancing, the woman who had thrilled me with her opinions, her independence, had vanished; in her place on my bed sat a depressed post-adolescent, a rejected teenager, a lonely, mixed-up kid. The gray afternoon light shone bleakly on my gray walls; even Francine's hair looked darker than bright.

Francine, round-shouldered on the edge of my bed, apologized. "You don't want to hear this," she said, shifting as if to stand. But I knew that was part of the reason she needed to say it—to know if, seeing the worst she could think to reveal about herself, I would still want to be with her.

Truthfully, I'd felt a terrible pang of disappointment, regret. Francine, it turned out, like both of my girlfriends before her, was kind of fucked up. I didn't know how badly, or what this would mean when we were together. Would she hate her body no matter how often I told her how beautiful she was? Would she think about food more than she thought about us? I didn't know. Did I want to be with her anyway?

"Here." I put up my shirt sleeve and wiped her face.

"You must really like me." She laughed through her tears.

"I do," I whispered. "I more than like you," I said, wrapping my wet arms around her trembling shoulders. "Actually," I added, clearing my throat a little, "I love you."

Francine turned to me, our noses nearly touching. "Do you think you can?" she asked, looking from one of my eyes to the other.

"Yes. I do," I told her. Her shoulders loosened. She leaned into me.

"I'm glad," she answered in a quiet voice, "because I love you, too." She closed her eyes and we held each other. I could feel her bones through her soft, gray sweater, and I wondered. She felt me feeling her body and wondering. She sat up.

"That's all done now." She looked at me intently, looking, for the first time that afternoon, like the Francine who had refused to kiss me for so long, the Francine who knew how to hold her own.

"What happened? Why?"

"A bunch of things," she said, matter-of-factly. She ticked them off on her fingers. "I hadn't had my period in nearly a year, and I got scared about that. I started seeing a therapist. I met Bonnie. I started being able to enjoy my body." Francine had told me once about how she had gotten together with Bonnie, a math geek and a distance runner. I'd imagined the two of them outlined against the bare, gray sky; between them, clotting, the milky clouds of their breath, the unsaid made visible.

"'Becoming a lesbian saved my life,'" I joked, framing my headline in the air.

Francine smiled. "I was ready to be myself. I didn't need the distraction of not eating anymore."

I nodded. Hadn't Terri told me she'd gotten drunk every weekend at boarding school so she wouldn't have to face her crush on her roommate? After she came out, she never drank a drop. Hadn't Glenn, before he came out, attempted suicide? Hadn't Mika become an obsessive, concert-level oboist? An eating disorder, in some ways, seemed fairly mild.

"So," I said. "You feel like you have this thing under control."

Francine cocked her head. She looked past me at the Jewish Museum calendar on my wall. The artifact of the month was a ring with an enormous metal house on top of it, a communal wedding ring. "The opposite. I've stopped trying to keep everything under control." Francine seemed restored. "You're sure you're not freaked out?"

"I'm from L.A.," I reminded her. "Half the girls in my high

215

school were either anorexic or bulimic." Francine stared at me. "Actually," I admitted, "my parents are kind of weird about food."

"Weird how?"

"They measure it." I coughed. "They weigh their chicken."

"Are they really skinny?"

"No," I admitted. "My mother is. But my father cheats." Francine looked concerned. "My dad likes to eat jam straight out of the jar. I used to find him standing in front of the refrigerator with a spoon." Francine laughed. Her laughter washed over me like cool water. She smoothed her forehead with the heel of her hand. Joyce had tried to annihilate her. She was still here.

I flicked on the light. My room filled with color again, Francine's hair auburn, her cheeks pink, my walls charcoal and white. I stepped into the hall. "Come on," I said.

Francine stood with her back to the stove while I rooted through my shelf in the cupboard, a chaos of canned pintos and Progresso soups. "Aha!" I plunged my hand into the darkness and pulled out an unopened jar of Bonne Maman apricot preserves. Holding Francine's shoulder, I hopped down and fished two silver teaspoons—Debbie and I had only four—from the silverware drawer. The jam jar opened with a satisfying *pop*. The shimmering circle of jam glistened orange-gold in the yellow light of the kitchen; it parted with a faint sigh when I split it with the spoon, scooped out a small, gleaming glob of jam and handed it to Francine, a whole slice of jellied apricot suspended in its amber. We clinked spoons. "To the future," I said.

"Amen," Francine licked jam from the round underside of the spoon. I slurped off the front of my glob. The jam tasted sweet and tangy; it tasted like fruit and flowers and the spring that was coming.

"Is this wrong?" I asked her.

"Eating apricot preserves?"

"You just told me about all your food and body issues, and here we are, stuffing our faces with jam. Am I co-ing you?"

"Co-ing?"

"You know. Being co-dependent. Enabling. Whatever."

216

"Where do you get this stuff?"

"Lesbian rap groups," I said. "Fiona."

"Right." Francine dropped her spoon into the sink. It rang against the old enamel like a distant bell.

That day seemed like it had happened a thousand years ago. Had Francine really wanted to marry me then? I'd written it off as insecurity. But maybe she had. The wind ripped through our hair. Down the field, twenty stunt kites danced a minuet across the cloudless sky. A huge Pooh bear, trailing a dripping pot of honey, billowed overhead.

Debbie squinted up into the sky. "You're getting married in three months. You two are going to need a *chuppah*." For thousands of years, Jewish couples have gotten married with the *chuppah* over their heads, a giant prayer-shawl, maybe, or a big piece of white fabric, raised at four corners by friends or relatives. According to Rabbi Loh, it was the *chuppah* that defined the sacred space in which that thing, that transformation from *lovers* to *beloveds* would take place, the same sacred space in which our parents, and *their* parents, had stood: the space of history, the space of timelessness. Debbie looked from me to Francine. "And I'm taking care of it." Her shoulders shone smooth and brown under the straps of her blue sundress. Could this be the same person who had told me there was no point in getting married if it wasn't legal?

I felt suddenly breathless. I opened my mouth, and the wind rushed in. "Wow," I inhaled. I knew she really was happy that Francine and I had decided to stay together indefinitely, but I didn't have any idea she would want to play a role in a wedding. "I thought you didn't really believe in lesbian weddings."

"Your wedding? Please." Debbie licked the salt from her fingers. "Anyway, I've changed my mind. Some people I know in New York are starting a group called Marriage Equality. This is starting to look like this might become our fight."

( )

"Did you see this?" Francine shook The Chronicle flat against the kitchen table. "There's an article in the Business section about your friend Charlie May."

"Charlie May?" I leaned over Francine's shoulder. Across the top of the page, the lead headline blared "Investors Go Gaga over IPOs."

Francine settled a finger on a much smaller headline in the lower right corner and read: "Arachnid Interactive, the Internet business development operation, filed for a $20 million initial public offering Thursday. Credit Suisse and Merrill Lynch & Co. are underwriting the IPO, blah blah blah." She skimmed the rest, a patois of numbers in the millions and billions. "Here." Francine jabbed at the page and continued: "Company CFO Charlie May said that Arachnid's numbers are very strong. 'We spin the web,' Mr. May told reporters."

"Wow," I said, though I realized, suddenly, a simple tenure-track position at Columbia or Yale, affairs with long-legged undergrads, fame of the provincial, academic sort would never have been enough for Charlie May.

"You know what this means?" Francine looked up.

That protean Charlie May was one of those people who knew how to be in the right place at the right time? That he probably would have been a Survivor? That he'd elevated to an art simply being Charlie May? "What?"

"Your friend Charlie May is a millionaire."

"No," I protested. He was lucky, I thought, but not that lucky.

"Yeah." Francine nodded coolly. "Probably." We both stared at the paper, trying to conjure the hidden smile under the studied, heavy-lidded gaze of CFO Charlie May.

"Poor guy." Francine folded the paper with a crisp snap.

"Why?" I asked, surprised. "You just said he's a gazillionaire."

Francine shook her head. "*Poor schmuck*. He always wanted you."

Poor Francine. I was glad she believed it. I stared at the dots that made up Charlie's face, then looked back at Francine, there in the flesh beside me, and told myself that all the money in the world could never equal what we had.

Which was a good thing, because we didn't have the money for the odd-sized envelopes our invitations required, and we were going to have to fold envelopes ourselves. Fortunately, Francine's best friend June and her girlfriend Trisha were suddenly *also* getting married. ("This is going to be such fun! Don't you realize? We can plan everything together!") These days, whenever June waved her hand, which she was doing quite a lot, her fingers sliced through the air with a blinding flash. That night, we planned to head up to the big family table at Betty and Sol's, the four of us, and get the envelopes done.

It had rained so much and so long that winter that everything on the edge of the park, instead of drying out to its annual golden stubble, stayed green, trailing vines of jasmine and trumpet vine twining around the stop signs near Sol and Betty's house. Francine pulled into the driveway, still carpeted with bright moss, Trisha and June in the back seat, the dappled light on their faces.

"It's so lovely to see you," June, parent-proper, gushed, while Betty took both of her hands. Trisha, towering next to Sol in front of the French doors, looked out over the green edges of the park like a king acknowledging another man's kingdom. Trisha turned to Betty. "You must be so proud—your oldest child getting married."

At that moment, Betty's smile stretched wider and froze there on her face, and she looked imploringly at Sol, who said, "Well."

Julia, I remembered.

We set ourselves up at the dining-room table, unpacking a thick stack of cream-colored paper, several glue sticks, and three pairs of scissors; a rubber stamp of our pomegranate tree, a pad of adhesive, a bottle of crimson embossing powder, and a hair dryer. June organized each article into its own tidy area, while Trisha sat at the head of the table, her white, waxed legs stretched out. In the kitchen, the discordant strains of the news sounded tinnily down the hall while Sol puttered around, preparing tea.

Francine picked up a creamy sheet of paper—a lightly speck-led French vanilla—and turned it over in her hands. Trisha, June and I watched as Francine held the sheet up, the three of us enchanted to a stupor by its shining blankness. We stared at the paper, the glue sticks, the fixative and the powder, as bewildered as if someone had demanded we turn them all into butterflies.

Like a sleeper struggling to wake, I, too, took a sheet from the top of the stack and squared it in front of me on the table. Slowly, Trisha took a sheet, and so did June.

Ten minutes later, we had not produced a single envelope.

Betty passed by, glanced into the dining room and stopped. June, looking up, twisted her diamond ring around her finger. I sat with my elbows stretched across the table, my chin perched against the heels of my hands. Trisha had uncapped a glue stick and sat twisting it all the way up and all the way down, the little torpedo of glue emerging and retracting like a remote-controlled phallus. Francine had let her sheet of paper drop, a frown of concentration creasing her forehead.

Without a word, Betty drew up a chair, pulled a fresh sheet from the stack of thirty-two-pound bond, swiveled it once left, then right, and began to fold. "Let's see," she said. In four quick folds, she had produced a neat, square envelope. She took the sample invitation between her fingers and slid it in, response card and all.

"Wow!" June crowed. "Mrs. Jaffe, you're incredible!"

"Now, if that were true," Betty answered, "Sol wouldn't still be in the kitchen, watching television." (I had never known Betty not to deflect a compliment, and, in that, she wasn't entirely unlike my own mother, who rarely missed an opportunity to interpret a compliment as an insult.) Betty straightened her shoulders, made a final, sharp crease and fit the sample invitation into a second, perfect envelope.

Trisha and I both reached for sheets of paper. Betty stopped us. "Girls, let's get organized." At her direction, June and Betty folded. Trisha glued. At the end of the line, I stamped the far right edge of each envelope with the rubber stamp dipped in fixative, and Francine dusted the sticky spot with crimson embossing powder, and we both watched in amazement as, under the hot blast of the dryer, the blood-red grains melted, swelled and settled into the smooth and shiny red form of our fruiting pomegranate. After ten envelopes, we stopped needing to throw every third envelope away; we were cranking them out.

Suddenly, there were no more envelopes. Francine and I looked up expectantly for the hitch in the line. But there was no hitch. In front of Betty and June, the white mound of paper had melted to nothing. Trisha had recapped her glue stick. At Francine's right elbow tottered three stacks of perfect envelopes, glossy red pomegranate trees bold on their far left edge like a Chinese imperial seal.

"Betty," I said, looking up at Francine's mother, her worry lines creased to softness at the corners, like a page that's been folded and re-folded many times. "Thank you," I said, true and simple gratitude flooding my whole heart for the mother of my fiancée, who had come in and, in her own straightforward way, put everything in order.

Betty stood, her magazine in her hand, turning to Sol's voice in the hall. She walked around the table, put an arm around me and an arm around Francine, drew us close to her tea-smelling cheeks and kissed us each. "I think I've done just about all that I can do," she said, lingering a moment before she left the room. "Now, go home, girls."

( )

Upstairs, in the red tile bathroom, my foot was peeling, thick, translucent sheets, the whorls and swirls of my print giving way to raw pink flesh underneath. And with the skin, I realized as I pulled the flat white balloons away from my foot pad, went my warts, the thick, painful nubs of them, where they'd pressed for months into my feet. Under the biggest one, in the depression it left, I found a tiny black splinter, small as a bee sting, which I gingerly picked out with the tip of the scissors.

By the eleventh of August, the first three response cards had arrived in the mail. Every day after that, cream-colored cards collected, slowly at first, and then in a windfall; they scattered like apple blossoms after spring rain across our little coffee table, where I hunched, checking off names against our list. By August 20th, we'd received over seventy replies.

"I hate to throw them away," I confessed, fingering the stack. I thought I could feel the idea of a wedding, and all the blind, lurching steps we had taken toward it taking shape in that compact rectangle, a pure, concrete reality, a moment about to be. I was good with the past. It was the future I could never see clearly.

"Here." Francine held out the recycle bin.

But, when I came down later, after peeling my foot, I found my beloved, a pair of dagger-sharp shears in her hand, slicing the perfect, crimson pomegranate tree from the crest of a reply card. A blood-red grove of trees spilled across the table. She looked surprised, caught in the headlights. "Our kids will love these things."

Our kids? The kids at the preschool? Or, *our* kids? I raised my eyebrows.

What else could it mean? Never a sentimental person—willing to throw out photographs if she thought the people in them looked bad—Francine wanted to commemorate our wedding; she wanted it to bear fruit; she wanted us to have kids together, and she wanted them to draw the long arc from the future back to the past. I decided not to rib her about the clutter.

And when, three days later, Francine suddenly lost interest in our children, and our wedding, and everything that went with it, I quietly piled the last dozen reply cards in the side-table drawer, saving them for the day when Francine might stock up her small, neat orchard of fruiting pomegranates against a future with which she could, I hoped, once again imagine filling our lives.

When the call came, I was crouching at the coffee table, stuffing a few late invitations—change-of-heart inclusions for my mother's side of the family. ("They won't come," my mother had assured herself, "but your father and I went to the son's daughter's bat mitzvah and we gave her a very generous gift.") Francine clutched the phone, mute, disconnected, in her hand. She moved toward the windows.

"My mom left."

"Where'd she go?" Two more envelopes, two more sets of stamps, two lines of glue stick.

Francine didn't answer.

I looked up from the clutter of my impromptu assembly station. Francine stood in front of the patio doors, the color drained from her face.

"What?"

Francine stared out the doors to the garden. Lit by the late afternoon, late summer light, she stood, a shadow, her mouth slightly open, her left hand clasped in a little birdcage over her heart. Finally, her dry lips parted. "My mom walked out on my dad."

I squinted at her figure, suddenly overcome by the contrast between the deep gold light behind her and the darkening shadow of Francine. *"What?"* The glue stick rolled off the table and hit the floor at my feet.

We found Sol hunched in his chair at the kitchen table, his forehead resting ponderously on the tips of his fingers. Wordlessly, he reached down to finger a piece of thick, blue paper. The note lay on the table untouched, inviolate as a murder weapon:

> *Dear Sol,*
> *It's time we faced the truth. I'm not in love with you. I never have been. I think we both realize, we should never have gotten married. I can't watch the rest of my life go by on my knees in that damned garden. I'll get in touch when I am settled.*
> *Betty*

Not a word or letter had been crossed out. It was either a letter Betty had practiced over and over in blue ballpoint on the yellow legal pads in the kitchen drawer, working at it, distilling it, until she had every word precisely measured, or it was a letter she'd been inspired to compose in a lightning strike of clarity, and gotten right the very first time. I stared at the page.

Francine looked up. "Was there something . . .?" she started. "Did you . . .?"

Sol turned, his palms up, empty, surrendered. He considered Francine, reached out his large, empty hand and filled it with Francine's warm cheek. At that moment, she looked very small. Sol looked very old.

I wanted to leave them alone. I left the kitchen and found myself wandering down the hall, past Betty and Sol's bedroom, down toward my own reflection in the mirror, watching myself get larger, the double doors to Betty and Sol's bedroom shrinking behind me to a point. When it looked as if I would have to step into the mirror to go any further, I slipped right into the passage to Francine's old room, the room where Betty and I sat together on Sunday nights after dinner, where Betty sewed, and I watched. It was a small room; when the door swung open, the walls sighed back with a hush. I don't know what I expected. The room was empty. Betty's sewing machine stood, silent, bowed, on the table. Beside it, in the sewing basket, threads from sheared pieces of fabric trailed out like broken veins.

"Where do you think she went?" I wondered as we drove home through the fog.

"She could be anywhere, Ellen," Francine whined, a razor-thin edge in her voice, "and we'd never fucking find her. She's spent the last twenty-five years helping women disappear!"

At home, the glue stick still lay on the living-room floor, underneath the coffee table littered with flayed envelopes I hadn't yet glued shut, the innards—invitations, reply cards, stamps—scattered across the table's cramped surface. Francine threw her keys down on top of it, stepped out of her shoes, and went directly upstairs to bed.

I felt cold, accused, immobile and terribly, terribly sad. I loved Sol and Betty, and now Betty had broken all our hearts. I quietly gathered up the reply cards and tucked them out of sight. "Come on," I whispered to the dogs.

The light was off in the bedroom, but I could see Francine's shape hunched under the covers in the streetlight from Broadway, unmoving. Lola leapt onto the bed and, with a turn, settled down at Francine's feet and heaved a deep, animal sigh of fatigue.

I didn't want to turn on the light, wash my face or brush my teeth, do anything that would suggest the world was normal, the same world we had gone to bed in last night, or the night before. Instead, I peeled off my clothes where I stood and climbed under the covers. "I'm so sorry," I whispered, taking Francine's lifeless hand in mine.

When I woke up, Francine was gone. Her side of the bed lay barren, flat and cool as a wound with the scab peeled off. I choked awake, inarticulate with fear, scrabbled into the bathroom and peered into the blood-red darkness: empty. The toilet, which had started to run, endlessly sighed. I stared into the mirror like a figure in a dream; billowing shirt, startled eye-whites, and floating hair gaped back.

Down the deep, narrow stairs, the early gloom gave way to pale, cool, yellow-blue eastern light seeping through the French doors. I didn't find Francine in the living room. I panicked, grabbed my keys, dropped them, knelt and banged my head on the back of the futon as I rose, softly cursing.

"Mmm." A groan from the couch arrested me. I held my breath, and made out dark, streaming tendrils of hair among the fringes of the crocheted blanket. I stared. Pressed into the crease of the futon where a dark emptiness had been, a breathing darkness now appeared: Francine, asleep, one pale arm flung up over her face. I reached down and shook her.

"What?" Francine croaked. Her pale, creased eyes opened in fear. When she saw me, her arms tightened around her chest, gripping the edges of her robe where they met, holding it shut over the bones of her breast the way Gramma Sophie's black seam had held shut the gaping doors of her heart. "I'm tired," Francine sighed, shutting her eyes.

Upstairs, in the dark bedroom, I huddled beneath the sink and shook, remembering: bright early morning light, white sheets with flowers on them, pale, hollowed with Gramma Sophie's shape, a smooth, oval moon scooped out. Three years old, I'd bolted up to Jacob's dream: a stream of firefighters in and out of the living room, heavy angels in burlap coats, black boots. I actually clung to my mother. Her white gown fluttered around me in the searing morning light. "Gramma Sophie had a heart attack," she said.

I huddled next to the dogs on the floor, long after Francine shut her eyes again and slept, and traced the ghost of the scar in my palm, and remembered the day Francine had told me she wouldn't leave me. Blocks away, a BART train rushed down the tracks, a wind whistling through a keyhole corridor, gathering speed, direction, distance, howling its fixed path away, away. "Listen," Sam murmured into the phone, three hours ahead. "This is a big loss." She spoke in quiet, capital letters. BIG LOSS. I thought of Francine, alone in the living room. "For *you*."

A week passed. Then two. Down our block, a line of pomegranate trees stood heavy with pale September fruit. I laughed at myself, bitterly, for never having noticed these trees, for noticing them now. Whether or not she intended it, Betty couldn't have chosen a more disastrous time to go. Had she given us a whole year, we might have mourned, ranted, coped and moved on. But with just six weeks to go before Francine and I were supposed to exchange rings, Betty had given us just enough time to doubt, and no time to recover.

I reached up. The fruit hung low enough to pluck. It was like the Persephone myth, but backwards. The mother had disappeared into Hades; the daughter, abandoned, spent her season in cold torment. Except, there was no fixed season for this grief.

I didn't touch the fruit. I didn't dare. I knew that this sadness, like all sadness for this one, archetypal loss, the mother loss, could go on and on.

( )

The High Holy Days loomed, taunting us with the idea of redemption and return. I wish I could say that we clung together, Francine and I, in those long days after Betty left, but something inside of each of us made us cling to our sadness harder, each to our own cold, cleaving blade of betrayal. We should have keened together. We should have released our grief, like a flock of dark birds, into the sky. But we didn't. When disaster struck, we had scattered. It was like she blamed me.

Debbie, June and Sam all said the same thing: Give her time. "We don't have time," I'd complained. "If we wait too much longer, we'll have to cancel the wedding."

"So," Debbie answered calmly, "you'll cancel the wedding. You'll try again."

"Cancel the wedding!" I screamed. "Have you ever planned a fucking wedding?!"

I suppose we could have gone on this way indefinitely, dodging calls from the florist and the DJ, had we not had our seventh premarital counseling appointment already scheduled with Rabbi Loh. Francine hadn't suggested we cancel. I think she wanted his blessing. We didn't talk much on the drive down.

Francine was the one who told him about Betty. I was the one who suggested postponing. Rabbi Loh templed his fingers. I expected him to close his eyes solemnly and tell us to take all the time that we needed.

Rabbi Loh didn't close his eyes. "In Jewish tradition," he told us, "a wedding takes primacy above almost everything. Even—" Rabbi Loh blinked—"God forbid, in the case of the death of a parent"—here Rabbi Loh looked deeply pained—"our tradition *requires us* to proceed."

Francine looked at him as if she hadn't heard correctly.

"We may stand under the *chuppah* crying tears of sadness as well as tears of joy," he explained, patient as a father, though he was the same age we were, "but Jewish continuity holds the celebration of Jewish unions above almost all things." He frowned like he was sorry, sorry he couldn't tell us just to cancel. He stared at Francine with eyes black and impenetrable as silt from the banks of the Vlatva.

On the way home, Francine and I fought. Underneath us, the Dumbarton Bridge rose up, unfurling its long track flat across the Bay alongside the big, blue flats of the old salt ponds. Francine looked weary. "The rabbis weren't talking about us. It was meant for straights. It's about having babies."

That was probably true. But it wasn't exactly what Rabbi Loh had said. And he'd said it to us. Not to heterosexuals. "Just because we're two women, doesn't mean we're not going to have babies." At this point, everything we said about our relationship, we said in safe generalities. Otherwise, I might have said, "You and I are going to have babies, don't you remember, Francine? *Our* kids."

"Having children is dangerous." Francine didn't take her eyes off the road. "Something happens to the kid, and the relationship is ruined. Do you really want to invest something else with that much power?"

That came out of left field. Then I remembered: Julia.

"Anyway," I back-pedaled. "We don't have to decide this now." I stared out the window at the water, the straight, dark sheet of the Bay, rushing by.

"We're supposedly getting married," Francine said. Her tone scared me; she sounded barely controlled, secretly frantic. I wished I were driving. "We do have to decide it now. Especially now."

"Your life is all about kids." I wanted to remind her that we had our own lives. She had her own life, apart from her parents.

"I know." Francine shifted gears with an alarming jerk. "Other people's kids."

I bit my lips. What would it be worth to keep her here, to keep her from driving, frantically, away from me? "If you don't want to have kids, we won't."

At its eastern end, the bridge practically sits on the water, four thin lanes dividing the waters to the north from the waters to the south. The car raced along between them like a skimming stone.

"You think you can say that," Francine answered, "but you can't, because when you start to want them, you can't stop. I've seen it."

Since when had my biological clock started ticking? Francine had wanted kids just as much as I did. Now she was pinning it on me, and there was no way to convince her of anything. "I don't know what you want me to say."

"Maybe we need to really think about whether we can make this commitment. Can we really promise we want the same things for the rest of our lives? Can anyone promise that?" Francine was the one who had always talked me out of questions like that. I didn't know what to say. Francine's words hung there, like the thin line of cars so precipitously streaming over the water.

I took a deep breath. The words to a Hebrew song popped into my mind: "Kol ha'olam kulo/Gesher tsar me'od." *The whole world is a very narrow bridge. . . . And the main thing is, not to be afraid.* "Francine," I said, calmly as a police officer talking someone down from a ledge, "This isn't about us. This is about your mother."

"Ellen." Francine shifted the car with another jerk and turned to me with an alarming coldness, a coldness I had never seen in her warm features. "Are you having an affair?"

"What?" The breathlessness of my terror at what was happening inside this car, at the speed with which we were traveling on such a narrow road, collided in an instant with my disbelief. "What are you *talking* about?"

"The whispered phone calls, the torn-up receipts," Francine answered without missing a beat. "I've called you at work, and you're not there." When I was with Anya. Tears rolled silently down her cheeks, but her face stayed cold. "You've been lying to me."

"No," I protested. "You don't understand." It was exactly the kind of thing a cheater would say.

"Don't I?" She smiled, a smile of inevitable sadness.

"Francine," I pleaded. "This is crazy talk. I love you. You love me." I shook.

"I'm not sure." Francine squinted into the rearview mirror. "I'm not sure that's enough."

( )

I'll admit right now, my reaction to this accusation wasn't logical. Instead of prodding me to contrition, to simple remorse, Francine's accusation inflamed a righteous anger in me that Betty's departure had already sparked. How could Francine even think I might have been unfaithful, when what I was doing was trying my hardest to keep a love alive? Anya's and Batsheva's. I had written a letter to Batsheva at the Rose of Sharon Home and heard nothing. And I'd almost let it go at that. But after Betty left, I thought: *Why do we have to accept this?*

I resolved to call Batsheva. But first, I had to tell Wendy. The baby was coming soon. It was time. "Do you remember Anya Kamenets?" I asked Wendy. "A woman you interviewed once, a couple years ago?"

Wendy, breathing a little heavily at her desk, frowned intensely behind her glasses. How on earth would she remember one old lady from another, simply by her name? Before she could cut in, I went on, "I know, we have limits—" Above Wendy's desk, Chagall's sad, *tallis*-wrapped Jew clutched his Torah of truth, pensive and alone. "I just wanted to let you know—" I took a huge breath.

"Ellen—" Wendy started. I expected her to object. I expected her to swivel her chair and adjust her glasses and remind me of what I'd come to think of as the Foundation's "Prime Directive"—an old phrase from Francine's and my *Star Trek: Next*

Generation days. In the 24th century: no interference in the development of other civilizations; in the Foundation's case, no involvement in the lives of our witnesses. I expected her, quite possibly, to fire me. Instead, Wendy gasped; she stood up in a gush of blood.

Lots of blood.

Instantly, I had the phone in my hand.

When I dropped it, I found Wendy on the floor, clutching herself. Her face had gone completely white. I tried not to panic. "The ambulance is coming—right now," I said. Then, because I wasn't sure what else to do, I stayed beside her and held her hand.

The good thing, it turns out, about working for a major Jewish organization in a major downtown area of a major city, is that, when you dial 911, about a million sirens start blaring at once. Wendy and I could hear them racing down Market Street, getting closer every second, and the tremulous wail of those sirens, threading down Market like a living umbilicus, helped us breathe when we couldn't breathe for ourselves.

The emergency caused confusion in the building, and everyone started to evacuate. By the time the paramedics had Wendy on a stretcher, the women from Development in their capri pants and the old ladies from the Post-Soviet Jewish Diaspora Project were already standing on the sidewalk outside, murmuring excitedly about a bomb. As I raced along next to the gurney, I caught a glimpse of Barbara from upstairs. Barbara saw me, and then she saw Wendy, and she broke out of the pack, running, her one short leg trailing half a beat behind. I held out my arm, expecting Barbara to reach out and clutch me, but she sprinted past, and as they lifted the stretcher, she vaulted straight up into the back of the ambulance.

"I'm sorry, ma'am." The paramedic waved his blue glove warningly.

Barbara from upstairs answered without missing a beat, "I'm her mother," and plunked down next to the stretcher, clutching Wendy's IV'd hand. I watched the doors shut on them; then the ambulance, casting its sanguine glow on the crowd, the sidewalk, the shining windows of the Foundation for the Preservation of Memory, drove, screaming, away. When I looked down, I saw that I had blood on my shoes.

I trudged heavily up the stairs with Mi'Chelle—it felt like an emergency; in an emergency, everyone remembered, you're not supposed to use the elevators—and picked up the phone and dialed the Rose of Sharon Home in Tel Aviv.

Seventy-five hundred miles east and nine hours into the future, dusky and ancient consonants murmured in the background: a nurses' station, possibly, bright with morning light off the Mediterranean, the crisp crackle of *Ha'Aretz*, the squealing of carts loaded with Galilee oranges. "A moment, please."

I was back in the ether, between worlds.

Then, the hush of an office, the voice of efficiency: "*Shalom. Slicha?*"

"Shalom. Hello. I'm trying to reach a resident, Batsheva Singer."

"Batsheva Singer?"

The woman at the Rose of Sharon Home in Tel Aviv sounded bored. "I'm sorry, Miss—?"

"Margolis."

"Miss Margolis. I'm sorry, Miss Margolis—"

There was a lag on the line, a transcontinental, trans-Atlantic echo, so that my first words crossed hers and I had to ask her to repeat them.

"I am sorry to tell you, Miss Margolis, that Mrs. Singer died nine months ago."

I got off the phone and rubbed my eyes. When I opened them, Mi'Chelle was standing in front of me. "Wendy's had an emergency C." Mi'Chelle started to smile. "But she's fine. They have a brand-new little baby boy." Tears sprang to my eyes. "Leo." Mi'Chelle looked about as pleased as if she'd popped Leo out herself. "Leo Micah Rosenberg. Six pounds, six ounces."

As soon as Mi'Chelle left, the telephone started ringing. It had already been an emotional day. I didn't know if I could handle any more. "Hey, Stranger." I couldn't place the voice, a young woman's. Only two young women ever called me at the office—Fiona and Francine. Fiona was long gone. And Francine?

My mind hung in the space between familiarity and recognition for an audible beat. But my heart, which had beat its slow, relentless dirge for the past two weeks, quickened.

"I haven't been away *that* long, have I?" asked Jill.

"I've never heard your voice on the phone before," I fudged.

"I've been so unbelievably busy," Jill started, misunderstanding.

"No, it's okay," I cut in, before she could apologize for not calling. "Me, too." I sat back in my chair. Same lonely Chagall print. Same old pile of magazines. Same old picture of Francine. Meanwhile, Jill had *schlepped* across the continent, started a new job, become a professor, object, no doubt, of a thousand crushes.

"I'm in San Francisco." Jill's voice rose over a sudden wave of other voices. "At *Mid-Century and Beyond*." At one point, a conference like that would be something Annie Talbot would have encouraged me to attend. "It's crazy," Jill said. "I'm moderating three panels and giving a paper."

"Wow."

"Listen," she cut in, "I don't think I can break away here. But I was wondering if you might be able to come to the hotel after my panel this afternoon." Then she added, "If it's okay with the Mrs." I glanced at Francine's photo on my desk.

"She's not the Mrs. yet," I answered.

Jill laughed. I didn't.

Neither one of us said anything.

"Oh," Jill said.

( )

The lobby of the Grand Hyatt in Union Square buzzed with the catchphrases of my forgotten, academic tongue. "If it were up to the New Historicists . . . ," a coiffed professorial type intoned, addressing her retinue. I could hear loud laughter as they disappeared down the hall. Grad students in Dockers and Oxford shirts in strange, shimmery blues glided along under twinkling chandeliers like fish in a tank. Thank god, I sucked in a breath, I didn't know any of them anymore.

Just then, Jill's sleek, dark head appeared around the corner. She was wearing a long, tan sweater jacket that fell open in the front; a necklace made of tiny steel dice gathered in the hollow at the base of her throat.

Jill and I fell into our own conspiratorial conversation, pressing shoulders as we wandered through the halls, gossiping about the professors in Jill's department, about people we both knew. Her face shone. As I talked to her, I tried to ignore the fact that Jill, in her long, tan coat and black boots, looked beautiful. Instead, I found myself blurting out the news of Sheva's death, confessing finally to my extreme over-involvement. Just telling Jill the entire truth felt like a betrayal of Francine. But why did that matter, when I'd already been accused of it?

"Are you going to tell Anya that Batsheva is dead?" As always, Jill went straight to the heart of it.

"I don't know," I admitted. "I feel like it's my fault. For all

236

those years, Anya probably thought Batsheva had died—an escape plan gone wrong—and then, when I told her that Sheva had submitted a death record for Anya, after the War was over, I resurrected her. Am I going to kill her *now*? And make her wonder why, after all this time, they never found each other before it was too late?"

Jill nodded thoughtfully. We'd made our way toward the hotel café and we let ourselves be jostled along toward the front of the line. "You don't think it's possible, do you, Ellen," Jill fixed her eyes on mine, "that two people who really love each other could knowingly spend their entire lives apart?"

I squinted under the hard light of Jill's stare, and couldn't decide whether I felt stripped, or seen, or both. Maybe I did need to believe that it's impossible for two lovers to deny a burning spark for a lifetime. Because, then, by some reverse math, it couldn't be possible to hide a lack of love for a lifetime, either, and Betty's note would have to be a lie. I was focusing on Anya and Batsheva, on Betty and Sol. But maybe I was purposely overlooking something else, something right in front of me.

I turned away from Jill. There, down the corridor that led toward one of the hotel's many ballrooms, Annie Talbot stared back.

My mouth opened, but no sound came out. I stepped out of the line and walked, trancelike, toward Annie Talbot's face.

"Ellen!" Jill called after me.

"Professor Oey!" a voice called out, and I heard Jill respond.

I stepped into the dark, spotlit hall, through the intermittent light, down the hush of the carpeted corridor toward my lost adviser's face.

It was Annie Talbot. Bigger than life. Propped on a tripod, a placard announced the publication of her last, posthumous book: *Martyrs to a Cause*. Below it, a caption announced, "*Annie Talbot's Brilliant Final Study of Self-Sacrifice*" and a talk at 3 p.m. that day by one of the professors who had given a eulogy at her memorial service. Once again, I'd come too late.

Jill caught me by the sleeve. "Did you know her?"

237

I turned to Jill in the near dark, my face palpably ashen. "She was my adviser."

I heard the murmur of Jill's name. "Professor Oey!" a pursuing voice called out.

"Come on." Jill grabbed my arm and started walking fast down the hall, away from the café and the plates piled with field greens, away from the voices of her students, away from the looming, unchanged face of Annie Talbot. At the other end of the hall, a green light beckoned: *Exit*.

Jill led me into the stairwell and up, floor after floor, through a dark corridor, past an abandoned room service cart and a heap of white towels, toward the elevator. We burst out onto the rooftop garden, the entire city laid out beneath us like the model of a city, and breathed.

Jill told me about her mother, who lived alone in New York and wanted Jill to come back. "First, it was just the Jewish thing. Now it's everything." Then Jill, who had just published a three-part article on social responsibility for *The Journal of Genocide Studies*, said, "Sometimes I do regret," flicking the long belt of her tan sweater, "that our moral fabric depends so heavily on the expectations of other people."

It seemed Jill and I stood, at that moment, just balanced on the skin of the earth. If you fix your eye long enough on some terrible, reason-defying scene—a mountain of shoes, for example, or a ravine, deep enough to conceal villages of the dead—your mind can go, eventually, to nihilism. You can go down into the meaningless dark, the dark that swallowed Primo Levi, that swallowed Annie Talbot. But it can go the other way, too: toward the manic freedom of the kind that lets you do anything you want, untethered by a world without meaning, without consequence, without God. It can happen to any of us.

What would it be like, I wondered, watching the Bay Bridge strung out over the dark gray gap, just now twinkling with light, to let go of Annie Talbot and her unquenchable depression—to turn back the clock, for a day or two, on Sol and his broken heart, on Betty and her secrets—to simply forget, just for a few hours, about me and Francine? What would it be like to give up the depressed kind of nihilism for the manic? To give in to the wild freedom of a world without meaning?

Jill and I stared out at the lights of the City. To the west, a white, obscuring fog hung low over the surface of the water, promising to obliterate the day's details; the towers of the Golden Gate hovered, unanchored, in the air. We stood over the city, watching each precise object—car, rooftop, suspension tower—turn into the shadow of itself.

Jill stood up, her sweater falling long behind her, and we walked silently back to the stairwell, side by side. When we got to Room 832, Jill paused. "This is me," she said. The hair from her bun stuck out at odd angles behind her smooth, dark head, the perfect symmetry of her teeth. Then she cocked her head into the nondescript bedroom, whose curtains hadn't yet been drawn against the night city. She tilted her head toward the big window through which the fading city looked ordered and still. She said, "Come in."

( )

Something always shifts in September, a morning every year that feels like school starting, a different kind of morning dark, when you wake up and realize: *Summer's over.* That was the day we found the letter from Betty, tucked in the flurry of fall circulars, postmarked Honolulu.

"Are you going to open it?"

Francine just looked at the envelope. In the corner, where the return address goes, Betty had written her and Sol's address in Berkeley. "Not yet," she answered, picking at the envelope with her nail.

We sat looking out the back window for a while. "I'm going to L.A. tomorrow."

Francine's head whipped around so fast, I thought she might turn into butter. I don't know why it didn't occur to me that Francine would be surprised by this news—maybe because I'd felt like we were so far apart at this point, real distance hardly mattered. Maybe because I'd already been accused of cheating, it didn't feel like betrayal. But I could see right away—before she'd managed to make her mouth look resolute—that she felt stricken, as if I'd actually struck her.

"I'm sorry," I backpedaled. "It, it just came up." (I'd gotten a call at the office that morning from a guy named Jeff Katz, "about a project we're starting here out of L.A. The world's largest data

240

base of testimony from the Shoah. We're looking for experienced oral historians to join our team.")

"It's just for the weekend." I didn't mention that it was a job interview. But, faced with the proof of my desertion—she'd known it, all along—Francine had already drawn back into herself, determined not to care. If only I'd recognized that stoicism for the terrified vulnerability that it was, we might have closed our distance, right then and there.

Instead, I found myself throwing dress clothes into a suitcase, contemplating a life hundreds of miles away from her. "How long will you be in L.A.?" Francine asked. She was lying on our bed, paging through *The New Yorker* while I packed.

As weird as the prospect of returning to L.A. seemed—really returning—it was nowhere as awful as the prospect of having a life in the Bay Area without Francine.

"Until Tuesday," I said, stacking up three clean shirts. "Listen," I told her. "I'm interviewing for a job." Then I added, as if it wasn't clear, "In L.A."

"Oh," Francine said; she'd looked up from the magazine. "You don't like L.A."

"I like L.A.," I countered. "I just don't want to live in L.A. again."

"Exactly."

"But if you and I aren't going to get married, I don't want to be here. I can't stay here if we're not together." As I lifted my black pants out of the bottom drawer, I tried not to imagine lifting out all of my clothes, packing all of my books, separating all of the things Francine and I shared and taking all of them away. I had never been able to pull off *goodbye* without leaving.

"Is this an ultimatum?" Francine rolled up the magazine, over and over, as it turned in her hands.

"Getting married—that's an ultimatum. You can't decide to spend the rest of your life with someone—you can't go through all of what we've been through to get ready for that—and then undecide it. We can't go back and act like none of that happened."

"You don't have to yell," Francine said quietly, pulling her curls back from her face with both hands. The magazine lay on the bed, defeated. "But you're right—" Outside, a car radio played the new Alanis Morissette song. "I need to think about it," she admitted, finally.

"Well, I'll be gone for two days." I shoved my shirts into the case. "You can think about it all you like."

"Okay," she said simply.

You're uninvited, Alanis sang. Then someone turned the car off and, outside on the sidewalk, the door slammed shut.

( )

The interview went ridiculously well. Which is to say, they offered me the job on the spot. "Do you have a family?" the woman—there was a whole team—asked me as she handed me the official packet. "We expect to have a lot, a lot of travel." Israel, Poland, England. A brilliant, career-boosting job, an ideal job for a single person. I'd be leaving Anya, too.

I didn't say anything about the wedding to my parents when I met them in Westwood that afternoon. Though, desperately miserable and miserably desperate, I'd wanted nothing more than an authentic, maternal voice to say, "I'm so, so sorry. It will all be okay." (Lured by the siren call of that hallucinated voice, I had already told my mother that Betty had left. My mother was in the pied-a-terre in Laguna Beach, packing for spring in Sydney. She didn't mince words: "You know, Ellen, children from broken homes are much more likely to get divorced themselves. Statistically speaking." My mother's voice was crisp. She was folding freshly ironed linen into neat, pastel squares. "You don't have to go through with this. It's not too late.")

Fortunately, during lunch, my mother didn't say anything negative about Francine. They didn't say anything about Francine at all. I think they were hoping that if they just never mentioned Francine, the whole thing, wedding and all, would go away.

As we waited for the *salade des tomates et mozzarella*, my father, who had been listening intently to the conversation at the next table, leaned in to my mother and whispered, "You have some jam on your lips." It was their secret code; it meant, "I'm eavesdropping; I'll tell you later." Then my father went on talking investments; my mother nodded along.

I thought about Charlie May and his millions; who said I needed to stay in scholarship at all? Maybe I'd peel off, like Charlie May, and make piles of money, and Francine would read about me in the Business section and feel deep regret.

"Have you thought about selling real estate on the internet?" I asked my father. These people, after all, might be all I had left.

"The internet." My mother made a pinched face. "It's just a craze."

My father slid an envelope across the table. "This is the money we promised you." For my wedding. He said it like I was holding someone he loved hostage. How ironic that they were giving it to me now, when it was probably too late.

I kissed my parents goodbye at the big lot on Wilshire, knowing that I wouldn't see them again until they'd come back from the other side of the planet, just in the nick of time for the wedding—or, possibly, just in time for nothing at all. Standing at the corner, my mother clutched me fiercely in both arms, as if trying to squeeze out the last few drops of something, then turned and walked away with my father without a second look.

( )

Out the airplane window, rolling brown foothills divided Hayward from the East. "Slam dunk." That's what the head of the Voices project had said; my graduate work in history, plus my professional experience, made it a "slam dunk." Could I come back for a kick-off meeting in October?

October. Our wedding date loomed, close as the rising hills, just four weeks away, all the big pieces in place, all the little pieces—pick up the rings, the shoes—hovering in the air like a swarm of bees, poised for the cue to swirl together into a single, directed vector of concentrated focus. But everything had stopped, and those little pieces, those hovering bits, now threatened to break apart. I peered out the window at the pink and white salt flats. I'd already begun to turn my despair into something like that, huge and salt-filled and dead, but beautiful, seen from a distance. We'd be landing in minutes.

I zipped *Tipping the Velvet* into my backpack and put the tray table up. Would Francine be home when I got there? Was I heading home right now? Or were the poles of my life about to reverse? I wasn't sure I could become an Angeleno again. I wouldn't be going back, I told myself. I'd be starting over. *Maybe*, I thought, as I shuffled off the plane behind a line of impatient commuters.

Someone grabbed my elbow; the passengers disembarking behind me mumbled obscenities and parted around us. "Ellen," Francine panted. She wasn't supposed to be there. She looked pale, white on white.

"What's wrong?" Had Sol done something desperate? Had he had a heart attack? Could our situation possibly get any worse?

Francine steered me toward an empty gate. Outside the big windows, the sun had just begun to set. "There was a crash," she said. "A bad one."

I didn't understand. *Sol? Who?* I gripped her arm.

"A plane crash," the words rushed out of Francine's mouth. "Just now."

Outside the window, an empty baggage train rolled past. I imagined Francine rushing to the airport to find out if I was alive or dead. I wondered if she was relieved, or disappointed.

Francine wiped her nose. "I'm not really explaining this well. The whole time you were gone, I couldn't stop thinking about that goddamned note. I needed to figure it out: Could I ever say to myself, or to you—" Francine fixed her gaze on me "—I never loved you, you never loved me?" Over the PA, Boarding Group A got called to gate 23. "I called my mother last night."

Francine looked at the flat brown carpeting. "I expected her to have some kind of answer, but, from the minute I called, it was all chitchat." Francine kicked at my bag with her foot. Her voice dropped to a fierce whisper. "I was so *pissed*. She didn't even mention my dad. Finally, I told her off, Ellen. I told her she needed to take responsibility for what she'd done to our family."

"What did she say?"

"Ha. Said she'd done that long enough, thanks. Said she knew it would take time, but I'd get over my anger. It's like she was just done with being my dad's wife, and done with being our mom, too, I guess. It's like she's gone insane."

"And then there was a crash?" I imagined Betty, wild-haired, careening her rental car over a Pacific island cliff.

Francine gently picked up my hand. "There's been a terrible plane crash. Near Canada. It went down in the ocean and no one knows why. I felt so, so scared. What if it had been you?" Francine gripped my hand so hard it hurt. *Could you trust the feelings that came from that all-or-nothing place?*

A line of twinkling lights stretched across the sky to the south; the closest wobbled and hovered, approaching, then materialized into an airplane and rolled smoothly onto the tarmac, slowed, turned and began its mundane taxi toward the gate.

"Listen," she said, "I don't know what's been going on with you." She put up her hand so I couldn't protest. "And this stuff with my mom—" I softened a little "—it's been confusing. But I think I can start separating us from them. I have to believe in us."

I looked out the big plate-glass window. A Southwest jet lumbered slowly back from the gate, a man with long orange sticks waving it on. "I wanted to walk away from you so I wouldn't lose you. But people can disappear," Francine whispered, "really disappear. Just like that. I want to hold onto you." She looked at me, but didn't take my hand. "If you want to stay."

I could still taste the stale airplane air in my mouth, could hear the thundering white noise of the jet engines, could feel the steady hum of flight under my feet. Francine stood up, waiting. She was asking me to trust her. "Let's go home," I said.

The house smelled like cedar and wood smoke.

"They offered me the job," I told Francine. "But L.A. was . . . L.A." For some reason, though I hadn't even gone there, my thoughts zeroed in, right then, on the house on Dunsmuir Drive; I was thinking of the long, dark hall to my parents' bedroom, and the distance between me and my mother, and of her hidden lace. I was thinking of my old closet, where Francine had stood in her underpants on the day of my sister's wedding, emptied of all of Gramma Sophie's things, emptied of all my things. I shrugged. "I can't go back."

Francine and I stood quietly together at the foot of our bed. She had met my parents at the house on Dunsmuir Road, and my Gramma Sophie. I wondered if she was thinking of her own home, and how much of it Betty had taken away when she left. "Come here," she whispered. "I'll be your home." We stepped out of our clothes, into our red bathroom, its rusty tiles red as the inside of the human heart.

( )

Two girls, young women, emerge from the shade of the pine forest. The blond girl's stray fingers pick leaves from the other girl's hair. Then thunder rolls through the ground. Over the Ninth Fort, the sky breaks into a thousand small pieces, the cry of old men, the first sounds of the slaughter. For the first time, the two girls fear something more than they fear discovery. They fly to the city, fly to their mothers. (Girls! Go back! Lovers! Back to the forest!) Later, after it is far too late to fly, the blond girl will have plenty of time to stare up from behind barbed walls, into the sky, which she sees now is perfectly empty, and wish for the stork that will come down out of nowhere to carry her lover—the dark one, the one no one will mistake for anything but a Jew—far away.

( )

Anya insults my shoes, so I know she's happy to see me. It's been longer than I intended since I've gotten over to the Rose of Sharon. But Anya doesn't ask any questions. She wears her straight blond hair, as always, pulled back. Her eyes and mouth, downward parentheses bracketing both sadness and love, as always, give nothing away.

We sit down on the couch. I've brought her late summer peaches.

"Did I ever tell you," Anya started, as I sliced into a peach;

247

deep veins of crimson ran red through the flesh. "About the first time I tasted an orange?" I shook my head. I hadn't heard Anya's story, though I had heard other people's versions of that story—the story that began with a disembarkation, a grocery stall on the streets of New York; the story that began at a busy Mediterranean port, Tel Aviv, the whole brilliant world cupped in one hand, fruit of the Galilee; the simple bright tang of life, antidote to ashes.

"Sheva brought it for me." I looked up, surprised. "We were teaching each other English, dreaming of America. A taste for a color!" Anya looked with unabashed longing at the photo of Batsheva, as if she could still taste that word, and the woman who had brought it to her, in her mouth. "We shared it," she said.

I handed Anya a slice of the peach, and she set the photo of Batsheva carefully, face down, in her lap.

"Have there ever been others?" I asked her. Who can account for my boldness? Did it matter, now that I'd broken all the rules?

Anya gave a curt, dismissive nod. "They all wanted to talk." Her gaze shifted to the window, the wedge of peach, a still life, neglected in her hand.

I considered the ripe fruit in that wrinkled hand. Then I shifted my gaze, too, toward the window, toward the huge blue sky. I had been right all along. Somehow, though, instead of triumph, I felt disappointment. I considered Anya, and her lifetime of waiting, and all of a sudden, I wanted to run, hard and fast, back to my own life.

Instead, I bit into the peach. The last of the summer burst in wild flowers across my tongue. I sucked the fiber from between my teeth. I wiped the juice dripping down my chin and glanced at the back of the photo. The little clasp on the back had worn a groove, a grayed-out rainbow, where it had been pushed open and shut many times.

In three days, it would be Rosh Hashanah, the time for return, the time for confession, the time for repentance. I needed to tell Anya that Batsheva had died. But I'd already waited too long. Instead, I slipped my hand into my bag and pulled out a piece of cream-colored card stock. Anya flinched. For the first time, I realized the shining crimson ink crowning the card was the color of blood.

"What do you want from me?"

"I don't want anything," I lied. But I did. I had never had the courage to come out to my own grandmother. I wanted something different. I slid the invitation across the transparent, unbroken surface of the table. "I'm getting married." Anya left the envelope between us, untouched.

( )

Sol looked the same, kneeling in the garden in his old corduroy pants, his gloved hand extended, finger pointed down with the cold poise of a surgeon, or a murderer, wrapped around the reedy tendon of a weed. When he pulled it, the entire weed came up with its roots dangling like a tangle of pale hair. "It's no good unless you get the root." He shook the loose dirt from the root back into the grass. "It'll just come back again." He kept on, working the ground with spade and glove, uprooting tenacious, stringy tendrils of dandelion and mint, whose crushed leaves smelled of dusky earth and chewing gum. As he plucked, he bundled his leavings into a careful pile.

I don't know what I'd expected. That the grass would shriek where Betty's knees no longer pressed it? That he'd let the garden grow crazy, overgrown with grief? Sol did, we did, what people do to survive: We just went on.

Inside, Francine got the plates out of the cupboard. Jigme swung in, garlic-and-chili-wafting bags of Chinese food swaying behind him like a censer. We'd returned to as close a version of normalcy as the four of us could bear: On Sunday nights, Francine and I and Jigme—and sometimes Jigme's new girlfriend Anne—all came over, one of us bearing take-out, and we set the kitchen table, and resumed, in our own, revised fashion, Sunday night dinner.

"So." Sol cleared his throat, reaching behind his head with one hand to smooth down the hair at the back of his neck. (Betty had used to cut it; now a tentative line had begun, covering his tanned nape with a budding forest of curling white tendrils.) It was a habit he must have acquired as a boy. "I called her today."

Francine set her glass down with an audible thunk. Anne and I exchanged glances. I liked Anne. She wore little wire-framed glasses, the same shape as Jigme's, and, before Jigme, he'd told us, Anne had dated Elizabeth.

Sol heaped a glistening mound of orange chicken onto his plate.

"You called Mom?" Francine worked to keep her voice neutral.

Sol frowned, waving his napkin in front of his face. "Your mother?" he answered. "Nah." He frowned. He waved the napkin as if to make the idea disappear.

"Who?" Jigme asked. He wound a chopstick expertly into a pile of *chow fun*, his lips shining with oil.

"Marion Silver," Sol answered as he dug into his *chow fun*, the noodles slithering away as he lifted them with a fork.

"Marion Silver?" Francine asked; she sat up straight, her chopsticks poised in her fingers like spears. I remembered Betty teasing Sol about his "old flame." Was something going on between Sol and Marion? Was that the real reason Betty had left?

"Mmm," Sol nodded, sounding gruff. Betty's letter hadn't said anything about infidelity, or an old romance rekindled. Had she been covering for him? "So many years," Sol mused, softening, his gaze focused out the window, into the dark folds of the hidden hills. I wasn't used to hearing Sol talk like that—about time, like it was an unmeasurable, viscous liquid, instead of something solid, measurable, stratified, with fixed periods, with fixed limits. "And we're still so much the same." Sol rubbed again at the back of his neck.

On the fridge, Betty and Sol stared, unseeing, out of the old photo of Francine's graduation day. Beneath the Rosie the Riveter magnet ("We can do it!") that had held it for so long in that spot, Sol had tucked a scrap of paper on which he'd penciled, in a scientist's precise hand: "Coffee/Oranges/Toothpaste."

Francine studied her father, the mound of rice on her plate untouched.

"Dad," said Jigme, who was more than forty years younger than Sol, the child of his old age, "you're turning into a real old fart." Sol laughed, and Francine started to eat.

"What did she say?" Anne asked. In the company of the family, Anne always seemed serious, but I'd heard her giggling uncontrollably behind Jigme's closed door.

"She has two sons." Then he murmured. "Back then, they said she could never have children . . ."

Jigme looked up. "Why?"

"Polio."

Jigme poked the black frames of his glasses onto the bridge of his nose with the tip of his index finger. Anne, watching, repeated the gesture.

"That's what they thought at the time," Sol repeated, reaching for his mug. Then he told us the details: how he and Marion had been high school sweethearts. How, after he'd enlisted, he'd written Marion a letter every week, filled with little clues meant to evade the army censors. How she'd stopped writing. How he'd panicked, convinced she'd met someone else, perhaps gotten married. How he'd gotten her parents' letter, telling him Marion had become partially paralyzed. How she'd written him herself, before his signal cryptography unit began its course through Italy, begging him to find someone else. His own parents' letter, following, agreed. "Then the War ended, and I met your mother." Sol turned to Francine, as if looking for Betty in her face. "She was a lot of fun, irreverent, a pixie."

(*A pixie.* According to, my grandfather's brother Jack, whom I met only once, at her funeral, my Gramma Sophie, too, had been a "pixie." Gramma Sophie with her soft curved nose hunched down in the center of her face like a fuzzy magnolia bud, Gramma Sophie with the one wild hair she pulled out every week from her chin. My Gramma Sophie had been a raven-haired beauty; my grandfather, his milk bottles rattling, had serenaded her, *"Fil sheyne meydelech - tsu dir kumt nisht gor-/Mit dayne shvartse eygelech un dayne shvartse hor."*)

252

"They were playing the Choo Choo Boogie." Sol smiled. "She was dancing with someone else," Sol told us, "and so was I, but Nat King Cole came on, and then we realized we'd been dancing with the wrong partners . . ." His voice trailed off here, where the story of romance became the family story.

"But she did," Francine recalled Sol. "Marion Silver. She got married. And had kids. But not with you." Francine appraised Sol with a scrutinizing glance, the one she used when she thought I hadn't apologized thoroughly enough for something I'd done. Did she blame him for loving someone before her mother? Or did she blame him for leaving her?

"Her sons are a little older than you." Sol gestured towards Francine with his chopsticks. "One of them," his face pinked up, "is gay." Sol lifted his eyebrows and blotted his lips with a paper napkin.

"You must both have gay genes," Jigme cracked, Betty's droll tone in his throat. Under the table, Francine braced her feet against the front legs of her chair, toes down, as if she might at any second spring up and sprint away. (She'd been running more, I suspected as much because there was something she needed to run away from as something she was running toward; still, she'd joked, aping June, "Those wedding photos are forever, baby. When I'm hauling a baby on one hip and an extra ten pounds on the other, I'm going to want *proof* that when you married me, I was *hot*.")

Sol, if he'd detected sarcasm, didn't acknowledge it. "If there is such a thing," he said, "and I think there have been some studies . . . " He returned to his element like one of those ancient sea turtles, sliding from the gravity-pressing ledge of a rock back into its weightless, liquid element. ". . . then, yes, I suppose it's possible that Marion and I might both carry a recessive gay gene."

Jigme loosely draped his hairless, brown hand around Anne's smaller, whiter one and pressed the smile out of the corner of his lips. "So," he said, "if you two *had* gotten married, your kids would have been *super*gay."

"Jerome," Sol barked. But Francine and I both exploded in a terse burst of laughter. Anne coughed into her napkin.

Francine stopped laughing. "Maybe you should invite her."

"Who?"

"Marion."

Sol told us that Marion's kids lived in different parts of the country. Her husband had died. I saw where Francine was going. And why not? We'd already paid the caterer for Betty's plate. "Where? Here?" He looked alarmed.

Francine wiped her lips, crumpled her napkin, and tossed it onto the table. "Invite her to the wedding."

( )

Francine and I lay on the couch in the living room together, quiet and thankful. We understood that we'd nearly lost each other. And we both felt that we'd returned, not slowly, but with the force of a planetary orbit.

Sol had told us once—it was a Sunday in February, just after Valentine's Day,—about the Near Earth Asteroid Rendezvous, a robotic space probe sent up to study the asteroid Eros. "The probe will use Earth's own gravitational field," Sol told us, "for a gravity boost. Which means," he continued, "that Earth's gravity will draw the probe toward it and then fling it out into space at a greater velocity than it had before."

Betty's defection was like a huge, dark planet with its own mass, its powerful gravitational pull, and Francine and I had found ourselves drawn under, into the dark shadow of its bulk. But then, we'd found ourselves just as powerfully flung out again, our trajectory changed, our velocity altered.

On the floor beside us sat six champagne flutes, still wrapped in bubble wrap. Every day now, the UPS truck arrived at our door with deliveries from Macy's and Crate and Barrel, white boxes tied in silver ribbon, proclaiming "A lifetime of happiness." Though these were gifts we'd picked out ourselves, their arrival nonetheless filled us with surprise and delight. Finally, we were being feted, initiated into a new, domestic life together, filled with domestic things. We mimed real surprise each time a package showed up at the door: *What? For us?* We loved the white, textured papers and the silver ribbon topped with little bells. I didn't want to open them, but Francine reminded me that we were going to have to write Thank You notes, and we'd better get started.

"Are you afraid I'm going to freak out again," she teased me, "and we're going to have to return it all?"

For the past three weeks, our gifts had piled up in the living room, big white question marks about what would happen after Betty left, a blank space growing, block by block where our future together had once been. Now the only absence they marked was Betty's.

"I just like how they look," I admitted, settling lumpily on Francine's belly. "I don't even care what's in them. The pretty boxes, the sweet, formal cards. I like the symbolism more than the stuff—you, me, together forever."

"I'd like seeing our living room floor again," she said, shifting her weight under me.

"Don't you like surprises?"

"Like you?" Francine looked at me. "Aren't you full of surprises?"

Surprises, did she mean? Or secrets?

That night in her hotel room, Jill and I sat on her bedspread in our socks, eating nuts from the minibar, and Jill pressed her back against the lacquered headboard, her leg tossed up on the spread, looking out at the darkening city. "There was a woman," Jill started, "who knew a story and a song; but she never told the story, and she never sang the song. One day the story said, 'Bahin [sister], this woman will never let us out. Let's run away.' 'You're right, Bhai [brother],' replied the resentful song, 'but let's do more than that.' So late that night, the story and song escaped. The next day, while the woman's husband was away, the story turned itself into a man's jacket, and draped itself near the door. The song turned itself into a pair of men's shoes, and sat partway under the bed. When the man came home that evening, he saw the jacket and the shoes, and accused his wife of unfaithfulness.

"But she hadn't cheated on him?" I'd asked Jill.

"No." Jill and I sat in the dark hotel room, huddled against the gathering night.

My father was right, I thought now, pressed into our couch with Francine: We all have compartments inside ourselves, compartments in which we seal parts of ourselves away. He was also right when he told me: *You have a choice.* We all do. But not about who you love. You have a choice whether or not to make a life out of silences—whether to let them become as solid as shoes under the bed—and about whether you flee. Whether to lose each other. You could sit across from someone, across a chasm like that, an omission, a silence, and let it grow until it was as deep as the ravine at Babi Yar. Howling. Or you could try to exhume it. Fill it. Bury the dead.

I turned to Francine. It was time for my confession. "I've been seeing someone. At work. Outside of work. Someone from work." *Work, work, work*—I kept repeating the word, as if the incantation of duty could prevent this from being personal. From being infidelity. Next to me on the couch, Francine tilted her head up awkwardly as if she couldn't believe what she was hearing and had to see it from a different angle. "An old lady!" I cried. Then I held my breath. Francine had already accused me of having an affair. I don't think this was what she expected. But how different was it? I was preoccupied with someone else. I was leading a hidden life.

Betty had excoriated me for "leaking." Now it would be Francine's turn to thunder down her disapproval, to tell me that I needed to confess to Wendy, to stop seeing Anya. Francine was the one who had sent me crawling to Wendy in the first place, trying to find in the Foundation a container big enough to hold all of my sadness and longing. Now she was going to tell me that I needed to quit my job. She was going to tell me that I had a problem and needed help. She was going to be furious at me for lying to her. Which—I sighed, ready to take on the onslaught—was a reasonable thing for her to be.

"The old woman who had a female lover?"

Francine's arm shot out to grab me as I toppled off the couch.

"You *knew* about Anya?" Of course she knew. How could I have thought she wouldn't? Francine knew everything.

"Anya? You never said her name." Francine chewed her cuticle, a habit that usually annoyed me, but which indicated a nonchalance I was too grateful for to mention. "You told me about her girl-friend." Francine prompted me as if I were the one who had forgotten Anya's story. *Girlfriend*—that seemed like such a strange word to use for Sheva.

"Sure—but, I mean, that was at work. I mean, I didn't say it was anything outside of work." I scanned my memory banks, trying to remember the exact words I'd used when I'd brought Anya up. *Old flames*, that's what we'd been talking about. Surely I hadn't suggested that I'd been seeing Anya at the museum, at her apartment?

"That's where you were when I called? Those were the torn museum badges, the florist receipts?" Francine let her fingernail drop from her mouth. She threw her arm around my waist and gripped me tight, her hazel eyes locked on mine. "Ellen. Were you *trying* to lie to me?"

"No," I squeaked. "Not exactly. I was just trying not to tell you."

Francine's forehead wrinkled. She didn't look angry. She looked sad. "Why wouldn't you want to tell me something like that?" It was like she was talking to her mother. It was like I had broken her heart.

I couldn't look at her when I answered. "Because I knew you'd be mad." I felt bad about hurting Francine. But, even now, it seemed like a good reason to avoid saying something when you could get by without. Not hurting Francine seemed like the very reason I had *not* told her about Anya. But maybe I was just concerned about hurting myself.

Now Francine looked confused. "Why would I be *mad* about you getting involved with this person?"

"For following an old woman around," I countered. "For getting too involved. That was the reason you made me ask Wendy for a job." I sat up. "So I would stop doing that."

"No, it wasn't." Francine sat up, too. She'd begun to chew her

258

cuticle again, furiously, like she was trying to solve a math problem. "I told you to call Wendy because you were depressed."

"Yeah," I prompted her. "And because of the old ladies at Safeway."

Francine squinted at me, as if she had no idea what the hell I was talking about. Then she spit out a piece of fingernail skin and held my face between her hands, one of them still wet. "Ellen, you think I don't know that you have a weakness for old Jewish ladies? You think I don't know you would follow them to the ends of the earth?" Was I supposed to say *yes* or *no*? Francine went on, "The *two* of us, apparently," Francine blinked back tears, "come from people capable of repressing the most intensely . . ." She scanned the ceiling. "The most painful and personal things, as if the goal in life is not to admit that anything has ever hurt you. But you, Ellen," she blinked again, "you've got this big, messy hole in the middle of your heart, and it's made you a generous and caring person. It's made you the person I love."

"Oh." The futon creaked. "I guess I misunderstood."

I blinked away tears, suddenly recalibrating all the conversations we had had about my grandmother, and the Safeway ladies, and the people I talked to at work. Rewinding in my head, I realized with horror that it had been possible, starting from this single misunderstanding, to have an infinite number of perfectly sensible conversations throughout which each person had an entirely different understanding of what was being said, and neither person realized it. Is that what had happened with Betty and Sol? One person said "For now" and the other heard "Forever," and it took them thirty-five years to realize the mistake?

As we nestled back into the crook of the couch together, Francine tapped my forehead with her nail. "I already told you I would love you, warts and all." It was a joke that didn't sting only because I'd finally rid myself of my hideous warts. The flaws in my personality would be harder to eradicate. Separating the selfish kind of silence from the selfless kind wasn't always so easy. Plus, I sensed that Francine's forgiveness came from her own loss. Had I told her that it was Anya right off the bat when the phone rang in our house that night, I wasn't so sure Francine would have been so generous. But, lying on the couch next to my future bride, I resolved I would try harder.

Beside us on the floor, a dozen packages tied with bells, wished us, over and over again, a lifetime of joy.

( )

Late Monday afternoon between Rosh Hashanah and Yom Kippur, I went to pick Francine up at school. Older children had invaded some of the preschool classrooms, hunching against the tiny yellow and orange seats. "What is holy?" a clear voice called out. I paused by the open door of Francine's regular classroom, "In Judaism, do we have holy places?" No one said anything. "Are the floorboards up in the sanctuary holy? Are the pews holy?" The students murmured disapprovingly. "No," the teacher confirmed, "because places can be destroyed. In Judaism, Time is holy. Can anyone ever destroy Time?"

Francine found me out in the hall. "Look," she said, pulling the preschool newsletter out of her backpack. Francine was shaking. "Here." She dropped her finger on the page under the black and white photos of the children dipping apples. *Mazel tov!* it read, *To teacher Francine Jaffe on her wedding next month to Ellen Margolis.* "Laura put it in." Francine's preschool director.

"That's . . . pretty fucking cool," I decided.

Francine looked ashen. "One of the families told Laura they won't be coming back next year."

I was confused. What did that have to do with . . . Oh.

I put my arm around her shoulders. "'The whole world is a very narrow bridge,'" I told Francine. "'And the main thing is, not to be afraid.'"

I'd been working a lot. Something about this time of year—the Days of Awe; the hour of confession; the blank, turning leaves of the Book of Life; the hovering wings of the Angel of Death—brought witnesses to the Foundation in greater numbers than at any other time of year. We booked appointment after appointment, making note of the names, the times, the dates, putting them down, sealing them.

"Ms. Margolis?" I had my head deep in a transcript when the phone rang. "This is Jason Klein." Jason Klein waited for me to recognize his name. "You interviewed my grandmother." When I still didn't respond—did he not understand that more than half the people I spent my life listening to were grandmothers?—he prompted me: "Ruth Klein. At the Western Home."

The Western Home. I remembered the old movie theater with the sadly urgent marquee: "Availability NOW!!!" Jason Klein was the grandson in khaki pants, the one who played Rummy Tiles with his grandmother.

"Yes," I told him. "I remember your grandmother." Of the present, Ruth Klein herself had remembered very little. Of the past, she had remembered enough, between slices of frosted lemon cake. "I hope she's doing well."

"Actually," Jason Klein coughed, "I wanted to let you know." He coughed again. "She died."

I pressed my lips together, touched my hand to my forehead, felt in my throat and eyes a familiar reflex. "I'm so sorry," I said.

Jason Klein coughed again. "I was wondering," he said, "if you might want to go out for coffee. Sometime."

"Oh."

I understood why Jason Klein called me. My mind flashed on the last Thanksgiving, Gramma Sophie behind the counter, frail, hiding behind the pots and pans, Francine in the other room. After this, no woman he met would ever have known his grandmother.

It would have been so easy to say yes. What did coffee mean? Coffee could mean anything.

I knew what coffee meant.

"I'm really sorry about your grandmother," I told Jason Klein. "But I can't. Have coffee with you. I'm getting married," I said, "in two weeks."

"Ah," Jason Klein answered. He'd been cute, I remembered. He'd played Rummy Tiles with his grandmother. "Lucky guy," he said.

My mind caught on the word. I opened my mouth to say something, got caught on the silence.

I was getting married. In less than two weeks.

"Girl," I said.

"Sorry?"

"I'm sorry for your loss," I told Jason. "Goodbye."

( )

Black is the color Jews, like Christians, wear for mourning. But white is the color you wear into your own grave. Because it is the color of spiritual purity, white is the color of the *kittel*—the pocketless, ceremonial gown—one wears on Yom Kippur. White is the color of the funeral shroud. It is the same color, sometimes even the same garment, a Jewish person wears on her wedding day.

I disappeared upstairs, safe from the eyes of my betrothed, to try on my wedding dress. Francine and I had gone back to Union Square, to the shining glass doors of Saks Fifth Avenue, to find out whether the waters would part, or swallow us up. (After my collapse there, Francine insisted I go to Kaiser. "Did you experience any uncontrolled movements of the arms and legs? Did you experience heart palpitations?" "I don't know. I don't think so. I hadn't eaten. I was shopping for a wedding dress." The doctor looked up from her checklist, her glasses perched on her nose. "You're planning a wedding?" She put her cold stethoscope against my back. "Go home," she said, "and have a glass of wine.")

Francine had pushed open the door and together we'd stepped back into the cool hush of the nautilus shell, everything polished and shining, entire worlds, above us, twisting up and up the moving stairs. My head felt light. Sweat broke out over my nose, my forehead and neck. But Francine had held my arm, warm in hers. As we stepped onto the main floor, I took a deep breath: perfume and powder. Suddenly, the fear broke. I'd stepped through it, cool and light, like a fairy-tale rag girl stepping through a mirror, turning princess.

Perhaps, when I'd fainted, part of my soul had split off and hovered there. Because something drew me on, something like instinct. Three floors up, scenting, blind, my fingers groped toward a sliver of cream-colored lace. "This is it," I announced, pulling the dress from the rack.

"That's the dress!" Francine exclaimed over my shoulder.

"Do you really think so?" I extricated the dress from its mates. It hung, straight, sleeveless, a sheer lace sleeve over a creamy, satin sheath.

"No." Francine shook her head. Her lips groped for words. "No, that's *it*. That's the dress I found for you in New York."

I'd stared at Francine, then at the dress. My dress. The mate— not matching, not clashing, she'd told me—of her dress. It was the only dress like it on the rack. Size 8.

Francine and I had walked out of Saks Fifth Avenue, the persistent horror of my childhood, bane of my wedding day, folded, finally and neatly, away; in its place, the form of my life to come: comfortable, sleek, light and shimmering as a pair of wings.

Now I stood at the far end of the bed, in front of the full-length mirror framed with a garland of leaves and vines: a housewarming gift from Fiona. Francine and I had just moved in together in our little craftsman bungalow, and I'd wanted Fiona to see all of this— the house, the life, the girl—and recognize me in it. She'd shrieked when she stepped off the plane, her huge green eyes brilliant with joy. The mirror, an object the three of us had admired at a boutique on Fillmore, had appeared after she left, Fiona's magnanimous gift. *Mirror, mirror, on the wall,* the card read, *who are my sweetest two of all?* It was the first gift in which we'd seen ourselves— literally, figuratively—reflected together as a couple.

Standing in front of it, I unzipped the cocoon of shimmery gray nylon that held my dress; the dress hovered up against the closet door in the darkened room like a spirit, waiting to be possessed. This was my own dress. My mother had not picked it out for me. My mother had not *seen* it—had not examined the label, pinched the fabric between her fingers, appraised it as "a knock-off," a fake. I hated that I knew my mother's criticism already. But it was practically written in the lace, patterned there, the thread of my mother's unfollowed passion, a lost life. It hovered in the space behind my own eyes, where I saw it, for once, quite clearly.

I pulled off my T-shirt and unbuttoned my jeans. Parting the nylon lips of the bag, I gently pulled the gown by the shoulders; I turned and unzipped it slowly. The fabric slid, cool and smooth, up my thighs, as my arms found their way through the openings. I couldn't manage the hook-and-eye at the very top, but it didn't matter. In the full-length mirror, garlanded by leaves and vines, stood a bride, her bare arms brown, her body with its gentle curves draped in shifting, subtle patterns of a single, classic line. Potentially my Achilles heel, my wedding dress had turned out perfect. Even more than perfect: I could wear it without panty hose. Even more perfect still: It was probably the last dress I'd ever wear.

( )

Though he didn't believe in God, or, for that matter, in religion, Sol believed in normalcy enough to go to Kol Nidre services on Erev Yom Kippur, the way he and Betty had every year for as long as they'd been married. "I'll meet you at the house," Francine reminded me, kissing me goodbye, a bundle of white clothes tucked under her arm.

I was standing inside the closet, trying on clothes and throwing them on the floor, which is why I didn't hear the phone until the dogs began to bark, and then to howl, a crazy, wailing sound that rang through the house like a *tekiyah gedolah*, the great, plaintive *shofar* blast that calls Israel to worship. *Arise sleepers! Awake from your slumbers!*

I dashed out of the closet, tripped over a pile of sweaters, and lunged for the phone. God knows why. The phone had begun ringing off the hook daily, the chorus of a professional pissing contest between the caterer and the DJ. Francine wanted no part of these conversations.

"Hello? Is this Ellen? Margolis?" A woman's hesitant voice accented my name on the second syllable, the first blurred. Brusque, thick. Israeli. "You called. About my mother."

"Batsheva?" I asked. "Batsheva Singer?"

"My name is Anat Singer. Batsheva was my mother."

I stared at the clothes heaped on the floor. "Yes." I'd been prepared, I thought, to tell Batsheva that Anya was still alive, still

266

loved her. And I had contemplated having to confirm that Sheva was, recently, dead. But the daughter? I couldn't exactly out Batsheva Singer to her surviving daughter. Probably, I realized, I shouldn't even be talking to Batsheva's daughter. "I work at the Foundation for the Preservation of Memory." As if that explained it.

"They said you worked there," Anat Singer answered, "but you never know. Those women," she added, "at Rose of Sharon, can be real bitches." I suppressed a smile. "You can't imagine how surprised I was to hear from that woman again, and my mother already dead nearly a year."

Of course she'd been shocked. What the fuck was I thinking, conjuring her mother's spirit up, like the Witch of Endor, out of *sheol*? "Your mother . . ." I started. Anat Singer listened quietly; these international calls had gotten insanely clear. "I'm so sorry."

"My mother escaped from Europe to come fight the war for Palestine. She was tired." Anat went on, the words with their strong downward slope conjuring the weariness of thousands of years of history. "The past was all she wanted to remember."

Wanted to remember. Why did Anat Singer say that? I wanted to press her here. I wanted to know: Had Batsheva talked about Anya? "Ms. Singer," I ventured, "I interviewed someone who remembers your mother." I stopped, unsure how to go on. "Someone who may have helped your mother escape from the Kovno ghetto."

"The Gandras?" Anat Singer asked. "The stork?"

I hadn't meant the *Gandras*, but, of course, Alina Sapozhnik was the one who literally helped Sheva escape. It wasn't necessarily something a survivor would talk about. "You know about the stork?"

"Only a little. From the letters."

There were letters. "The letters?"

"Yes. After she died, I found some letters among my mother's things." Before I could ask Anat Singer about her mother's letters, she continued. "I always suspected there had been someone else. Someone before my father. Why not? My friend Devorah's mother came from Warsaw. Later, she found out, her mother had had a husband, and two children before her. Killed in the War. Why not my mother, too?

"When she died, I looked through her things. There were the two letters. And a photo of my mother as a young girl, and another girl. A school friend, I think."

Anya. It had to be Anya. "The person I interviewed," I tried to keep my voice steady, "might be able to identify the other person in that picture."

"The *Gandras*?" Anat Singer asked.

The *Gandras*, like Sheva, was dead. But why complicate things? "I'm not sure," I lied. "Can I get your number?" I'd leave it in Anya's hands. Francine and I had agreed: This had gotten way too complicated to keep hidden any longer. If Anya wanted to tell Anat her story, she could. I had already done too much. "Is there a country code?" I pictured early light, a cool, modern apartment block, a bowl of oranges, the sky outside bright, the world already slipped into morning, spinning fast.

Anat Singer cleared her throat. "I live in Chicago." Not Tel Aviv. A woman in a dark apartment, late on Erev Yom Kippur, overlooking the black, windswept shore of Lake Michigan. My mind whirled to catch up. "I grew up in Tel Aviv. But I met someone here," she added. "It would have been awkward to return together to Israel."

A non-Jew, I guessed. She'd met a Gentile, with whom her marriage would not be recognized by the State of Israel—possibly not by her mother, either. So they'd stayed here. Francine and I didn't have that choice, I thought, to live in a country where we'd be acknowledged. But then, I thought, tamping down my right-eousness, Anat Singer was also an exile. So I asked, "He's not Jewish?"

Anat Singer didn't say anything. Had it come out wrong? Like an accusation? All she knew about me was that I worked for the Foundation. Probably, she assumed I was judgmental—the voice of institutional Judaism, guarding its past, lamenting its future. "I mean," I added, trying not to get into any more trouble before the hour of repentance, "I know that can be tricky."

Anat Singer corrected me. "My partner is a woman."

( )

"Surely," Anat Singer cleared her throat, "this can't make any difference for my mother's case."

How could I explain what kind of difference it would make? My mind raced, but my mouth stayed shut.

Misunderstanding, Anat challenged me. "You live in San Francisco." The words came out thick. "Do you mean to say, Miss Margolis, you haven't met any lesbians?"

"No—no," I rushed to correct her. "I mean, yes, of course." *Some of my best friends are lesbians.* "Anat," I started over. "My partner is a woman, too. We're getting married in two weeks."

"Married?"

Inspiration struck. "Come," I told her. "To the wedding. It's short notice, I know. But it would be wonderful," I told her, "if you could meet Anya." I got it, then. Anat, Anya. Batsheva had named her daughter after Anya.

"Anya. That's unusual. Anya is your partner's name?" Anat asked politely.

I squinted through the blinds, peering through the endless, small, stiff fronds of the redwood tree outside the window. "Anat, Anya Kamenets is the girl in the picture. Your mother's friend."

She didn't get it. Just like I didn't get it about her. Just like she hadn't gotten it about me. How many opportunities for happiness, I wondered, had disappeared in these misperceptions, how many histories vanished, unwritten? "You're her namesake."

"Perhaps she'll know who sent the letters."

"Yes. Bring the letters."

"I was right about my mother, you know." My heart stopped for an instant. Did Anat already know? "There was someone," Anat told me. "Someone who burned in my mother's heart. A

269

ner tamid. An eternal flame. The person who wrote in the letters: 'All these years, Sheva, I have dreamed about the *Gandras* who carried you away and wondered, would another stork ever carry you back to me?'"

All these years? I'd assumed that the letters came from before the War. *All these years?*

What the ever-loving fuck? All these months I had been searching for Batsheva, when Anya had already found her.

( )

That night, Francine and I stood up in the pews beside her father and her brother as the violin cried its first, stirring lament, as the long, pleading voice of the cello stretched out its supplication, a note long and low enough to reach across generations, across worlds, and I couldn't help thinking, again, of the folktale about a woman who knew a song she wouldn't sing, who knew a story she wouldn't tell. I lay awake that night, the Gates of Heaven open, this one night, somewhere in the universe, and I couldn't sleep.

( )

"I've got to go into the City."

"On Yom Kippur?" Francine looked up from the paper, the little kitchen table for once empty of jam jars.

"It's Anya," I told her.

Francine looked at me like I'd just said I was meeting my dealer. But we'd already been through so much. She let her hand fall to my shoulder. "Do what you need to do."

I needed to see Anya. I needed Anya, finally, to tell me the truth. I needed to extract confession.

The halls of the Rose of Sharon Home had emptied for the day, their occupants drawn into the converted dining hall by the call for prayer, the call for redemption. Who knew whose last chance this might be?

I didn't expect to find Anya in there.

I took the elevator up, instead, to the eighth floor, walked alone down the empty hall. "Warning, Oxygen in Use," read the black and red sign outside Mrs. Linde's door. The door stood open, her oxygen line lying on the floor inside her doorway, a thin, transparent vein, while, ten paces away, Mrs. Linde leaned against the wall, sucking a cigarette between hungry lips.

As always, Anya refused to seem surprised to see me. "Cake?" she asked, stepping into her little kitchen.

"It's Yom Kippur."

Anya frowned. "I had no idea you were so *pious*." She squinted, the corners of her lips turned down.

"You're not at the Museum today," I observed.

"It's Monday."

I wandered over to my usual place by the window. My wedding invitation lay on the table where I had left it, untouched, unopened. That wasn't like Anya, to leave something lying out on that table. She'd left it to tell me she couldn't be bothered. It stung enough to make me careless.

"Tea?" Anya asked.

I picked up the photo of Batsheva. "I spoke to Anat Singer last night."

Anya's shoulders, upright in front of the sink, filling the kettle, went rigid. "I don't know this person Anat Singer," she said.

"Batsheva's daughter," I offered quietly. I was tired of evasions.

Anya, pausing over the stove, seemed to freeze. Underneath the kettle, the gas starter clicked, like a bird's small, fast heart, over and over. The smell of gas rose up, started to fill the kitchen. Anya's hand turned with a jerk. The flame spurted up, blue. I'd already waited patiently a very long time. "You knew Batsheva was alive. All this time. You wrote her letters."

Anya's head whipped around. Her fierce squint bore into me, her eyes little curved daggers of pure hatred. "What, gives you the right—" her hand flew out over the countertop. She slapped

272

it down so hard, I thought she might break it. "What gives Wendy Rosenberg," she spat the syllables of Wendy's name out like bones. "The right," Anya spat, clattering the kettle down against the flame, "to go, dig up old people's past? Is that what your Foundation is for?" She stepped out from behind the counter and into the living room. She was staring at the wide open sky. "Preservation of Memory," she pressed her lips over The Foundation's name as if she'd spoken a curse.

Anya's anger frightened me. I had wandered over to the coffee table and picked up the photo of Batsheva. The frame of the photo, tight in my hands, cut against my palm. Then I realized: *She's afraid.*

My heart raced unevenly. "It wasn't Wendy. Or the Foundation. It was me. I looked for Batsheva. I thought you *wanted* me to find Batsheva." I was shaking.

Anya turned from the window with incredulity. She thrust out her hand. The photo. She wanted it back. "Why?" She frowned, all the lines of her face pointing down toward the center of the earth. "Why would you think that?"

Why *wouldn't* I think that? I stared at the photo I had laid, face up, in her palm. As if the photograph were proof enough. "You loved her," I whispered, fiercely, as if not wanting even Batsheva, in my hands, to hear us. Anya herself had never exactly acknowledged this. "I did it because I knew you loved her."

Anya's face folded inward. "Hm!" she said. A thousand upwards parentheses sprung up around the big, down-turned parenthesis of her mouth. "Well." She reached for a dish towel and plunged the corner into the corner of her eye, as if wiping away something that had blown into it, an ember, a little floating piece of ash. She pressed the dish towel into her mouth and didn't breathe.

I held my own breath. Like the third Chinese Brother, the one who had swallowed up the sea, I was afraid of what would happen if I tried to speak. Love, fear, devotion. We never spoke about these things. Except, I had. I had broken the rules. "Anya," I whispered, willing myself not to cry. "When you wrote to her. What did she say?"

273

Anya shook her head. I didn't understand. Anya had been meant to go, Anya, to fly with the *Gandras*—Anya with Alina Sapozhnik, two blonds, two blue-eyed Jewish women who could pass, who could blend in, who could disappear. What fervent, whispered negotiation at the gate, what transaction had persuaded the Gandras to take this other one with the raven-dark hair, the girl she'd have to hide? What else, besides her own life, had Anya given up? Anya shook her head, a curt, final shake and glanced up, not at me, but at the big blue panel of sky. I looked up as a gull crossed the window: a brilliant, chalk-white mark sketched against the pure blue slate of Anya's sky. White as a letter on which no words are written, the bird sailed on.

She set the photo down. Anya and Batsheva stared back at us, islanded in the past. And then I understood. I stared at those beautiful girls whom neither terror nor death had parted, could not part, and with a terrible, sinking sadness, at last, I understood.

The one Batsheva had found herself thinking about most was her father, the shochet, *the butcher; he'd showed her once how he held a blade, not a single nick on it, to the thin parchment of the chicken's neck, how he drew it across, one swift line, barely visible, before the dark ink of the body beaded up across it, how he drained it of its life, completely, and according to the laws of Moses. Anya didn't understand about that. Anya's father had written stories for* Yiddische Stimme. *Sheva thought of her father's veined hands, and the whiteness of that thin line, just before the blood flowed, and thought about what she owed him. A husband. Jewish children. A return to the Promised Land. A life lived according to the traditions of Moses and the Jewish people. One thin, white line.*

I drew a long and painful breath. Then I blew it out toward the blank, white ceiling. Anya had written to Batsheva.

But Batsheva never wrote back.

I would have liked to pretend I knew nothing about these endings. But I had grown up, too, in an age of shame. When Liz and I had parted, there'd been no last words of love, no promises. So why did I feel that my heart was breaking? What had I done?

Downstairs, eight stories down, in the big, carpeted dining room, where the janitors and nurses had set up rows of folding chairs, *Avinu malkeynu*, the melody of the reconciliation, the plaint for mercy, swelled over the hiss of Mrs. Linde's two-pronged oxygen line, leaking into the hallway. Blocks away, across the City, under the great dome of Temple Emmanu-El, the melody rose up before the jeweled ark. Along the boulevards, across the Bay, under red-shingled roofs, under arches, under the spires of converted churches; inside the homely clapboard of prairie *shuls*; across the cool marble floors, before the panels of blue and gold glass of the Chicago Loop; under the perched, gold eagles of Harvard's Memorial Church; across the oceans, around the world: Voices rose up, the three-thousand-year cry, *Imaynu malkateynui*, the eternal plea.

Our Father our king, Hear our voice.
Our Mother our Queen, We have sinned before you.
Be gracious to us and answer us.
Our Mother our Queen,
Hear our voice. Hear our voice...

"Anya—," I started, but I didn't know what to say. My face burned with a thousand kinds of shame. This was my fault. I was getting married and I had wanted my grandmother. I had wanted her to bless me. And so I had made a terrible, heart-breaking mistake. I had done this. Not Anya. But me. "Anya. I'm sorry." Avoiding Anya's eyes, I stared down into the depths of the coffee-table glass, even though I knew I would see nothing there.

In it, I caught sight of my reflection: my dark eyes, my black bag, my dark coat. I glanced at the picture. At Batsheva's dark eyes, her dark hair. I felt, suddenly, as if I were trapped inside the glass, as if something Anya had said or done had charmed me, had caught me there. Why hadn't I considered that seeing ghosts could work both ways? I wondered, suddenly, whether Anya had sought me out because she wanted me, or if she really just came for Batsheva. We were trapped, the two of us, wanting the love that had left us.

I shook my head. My reflection moved. But Batsheva, all those years ago, remained frozen in time. I was the woman in the glass. But I wasn't the girl in the picture. Everything—past and present, present and past—had become so horribly confused. But I wasn't Batsheva. And Anya wasn't my Gramma Sophie. And maybe that was what *both* of us had needed all along. Not the women we had lost. A way to do something different. A way to repair a broken heart.

Batsheva had been trapped, a woman who couldn't tell her story, couldn't sing her song. But I knew something Anya didn't. "She kept your letters. Even though she didn't write back to you. She treasured them. She thought about you," I told her, "all the time."

(What had Liz done with my unanswered, final letter, I wondered. Had she read it and thrown it quickly away? Or, had she tucked it somewhere away in a drawer, its pale leaves crushed, like the faded petals of the sweet pea I'd saved all these years?)

Anya shrugged.

"She had a daughter," I reminded Anya. "A daughter she named after you. Anat. Anat . . . ," I paused. I was searching for the words, words you could say without saying anything, words you could hear, if you wanted to, without hearing anything, words that would fall, if you wanted them to, like a stone disappearing without a ripple into the sky—the only kind of words I thought Anya could hear. "Batsheva's daughter is . . . a friend. She's coming. Here. To meet you." My legs were shaking as I rose for the door. I had to let her be, to measure in her own scales the weight of silence against the weight of words, and decide which was heavier to bear. But I believed she was tired of disappearing.

I was tired of disappearing, too. I had been a coward and a liar.

I had told myself that, if only my Gramma Sophie were alive, I would ask for her blessing. But I would never have asked. Because I didn't believe she would have given it. She was the one person in my life whose love had been unconditional. But in my heart, I knew there were conditions. I was shaking harder when I told Anya, frowning to stave off tears, "She's coming. To my wedding." I bent and lifted my invitation from the table. For all I knew, Anya thought I was marrying a man. Not because I loved one, but because, like Batsheva, like so many others, I preferred lies to the truth. I ripped the back flap open and held out the card so Anya could read it: *Ellen & Francine.* "I want you to come, too." It was all I had to offer, and I offered it for my own ravenous heart. I couldn't fix the past. Just like Anya couldn't fix mine. It was never mine to fix. I could only be here, and be myself.

I waited until I stepped out of her apartment, out of the elevator, out of the building, out onto the street, until I started to cry.

( )

Right before the wedding, Francine cut her hair. I found her with Debbie and June in our living room, sorting through cardboard boxes full of vases, tall vitrines in which, filled with small pomegranates and leaves, we'd float white votives. June had read about it in *Martha Stewart Wedding*. June held one of the vases, scrutinizing it in the afternoon light, squinting through her glasses, wrinkling her nose. "Wash," she declared, and tucked the vase into a carton half-filled with vases just like it.

I looked from June to the back of Francine's head. I could see the dark line of hair at the pale nape of her exposed neck. "Ahh . . ." June's mouth hung wide.

Francine turned her head slowly. "Don't freak out," she said.

I stumbled over Francine's clogs and my butt hit the door with a thud.

"She freaked out," Debbie announced.

Francine, pleased with herself despite me, shook her head, sending the curls in a jumble behind her. "I needed a change," she said. This wasn't just about the hair. "Sit down," she said. "I'll get you a drink."

"Big change," June commented, heavily, as Francine walked out.

But Debbie hissed, "What's your problem?"

"Shouldn't she have asked me first?"

June's thin, feathery eyebrows rose.

"Warned me, then," I corrected myself.

"Goddammit, Ellen." Debbie smacked her hands down on her pants with a vehemence that stunned me. On the rug next to her foot, two of the vases wobbled dangerously. "I introduced you two. I told you to stick it out when you thought she didn't like you. Francine can shave her head if she wants to. But you are damn well going to get married, and you are going to thank me for helping you do it."

June stared with appreciation, as if she'd never quite seen Debbie clearly before.

"So," I said, taking in Debbie, her sweaty upper lip, her intense, scholarly gaze, "this is all about you?"

Debbie didn't smile. "Fuck, yes," she answered. "Who *else* do you think is going to hold you two accountable to each other?"

Francine came in from the kitchen, a glass of fizzy water in her hand.

"Marriage is a *social* contract," Debbie, our civil rights lawyer, went on. "So, you love each other." Debbie waved her hand dismissively. "That's wonderful. But you're asking for more than that." Debbie looked from me to Francine. "You've asked us all to watch. For a reason. This is a social contract. Between you, sure. But also: between us and you—your community and you." She appraised us with the solemnity of a judge. Then her nose flared. "And I plan to hold you to it."

( )

That evening, after Debbie and June left, Francine and I went up to our bedroom to put on our bathing suits. The heat we'd hoped would return in October had rushed in with a vengeance, like a rogue tide. I couldn't wait to get into the water.

"I've got a million short hairs down my back," Francine complained, pulling off her shirt and scratching vigorously between her shoulder blades; red lines materialized across her back like ghost writing. She caught my eye in the mirror. "Do you really hate it?" she asked me. Her chin dimpled in worry.

"No," I reassured her.

279

"It's just a haircut." Francine looked wounded.

"I know. You're beautiful. It's fine."

Francine, still a little wounded, stuck out her tongue.

"Hmph," I grunted. I was too hot to protest. Francine stepped into my arms. "Let me help you with that." She pulled my bathing suit out of my hands and slipped her hands under my shirt, slipped it off over my head. Then she wrapped her arms around me.

"Look." Francine turned me in her arms to face the mirror. She stood behind me, her face peeking out over my shoulder, her arms pale around my naked waist. Looking into the mirror, we were not what five millennia of Jewish life and culture had imagined as its survival. And yet—living Jewishly together, after two generations of assimilation—that is what we were. Twined in each other's naked arms, we were not what our parents and grandparents, heaping our unfused heads with hope and blessing, had imagined for each other, *bashert*. And yet—following generations of loving couples—that is what we were. In any iconography of any culture, that was clear.

We showed up at Trisha and June's door hand-in-hand.

"Well," June crowed, insinuatingly. Like she had x-ray vision into the recent past. She appraised us with greedy eyes. "Honey!" June called into the apartment. "Our friends have been practicing for the honeymoon!"

"It's getting close to D-Day, girls." Trisha walked in, balancing a tray of champagne flutes.

I reached into my old black satchel and unwrapped a secreted object as carefully as if it were the Holy Grail: the glass I'd smash at the end of our wedding ceremony.

June hefted the goblet and pinged it with her fingernail. "Are you planning to wear steel-shanked boots with that dress?"

"What do you mean?"

"Honey!" June's eyes rolled sympathetically. "This is the kind of glass they serve ice cream sundaes in. You're going to need a sledgehammer to break that thing."

"Come on," I argued. "It's a wine goblet." I'd rejected Rabbi Loh's suggestion of stomping a lightbulb—all bang, no substance.

"I've seen Ellen do squats," Trisha offered. "She can power through it."

June shot her a practiced glance of arch warning. Then she stood up and disappeared behind a cabinet door. "Here." She returned with a thin-stemmed wineglass with a large, round bell. It wasn't quite as curvaceous as ours, but it was traditional. June tapped the glass with a fingernail; the bell rang a long, soprano note. "Use this."

Francine reached out and took the glass. We took turns sliding our fingers down into the bell. The glass's long beveled stem was at least half an inch thinner than the one on our glass; it would snap easily when I stomped on it in my dyed-to-match ballet flats.

I hefted our goblet again in my palm. I pinged it. It emitted a short, low tone. I slid my fingers up the sturdy crystal stem. June was right. Our glass was unusable.

June nodded. "Take it. We have dozens of them."

Trisha settled right next to June on the couch, smiling sweetly as the first notes of Anita Baker's "Rapture" began to play. "Thanks," I said, something curiously like relief breaking over my head and shoulders. I raised my eyebrows toward Francine. "I think we just got something old, or borrowed. Or something."

"She's so traditional." Trisha tilted her chin demurely to Francine, who turned confidentially back, folded one of my hands between hers in her lap and said, "I know. It's kind of sweet, isn't it?"

( )

I woke up early, the morning light bright on the empty bed. We had seven days left, and, like the miller's daughter, more straw than we could possibly spin into gold.

I grabbed our final checklist—I was never without it now—and wandered downstairs, where I could hear Francine stirring tea in the kitchen. Light flooded the living room. Even the clatter of the spoon against the mug sounded bright. I stared out the French doors at the bricks and the blazing blue. If the weather held, we'd have a perfect, cerulean wedding day, the sky warm and deep as waves. I stood entranced, our little world of domestic peace spread before me like a kingdom, when—*crack!*—something sharp struck the glass.

Adrenaline surged through me; my legs shook. I looked down, straight into the beady eye of the world's smallest velociraptor, gasped, and leapt away.

Almost every culture in every part of the world tells at least one tale of an animal bride, of a man who marries a bear, a monkey, a horse, instead of a human. Almost always, in the end, the animal reveals itself as a beautiful woman. Almost always.

The beast stared at me with its auburn-feathered head. Francine had been turned into a chicken.

Then I heard the pages of the Sunday paper turn. "Francine!" I cried, fleeing. I just wanted to hear her human voice.

Francine looked up from the paper. "It was standing by the side of the house. It looked terrified."

I stared at Francine, her hand loose around her mug of tea, her bony ring finger bare, but not for much longer. Of course, she'd brought home the chicken.

I shook the list in my hand. This chicken was not on it. "We have to pick up our dresses from the tailor." I ticked off task after task. "And we're having lunch with your father today." Our one thousand and one tasks stared me, hard, in the face. "We're getting married," I whispered fiercely, so the chicken couldn't hear. I could just picture it now, my friends and parents showing up, and a crazed chicken roaming our yard, out for blood.

"We'll make some calls." Francine kept reading. Betty was gone; the worst had already happened. "Don't worry about it."

( )

Francine and I sped toward Tiffany's Bridal Boutique, our checklist clutched like a magic hanky in my hand. We were going to pick up our hemmed dresses and the pair of dyed-to-match, cardboard-soled peau-de-soie ballet flats I'd ordered in defeat after trying six dozen pairs of flats, sandals and pumps in every shade of off-white, cream and ivory but the right one.

(Early on, not long after I started spending nights at Francine's little wisteria-covered bungalow in East Oakland, we stepped out of the chain-link fence in the morning together. It wasn't a great neighborhood: Broken bottles lay in the street, syringes. But it had been a grand old neighborhood once, filled with huge, three-story, gabled houses. Francine and I stood on the corner, squinting up into the light. Shared mornings were new for us. The shingled rooftops glistened. I followed Francine's gaze. Way above, atop a brown-shingled house four stories high, a pale white cat stepped out a dormer window, lithe as a spirit. "Look at the cat," I said. Because, when you're just in love, you say all the obvious things. Francine looked at me. A wry smile curved her lips.

"When you look around," she said, like someone who has finally come to accept a critical but counterintuitive fact about the world—like, say, gravity, or the fact that, even though we can't see them, the stars are still out there, even in the daytime—"I'm really the only woman you see, aren't I?" I turned and looked. There, lounging and grooming and stepping and sunning, twenty or thirty or forty cats, blond, brown, black, fat, narrow, dotted the rooftop. Cats had slithered in and out of the dormer window as we watched.)

The ballet flats were an admission of defeat. At least, I reminded myself, my warts were finally gone, sheet by sheet of peeled skin, thick as a manuscript.

But when we got to Tiffany's, there was a problem with my dyed-to-match shoes. They hadn't been dyed.

The saleswoman—Tiffany herself?—eyed me and Francine over half-moon bifocals as she fingered through her file box for our receipt. "You two—sisters?"

This again.

"You," the saleswoman jerked her head toward me: "the bride?" She followed my rolling eyes to Francine. "Who is the bride?" She pulled our receipt. "One shoes. No dye."

Francine and I looked at each other. "We need them dyed by Friday."

"Friday?" The saleswoman's big, flaccid face frowned with uncertainty as she peered at us over the rims of her glasses. "Dye takes *three* week!" She held up three fingers in front of our incredulous faces.

Francine and I sped up Piedmont Avenue in a blur of panic. In their box, the ballet flats thumped, soft and dull, heavy as dog turds. I felt close to hysteria. I was a bride: At this point, why the fuck not?

"Hang on." Francine swung the car around and pulled up in front of a cobbler. Clutching the box, I ran in while Francine waited in the car like Thelma waited for Louise, engine idling, ready to peel off.

Inside the cobbler's, an acrid little hole-in-the-wall reeking of brain damage and birth defects, the shoemaker lifted the shimmering white shoes with blackened fingers. "Can't dye these," he declared. At the tip of his finger, where the satin met the cheap sole, a blob of translucent glue had oozed out and hardened. "They'll just fall apart." I stared at the shoes, willing the soles to fuse to the satin with my mind.

"Look," I pleaded with him, "I'm getting married next week."

The receipt flapped in my hand as I raced to the car. "We'll know on Wednesday," I told Francine, as she knocked the car into gear and we sped away.

"Sorry we're late," Francine apologized as she kissed her father. "It's been kind of a crazy morning."

"No hurry, girls." Sol answered. "Just an errand." He looked at Francine. "Something I used to do with your mother . . ."

My mother used to take me and Rebecca to do errands with her—"Daddy's" jobs. These usually involved going to the bank, into the steel-doored vault, where in the privacy of the sealed, faux wood-paneled booth, my sister and I watched as my mother clipped bond coupons. Afterwards, she'd put back the safe deposit box, slide it into its place in the tidy columbarium of wealth, secure inside the foot-thick doors of the safe, a box inside a box inside a box.

What could Sol and Betty's job have been?

Francine and I, still trembling with adrenaline, waited by the car, toeing the moss that was growing up between the bricks, a stunning border of deep emerald that was threatening to over-take the shaded path. Gazing at the living track of green, all I could think of for a second was Fiona's eyes. As my gaze traveled the bricks, the thick margin of moss became the ancient residue of crumbled monasteries, their Gothic arches half moldered over, slow and seeping as time itself, a sign not so much of growing back, as growing over.

"They need to get rid of this stuff," Francine murmured, "it'll get slick when it rains." Then she caught herself. "Shit." She crossed her arms and sighed. I thumped onto the door of the old Volvo beside her. Francine leaned into me. There were things we'd never stop worrying over—Sol, alone; us, the possibility of two

285

people together, making it—but as we stood by the car in the sun, the moss lush and green, our eyes smoldered. Because we're always discovering what the Romantics already knew: that what's ruined can also be beautiful. The way that tumbled, roofless walls, stripped and broken, uninhabitable, given time and covered over with green, can become a lovers' cloister.

Sol came back from the house carrying a pitcher of water and a towel he set by the front door. Then he bent down in the garden and picked out two, smooth, flat stones, and slipped them into his pocket. I looked sharply at Sol. For once, he avoided my eye.

We wound down the hillside, across the east side of campus, where we found ourselves clogged behind a line of belching city busses toward the stadium. Sol's fingers disappeared into his pocket, where they worried his memorial stones.

It wasn't until we were headed down Claremont, the big cranes of the Port of Oakland stretching their primitive claws against the skyline, that Sol cleared his throat. "Here," he told Francine. We had nearly reached our own house. "We're going to Mountain View."

( )

Mountain View sits just on the margin of Oakland and Piedmont, a big slice of the old ungridded hills, its huge iron gates
open at the top of Piedmont Avenue. It was one of our dog-
walking spots, a big urban greensward, trekked by clusters of
women with strollers, old people meandering in pairs. On drizzly
mornings, the dogs ripped across the lawn to throw themselves
on the grass, tossing up clods with their muzzles. Once, turning
a corner in the fog, Francine and I had encountered a full herd
of deer on the hillside, one shy form after another stepping out
of the mist. Pass through the arches, cement and brick ginger-
bread Gothic, and what strikes you most of all is its vastness,
ascending green hills everywhere you look, islands and mounds
and seas of green afloat with obelisks and stones: endless green
registers of the city's historic and its unremarked dead.

Sol's neck reddened visibly. "Your mother and I always went
together, but . . ."

Francine looked confused. "You and mom always went to the
cemetery . . . ?"

"On the *yahrzeit*. Once a year." Sol sounded embarrassed. "It
was all before your time. We didn't want to bother you kids with
it. Maybe that was a mistake," he added. "I don't know."

Inside the cemetery gates, the leaves of the birch trees flickered bright as pennies, the high paths hovering over pristine
views of the entire city. Tumbling across the hillsides, Chinese

grandparents peered from oddly colored photos, behind shining, tilted pinwheels. The Jews, in death as in history, lay apart: Just inside the cemetery's gates, ancient letters traced the names of our own tribes.

"Here?" Francine asked, looking uncomfortable.

Sol shook his head. "Your mother thought that was too close to the road."

Francine piloted the Volvo up through the narrow lanes, up past the fiery, turning maples, past the lone, disconsolate angel inscribed with slow and heavy hand, "REST, DEAR ONE."

Francine's Volvo shuddered as it mounted the hill. Behind us, like a map of everywhere we had ever been, lay all of Oakland and, beyond it, in a haze of light, the pyramid-spired City. The Bay Bridge spiderwebbed across the water, touching down on Treasure Island; the Golden Gate barred the western horizon. Inland, Lake Merritt, spreading blue under the colonnaded city government buildings, filled like a cistern of tears. And all along the horizon, stretching to infinity, the Bay's bright water reached endlessly south, shimmering, an unbroken plain of light.

There, at the top of the hill, Sol motioned for Francine to park the car. We'd come over the crest. Here, on the back side of the cemetery, the margins of the graveyard and the world outside were much closer. Below, you could see the gas station on Broadway Terrace just two blocks from our house.

The Volvo's heavy doors opened reluctantly. Sol led us down through the graves. As we crossed the wet grass, I picked up Francine's hand. Francine pursed her lips, and the little dimples in her chin stood out.

Sol looped up, disoriented, then back down the slope again. Then, suddenly, we were standing directly over the grave.

Julia's stone wasn't much, a pinkish rectangle of flecked granite set into the grass:

Julia Michelle Jaffe
March 21, 1962–August 23, 1963

Across the bottom, the plaque read simply: "Our Baby." It had been thirty-five years since Julia had died, thirty-five years the week Betty left. Thirty-five years since this little parcel of dirt was the open hole into which they'd lowered their only child's body. On the upper left corner of Julia's polished pink marble sat a round, black stone like the two in Sol's pocket. "Your mother's been here," Sol said, drawing the stones out of his trousers. He handed one to Francine. The second he set, still warm from his body, on the grave marker next to Betty's.

Could all the years of suppressed loss have coalesced around a single point, a place where the rupture between the past and the present and the future-that-might-have-been collided at a major fault line: Betty couldn't bear to see her younger daughter marry before her first?

Francine bent and set her stone on the grave with a shallow click. Sol brushed a little cut grass from the edge of the stone. Francine stuffed her hands in the pockets of her jeans, looking down the hill toward the gas station. I couldn't tell if she was angrier at Sol for bringing us here, or for not having brought her all these years. She squinted. "Do you miss her?"

Sol, who had stood at this grave when it gaped, who had filled it with rough clods of earth, scuffed his shoes in the thick, trimmed grass, stuffed his elderly hands into the pockets of his corduroys, looked out over the hills, and smiled.

Between us, their silence rose up until it stood, shoulder to shoulder, like a fourth person.

When I said, "I'll meet you down there," neither one of them looked up. They were still standing there, unmoving, when I crested the hill, probably there, still, as I wandered down the steep road toward the cemetery gates. I had my own deep grief to meet, the price of going forward, always, that backwards glance.

( )

Three days after Valentine's Day in 1992 we buried Gramma Sophie. It was a little coastal cemetery west of Ojai, a bit of rolling green earth right at the edge of the ocean, flagged with spreading palms. "Unbelievable," my father muttered. "Untouchable, prime real estate," he breathed, when the ocean rose up into view, slate gray, brooding, as we drove through the rustic gate. He meant: doubly sacred. His eyes gleamed with regret.

The rabbi, someone Uncle Irvin had found in the phone book, wore a tweed coat with elbow patches. Three jump-suited men leaned on shovels behind the grave. The mortician's apprentice, a gray man in a gray suit with a long face and fingernails thick with fungus, stood solemnly by the hearse.

The day of the funeral was overcast, those low coastal clouds that might burn off, might bring rain. My father pulled the car up too close behind the hearse, then backed it with a jerk. Rebecca, Ted, and I climbed over the front seats, out onto the grass where Uncle Irvin, Aunt Leah, and the tweed-coated rabbi stood beside the cemetery men. We had returned, all of us, to the origin of time: a hole in the green earth, my Gramma Sophie's body.

My mother and Aunt Leah clung to each other, clutching rumpled tissues. Rebecca stood by Uncle Irvin, her eyes, like his, bloodshot but dry. The mortician waved us forward, and my father and Uncle Irvin, Rebecca, my mother and I hauled the plain pine box together from the back of the wagon; we struggled it over the curb, my mother and Aunt Leah barefoot, their shoes abandoned behind them, planted in the soft, clinging earth.

Our throats closed over our grief; open them, and what shrill, animal keening would have issued forth, what primitive howl of pain? All around us, the earth below and the sky above poured forth their funereal music.

The rabbi murmured ancient words, warm and smooth as stones—*v'yitgadal, v'yitkadash*—to the ragged ululation of a hidden bird shrouded in the overhanging oaks; the low cry of a train winding its way along the coast, wailing down the distance, faded and disappeared. We pressed on black ribbons and tore them. My father pushed his *yarmulke* to the center of his crown. Then the cranks wound down, their indecorous, mechanical clicks loud as they lowered my Gramma Sophie's box into the ground.

And what did I remember about that day, now that the twin filters of time and grief had strained my memory clear of the debris of its details? The rough thunder of dirt bursting against the top of the rough pine box, subsiding to a thud, ascending to a soft, clay rain; explosion, thump and sigh. The length of the slowly filling coffin, pale as a blank sheet of paper. The whisper of my father's rough fingers fumbling to caress the coffin, a child for the last time at his mother's side. The liquid clench of my own jaws as, in the family way, I strangled back tears. The silence of the drizzle, then, as it started, blending the gray gauze of the sky down into the horizon, curtaining the landscape around us, a mist into which we disappeared, car doors closing, earth subsiding to rain, and rain to earth. I walked the path to the curb alone.

I thought I'd left my sorrow for my Gramma Sophie at Anya's door. But I hadn't. I walked alone now, away from Sol and Francine, away from Julia's grave, tumbling down the winding lanes that flowed like tributaries, rivulets, rills, all joining together as they wound down the valleys of the dead. Grief and guilt wrestled for my heart. The moment I had realized that Gramma Sophie's death had to happen for my life to move on was the moment I felt I had killed her myself.

But that wasn't right. It couldn't be. Love, too, has its tributaries and its deltas, its rivulets and its rills, its thin branches, threatened with desiccation, loaded with salt longing for fresh. Love—my feet thudded downward; my blood pounded in my ears—has its floodplain; Love has its spring, a starting point, the source from which all of its streams will flow, and a destination all its streams will join at points below, indistinguishable from one another.

I looked back again, and this time, instead of earth showering into an open hole, I saw water:

When we move, the water folds in slow-moving wrinkles against the tile. A rich, chemical fog rising off the pool mixes with the green perfume of cut grass and dissipates, evaporates. Floating, my head half-submerged, I try to lie perfectly still, while Gramma Sophie's hand presses up against the small of my back. She balances my whole weightless weight on five fingertips, while, with the other hand, she absently picks leaves off the surface of the water. "Keep breathing," she says. Above, the sky, a whole inverted bowl of water held back by a breath. When I close my eyes, I can't feel my skin. The trees throw sudden, dappled patterns against the backs of my eyes, little spots of shaded cool freckling my chest. She says, "Now, float," withdrawing her hand, and I do.

I reached the bottom of the hill. When I turned back, toward the eastern hills, a pair of Japanese maples stood at either side of the lane like flames of fire.

I wandered toward a marker with the photo of a boy at the top, set into the stone like a jewel: a teenage boy knee-deep in gray waves, his eyes gray as the sea. And I couldn't help thinking, waiting for Francine and Sol: The real tragedy of the dead is that our lives go on without them.

Then I spotted the Volvo winding its solitary way, bone white, down the lane.

( )

"Will you feed the chicken before we leave?" Francine had collapsed on the futon. She was sorting through the mail.

I glanced skeptically out the window. Huddled against a low fern, the prehistoric creature stared back, its beady black eye coldly appraising. I stepped out with a fistful of Cheerios and the lunatic bird dove at my foot, driving hard into my sandals. "Shit!" I flung the Cheerios into the corner of the yard and dashed in.

Francine held up one of our response cards. (I'd invited Fiona to the wedding. And Duncan Black. But we hadn't had a reply.) "Who's Jill Oey?" *Jill.*

"A friend." I pronounced the word in the clearest way I could, debating whether it was necessary to say any more than that. The phone rang. I darted off to answer it.

"I'm calling about the chicken?" A man's voice, rich and delighted, poured into my grateful ears. He'd seen my posters. *Found, live chicken.*

"Yes!" I answered, eager. "Is it yours?"

The man hesitated. He sounded confused. "You mean there's *really* a chicken?" The smile faded from his voice. "I thought it was performance art."

( )

It was still light over the pointed spires of the City, a dark Oz in the Indian summer dusk, as we drove across the Bridge to Debbie's. (*A short trip, but the psychological distance*, as Francine liked to say, *is enormous.*)

Debbie's cat met us at the door. A small, dark chocolate Burmese, Godiva wound herself around our legs, then trotted after us as we followed Debbie into the apartment. We were all in the kitchen, dicing basil, when from Debbie's bedroom came a sudden shower of little bells tinkling.

"God!" Debbie called, wiping her hands on a kitchen towel. "Here, God!"

"Do you have a belly dancer hiding in there?" Francine nodded toward the bedroom. After all, we hadn't had a bachelorette party.

Debbie looked from Francine to me. "I have a *chuppah* in there." She raised her eyebrows. "Would you like to see it?"

We followed Debbie down the little hall into her bedroom. There, spread out across the queen-size bed, lay what looked like a handmade quilt, bordered on all sides with a fringe of tiny silver bells. Large, colorful squares, each one different, lined the edges around a large, rectangular panel of thick, cream-colored silk, in the center of which had been sewn a huge pomegranate tree— our pomegranate tree—in rich crimson velvet. Francine gasped.

We stepped closer to the bed. The side panels, one-foot by one-foot squares of fabric bordered in red velvet, were not simple multicolored panes. I reached out to touch the closest one with my finger. Against the red, corduroy suspension cables of the Golden Gate Bridge stood two corduroy dogs with shiny, black button noses. Below them, stitched in gold thread the color of warm sand, a line of sloping letters read *Love, Rebecca & Ted*. My sister!

Francine was studying a panel near the corner. Two slightly faded photos had been printed side by side onto the white cotton fabric: In the first, a fat-cheeked girl of three or four, her auburn curls pulled back, straddled the sand, hands on her hips.

Next to her, my six-year-old self in a straw cowboy hat sat high in the branches of my cousins' old oak, bare feet dangling down. "I lost TV for a week for that," I murmured, remembering my mother's harsh cry.

"For climbing up so high? Or for going topless?" Francine smirked, sliding her fingers under the hem of my shirt.

In the margin, my cousin had written in purple Sharpie: *"Free to be . . ." Love, Nathan & Amy*

Francine turned to Debbie. "Where did they get my picture?"

"Your mother," Debbie answered, not taking her eyes off the quilt. Francine reached out and stroked the picture with the tip of her index finger.

"Look!" I exclaimed, turning to an exquisitely quilted mandala, its concentric circles stitched from colorful, silky fabrics I guessed were Tibetan. In the center of the circle sat a perfect, red lotus. Of course, I realized, Jigme could sew.

Francine turned into Debbie's arms. "This is amazing!" she gushed.

"It's incredible," I agreed. "Did you sew all the squares together yourself?"

Debbie frowned. "Are you joking?"

I remembered walking into Betty's sewing room, how her hands flew to cover a pile of scraps in the basket, bits of red velvet peeking out.

"It's the most incredible thing anyone has ever done for us," Francine told her.

I admired our *chuppah*, a quilt of friendship, a quilt of the future. I noticed there wasn't a square on the quilt from Fiona; I didn't want to ask. Fiona was gone—at least for now; Fiona had disappeared, the way so many people disappear; one day, I hoped, she would come back. Until then, I was just going to have to get by without her.

Francine and I inspected the *chuppah*, pulling the far corner toward us to the shimmering of tiny bells. Wendy had quilted her square; on top of a simple checkerboard pattern, black thread spelled out the words, *Ravish my heart, my sister, my bride.* "When on earth did she do this?"

"Wendy's was the first square in," Debbie answered. It figured. "Do you want to try it out?" Godiva batted at the *chuppah's* tinkling fringes as we lifted it with outstretched arms above our heads. It was heavier than I'd expected. There, in front of Debbie's white bed, presided over by Debbie and her little cat God, Francine and I stood alone together under our *chuppah*, our arms raised to the sky. The underside had been lined with silk the color of twilight and scattered with stars.

I blinked rapidly at our Technicolor dream quilt, our amazing and inimitable, button-spangled, bell-decked, silk-and-velvet wedding canopy, and tried to take in the fact that, for weeks, every person we loved had secretly worked his or her feelings about me and Francine into a single square foot of fabric, and that Debbie herself, the friend who had brought us together, and Betty had joined all of these squares together into a canopy that would shelter us. I blinked again, so that I could really, fully see it. The wedding canopy is supposed to be the place where the past stretches out its arms and becomes the future. Our *chuppah* already was.

( )

Our list, ink-smeared, food-stained, road-rough, curled like an autumn leaf.

A bottle of kosher wine for the ceremony. *Check.*

Cloth napkin for the wine glass. *Check.*

Check for Rabbi Loh. *Check.*

And now it was time to call Anya, while I still had one trump card to play.

"Anya," I asked her without alluding to our emotional parting; that wasn't how we did things, either Anya or I; we gave each other privacy. Dignity. "Are you coming to the wedding?"

"Am I coming," she tossed the question aside. "Is *she* coming?" She? *Anat.* Batsheva's daughter.

"Anat's coming," I told Anya, fairly certain she would balk at meeting her, fairly certain she was dying to. "I'd really like you to be there." And I meant it. Even though, if Wendy came, I'd find myself with more than a bit of explaining to do. In that way, at least, I felt determined, once and for all, to start naming things for what they were.

Anya sighed, a weary sigh meant to conceal that fact that she'd finally gotten me to admit I cared.

"The caterer," I pleaded practicality, "needs to have the final count."

Anya's voice revealed her interest was piqued. "I didn't know it was going to be a catered affair!"

( )

Dina, the cellist from our *klezmer* trio, called about the processional music. "Sorry. Everything's been a little frantic." I rattled off half of my to-dos. "And on top of it all"—I peered out the back windows, where the chicken, tired of Cheerios, threatened to mount a glass-pecking revolt—"we've got to unload this crazy chicken."

Dina, a wide-hipped redhead with sad, *shtetl*-brown eyes and red kewpie-doll lips, who didn't have much sympathy for the problems of the modern bride, sparked to life. "A chicken? Can you bring it up to the Julia Morgan tonight by seven?"

Hallelujah.

That night, an unfamiliar silence descended on our home. "Enjoy it," Francine advised me, plopping down on the couch. "It won't last."

As if on cue, the phone rang. It was Fiona. I didn't know what to say. "Don't say anything," she commanded me. "Look, I know you're mad." Fiona was married. She was in L.A. Duncan Black was in Ireland. It was complicated. "But you're getting married. Can we put it aside?" *Could* I put it aside? I didn't want my wedding to turn suddenly into the Fiona Show. And I only had a Fiona-like instant to decide.

"We all have little compartments ..." Francine raised her eyebrows at me and shrugged.

Damn, she was good.

"Of course," I told Fiona, even though it wasn't something I felt entirely sure about at all.

( )

The next day, our friends and family began to arrive. Saturday, late morning, Francine and I strolled down Manzanita Court with the dogs to find Fiona making her own way toward morning buns and café lattes. The minute Fiona saw us, she threw her arms out and started to sing, loud, clear notes that sailed down College

Avenue: "I'm going to the chapel . . ." She broke into her effervescent smile, "and I'm gonna get ma-aa-rried!"

Francine and I groaned. Fiona held out her arms, theatrical, open. "It's very clear," she sang, "our love is here to stay." Fiona had always loved to sing. Maybe we had to sing in order not to talk, but who cared? Why had I doubted her ability to be happy for me? In the morning sun, Fiona's face, lit with music, shone.

A couple pushing a stroller applauded. Fiona called after them, "They're getting married tomorrow!" The couple took a double take, smiled—a noncommittal, Bay Area liberal smile—and moved on.

That afternoon, Trisha and June pulled up in their new silver Jaguar, Francine's "best girls," to whisk Francine away for her last spa day as a bachelorette. "Consider it my *mikveh*," she suggested. I kissed her goodbye and then, sealed up in their silver pod like astronauts or time travelers, they sped away.

I was the one who had wanted a *mikveh*. "Collection," the word means, literally, a collection of water. Immersing in ancient pools, rivers, streams, Jewish people have sought ritual purity in water ever since Adam and Eve, banished, sought renewal in the river that flowed out of Eden. Jewish brides and bridegrooms traditionally immerse before they marry to wash away the past, to come together cleansed, new.

That wasn't exactly the way it seemed to me. I thought of the traditional basin, filling drop by drop with 200 gallons of rain; those deep blue wells held for me, not the clear, rinsing blue of a Diebenkorn sky, but the slow, brimming drops of Time.

Coalescence. Accumulation. What do we rinse ourselves in, if not the quivering liquid of every drop that has fallen before?

( )

Debbie, Sam (just in from Toronto), and I met up in the parking lot at Strawberry Canyon. In the West pool, lap swimmers plashed up and down the marked lanes. Beyond it, hidden, the

East pool sat dormant in the shade of the shedding redwoods, deep and blue. As Debbie positioned her materials—little bottles of oil, candles, white pages printed black—I considered my two dear friends: Sam, lounging in long surf-shorts at the edge of the water, Debbie, throwing her head back, white teeth flashing like a wave, and realized—I had already been blessed.

We were still in our bathing suits, filing out past the West pool, the chemical tang of chlorine mixing with the dusty smell of the hillside and the Indian summer afternoon, our damp heads nearly touching, when I glanced over my shoulder into the huge blue eyes of Charlie May, advancing toward us on the path. He was shirtless and bronze, his Greek stature, I thought, particularly suiting, now that he was filthy rich. Thinking of Francine, I reminded myself: I was rich, too. "Hey, Charlie!" I called. "Enjoy the water!"

"Ellen!" Charlie May exclaimed. His big round eyes opened bigger and rounder, blue on white. "How are you?" Sam and Debbie stopped, Debbie frankly appraising Charlie, and looked back at me with a questioning glance.

"I read about Arachnid in the paper," I admitted. "Congratulations."

"Thanks," he said, nodding his head, practically a bow. "I've left the company," he said. "I'm thinking about starting a few other projects on my own." His gaze settled with disconcerting intensity on my face. "But what about you?"

"I'm still at the Foundation." I bowed back at him; I didn't have to apologize for not being rich; I'd stayed true to myself. "I'm still getting married. Tomorrow."

Charlie's eyes bugged comically. "Congratulations!" he reached out, half as if to shake my hand, half as if to poke me in the ribs, but didn't do either. "The red-haired girl?" he asked. I nodded. I wondered if he remembered telling me not to be a pussy. I owed him for that.

"It's good to see you," I told him, stepping away. Ahead of me, Sam had already pushed through the turnstile to the parking lot.

"Ellen—" I turned back. Charlie dropped his voice confidentially. "There's something I wanted to talk to you about."

Charlie's lips looked white against his tan face. Sam and Debbie waited in the parking lot, leaning in the late afternoon sunlight against the cars. "I've been thinking about you lately, Ellen." Charlie stared at me with unmodulated intensity, the way he had sometimes at Caffe Roma when he talked about the Peloponnesian War and the War in Iraq, his big square hands spread wide across the table. I resettled my bag against my hip, uncomfortably aware, all of a sudden, that I was standing there half naked, a towel wrapped around my waist. Francine had always claimed he had a thing for me. That was the last thing I needed her to be right about.

Charlie's face was still and serious. "I didn't just leave Arachnid, Ellen." Charlie gazed at me appraisingly. A wry smile lifted the corner of his lips. "I walked out of that company with enough in options to build myself a brick shithouse."

I had no idea what that meant, or what it had to do with me. And I felt uncomfortable: When it came to talking about money and cash and capital and shithouses, I was neither my father nor my sister. My face felt fixed, like a mask.

"I want to start my own archives, Ellen. A record of our own times. This is the new wild, wild West. And I don't want to miss it." Charlie eyed me, then gazed over my shoulder toward the pool. His voice softened. "I need someone, Ellen. Someone smart, like you." Charlie stared at me, unblinking, his face stony. "Listen," he said; his nostrils flared. "I've already incorporated the May Foundation as a 501(c)(3). I'm looking at office space South of Market. Ellen," Charlie frowned, swallowing, "I want you to run it."

My hand, which had been twisting my hair into a damp rope, stopped in midair.

Charlie went on. "It's going to be a huge project, but you could ramp up as slowly or quickly as you wanted." He smoothed the air in front of him with all-encompassing hands. "I'd be in the background; you'd be directing the whole thing. I'm prepared," he added, "to offer a competitive package."

A little jolt of mercury, icily silver, flashed through my nerves, both fear and excitement. Saying *no* to the Voices Project in L.A. had been easy. But a competitive package? Right here at home? "I don't know what to say." I was getting married tomorrow. And here was another proposal. A proposal to make it big time, the way my parents always wanted me to. How could I say no? I squinted through the golden, dust-thick air spreading slowly over everything, past the white stone spire of the Campanile, out over the Golden Gate.

The soot of Treblinka settled down. The faces of Wendy, of Anya. How could I say yes? "I'm . . . flattered," I began, pulling my bag higher up on my shoulder.

Charlie looked at me with liquid blue eyes. "Ellen, you're the first person I've asked. Here." He reached back into the pocket of his bathing suit and pulled out a card. "Get married. Then call me and tell me what will make you say yes."

He was the same Charlie May, I thought, as he'd always been, but smoother, the grandiosity and love of pretense that had made him seem too big for his paws in graduate school refined, through the rock tumbler of time and money, polished to the high gloss of adult success. He had become something.

"It's compelling," I said, recovering my composure. "I'd be lying if I said it wasn't."

We weren't students at Roma anymore, arguing over lattes and biscotti. Charlie had become adept at moving people, and more subtle. "Contribute."

I squinted into Charlie's face, confused.

Charlie's shoulders hung, loose and massive, from his jutting collarbones. He looked relaxed, confident. "You. Contribute your own story. Say something. Anything."

"Why me? I haven't worked in High Tech. I'm not one of your Miner 99ers, or whatever." What did I have to do with "our times"?

"You're part of a cutting-edge social movement, aren't you?" He raised his eyebrows and glanced pointedly at my friends, gathered in the parking lot under the crunchy apostrophes of the oak leaves. Charlie smiled; his brown cheek dimpled winsomely.

"Get married," he tossed his head toward the parking lot, "then interview yourself about it. And call me."

My head felt like I'd just sucked in a balloon full of helium, light and swirling, and I ran toward the parking lot like the same balloon untied, shot through the air. As I ran, the idea of Charlie's job offer shed its particulars until it had become nothing more than light energy, the excitement of the offer itself, the possibility of the proposal, any proposal, blurring, as I ran, my hair flying behind me, with the excitement of the wedding. And as I ran toward it, the wedding, the whole idea of the wedding, began to form itself into words—as Charlie May had certainly known it would.

For a fleeting moment, I allowed myself to consider that The May Foundation might offer what the Foundation for the Preservation of Memory never could: the future.

( )

Our little house on Manzanita Court trembled with anticipation,
friends and relatives pouring in and out of the French doors like
atoms of the evening air, visible in the growing dusk. Scattered
in the grass, trodden Cheerios, the last remnants of the fugitive
chicken, gave way under the feet of our friends. Nathan and
Francine consulted over lighting the coals. Sol and Amy huddled
in a corner of the garden talking about the Hubble. "They've just
taken photos from a clump of galaxies that reveal what those
galaxies looked like when they were only 700 million years old."
I smiled, as if this meant something to me. Just the last century
seemed more than I could manage. "If you can look far enough
away, distance becomes time. They're images from the origins of
the universe." Sol's eyebrows rose.

I remembered what Anya had said, about *pentimenti*. Images
from the past. Repentance.

I left them, thinking about how far back you would have to
look to see into the origins of things, and the way that the past
could still live, could still unfold before you, if you were able to
move out far enough from its source. I was still thinking about
that as I floated through my friends, clustered together in the
house, in the yard, among them but, somehow, apart from them,
and I was relieved when I found Jigme, a bunch of irises clutched
in his hand, poking around the kitchen, ostensibly looking for a
vase, but holding Gramma Sophie's cookie tin.

"Good idea," I told him, reaching into the cupboard for a mixing bowl.

Jigme protested, "You have a thousand people here."

"Exactly," I said. "Everybody likes cookies." I was already pouring sugar into the bowl. "Can you go out and see if there are any oranges?"

I broke an egg. Then another. The clear, viscous fluid ran down the side of the bowl. I could hear Uncle Irvin arguing loudly with Trisha about land values out in the yard. My parents hadn't arrived, and wouldn't until the next day.

Jigme came into the doorway, trailed by Francine. Seeing her, my heart felt suddenly as big and warm as the orange Jigme held out to me in his hand.

I had the orange zested, the flour sifted and the dough finished in ten minutes. Then I went out to the garden and found Debbie. "I've got a job for you," I told her.

Debbie stood over the cookie sheet with me, shaping dough into little, triangle-shaped cookies. She had a way of crimping the edges with perfect, artistic little twists. "You're going to overfill it," she warned me, gesturing toward my spoon, quivering with a big, ruby dollop of jam.

"Intellectually," I conceded, "I know you're right. But when I look at that tiny little spot of jam on the tip of the spoon, it just doesn't feel like enough."

"I'll get you a salt spoon," Debbie said. "You can load it like a Mack truck."

When the cookies came out of the oven, everyone went for Debbie's perfect little tarts—everyone except for Uncle Irvin. "*Hamentaschen*," he said, sweeping an entire cookie into his mouth and reaching for a second. "Gramma Sophie's." He was wrong. My bursting little cookies were nothing like Gramma Sophie's. But just hearing her name tonight was nearly enough.

"Phone!" Jigme called out. I was loading up a plate when Jigme appeared, the phone cradled in his hand, as if to protect the tender spot where its umbilicus might have been. "For you," he mouthed. Behind his glasses, both his eyes blinked.

I took the phone into the living room, reconsidered the crowd moving back and forth through the French doors, and made my way up the stairs. The bedroom lay quiet; I held the phone, gazed at the light on the bed, waited.

"You'll wear white, I suppose." The wary voice, lined with all the rivers and roads of an ancient map, I recognized at once as Anya's.

"Cream," I told her. I wasn't sure what she wanted me to convince her of. Our faithfulness to tradition, or our departure from it?

Anya sighed. But it didn't mean anything. It was just the role she liked to play.

Then it dawned on me: She had my home number. "Anya, did you call me at home? A long time ago?"

Anya blew into the phone. "Why would I do that?"

But we both knew why she would do that. I answered with a question: "How did you know?" I guessed that she had seen me when she'd been at the Foundation, probably seen me in and out of the Rose of Sharon, but, aside from my resemblance to Batsheva, what had made her so sure I was the right person to talk to? How had Anya known about me?

Anya suppressed a very dry chuckle. "I have eyes," she said.

Downstairs, the dogs erupted in a frenzy of barking. A cacophony of voices filled the hall. Someone had arrived. Something was changing.

"Anya." I realized, suddenly, how far the Rose of Sharon was from Tilden Park. "Do you need a ride?"

Anya tsked. "I don't need a ride," she protested. "She's going to pick me up."

Downstairs, the trail of voices had drifted together into the garden. Debbie and Sam rushed into the house and out again, cradling a bundle. It tinkled with celestial music as they carried it out into the yard. They held the *chuppah* by its corners to show

306

everyone their places in the tapestry our lives had made. Francine and I crowded under it. Then Sol, sounding, for a second, a lot like Betty, asked, "Does anyone have a camera?"

I ran into the kitchen for film—we kept the canisters inside the butter compartment in the fridge—and Fiona, still anxious to be the best friend, to do the right thing, to stay by my side, rushed to follow.

"Can I get it for you?" she was asking me for the third time.

"Really," I said, "we've got it—" I was about to say *under control* when I uncapped the cold black film canister and turned it over into my palm, releasing a tiny landslide of earth. I gasped. Fiona, wide-eyed, stared at my hand and then back at me. It was the dirt my father had scooped up on his roots trip: earth from Ponar, from the clearing in the woods where the Jews of Vilna had been shot, plowed under, erased.

Fiona's huge, green eyes locked on mine. Despite all our recent strife, I knew Fiona and I were thinking the exact same thing at that moment: about how many molecules of how many thousands of Jews I had just tumbled out into my palm. Every atom of that Ponar earth, a soul. "Oh sh—!" I dumped the earth back into the canister, dusted the grains from the life line of my palm, snapped the top back on. Only then did my hands start to shake.

Fiona and I clung to each other, giggling. It was one of those strange, sudden, hysterical moments, the kind of laughter that could just as easily become tears. I felt so grateful to have Fiona with me then, alive on earth, my oldest friend. On the way out the door into the garden, I couldn't help thinking about Gramma Sophie. About Annie Talbot. About Liz and Betty. About how, when a person dies, the body goes back into the earth; but when you love someone intensely, and then, suddenly, the person is gone—where does it go, all that love? Can it really just be gone?

( )

"Sweetheart, it goes back into the humus, into the deep, rich soil of the earth, just like everything, to feed the person you've become." Night has fallen. We're together, alone. "Come to bed," Francine begs me. "You've been up all night."

"Just a little bit more," I tell her.

"Sweetheart, it's our wedding day."

Francine lies in bed. Her hand flutters, smoothing out the place on the clean white sheets where I belong. Behind her head, the dogs lie curled, open quotations.

Papir iz doch vays un tint iz doch shvarts.
Paper is white and ink is black.
Tzu dir mine zis–lebn tsit doch mine harts.
My heart is drawn to you, my sweet-life.
Ich volt shtendig gezesn dray teg nochanand . . .
I could sit for three days, one after another,
Just kissing your sweet face and holding your hand.
Last night I went to a wedding
And I saw many pretty girls there,
Many pretty girls, but none of them compared to you
With your beautiful black eyes and your raven-dark hair.
Dearest God, hear my plea
To the rich you give honor and an easy path
But I ask only for a little house on a grassy green
In which my true love and I can dwell.

"I'm almost done," I tell Francine.
But this is not the end of our story.

( )

The old *kabbalists*, Rabbi Loh told us, wrote that a bride sees with special eyes, that once the veil has been drawn and she begins her walk toward the *chuppah*, she not only walks there with, but also *sees* her descendants, all of her generations stretched out before her, like Banquo's trees, stretching out to the crack of doom.

As the thinnest veil of dawn draws light across the Oakland

308

Hills, across the flat lands of Berkeley, down to the still, shining panels of the dark Bay, what do I see? What future stretches out before us?

Today Francine and I will wake up late. We'll have breakfast in our little garden, with friends. Today, early, with the precision of a team of astronauts moving toward launch, my parents Marilyn and David will walk off a plane side by side, clutching the black garment bag in which she's hung her 1925 Fortuny beaded silk dress, cream-colored—a little bit too bridal; a bit, in fact, more than one guest will comment, like my own gown—a nice dress, an expensive dress, a rare and beautiful dress, though not the dress she might have chosen had this been another kind of wedding. All down the aisle and all through the ceremony, she will hold carefully onto the tips of my father's fingers.

Across town, Francine and I will race to get our hair done; a song we both like will come blasting like a willing spirit through the speakers. We will roll down the window, our hair flying, the car flying, everything within us taking flight.

Later, up in the ancient hills, among the redwoods, I will step out into the big, wood-paneled room hung with green and gold. Francine's dress will shimmer in the fall's afternoon light; her hair will float around her head like seaweed; the green flecks in her eyes will glow like emerald islands. Francine will gaze at me as I cross the floor, curiously, as if I, in my off-white dress, am a creature of the clouds. We will clasp hands to make sure that neither of us floats away. We will look out the windows together as the people arrive.

Anya will come very, very early, dressed in mother-of-the-bride charcoal gray, with seed pearls stitched into her jacket. She and Anat Singer will find two white folding chairs and sit, facing each other, talking. We will wait for Rabbi Loh to arrive, Francine and I hidden inside the Brazil room, our family, our friends massing like brightly colored birds on the stone porch. Jigme and Rebecca will practice marching together with the

309

chuppah poles down an imaginary aisle. They'll step slowly, the fabric gathered between them, and then, on cue, step apart.

Across an ocean, escaped, yet caught in a twining net, Betty will make careful note of the time and start a very slow game of Scrabble, playing both hands.

The musicians will come, and tune up, a scattering flock of notes, and wait.

Francine will squeeze my hand.

Then, smiling his freckled smile, Rabbi Loh will walk in the door.

At the table near the window, Francine will place a wreath of flowers on my head, and I on hers. *Bedeken*. We will be veiled. We will see, with special eyes, the things that lie before us. We will see children. We will see our parents' parents, feel their spirits swelling, under the *chuppah*'s pale sky. We will step out onto the flags. The *klezmer* trio will play. A little warm breeze will lift the corner of the *chuppah*, a small melodious tinkle of the bells. Francine will slip a ring onto my finger, the finger whose vein, according to medieval Jewish tradition, runs straight to the heart. I will do the same.

And under that piece of fabric, stitched together in Betty's little sewing room, something will happen to us, something invisible, but something nonetheless real; like moving through a membrane, something will shift; the words we say will change us. We will be changed. Then I'll drive my heel down through the napkin, down through the wineglass, straight through to the river-stone flags, shattering the shape that filled the napkin, turning it into the fragments of something else.

( )

October 1998

Dear Charlie, this is a very belated way of saying, politely, deferentially:
As much as I may be tempted to join you, the world will lose its Sur-
vivors. And then what? (We each have a voice that passes into silence.
We each have just a moment that becomes the history of our life on earth.)
I dread with all my heart what the world may become when those voices
have left it. I'm a Jew of the late 20th century, Charlie. That history is
still my burden.

As is this. Take it as a hedge against that other hoped-for day when
the world has changed so much that the idea of our inequality becomes
otherwise unbelievable, when acceptance comes to look, dangerously,
wondrously, a lot like invisibility.

Take it, Charlie, and make sure the scholars of the 21st century
understand, despite the limits of our time and place, that this *woman*
of the late 20th century met a young woman, and fell in love and,
despite what the books of law still say: Here, in the hills of Berkeley,
in Tilden Park, on October 11, 1998, surrounded by family and
friends, and according to the laws of Moses and the Jewish people,
Charlie, I married her.

(Postscript: In the summer of 2008, I married her again in Oakland
City Hall. Our two little girls held the flowers. Their names, Charlie,
are Sophie and Annie.)

311

About the Author

Hilary Zaid is an alumna of the Squaw Valley Community of Writers and the Tin House Writers' Workshop and a 2017 Tennessee Williams Scholar at the Sewanee Writers' Conference. Her short stories have appeared in publications including *Lilith*, *The Southwest Review*, *The Utne Reader*, *CALYX*, *The Santa Monica Review*, and *The Tahoma Literary Review* and have been twice nominated for the Pushcart Prize. A graduate of Harvard and Radcliffe, and of the Ph.D. program in English at the University of California, Berkeley, Hilary lives in the Bay Area with her family.

Acknowledgments

When I sat down many years ago to write this book, there was only one person who mattered: you. I hoped that one day this book would find you, as so many quiet novels had found me and spoken to me and lit up my world with the warmth of another mind, an imagined world that made me at home in mine. Scrawling these pages in the pages of notebooks, I hoped, one day, that they would meet you.

I'm so glad you're here.

Writing is solitary. Bringing a book into the world is not. This book would not be in your hands without the love, generosity and support of the following people: Rachel Adams, Kevin Allardice, Lisa Alvarez, Elizabeth (Radar) Anderson, Camille Angel, Shona Armstrong, Chris Augusta, Damir Augusta (z"l), Karen Augusta, Phillip Augusta, Jessie Austin, Ramona Ausubel, Karen Bender, The Binders, Lucy Bledsoe, BLOOM, Barbara Boardman, BGN, Rachel Borup, Sylvia Brownrigg, Dani Burlison, Bywater Books, Alexander Chee, Lance Cleland, Leland Cheuk, The Community of Writers at Squaw Valley, Congregation Sha'ar Zahav, Karin Cecile Davidson, Ilana DeBare, Mavis Delacroix, Jo Levi DeSanti, Dr. Dixon, Pat Dobie, Erika Dreifus,

East Bay Booksellers, Charles Flowers, Janet Frishberg, Craig Foster, Amina Gautier, Elizabeth Gessel, Francoise Guigel, Rachel Hall, Jane Eaton Hamilton, Sam Hiyate, Carolyn Hutton, Susan Turner Jones, Jody Joseph, Brad Johnson, Carmel Kadrnka, Sarinah Kalb, Deborah Kalb, Nancy Kates, Anna Katz, Judith Katz, Rose Katz, Rosalie Morales Kearns, Cherry Kim, Nina Klose, Georgia Kolias, Jed Kolko, Cheryl Krisko, Ida Kuluk, Chaney Kwak, Jean Kwok, Adam Latham, Kiese Laymon, David Leavitt, Dora Lee, Lois Leveen, Lilith Magazine, Rachel Maizes, Marianne K. Martin, The Martinez Family, Jane Mason, Jackie Mates-Muchin, Richard May, Jamie Mayer, Jill McCorkle, Alice McDermott, Yona Zeldis McDonough, Ann McMan, Nayomi Munaweera, The Oakland Public Library, Aline Ohanesian, Chinelo Okparanta, Morgan Parker, Joe Ponepinto, Peg Alford Pursell, Crystal Reiss, The Rights Factory, Jennifer Robinson, The Rockridge Library, Cassandra Rodgers, Meredith Rose, Elizabeth Rosner, Bob Ross, Emery Ross, Rob Saarnio, Deborah and Mike Sabin, Saints & Sinners' Literary Festival, Mo Saito, Anne Schmitz, Susan Weidman Schneider, Diana Selig, Wendy Sheanin, Hilary Sloin, Kelly Smith, Connie Sommer, Rachel Spengler, Adrian Staub, Luan Strauss, Nancy Squires, Molly Talamontes, Mariko Tamaki, Jenny Teaford, The Tin House Writer's Workshop, Andrew Tonkovich, Kern Toy, Alicia Upano, Jen Vetter, Paul Vetter, Jess Walter, Mike Waters, Steve Yarbrough, Amy Waldman, Rebecca Weiner, Ellen Weis, Salem West, Amy Weston, Jessie Williams, Angelica Zaid, Blaine Zaid, Gavin Zaid, Gerald and Shirley Zaid, Jon Zaid, Mel Zaid, Pam Zaid, Ryan Zaid, Spencer Zaid.

Most especially: Lauren Augusta, my spouse and my love, without whose perfect faith in me nothing would be possible. My sons, who broke open the world. No creation will ever be as beautiful as you are to me.

History is incomplete. Behind and between these names are others whose stories sustained me and those whose names have not been written. Whoever you are, holding me now in hand, I hope you have found some bright shard in these pages to sustain you and to light your way.

Bywater BOOKS

At Bywater Books we love good books about lesbians just like you do, and we're committed to bringing the best of contemporary lesbian writing to our avid readers. Our editorial team is dedicated to finding and developing outstanding writers who create books you won't want to put down.

We sponsor the Bywater Prize for Fiction to help with this quest. Each prize winner receives $1,000 and publication of their novel. We have already discovered amazing writers like Jill Malone, Sally Bellerose, and Hilary Sloin through the Bywater Prize. Which exciting new writer will we find next?

For more information about Bywater Books and the annual Bywater Prize for Fiction, please visit our website.

www.bywaterbooks.com

CPSIA information can be obtained
at www.ICGtesting.com
Printed in the USA
FSHW01n0708190618
49582FS